THE
STRANDED

THE
STRANDED

SARAH DANIELS

sourcebooks
fire

Published by Sourcebooks Fire, an imprint of Sourcebooks
P.O. Box 4410, Naperville, Illinois 60567–4410
(630) 961-3900
sourcebooks.com

Originally published in 2022 in Great Britain by Penguin Books, an imprint of
Penguin Random House UK Ltd.

Cataloging-in-Publication Data is on file with the Library of Congress.

Printed and bound in the United States of America.
KP 10 9 8 7 6 5 4 3 2

For my husband and our children.

PART ONE

THE *ARCADIA*

Good evening. It is 17:00 hours on Sunday 24 October 2094.

This is the captain of the cruise ship Arcadia.

We are currently experiencing strong northwesterly winds, a high of 50°F and a wind-chill factor of 25°F.

All passengers please be prepared for high seas.

Daily reported Virus cases: zero.

Days at sea: 15,934.

CHAPTER 1

ESTHER

I shiver against the wind that threatens to take my homework over the ship's railing and into the sea. That's the last thing I need. I don't want to pull an all-nighter, and this close to graduation, I can't afford to let my grades slip, so I weigh the loose pages down with my digiscreen. This model was already old when I got it, and that was five years ago, the glass face sliced across by a crack like a rivulet of ice. You can feel the sharp edges with your fingers.

It's aching cold this evening. Autumn cold, getting us ready for winter. Storm season on the ship feels never-ending. Last year, we endured night after night of thundering waves. Snow piled up on the deck in great mounds, and the chill seemed to enter every salt hole and frayed seam in our clothes.

Even the memory of it makes the skin on my arms pucker with goosebumps, so I shake out the blanket from the back of my chair, wrap it around myself, and try not to think of bugs. Crumbs and splashes of dried food crust the surface of the wool. By the end of this year, with any luck, I'll be miles away before the worst winter storms come; I'll be on dry land, sleeping in a warm room, with nothing to worry about but passing my first-year exams.

At least, that's the plan.

The Lookout is packed with customers huddled around tables. Sim, the café's stubble-faced owner, makes greasy food on a camping stove, separated from the rest of the Lookout by a counter of tacked-together planks. The café furniture is a mishmash of styles scavenged from around the ship: Plastic chairs taken from the staff cafeteria. Ornate velvet-covered dining chairs from the expensive upper-deck restaurants. A variety of faux-leather tub chairs stolen from the cabins, cracked and faded from exposure. They've all seen better days.

The café itself is a broad, semicircular disc of planks built out from Deck Eleven, landward side. From the decks below, you can see it's all held up by a mess of scaffolding poles and oars and planks. It's so rickety, it creaks in the wind as though it could collapse into the sea at any moment. In all, there are fourteen residential decks layered above the *Arcadia*'s waterline, and each deck is separated into cabins. A few big, fancy cabins per deck at the top of the ship, and then, the lower you go, the smaller and less fancy they get, until you hit the waterline. That's where the really bad neighborhoods start.

The Lookout's appeal for most patrons is the cheap food or even cheaper bitter, reheated coffee. But for me it's the view. Every icy chair faces the land. Even when it rains—which it does a lot out here on the Atlantic coast—you can still see the city. This evening the sun is slung low behind the skyscrapers, and the coast is a jagged silhouette dotted with hundreds of brightly lit homes. My eyes trace the outline of the sun-backed buildings, drinking in every familiar detail. The shipyards, the low-lying suburbs, the towering midtown. And on the fringes of the city, right at the edge of my vision, the university campus. That's the place I'm aiming for. Up here, I can forget the waves that separate me from the city. Up here, my new life is within reach.

Ten more minutes, then I'll head home.

At the next table, a group of teenage girls chat in Arabic, then slip seamlessly in and out of English. One of the group pulls aimlessly at a hole in her coat sleeve while she gazes at the badges on my uniform. I squirm, suddenly aware of how stiff the collar of my jumpsuit is, and find myself pulling at the neck. I stare down into my coffee, cheeks burning with embarrassment.

A shadow passes over the table. "Anything else?" Sim says, wiping a hand down the grease-stained apron he always ties around his waist. His face has the deepening lines of someone who spends most of their time out in the elements. He takes my plate and tops up my mug with watery coffee. The mug is an ancient ceramic thing, cracks in the white glaze like cobwebs, and stained by the thousands of coffees it's held before mine.

"No thanks," I say, and I hold out my hand to him.

Our comgloves cover most of our hands, but the fingers are free. When we hover in an almost handshake and wait for the funds to transfer, I can feel a hint of warmth. The gloves beep in unison as my ration credits are transferred to pay the bill. I flip my hand over so that I can see the flexible rectangular display on my palm.

"Hey, Sim, you didn't charge me enough."

"It's…a thank you, Esther…for the rush on my Virus swab last week. Can't afford to close up while I wait."

"Just doing my job," I say. "But thanks."

"Well, you didn't have to help me out so…thank you. Captain's announcement said it's going to be a rough night, but it'll be clear tomorrow. You'll get a good view of the city. And it's ration day, so there'll be bread."

My mouth waters at the thought of fresh bread, crisp on the outside, soft as a cloud inside. "I'll be in after class—you'll save me some?"

He gives me a half-smile, which is as much emotion as you get from him most days. "You're my most regular. It'll be behind the counter for you." He lingers, eyes resting on the pile of handwritten paper on the table. "Can't be long until it's your turn to graduate. How's the exam prep going?"

My jaw tightens with anxiety. "Same as always," I say. "We study. We're tested. We study again. At this point, I know more about contagious diseases than most doctors will ever need to. Still might not make the cut though."

The girls at the next table giggle, and I can't help looking up to see if they're talking about me. One of them whispers behind her hand. When I catch the word *collaborator*, I sink further into my chair, wishing the deck would swallow me up. Tears prick my eyes. It's not like I've never heard it before—plenty of people resent me because I wear this uniform—but it still stings, and it's mortifying that this is happening in front of Sim.

He looks briefly at the girls, then he rests the antique glass

4

coffee pot on the table. There's a crack down one side, weeping coffee, so he carries it with a tea towel pressed against it.

"Now listen to me. There's not a person aboard this ship that hasn't taken something they've needed from the Federated States. But that won't stop them dragging you down. You ignore them, you hear? You've worked damn hard to get where you are. And when you graduate, I'm going to put your picture up behind the counter and tell everybody it was my coffee you were drinking while you studied. Got it?"

"Got it," I say.

Sim takes his coffee pot and moves to the girls' table. "Who's up for some collaboration coffee? Fresh from the Federated States last week." His voice booms.

The girls scowl at him, but let him refill their cups, reaching their hands out to his, one by one, to pay. He winks at me over his shoulder.

At least I've got a shot at getting out of here. Sim's a whole-lifer, like almost every other person onboard. He was born here, and he'll die here, like all the Stranded.

There's a ping from my comglove, the wrinkles and frayed cuff of the graying fabric so familiar it feels like a part of me. It's a joyful noise for bad tidings. Glowing green text scrolls from the heel of my hand to the folds of my fingers.

Esther, it's getting dark. Are you in?

I've stayed too long. Again. I sigh louder than I'd dare if Mom was in earshot, wipe my fingers on the blanket, then use the middle two on my left hand to tap out a lie.

With Alex, home soon.

Irritation nudges at me as I pull my med bag over my head and stuff my homework in among the bandages and syringes. Mom means well, and without her help, May and I wouldn't be leaving the ship at all. She taught my sister and me everything, from how to ace our entrance exams to rigging up a desalination system so we're never thirsty when the freshwater shipments are delayed. It's just that she winds her worries so tight around us that we can barely fill our lungs. And May gets off easy. She's free to stay out after dark. Or eat dinner alone without someone keeping tabs. It all makes me want to scream.

I get up and weave a path between the sticky, plastic-covered tabletops, making my way to one of the exits.

"Hey!" someone yells from the deck above the café.

My eyes snap up in time to see a pale hand hanging over the railing, clutching a small white rectangle. The rectangle swings through the air and shatters into a hundred sheets of paper that curl out and down toward me, catching the last of the day's light as they fall. Making them flash.

I'm caught in a leaflet drop.

Aboard the *Arcadia*, news is strictly packaged and sanitized. Anything that doesn't come from the Federated States is propaganda or hearsay or outright lies. Writing it down will get you arrested. Giving it to other people will get you arrested. Reading it, holding it in your hand, standing next to it will get you arrested.

They'll be here soon. I should run, but instead I watch the paper drift to the ground, my heart beating in anticipation.

The air is supercharged with excitement. People grab at the leaves as they arc to the ground. Above me, hands throw ream after ream. Paper litters the floor and the tabletops and settles on the mismatched chairs. A black-and-white snowdrift lined with text.

I anchor my feet to the deck and shove my hands into my pockets to stop them from reaching out. The voice in my head that sounds like my mom says, *Don't even think about reading that message. Don't blow your chances.*

I watch the girls from the next table holding their hands out as more and more paper rains down. One girl snatches a leaflet from midair and starts to read, the others gathering around to see what it says.

Just one look. My hand trembles as I reach for a leaflet. A spark of something unfamiliar and not totally unpleasant flickers inside me. It's anticipation mixed with anxiety. It's fizzy. I spin to face the sea, hunching my shoulders to shield the forbidden rectangle from view. A blurry grayscale image of a cruise ship floats in the center of the paper. Not my ship. I'd recognize the *Arcadia* from any angle. It must be one of the others. Smoke billows out from the hull, and it keels sickeningly toward the water. Underneath the image, the text reads:

CRUISE SHIP *OCEANIA* CLEARED!
HUNDREDS DEAD!

"Coalies!" Sim yells behind me.

They're here.

A collective whimper from the café's patrons. I squeeze the leaflet into a tight ball. It whispers, and when I open my fingers, what's left of the paper drifts away on the breeze, leaving a smudge of gray dust on my skin. Recycling paper. Smart.

7

"It degrades!" I shout.

All around me, people scrunch up the sheets, letting the ashy powder blow away, clapping their hands to get rid of the residue. When the leaflets are crushed just right, they recycle in a hushing chorus that sounds like waves on shingle. There are still hundreds of them strewn across the floor, and no one wants to be caught next a batch of illegal words. No one wants to be scanned, to have their proximity to the drop entered on their permanent record. No one wants to be taken.

Chairs screech against the wooden deck. People leave steaming drinks and half-eaten plates of food. We shove each other in our need to get away. A table topples, showering the deck with plates and cups, the silverware falling like rain. Sim's coffee pot ends its life in a glassy tinkle.

My need to escape surges with every heartbeat, but each step brings me up against a new obstacle: a chair leg crunching into my shin, an abandoned bag blocking my feet. People scramble around me. The tables and chairs of the Lookout heave as though moved by a churning sea. Ten steps feel like ten miles, but I make it to the Lookout's closest exit. People bottleneck, squeezing through the single-file opening that leads to the next stretch of narrow deck.

A sour film coats the back of my tongue. Epinephrine. My adrenal glands are working overtime, getting my body ready for fight or flight, pushing blood to my muscles and making my heart work harder.

There's a dull thud, a groan, and I look over my shoulder to see a girl lying flat on her face, papers fluttering around her. My instinct is to help. But in the second it takes me to turn back, a wave of black uniforms surges through the entrance on the oppo-site side of the Lookout.

The world pauses like a held breath. The Coaly uniforms and weapons are so black they seem to consume light. The mirrored visors of their smooth helmets pan left to right, taking in the scene. The people and the overturned chairs. The piles of for-bidden knowledge. A static crackle precedes the Coaly's digital voice, fed through the helmet to disguise the person inside: "You are in contravention of ship bylaw sixty-two B, forbidding the creation, dissemination, and possession of inflammatory written material. Remain where you are."

Panic stretches the girl's eyes into glassy marbles. I've seen that collision of dread and resignation before. Our neighbor didn't fight when the Coalies searched his cabin. He stood by his front door with his arms loose at his sides, his body slack. But his eyes didn't rest. They darted from face to face, searching for a clue—something, anything—that would save him.

Strands of soft brown hair stick to the girl's lips, puffing and sucking in time with her breath. She can only be sixteen, my age, but her face is weathered and her lips raw and cracked.

The Coalies spread into the café, pouring between the tables. They catch the stragglers that have been too slow to run. One Coaly throws a man down; another shocks him with a taser. The man spasms, boots drumming against the deck.

The girl's marble eyes are locked on to mine. They make a des-perate, unvoiced appeal for help. Why hasn't she gotten up? Fear? She's paralyzed. I could help her—there's still time. She'd move if I pulled her up.

There's not *enough* time. People rush past me, through the opening and down the deck to safety. And the voice in my head, the one that uses my mom's tone, says: *Don't get involved. Look after yourself. Let her escape—or not—on her own. She wouldn't help you.*

I ball my fists. You put your own life jacket on first—everyone knows it.

I leave her behind.

CHAPTER 2

NIK

'Ve never been this pumped. I'm not kidding—my heart is going like you wouldn't believe.

News will spread fast. Now everyone's going to know what went down on the *Oceania*. Pulling a drop like that is all kinds of illegal, but it's my duty to shake things up. Clearance is coming. Got to be ready.

We've been zigzagging down the ship, making sure we're not being followed, and now we're walking beside the cabins on Residential Deck Seven. Beyond the three-bar railing, there's a view of the sea, churning and gray. I'm trying to play it cool. My smile's a dead giveaway, but I can't help it—it keeps breaking through. May's beaming too. Her eyes are all glisteny. I want to grab her hand and run.

"See you later for debrief." She jogs away, then hops back and grabs my arm. "We did it!"

I turn in the opposite direction. Time for us to split up. We'll take different routes home to our cabins and—crap. Coalies. Twin uniforms striding along the narrow deck. Far enough away that they haven't spotted us yet, but there's no way past. On one side, there's a row of cabins, a pattern of porthole-door-porthole-door that's repeated on every residential deck on the ship. On the other side, the railing hems us in. Those Coalies aren't going to let us pass if we act nice. And walking back the way we've come won't do any good either. By now, Hadley will have put out an all-ship alert. They'll be rounding up everything that moves. At this point, even just walking away will have them after us faster than a drone chasing a pickpocket.

May spins back to face me. Her grin's gone, and the color has washed from her face. She lays her hands on the top rail, one foot resting on the bottom. I take up position next to her. Pretending we're only here for a chat. The sea and the sky blur into the same twilight gray, and even though it's dropped cold, I'm sweating under my hoodie. My palms are clammy against the crusty white paint.

"Don't freak," I say from the corner of my mouth.

"I'm not going to freak."

"All right. I'm just saying, don't freak."

"Look, I'm trained for this. You're far more likely to freak than me."

I sigh. May always needs to be top dog, even when we've got Coalies stalking toward us. But I like that about her. "Your military training. Sure. So, what's the plan, General?" I say.

May turns her back to the sea and rests her elbows on the railing.

She glances at the Coalies. "We can't let them scan us, not this close to the Lookout. Not together."

"That's affirmative, sir."

"Stop fooling around. This could be life or death."

"OK, give me the plan."

"The plan is we run."

"That's it? Five years of cadet training, and all you can come up with is *we run*?"

"We run, really fast, away from the Coalies," she says.

They must have seen us by now, but they're not moving any quicker. "Where to?"

"That's your department. You've got the shady underworld contacts."

I take a sideways look at the Coalies. "We split up," I say, and I can predict her response before she opens her mouth.

"No way."

"If they stop you, high-flying cadet, you can talk your way out of it. Flash your comglove ID. Tell them you're on your way home from class. If we're together, they're going to start asking questions."

"And by yourself, you're just another kid stopped without cause. They'll arrest you and haul you off for interrogation."

"You can use your privilege to get me back, can't you?"

"I have less sway than you think," she says, and she picks at a bubble of rusty paint with her fingernail.

"Look, don't want to pull rank or anything, but I'm your handler, and it's my call. You go first. Walk as fast as you can without looking like you're running. I'll wait here until you get up the next staircase before I make a move."

"You're ordering me to pretend we don't know each other, make my escape, while you stay behind and distract them?"

"Never know, we might both get home without being stopped."

May fixes me with a hard stare. I've lost this fight. She curls her fingers around mine and, while I'm distracted by how warm her skin feels, she holds our hands up in the air. Now the Coalies won't fail to spot us—and see we're together.

"That was so stupid," I say, pulling our hands down without letting go.

They've noticed us. Target acquired. Their stride lengthens to a march, and their hands tense around their weapons. Gotta keep my nerve. Once they see us run, the game starts. We can't try for home. That'd lead the Coalies straight to us and our families, and no one wants a visit from the ship's official police force in the middle of the night. Need to lose them first. Lucky for us, this boat's riddled with nooks and crannies and whole sections below deck lorded over by Neath gangs. There are places even the Coalies won't go without riot gear.

"OK. Stay close—don't want to slow down for you," I say.

"Sure. Because you're so much faster than me."

We walk, easy as you like, away from the Coalies, back toward the nearest staircase. Fast enough to keep some distance between us and them, not so fast that we look suspicious.

"Head down the staircase and along the main service corridor. We aim for the rear of the ship. Once we make Neath territory, we'll be home free," I whisper.

"We're going below deck?"

"It's the only place the Coalies won't follow us. Worried?"

"I'm worried because every time you take me down to Neath territory, people act like I've got two heads."

"They're not used to seeing ticket holders down there. And anyway you're going to have to deal with it, because we can't make it all the way to Enid's with them chasing us. We need somewhere to hide until the dust settles."

"Fine. But you'd better be right about them not following us. It's bad enough that we're going into gang territory without an invite. God knows what they'll do if we lead Coalies down there."

"I can handle it. I know people," I say.

But she's not wrong. Silas Cuinn. Gang leader. Controls everything below deck. Mean streak as long as the *Arcadia*. And whether he helps us, hides us, or hands us over to the Coalies could depend on which side of the bed he got out of this morning. Heading into his territory uninvited has me feeling more than a little nervous, though I'll do my best to hide it from May.

"You got your memory scrubber in case they take you?"

"This isn't my first day as a double agent."

"May—"

"I've got the scrubber. Not that I plan on getting caught." She smiles, broad and toothy, like she owns the world.

"All right. Let's go," I say.

We both pull our scarves up over our faces—nothing suspicious about that; you've got to protect your skin from the salt. All I can see are May's big eyes and a few wisps of hair. She squeezes my hand, and the hammering in my chest gets worse. Two well-armed, well-trained Coalies are following us. We're about to run for our lives. And I'm still thinking about her fingers twisted into mine and the skin on my palm buzzing. I hold my breath.

Soon I'll have to let her go.

"Go!" May shouts.

"Stay where you are!" a Coaly barks.

We run. Along the wooden boards of the deck, through the swinging door, into the covered staircase. They're the same all over the ship, metal stairs connecting the tiny landings. A big white number stenciled onto each door tells you which deck you're on. We plunge downwards, two steps at a time, shock waves striking through my legs. A short stretch of steps, then circle around the landing and take the next set of stairs down.

Somewhere above us a door slams, and then there's the heavy tramp of boots on metal, and I know the Coalies are just behind us. I jump, use the handrail to swing myself around a corner, and for a second I'm airborne. May could trounce me in any race, but she stays a step behind, a human barrier between me and the Coalies. If they start shooting, she'll put herself between me and the bullets. That's who she is.

I count the doors as we pass them, the numbers getting lower the further down we go. Deck Four. Deck Three. Deck Two. Sweat sticks my shirt to my back. My chest rages from running.

"Next one," I say, wheezing.

There's a bang like a crack of thunder, and something thuds into the wall right in front of my face.

We both duck, clinging to the wall. "And now they're shooting," says May, panting.

There's no number on the next door. Instead, the word

SERVICE has been stenciled on to the blue paint. I yank the door handle, swing it open, feel the pressure of May's hand pushing me in front of her. She lets the door slam behind us. For a second, I think about trying to block it, but then I hear another round of muffled gunshots. No time for anything but running.

We race into the service corridor. The ship's main thoroughfare is wide enough to drive a truck down and so long you can't see the ends. It runs down the middle of the ship like a spine, connecting every part. It's the quickest way to get somewhere in a hurry, if you don't mind taking your chances with the muggers and pickpockets. Once upon a time, it would've been used to move supplies and staff around without the ticket holders upstairs having to set eyes on the help. Now it's the domain of Neaths—ship folk from below deck—and some of the more adventurous above-deck ticket holders.

"Keep left!" I shout. We launch ourselves along the corridor. It's so jam-packed with ship folk you can barely move. Air ripe with music and shouting and the warmth of hundreds of Neaths squished into a small space. I map out the escape route in my head, aiming for one of the hidden entrances to Silas's territory. There are lots of ways to get down to the lawless places below deck, some official, others secret. Just have to know where to look.

We dodge around a guy leading a goat on a rope. May ducks under a kind of makeshift tent made out of tarpaulin and emerges on the other side with the owners shouting after her. I catch my foot on a stray box, stumble. May steadies me, and we're off again. There's no organization down here. No planning. No rules. People set up shop wherever they find a space. It's the perfect place to get lost.

"Where now?" May says.

"Up ahead. Last elevator on the right."

The elevators that line the walls on both sides of the corridor are enormous steel boxes. Doors jammed open, buttons unlit—well, all except the elevator we're heading for. They haven't moved in living memory, and it's a good thing because they make good sleeping places and good cooking places, and almost every one is crammed with people. It's like one long bunkhouse.

"You better be right about them not following us down," May says through ragged breath.

I don't answer. There's no plan B here. We can't keep running forever. But the Coalies are lagging behind, weighed down by their knife-proof vests and shiny helmets. They're having to jump around the pedestrians that keep getting in their way. We might just make it.

An old woman is shuffling between us and the open elevator doors, pushing a shopping cart with a mountain of junk on top. Her red, wrinkle-folded face peeps out from under a hood, and she's hunched, covered in blankets.

I pull hard on May's hand and swing her forward past the woman with the cart. "In there!" I shout. "Use the cable!"

May speeds ahead. Still running, I feel in my trouser pocket for an air grenade, dropping it into the old woman's cart as I pass. I make a grab for the handle. It swings away from her easily enough, then a wheel gets stuck and it topples sideways. The grenade explodes. A plume of smoke shoots out, the contents of the shopping cart go clattering over the floor of the corridor. Scrap metal, rags, bones, frayed rope.

The old woman shrieks, mouth stretched into a gummy O with her purplish tongue wriggling inside. Everybody else hits the deck. That'll slow the Coalies for a few seconds. Might be all we need.

May leaps through the open door, catching herself on the thick metal elevator cable. She hooks her elbow around the cable and shoots down into the empty shaft. I skid to a halt a quarter of an inch from the drop and teeter, grabbing on to the outside wall to stop myself from toppling down. It's only one deck, but a fall like that onto concrete would be nasty. At the bottom of the shaft, May touches down in the murky darkness.

"Come on!" she shouts.

Metal pounds into metal. A spatter of neat bullet holes opens on the wall next to me. Head height. My distraction didn't slow them down. And they're shooting to kill.

Not gonna wait around to see if their aim gets better. I leap and grasp the cable, then pause to see if my grip holds. The metal of the cable is twisted and fibrous in my hands. I wrap my feet around it to stop myself falling. For a second, I'm swinging, the cable creaking by my face. Cold air rises through the elevator shaft. The taste of mold and rotting metal coats my tongue. All I have to do is slide down, but I'm looking back into the corridor, right into the black, blank visors of the two Coalies. They raise their weapons. My face flashes in their visors: fear staring back at me.

They open fire.

CHAPTER 3

ESTHER

My legs shake from running. Or adrenaline. Or guilt. The look on that girl's face is burned into my mind. What kind of person runs when others need help? *Someone who survives,* my mom would say.

That girl would have done the same thing if it was me lying on the ground.

I push a heavy metal door with my shoulder, leaving the cover of the staircase for the open-sided deck. My eyes blur with tears, and I bite down on my lip until the skin breaks. Gulping air through strangled sobs. That was too close.

Pull yourself together. Wipe your face.

Where am I? When I saw those Coalies, I ran so fast I didn't even think about where I was going. Now it's almost dark. I'm at the top of the ship, that much is clear. The sea seems miles away. Every front door is the same cool blue. Every cabin is flanked by shrubs in ceramic pots the size of my head, trimmed neatly into a sphere, and some of them have the beady eye of a security camera watching over the deck. A quick glance upward and I realize these cabins are two stories high. I've stumbled on to Deck Thirteen.

My breath still forces its way out of my mouth. Hot and uncontrollable. OK. This is no problem. I shouldn't be here, but I've done nothing wrong. The people up here, with their huge cabins, don't like nonresidents exploring. Some neighborhoods employ a watch to make sure those of us from the lower decks don't come up here. There are even restaurants on some decks, glittering and exclusive, and definitely not for the likes of me.

The horrible squirm of fear in my stomach tells me I need to get home by the quickest and safest route. If that means being yelled at by the DIY security guard of an upper-deck neighborhood, then so be it. If I sprint all the way along this deck and into the farthest staircase, I'll be home in no time. It's a safe staircase, as they go. I've never seen a Coaly patrol in there, or any Neaths for that matter, so the danger of getting mugged is minimal.

This is nothing. No distance from here to there. An eighth of a mile. May would do it without flinching.

My comglove starts a high-pitched ring that shatters the silence. Incoming call, Alex.

If I answer, he's going to be worried. But I could really use someone to talk me through this, so I tap the answer icon.

"Where are you?" His voice is sharp with worry. "Open a video link, will you?"

I tap the video icon on my comglove, and Alex's face flares into view, flat on my palm. Square jaw, gentle eyes, blond hair swept back and parted on the side. Behind him, I can see his tidy bedroom. The bunk turned down. Textbooks arranged by size on the bookshelf.

"On my way home. Deck Thirteen," I say.

"What are you doing up there?"

"Thought I'd take the scenic route home," I say.

"You're only a few decks away. Come over. Want to see you," he says.

My cheeks tingle, and I suppress a smile. With him on video, my fear of the open deck lessens. "What do you want, Hudson? I've got homework to do." I rest my free hand on the railing as I walk. Forcing myself to move. Acting like there's no danger in the world.

"I was worried you'd gotten picked up," he says.

"Picked up? For what?" I say, playing the innocent.

"There was a leaflet drop near the Lookout."

I shrug, shake my head, pray I'm not giving anything away. "No, I'd have called you if I was in trouble. Wasn't anywhere near it," I add, the lie coming easily.

"OK," he says, although he doesn't sound entirely convinced. "I've got a couple of kids to tutor tonight, but I can slip out to meet you beforehand."

"No, I should get home and finish my assignment."

"I don't like you walking around by yourself."

"I'm fine. Really. Let's grab breakfast on the way to class tomorrow, though. Meet me in the market?"

He grins. "Sounds good. Listen, if you change your mind, message me. You know they always crack down when something like this happens. I'd prefer if you weren't out alone."

"What good would it do if we were together? It'd just mean two of us getting arrested instead of one."

He brushes his hair back with his glove-free hand and looks away from the camera. "I know. But if it's going to happen, I'd rather we were together."

I would, too. On the *Arcadia*, we live under the constant threat of being arrested. Look at a Coaly wrong: arrested. Break a rule in front of one of the many surveillance cameras: arrested. Stand too close to someone doing something shady: arrested. *Wrong place, wrong time* is basically the ship's motto. And, once they've got someone in custody, it's anyone's guess what they'll do with them. They might interrogate them. They might release them back into the ship. Some people just disappear without a trace. It's a harsh system, but before the Coalies, the gangs ruled, and from what my parents have told me, things were even worse back then. If I'm going to get arrested, the thought of being locked up with Alex is way more appealing than the thought of being alone.

"Hey, you want to hear something funny?" he says, filling the silence.

"Sure."

"My mom went to the captain's offices today."

"Yeah?"

"She says it's time for us to be serious about our future."

Nausea grips me. *Serious. About our future.*

Alex holds a piece of paper up in front of his camera, too blurry to read, but neat and official-looking. As the image resolves, I catch sight of words that freeze me to the bone: *marriage license.*

"She says married candidates get stationed together. They'll send us to the same hospital after college, and we'll get joint quarters. End of term's only a few weeks away now, so we need to make plans. Doesn't have to be a big deal, but we'll have to do it before graduation."

I can't speak. *Married candidates?*

"Isn't that hilarious? Our very own marriage license. Look, it's got your name on it."

I stare at the image of Alex on the digiscreen, feel myself blinking mechanically, but I'm too shocked to speak.

As my silence stretches, Alex's expression turns to mortification. "I mean, I didn't think we would so soon. But—"

"We're sixteen," I say, cursing the quiver in my voice.

"I know," he says, and he looks so embarrassed I could cry. "Let's talk about it tomorrow."

"Alex—"

"No, it's OK. It's fine."

Marriage. Plans. Was that a proposal?

Halfway down the deck now. The deck lights give off a cozy glow. The smell of cooked food seeps from each cabin, and I can hear music coming from inside some of the homes.

Neither Alex nor I hang up. I walk with him looking out from my hand, while he pretends to be sorting things on his desk.

"This is excruciating," I say.

"Yep. It is."

"Can we change the subject?"

I want him to say yes. I want us to brush whatever that was under the carpet and leave it there until I'm ready to deal with it. Instead, he frowns at the digiscreen. He turns his head so that he's closer to the camera, and I get a view of the short, neat hair over his ears. "What is that?" he asks.

My stomach drops. What I've been too preoccupied to take notice of is a constant buzz. The sound of an insect, getting closer. My anxiety rushes back, so intense I can feel it spinning in my head.

"Is that a drone?" he asks.

"Yes."

I lick my lips and try to shuffle the strap of my bag so that the Federated States flag sewn onto my left sleeve is visible. I tell myself to keep walking, that the staircase can only be a few more yards. But my legs seize with each step, and—no matter how hard I try— my knees move in jerks. Everything in me wants to hide.

"Is it watching you?"

I let my eyes drift sideways and immediately wish I hadn't. It's gliding slowly through the air, hovering above the ocean. Matching my pace perfectly. A ball with four propellers sticking out on arms. On the underside, a camera lens swivels until it's looking at me, like a single beady eye. I snap back to Alex. Give a tiny nod. Try not to let fear overtake the normal functioning of my body.

On my hand, I see Alex sit up straighter, see his face tighten, his eyes narrow.

"Don't run," he says.

CHAPTER 4

HADLEY

Hadley launches a drone from the small, inaccessible docking platform at the prow of the ship. In the air, out of view, the drone flies toward Hadley's location. He uses his finger and thumb on the control digiscreen to set its course, forcing it away from the ship and out into the night, so that he gets a broad view of the ship.

The *Arcadia*. It's pushing a hundred years old. One of a class of megacruise ships, a floating city designed to give its thousands of wealthy ticket holders the luxury cruise of their dreams. Now it heaves and creaks with the swell of the Atlantic.

Hadley directs the drone to circle the ship. The Lookout café is attached to one side like a shelf fungus, empty and unlit after the unrest of the afternoon. From above, he can see the layered surfaces of the *Arcadia*. The market, the arboretum, the captain's offices, each occupying its own patch at the very top of the ship, separated from each other like islands.

He pushes the drone downward so that its light floods the flotilla: the tangle of low rafts and barges extending on all sides from the main ship like tentacles. Ragged edges reaching into the ocean for 150 yards all around. He draws the drone upward from the water, skimming deck after deck. This part of the ship is easy to patrol. It's an apartment building turned inside out. The cabins are lined up, nice and neat, along an open deck like a long corridor. Staircases connect the floors. There are no open spaces for people to congregate in, no reasons to loiter, no places to hide. Home to ticket holders only.

The stairwell he's currently standing in is good and bright, but so cold he can see his breath clouding. Before he opens the door out onto the deck, he checks the drone display once more. There's someone there.

He watches a girl on the digiscreen in his hands, a grayscale figure walking quickly along the deck. She's talking to someone on her comglove, her free hand skimming the top of the railing. In the dark space between deck lights, she's almost a shadow. But, in the moment she passes into full light, his drone camera picks up the shape of a patch on her left sleeve. The Federated States flag. She might be a medic or a cadet. Neither would be out of place here on the upper decks. These people educate their kids.

If she doesn't go into one of the cabins and continues on into this stairwell instead, she'll see him. Hadley reaches up and unscrews the light bulb hanging from a cable above the landing, then climbs up half a flight and finds a corner to lurk in. He has no intention of being recognized tonight. Under normal circumstances, he'd arrest her, but she could say anything under interrogation, and people might start asking him why he was up on this deck at all.

Let's get a closer look. See if he can't persuade her to change course. The drone had been up high, giving him a wide view of the ship, but now he brings it down, making it swoop close to the girl, staying level and slow, so that she knows it's there. Knows someone is watching.

He needs to get to Neath territory without anyone recognizing him. That's fourteen decks to navigate incognito from his head-quarters at the back of the ship, and he's not even halfway down. He can't afford any screwups if he's going to get off this godforsaken ship and back to the real world.

He returns his attention to the girl on the digiscreen, following her small figure with the camera at the bottom of the drone. Not technically an authorized use of equipment, but he had his needs. And he needs his meds.

She hasn't entered a cabin, and she hasn't been deterred by the drone. *Dammit.* The girl's last chance is if she goes down the stairs instead of up.

As she pushes open the door with her shoulder, she disappears from the viewscreen. She hesitates in the darkness. Hadley imagines her deciding which way to turn, imagines her peering into the gloom. Yards away. He holds his breath.

The next second, she's clipping down the stairs away from him.

Lucky girl.

The timer on his wrist sounds, shrill as a banshee in the dingy light of the stairwell, bouncing off the metal stairs, the bare white walls. He curses under his breath.

The girl's footsteps stop. He imagines her looking up and back, over her shoulder, trying to figure out what the noise was. If she's in danger. Then her footsteps clatter away, running like the hounds of hell are chasing her, and somewhere below there's the sound of another door slamming.

Hadley rests the digiscreen on the ground next to his boots and searches his pocket for a syringe. He pulls off the lid with his teeth, holds his breath and jabs the needle point through his coarse trousers into the skin underneath. Into the flesh that's already dappled with purple-and-green circles from his pointless daily injection.

1,836 days aboard. 1,836 syringes. 1,836 pinprick bruises.

He picks the digiscreen up and runs the drone from one end of the deck to the other, checking that it's clear. Checking whether he can continue. He swings around the back of the ship where it rises in steps from the water, and then upward, over the closed-up market, over the captain's offices still lit from within, over the bridge at the front of the ship that's like a visor pointing out to sea. *It looks like a face,* he thinks. *It looks like eyes.*

The *Arcadia* is in good shape for a ship that's been sitting in salt water for forty years. For all his faults, the captain keeps it well maintained. He stops it from being torn to pieces by the vermin that live on board, the ones who would break her up for scrap. It's been repainted in the past decade too, although now it's showing lines of rust—like dried blood—on its black paint.

He knows this ship inside and out. He's seen most of it, heard about the rest. He knows about the Neaths living in the bottom of the ship, who never come up into the sunlight. Left behind and forgotten. He knows the lower decks where poverty keeps them one missed food shipment away from starvation. He knows about those in the middle who've managed to get jobs and feather their nests and tell their kids that they've got a chance of being accepted into the Federated States. The free schools they've set up in tiny back bedrooms. The community gardens that fill empty bellies. The secret libraries that pass dog-eared paperbacks from person to person. He understands this ship's can-do attitude.

And, if it was up to him, he'd punch a hole in its hull and watch the whole thing go under.

CHAPTER 5

ESTHER

When my feet touch Residential Deck Seven, I glance back; the coast is clear. No mirrored faces have followed me home. I stop, chest aching, and lean against a section of wall that's been planted with samphire. Its pungent, earthy smell invades my nose.

Maintain control, Esther.

When I finally pull myself together, the last sliver of daylight has been replaced by a desolate night sky. Still shaking, I push away from the vegetation-encrusted wall and start the walk home. It's comforting just being in the right neighborhood. Everything is completely normal. There are no strangers and no surprises. I walk on a familiar wooden deck, kept varnished by the Deck Committee, and step over the shuffleboard that's repainted every spring before the weather gets nice enough to play. I know all of my neighbors by sight, and they know me. I'm home.

If I can get into bed without letting May and my parents know what happened in the Lookout, how close I came to getting arrested, I can sleep it off. By tomorrow, it will feel like a bad dream.

The cabin sits lifeless at the end of the deck. I'm the first one home. Ours is a tiny cabin on the seaward side of the ship, where we have an unbroken view of the Atlantic. The *Arcadia* is half a mile of floating metal. As high as the Statue of Liberty, which my Federated States history class taught me is located somewhere north of here, but which I've never seen in real life. Maybe one day I'll take a day trip to Liberty Island and see her for myself.

As I get closer to the front door with its familiar porthole window in the center, I notice our pocket-sized solar panels are still hanging outside where they've been charging all day. The sun's so weak this time of year that we might only get a couple of hours from each. I choose the ones with the highest energy levels, four with green charge bars, a couple more showing yellow, and hug them to my stomach while I unlock the door. I slide a charged panel into the lantern closest to me. Shadows stretch around the cabin, and I'm reminded how lucky we are to have access to some of the Federated States' technology. Along with our uniforms and badges, May and I were given these lights when we were accepted into our training programs.

My foot hits something as I step inside, and I stoop to grab a paper bag lying on the doormat. Once all the lanterns are lit, I close the door and rest my back against it. There's a message scrawled on the bag in Alex's neat handwriting: *Brain food*. Inside are six apples. Real, actual apples—plump with shiny red skin. My mouth waters. These aren't the stunted billiard balls that are forced out of the trees in the ship's arboretum. These are eaters that can only have come from the land. Alex must have worked for hours to get them.

In the dim light from the lanterns, our cabin is claustrophobic. At the front, one room contains our tiny kitchen with a single-ring stove, square cupboards above the stainless-steel sink. We have two saucepans hanging from hooks on the wall, a collection of blunt kitchen knives on the counter, a kettle that's stained brown from the stove flame. The other side of the room is taken over by the couch, a rough red cotton affair that pulls out into a bed for my parents. On the wall above it is the Federated States flag, hand-sewn by my mom. An ostentatious show of loyalty to the country May and I are desperate to be a part of.

I squeeze through the corridor that's too narrow even for a single person. Our family pictures are framed and hung on nails. I straighten the one of Grandma and Grandad Crossland as I pass and feel the tug of missing them in my chest.

I never really knew Grandad, but I had Grandma until I was seven. This was their honeymoon cabin, and there are traces of her everywhere. The pots and knickknacks that she collected during her life. The big crocheted blanket my parents still sleep under. My grandparents were on board the *Arcadia*, waiting to set sail after their wedding, when war broke out in Europe. Nobody really knows which of the European powers pressed the button first, but within hours, missiles carrying biological warheads were being traded across the continent. The Virus inside the missiles spread at a terrifying speed, wiping out millions of people in a week.

As well as the ticket holders already on the ship, the captain managed to squeeze on hundreds more who were fleeing for their lives. They made the terrifying journey west, but, when they got here, hope turned sour. It's been forty years, and fewer than five hundred refugees have ever set foot on dry land. Right up until she died, my grandma still clung to the hope that she'd be able to leave the ship one day. She'd have been over the moon that her two granddaughters were about to make it.

At the end of the corridor is the room I share with May. Our bunk beds take up most of the space, the only other furniture squeezed in being a chest of drawers that doubles as a desk. I climb onto the bottom bunk, grabbing a textbook from the desk to start my revision. Or at least pretend to. If I'm studying when the others get home, no one will disturb me. If the leaflet drop comes up, I'll deny I was there. I can't let the Lookout be added to the long list of places I'm not allowed to go by myself.

A jangle of keys. The sound of the front door closing, footsteps through the front cabin, and then the swish of the bathroom door sliding closed. Two minutes later, May appears, hair wrapped in a towel. She stuffs a ball of clothes into the drawstring laundry bag that hangs by the door. Over my textbook, I watch her combing her hair as she paces: step, step, turn.

"You showered?" I say eventually.

"And?"

I bite my lip and try not to speak. The sun can only heat so much water, and today that two-minute tank belonged to me. She stole my shower.

"You showered yesterday. Today was my turn."

"I spilled coffee. I needed to shower. Get over it."

Her face is hot-water blotchy. She throws the comb down onto the desk. It lands among the jumble of books and brushes and pens that litter the top of our shared workspace. The three-rung ladder creaks as she climbs up and thumps her pillow into shape. Silence thickens around us. We can't see each other when we sit like this— her in the top bunk, me in the bottom. But I can feel her seething. I won't apologize first. I won't.

My eyes skim the lines of the textbook without taking anything in. I can't concentrate. I find myself drawn back to the Lookout. Where is that girl now? Is she at home in her own bunk or—

"Sorry," May says. "Long day."

I take an apple from the bag and throw it over the edge of the top bunk so that it lands on May's blanket. Her face appears, upside down, the dark hair hanging in a wet curtain. I've always been envious of May's hair. The way it frames her face in thick waves that look polished no matter what she does with it.

"Alex?" she says.

"Alex."

"He's a keeper, that one. It's cold—scoot over." Apple between her teeth, she swings herself down on to my bunk and pushes icy feet under my blanket. "Say someone got hurt, and they were bleeding, how long would they have?"

"Depends. Is it like they cut their hand, or like they lost a limb?"

"No, more like they got shot."

"Shot?"

"Or stabbed."

"What are you talking about?"

"Nothing. Doesn't matter." She takes a tiny bite of the apple, leaving a circle of toothmarks in its skin, and rests her head on my shoulder.

Turning the page of my textbook, I try to act like I didn't come within seconds of getting arrested today. My movements feel too big. Like they've been rehearsed.

May takes my hand, and I freeze, seeing for the first time the thing she's noticed. A dirty gray smudge on my comglove. The telltale residue of recycling paper. She runs her thumb over it, and when it doesn't disappear she applies more pressure.

"Is that—did you go to the Lookout today?"

Don't look at her. Act normal.

"No, came straight back after class." I flip a page with my free hand.

She stares at the smudge. There's no reason for her to doubt me, but if she looks at my face, she'll know I was there. You don't spend sixteen years in the same cramped space without learning how to read your roommate.

"And now you're lying."

I slap the textbook closed and scooch to the edge of the bunk. "I'm going to get some wood from the store."

"It's dark out."

"And?"

"And it's dark out. I'll go."

I don't need her to go for me. I don't need the third degree about where I've been today. Envy bubbles up inside me. May gets to go where she wants, when she wants, and no one bats an eyelid. She's the self-possessed military cadet, and I'm the weakling medic who needs to be chaperoned and watched like a toddler. "I need some air."

"Not this late, you don't."

"Excuse me?"

"You're acting weird, and you're clearly lying about where you've been and what you were doing. I'm not letting you go out alone."

"You're not *letting me*," I say, my voice irritatingly squeaky. *Way to show your robust side, Esther.*

"I can't protect you if I don't know where you are. I expect you to be here, at class, or at Alex's."

"It's not your job to protect me. I'm not a kid."

She raises her eyebrows.

"This is exactly why I don't tell you where I'm going the whole time," I say.

I can feel the room getting smaller. I need to get out. Out of this room. Out of this cabin. Off this ship. I spin on the spot and barge out of the room, wishing it wasn't a sliding door so that I could slam it behind me.

I press my hands against my temples. My head's fuzzy with all the things clamoring for attention: The girl with her pleading face. Alex's sort-of proposal. School. May's questions and orders and demands.

I'm going to Alex's, and if I run into the Coalies, I'll flash them my Federated States badge and explain who I am. I don't even know why I ran from the Lookout in the first place. Obviously, they'd let me go. I'm almost one of them.

I grab my bag from its place next to the front door and swing it over my head. When I get outside, I break into a run. Within seconds, my face is coated with needles of icy salt water. Running makes me feel like I can escape this ship and this suffocating life. It makes me feel as if I could go somewhere new.

It's good to move. To feel the air rushing into my lungs. I realize there's no point stewing over May. She's going to try and protect me however much I struggle. And there's no point agonizing about what happened to that girl. It wasn't my fault. It was the fault of whoever dropped those leaflets in the first place. In the hierarchy of blame, I'm way down the list. If she's innocent, she'll be released without charge, no harm done. And Alex is the *only* choice. Who else would I end up with? The whole marriage thing took me by surprise, that's all.

As I near the end of the deck, my feet pound in time with a new mantra: *Don't look back. Commit to Alex. Graduate. Commit to Alex. Graduate. Don't look back—*

Something hits me in the stomach so hard the air erupts from my lungs. I sprawl on my back. Some idiot blocked the deck, and it's so dark I didn't see it. Tears blur my vision. I try to breathe through the pain that's taken over my body.

Dark silhouettes crowd above me. There's a pair of worn boots right in front of my face. The laces snapped and reknotted.

Someone saw me fall. They're coming to help. Humiliation and pain coil in my gut as I try to push myself up. May will love this. She'll have a field day when I tell her I fell over on deck.

A man's hands, fingers fat and gloveless, a rope snaking between them. Panic rises in me.

Rough fabric drops over my face, and instead of air I'm breathing cloth and ancient dust. I try to move, to pull my hands apart, to fight, but a rope bites into the skin at my wrists.

Still dazed, I'm hauled up and slung over a shoulder like a water-logged net. The blood rushes to my head. My lungs are pressed against the man's shoulder so hard I can't breathe. I kick my feet desperately, but hit nothing. With each pointless kick, fear pulses through me like it's carried in my veins.

This is happening.

My boot makes contact. The man carrying me grunts like an animal. Feeling the heat of triumph, I seize the moment. I twist at the waist. I kick again. I smack my tied hands against the back of his head.

He's thrown off balance, and we drop to the deck, pain exploding through me. My teeth slam together so hard I'm surprised they don't shatter. I scream. Loud and hard and with everything I have. The noise is swallowed by the hood. Someone will come. Someone has to come.

"Get her feet," a man's gruff voice says, like a match striking close to my ear.

He huffs with exertion. I can smell his breath: spicy tobacco, stale food. Arms wrap around my shoulders, more around my legs. I shout again, but this time a hand clamps over my mouth, pushing the fabric hard against my lips until I taste blood. I struggle, and it's as futile as a fish flopping on the deck. My muscles burn out. My last scrap of energy fades.

I let them carry me.

CHAPTER 6

HADLEY

Hadley pauses when he reaches the lowest deck. He stares straight down through a hatch, steeling himself for where he's going next. Here, at the waterline, the staircases of the upper ship are replaced by ladders leading down into inky darkness. Stagnant air muffles his senses. The drone's been his companion, a safety net, letting him check for danger. But he can't get a connection down here. He slides the drone controller into his pocket, takes hold of the top rung, and starts his descent.

How long before he, commander of the *Arcadia* security forces, was missed? Hours? A day maybe? Too long for anyone to help him even if he could tell them where he was.

His feet touch the ground. These would have been the staff areas. Right in the middle of the ship. A maze of corridors and storage rooms. Something scuttles in the darkness. Instinctively, he turns his back to the ladder, feeling a rung press into his shoulder blades, and uses his comglove to flash a light into the darkness. Boxes. Rubble. Nothing moving. A slime of black mold climbs the wall opposite him, reaching up from the floor and over the ceiling. Dust and spores so thick he can see them flowing in the beam of light. Feel them settling in his throat. Like the ship is becoming part of him. Sometimes, he wonders if he'll ever be able to extricate himself. If he'll ever really be free of it.

When he was a kid, before it even entered his head to join up, he had a mortal fear of the ships. News footage showed people weak from starvation, teeth brittle and cracked from lack of sunshine. It's not exactly what he found on the *Arcadia*, but damn close.

He sweeps the light back and forth once more. Nothing there.

Get on with it, Hadley.

Moisture drips from the ceiling, playing an eerie, echoing soundtrack. When he gets to the door he's looking for, a thin sheet of plastic nailed over an opening, he raps his knuckles on the door frame. The sound is muffled by the dampness of the wood.

A light appears behind the plastic sheet, blueish and ghostly. A kid pokes his head out. He can only be eight or nine, but his lips are sucked inwards over his gums, and he has a purple hue to his skin. Repulsive.

"Tell him I'm here," Hadley says.

The plastic curtain swooshes down behind the boy.

"Nice to see you," comes a man's voice from the other side, raspy and wet enough to make Hadley's skin crawl. The man's cheeks are sunken, skin pulled taut over the bones.

"Give it to me."

The man nods and hands Hadley a manila envelope.

Hadley opens the tattered edges to check inside. "This is half my usual," he says.

The old man squints at him. "Problem is, one of my deliveries was delayed at security. It's the domino effect, isn't it?"

"I need more than this," Hadley says. He's trying not to let the weakness of panic seep into his voice.

"Then make sure no one goes poking around in my next shipment."

"I don't make security decisions based on the needs of a lowlife drug pusher."

The man sneers. "If you want your medication, you do," he says.

Hadley's close enough to see his peg teeth, stained tobacco-yellow in the cracks, smell the old sweat and leather of him. How can anyone smoke down here? How can anyone *live* down here?

Hadley takes the man by the collar, fingers skimming the sagging, raw-chicken flesh of his neck. "When I ask you for something, you supply it. Or have you forgotten who's made it possible for you to run your smuggling operation all these years? While everyone else had their freedoms stripped away, you got to continue without any security checks. If you can't supply me anymore, you might find the Coalies take more interest in what you're doing."

The man grins, throwing Hadley off guard. This isn't how it works. This is not how people respond to his instructions.

"Rumor has it you're losing your grip. People are saying your time's up."

Hadley tightens his grasp on the man's clothes, pulling in and up so that they're nose to nose. "Who? The gangs?"

But even as he says it he doesn't believe it. They behave, and he keeps out of their business—for the most part. It works, and it's how he likes it. And it gives his superiors the impression he's got everything under control.

"Couldn't tell you who, just that's the rumor. You might not be giving out orders for too much longer." The man shrugs him off and ducks under the plastic sheeting, the light within fading.

Hadley sweeps the sheet aside. "There's not enough here to last me through the week. You need to get more!"

"Sorry, nothing doing," the man says over his narrow, bird-like shoulder. He's moving away from Hadley, through another doorway, another sheet of plastic. Out of reach.

"What am I supposed to do?"

"Guess you'll have to face whatever it is those meds help you forget," he says.

CHAPTER 7

ESTHER

Everybody wants something, Esther, my mom's voice whispers.

The ends of my bones grind together with every step the big man takes. The men carrying me shift me around. Sometimes sharing the load, sometimes taking turns carrying me. Right now, my arms dangle over the man's back. I hear him grunting and snuffling. I smell the stale sweat of his armpits. His shoulder presses into my gut.

What does he want? My death? No, he'd have given me to the sea already if it was that.

I've stopped trying to remember which way he's brought me, the hood over my head blurring the journey into endless staircases. Every neuron in my body fires pain.

There's a metallic wheeze and the clunk of a hatch sliding shut. I'm planted on the deck. Terror forces me down, and I wait for whatever's next, clinging to the passing seconds. The hot air is tainted by the smell of rust and less pleasant human smells. Urine and sweat.

"You got her," a woman's voice says. "What happened to you?"

"Stupid bitch kicked me," the man says. He sniffs, and I imagine him wiping blood on the back of his hand.

"I told you not to hurt her," the woman snaps. Her voice is deep and glacier-smooth. She's in charge. She's the one who will let me live or not. "Get that hood off her. He hasn't got much time."

Strands of my hair snag and are pulled out at the roots as the hood is lifted. I gulp in air. My eyes burn with the new brightness. When my aching vision adjusts to the light, I see I'm in a narrow room with a metal floor. Machinery and pipes line the walls like veins. Lidded vats, taller than a person, squat in a row with their bare metal flesh showing through cracked paint. There's no steamy hiss or hum of work. The machinery is dead.

Freed from the hood, I see that the man is mountainous. The lower portion of his face is covered by a smooth leather mask, black, with metal-edged holes for breathing. His eyes move fast and are bloodshot and full of malice. A red crescent crowns the bridge of his nose with a stream of tar-like blood running under the edge of his mask. His breath rattles through mucus.

Despite all the despair and panic, I feel a tiny spark of satisfaction. I did that to him.

The woman's face is covered so that only her eyes are visible, edged by delicate crow's feet on dark skin. Silver-streaked hair pokes from the edges of her hood.

These are Neaths. Who else would do something like this?

"Help him!" the woman orders, pointing at a figure lying on the floor at the end of the room. A tube light flickers on the ceiling, picking up the edges of rags folded on his chest. There's a cloth covering his face that is sucked in with each painful breath. He's alive, but not for long, given the slick of blood on the floor around him. Now I know what they want.

We've got minutes.

I move toward him, but stop when I feel the tug of the rope around my wrists. Keeping my eyes on the patient, I raise my hands. The man ambles over with a knife lolling in his hand. No comglove, so I can see the fleshiness of his fingers around the handle. He pauses, the blade level with my face.

When the metal grazes my skin, cutting the ropes, I can't suppress a shudder. Blood rushes back to my hands with a thousand pinpricks. The man's eyes crease at the corners. He's smiling under his mask. I rub the skin on my wrists, scraped raw where the ropes held me.

Careful not to let my knees dip into the pool of blood, I crouch by the figure. I'm not fazed by blood—I've seen enough in training—but this is the first time I'm supposed to work on a live person with such catastrophic injuries. I've sewn my share of bullet wounds, but now the clean, cold disinfectant smell of the training room at the infirmary has been replaced by warm metallic blood radiating from the body on the floor. This is not how I dreamed my first emergency would go. With so much blood, and the metal floor pressing into my knees, and the circulation flowing painfully into my recently untied hands. And the woman staring intensely. And the man who brought me here still trying to intimidate me.

It's going to swamp me. I try to breathe, and force myself to touch the inside of the patient's wrist. My own pulse hammers so loud I have to close my eyes. Pressure builds in my head. *I can't do this.*

Corp's voice breaks through the hum of panic in my mind: *Keep your head and people keep their lives.* She's standing at the front of the training room with her hands clasped behind her back, commanding the room in her standard-issue medic's jumpsuit. Her black corkscrew curls are pulled back from the warm bronze serenity of her face.

My classmates and I stand behind our benches, each with a cloned body part resting on a plastic tray. I have an arm, cut off seamlessly just below the shoulder. The fingers move restlessly, caressing the air in perfect imitation of human motion, but the smell from it is raw meat and bleach. Corp's hand emerges from behind her back. She presses the timer button and smiles. "Go."

Checklists flit through my head, and I snatch at one. I know exactly what to do. I'm trained for this. It's not what I expected, but it's what I've got.

Step 1: assessment. From what I can see of his eyes and forehead, the patient is young, probably about my age, and male. His brown skin is pallid and clammy, but there's flesh on his bones and no signs of malnourishment. Judging by the amount of blood, I'd say he has a serious chest wound, and his breathing is hindered by the bandana covering the lower part of his face.

I move to loosen the saliva-dampened cloth. The man grabs my hand and twists it away, sending fresh pain shooting through my elbow.

"No, leave him covered," he growls.

I grind my teeth and yank my arm free, anger overtaking fear.

I've never been the voice of authority in a situation before. But he put his hands on me again. He stopped me doing my job, and I can't control the urge to stand up to this man, even though he's holding me against my will. "He can't breathe," I say.

"He'll have to manage."

The woman drops to her knees on the other side of the boy and pulls the cloth upwards, holding it so that it blocks my view like a curtain. Her hands tremble. Tiny shock waves quiver through the fabric. Her neatly trimmed nails are clogged with blood, and there are reddish-brown splashes on her comglove. Definitely not a Neath. They don't wear comgloves. And she cares more about this boy than the man does. Maybe I can use that. There's no room for panic now. If I let fear get the better of me, like I did in the Lookout, I'll be lost.

The flashing of the strip light above my head is distracting. Every blink and pop sets me on edge and breaks my concentration. "I need light," I say, and my voice holds a faint quiver. "And my bag, is it here?"

The man dumps it on the floor next to me, rippling the pool of blood and sending a shiver creeping down my spine. But the rough canvas of the med bag feels solid and familiar. I can open the leather and metal buckles without looking at them. It's comforting. A life-saving piece of driftwood on an unforgiving sea.

I unpack the things I'll need.

You treat the patient first. Focus in until there's no place left for panic. It's one of the first things Corp taught us.

I need to see the wound so I lift the rags covering it. They're candy-cane striped: white rags, bloody stripes. The boy's chest is pierced by a clean black hole an inch beneath his heart. A gunshot wound. Blood oozes from it, but it's not gushing, and that's a good thing. I slide my hand underneath him, feeling with my fingers. There's no hole on the other side. No exit wound means the bullet's still in there. But this isn't a straightforward case.

I touch the skin around the black hole of the wound. Dark blue tendrils reach out from it, spreading a network over the skin of his chest and up to his neck. A poison-laced bullet. They're illegal unless you're law enforcement. No surprise; these people are on the wrong side of the law. Whether they're from the Neath gangs or smugglers or petty criminals, I don't know, and it doesn't matter. We don't fly the same flag. They're enemies of the Federated States.

The poison already making its way through the boy's circulatory system is my golden ticket to survival. No matter how well I patch him up, he'll die without the antivenom. That's what will save me. And, even though my rational brain tells me I should dread playing such dangerous games with a bunch of criminals, I can't help the spark of excitement in my chest.

I drop the rags back over the wound and set my face. Don't let them in on the secret until the right moment. My mind whirs with energy. My hands move through old habits, dipping into the sense memory built from years of training.

Step 2: treatment. I unscrew the bottle of wound sterilizer from my bag and douse the boy's chest. The sight of it bubbling out of the bullet hole is sickening. I've racked up a hundred hours of practice, but this is different. He's softer, more fragile. He'll die if I mess up.

When I press my field scanner over the bullet hole, it scans my thumbprint and hums to life, giving a clear picture of the damage. He's lucky; the bullet lodged in his fifth rib. If he'd been any closer to the gun, the bullet would have smashed right through to the delicate organs inside. He'd have been dead before I ever set eyes on him.

I know what to do. I know how to escape. Turns out I'm a competent medic.

The woman holds the boy's hand to her chest like she can force life into him. The man lingers in the shadows.

I roll up my sleeves and get to work.

CHAPTER 8

NIK

No clue where I am.

There's a fist of pain right under my heart. It drags through my veins like barbed wire.

A streak of light blinks on and off above me. My fingers sway in something wet. Everything's wet.

May's here!

Light flashes behind her head. Her shape burns on to the surface of my eyes. Like staring at the sun. May is the sun. May is—

She's pressing at the pain. I cry at her to stop, but the sound gets tangled in my throat. May's never hurt me before. May's never—

Why did she change her nose? And the shape of her eyes? To get away from the Coalies. Clever May. Clever May. She needed to get away, so she threw on a disguise. Stretched her nose a little longer and made her eyes a little rounder. Covered that mole on her cheek, the one that bobs up and down when she smiles.

May would never hurt me. She leans forward, and there's no expression on her face. Flawless. Blank.

It's not May. It's not May.

My lungs are too heavy. Drowning. My voice gurgles through water, and the girl can't hear me over the pool in my chest. She won't stop.

I don't want to die.

She keeps stabbing and stabbing.

It's a trick. It's a trick. It's a trick. It's not May.

I'm going to die on the ship. We're all going to die on the ship.

CHAPTER 9

HADLEY

His ship is next.

Hadley slips a blue tablet onto his tongue and lets it dissolve to powder. His eyes skim the digimap of the coast that's suspended in front of him. The immigrant ships sit like pustules on the flawless skin of his country. To the north, five ships flicker red against the blue-gray of the digital ocean; to the south, there's a straggling line of black ships. The *Arcadia* is next in the cascade of clearances that will see the rotting hulks unbuilt: dismantled piece by piece until there's no trace left of them or the human dregs that inhabit them.

There were ten to begin with, spread out along the six-hundred-mile coast of the Federated States. All have jarring, saccharine names. *Arcadia. Oceania.* The *Azamara Quest* crossed the Atlantic Ocean all the way from Lisbon. The *Jørgenson* was cruising Iceland with a few thousand rich sightseers when the Virus took hold, and it couldn't go back to Denmark. This one, the *Arcadia*, spent weeks limping from Liverpool to here. Weeks of open water, buffeted by waves the height of skyscrapers. They thought the Federated States would throw open its borders and let them in. But, by the time they realized they wouldn't be receiving a warm welcome, it was too late. Within a generation, engines fell into disrepair. Hulls rotted. The Stranded weren't going anywhere.

It's taken years for the antiship elements of the Federated States government to outmaneuver the proship contingent. Finally, a vote went the right way, and the decision was made: the ships had to go. Five have been destroyed so far, the inhabitants sealed in quarantine camps on land where they're made useful. There are complaints about inhumane conditions in the camps, but the ship folk can't be set free. They expect a free ride that the Federated States isn't in a position to give. In any case, the prison corporations always need more workers.

He'd watched the first ship burn from the shore, standing shoulder to shoulder with the other unit commanders. The waves were high that night, and he planted his feet on the barnacle-crusted rock, too excited to notice the icy spray that soaked his trousers. Smoke and salt sharpened the breeze. Rising flames were reflected on the oil-slick ocean, and gunfire clattered around the bay, signaling death for the handful of insurrectionists still fighting. Grime scraped away by government forces.

Hadley never had any romantic notions that a career with the Coalies was his calling. He joined up because jobs were scarce, and the pay was good. But, as that ship burned down to a smoldering skeleton, a spark of desire took hold inside him. A desire to purge the land and the sea of every ship and every invader.

Hadley flicks the digiscreen with his finger. The map fades, and a series of mugshots rises to replace it. These are the prisoners his team picked up after the leaflet drop in the Lookout. He's looking for any clue that one of them might be responsible for the propaganda. But there's not a single criminal record between them. Not a single known association with criminal groups. He pinches the top of his nose in an attempt to stop the spread of a headache and turns his back on the roving camera that monitors his expression. His superiors are watching. They want to see control. He's worn this mask of dispassion so long, he can't remember what's underneath.

All units are out patrolling, leaving him and a new deputy alone in what passes for HQ. As poorly provisioned as it is, this is the most secure place on the ship. No proper offices, just a tiny shared room with a coffee station set on top of a filing cabinet and the end wall given over to a digiscreen. The furniture's from the original ship. Decades-old wooden desks, all scratched and etched with graffiti. Office chairs missing half the stuffing from their seats, and with so many stains on the fabric, it looks patterned.

Hadley has a couple of cells at the back to keep his prisoners in before they get transferred to the mainland. He lives in that part, too, in a shoebox cabin that's barely fit for a human. There's no air in there.

This piddling act of civil disobedience is the first peep of trouble he's seen in weeks. If a leaflet drop is as far as their resources stretch, they're no threat. A handful of leaflet-dumping civilians won't put up much resistance when the clearance order comes.

The words of his supplier drift back. *Your time's up.* He shakes the memory away. There's no one strong enough to challenge him, not seriously. Not Silas Cuinn and his army of Neaths. The other major gang leader is Enid Hader, and she rules over a territory that's literally built out of trash.

No, he's done well here, and the *Arcadia* has got a reputation for being under control. Quiet. Especially compared to the other ships down the coast where drugs and crime and escapees break over the nearest cities like toxic waves. He credits it to the atmosphere of suspicion and surveillance he's cultivated. The drones and spider-legged bots he patrols with have got them all thinking they're being watched the whole time.

Six months—ten at the outside—until clearance. Still, wouldn't hurt to investigate this leaflet drop. Get his ducks in a row before the clearance order comes. He scratches at the complicated scar that runs through his top lip, his nails scraping on stubble.

"Anything?" he asks, turning to the deputy occupying the nearest desk.

The kid's just out of the academy, his chin still dotted with purple zit scars that he picks at when he's concentrating. Eagerness lights him up from the inside. His spark will go out soon enough, the first night he spends guarding the sewage tanker.

"Nothing on any of them, Commander Hadley, sir," the deputy says. His pointy Adam's apple bobs. "But Grimson and Dennis gave chase to two suspects near the Lookout—"

"Why were they suspects?"

"Sir?"

"What was suspicious about them?" Hadley sighs and rubs at the star of pain throbbing between his eyes. "Doesn't matter. Did they get them?"

The deputy deflates. "Well, no, sir. They chased them along the service corridor and lost them going into Neath territory at the aft end of the ship. Didn't want to follow without backup."

"No." His team knows better than to wade into trouble by themselves. Neath gangs are unpredictable. And drug-addled. "Circulate their descriptions to all units."

"They didn't get a good look at them, sir. Faces covered," he says. "But Grimson thinks she shot one of them."

"Tell me they were packing toxic rounds."

A grin spreads over the deputy's face. "Yes, sir."

Hadley suppresses a smile. A minor success. "Get me a list of every black-market contact we have. And do it quietly, no spooking them. If anyone on this ship even thinks about antivenom, I want to know. Got it?"

"Yes, sir." The deputy taps at his digiscreen, dripping eagerness.

Hadley turns back to the mugshots on the wall and flicks through them with his finger. Dirt-streaked. Half-starved. Toothless. The usual. But then—a girl, mid-teens, greasy hair straggling over her face. Pretty if she was from anywhere else.

"Process them all, except for the girl," he says over his shoulder.

"For release, sir?"

"Decontamination and quarantine for transfer to prison camp." Might as well start cleaning up before the clearance is announced.

Hadley turns to find the deputy open-mouthed. "Problem executing my order, Deputy?"

"No, sir. But—"

"But what, Deputy?"

"It's just that she doesn't seem to be the type, sir. She's not—she doesn't look like—"

"You mean she doesn't look like a rebel hell-bent on undermining our control of this vessel?" Hadley squares his shoulders at the younger man.

"Yes, sir."

Hadley grabs the deputy by the shoulder and maneuvers him until he's facing the digital mugshot of the girl, digging his fingers into the young man's collarbone.

"Have a look at her. Tell me what you see."

The deputy licks his lips. "A kid. She's thin—"

Hadley squeezes his shoulder. "What I see is *potential*," he says. "Every single one of them's got potential. The next leaflet drop. The next quarantine breach. The next murder. She'll be a criminal eventually. So we treat them like they've already done the things we know they're capable of. That way we get to stop all the damage they would do given half a chance. Don't let them get under your skin, Deputy. They'll exploit any weakness. Now take the girl to Interrogation Room One. Loosen her up a bit." Hadley lets go of the deputy's shoulder.

"Loosen her up, sir?"

Hadley sighs. "Ask her the standard questions," he says. This recruit needs toughening up. No place for weak links on Hadley's team.

Hadley refills his cup from the jug in the corner of the bullpen. The coffee's cold and sour, and the boxed milk gives it a fruity tang. He can almost remember real coffee in a real coffee shop. With cream. There was cream in his apartment in the city. A plastic pot on the top shelf of the fridge. On the morning of his disciplinary hearing, he took it out, sniffed it and put it back. He never saw the sentence coming. If he went back now, that cream would still be there.

The roving camera takes a clumsy path along the wall, its Cyclops eye fixed on him. That tinny *clack-clack* footstep invades his sleep; he knows the thing crouches next to his bed at night. The metal-rimmed eye draws level with his face. It folds its legs under its body and swivels its lens so that Hadley sees his face reflected. Colorless and fish-eyed in the rounded glass. Lint-gray skin against the black of his uniform. He could swat it off the wall and crush it with his heel. He could unholster his weapon and put a bullet right through it.

No. He's been here seventeen years. He can wait another six months. Ten at the outside. After that, there'll be a new post. Freedom. Maybe even forgiveness.

***

The camera skitters into the interrogation room a second before Hadley closes the door behind him. Fetid air clogs his nose. There are no windows, and the prisoner's personal hygiene isn't up to much. She's waiting for him beneath the naked bulb that hangs from the ceiling, perched on a hard, backless stool. Sweat glistens in the creases of her nose.

Hadley takes his seat next to the deputy. The girl licks at the cracked corner of her mouth and stares at Hadley's cup. He takes a gulp of coffee and rests it on the floor by his chair.

The deputy gets up to leave. "Stay, please," Hadley says.

The youthful color drains from the deputy's face, and he presses his lips together as though trying to keep his digestive system in check. He takes his seat and stares at the white mounds of his knuckles.

This one's unnervingly still. What kind is she? One that's too stupid to realize what's happening? Or one of the defiant ones?

"Deputy, read out the prisoner's details and charges."

"Margarite Stenson. Deck Three. Age fifteen. Charged with possession and dissemination of propaganda damaging to the Federated States."

Hadley looks at the girl's eyes. They're clear, but there's a hard edge to them. It's like looking at the horizon. Immovable. Inviolable.

Let's see.

"Has she told you anything?" Hadley asks the deputy.

"Don't know anything," the girl spits.

Hadley bristles. They've hooked a live one. He checks the excitement rising from his gut, but it reaches his head in a dizzying wave. The deputy fidgets by his side.

"Margarite Stenson, you will be found guilty on all charges and detained indefinitely. But I figure we can help each other. I need to know who dropped those leaflets."

It flashes across her face. The cunning. The *what can I use to save myself?* She hasn't had enough practice to hide it yet. Not like Celeste—

Stop. Hadley slams the door shut on that thought before it can get a foot in.

The girl grits her teeth; the muscles in her jaw twitch. "Told you I don't kn—"

Hadley stands up and moves closer. She passes into his shadow, and her pupils dilate in response to the changing light. He lifts her chin, her skin unexpectedly soft against his fingers. He enjoys the pliability of her.

"Sir, I don't think she knows—" The deputy's voice squeaks.

"Shut up," Hadley says with a growl.

He picks up the girl's hand and eases the woolen glove from her fingers. She stiffens. Her lips whiten. Hadley checks the location of the roving camera, pausing while it gets into position and whirs into focus.

Let them watch. Let them see what he's become. Let them see he won't show mercy a second time. He won't be tricked again.

He takes the smallest finger. Suddenly he forces it out, then up. Soft tissue tearing under skin echoes through his fingers, and there's a satisfying pop when the bone leaves its rightful place.

The girl's scream sets his nerves alight. He breathes deep, eyes closed, waiting until the last taste of it fades. His encounter with the dealer made him disoriented. Shook his confidence. But now he's back on his A-game. He takes the next finger.

The deputy's vomit splashes onto the floor next to Hadley's coffee cup.

CHAPTER 10

ESTHER

I grasp the bullet with the extractor forceps and keep my breathing steady as I ease the bent and twisted casing out of the boy's flesh. I don't know whether I've done enough to save him. If his chest stops its agonizing rise and fall, they'll kill me. If his heart fails, they'll kill me. If his brain function disappears, they'll kill me. Our survival is threaded as close as the strands of a net. Me and the boy lying in a pool of his own blood.

I wrap the bullet in gauze and set it on the ground by my knee.

My tongue's like sandpaper. I swipe at my forehead to keep sweat from dripping into my eyes and circle my head to work out the cricks in my neck. It's like operating in an oven.

Another man enters, bringing cooler air rushing into the stagnancy of my operating room. He hurries over to where I'm working, crouches, and places a hand gently on the boy's face. I don't dare look up at him, but I hear the words when he speaks close to the boy's ear. "It's going to be OK." He must have a modulator sewn into his mask because his voice has a robotic, discordant quality making it impossible to recognize.

He turns to the woman. "I need to talk to you," he says. They move to the edge of the cabin, still close enough for me to listen if I can quiet my breathing.

"What were they doing?" the man asks the woman. They're holding hands in the space between their bodies.

"They were being insubordinate," she replies. "Spreading information about the other ships because they think the truth needs to be told. They were risking exposure."

"They're teenagers, and they didn't think it through. This could have been much worse. They could be in one of Hadley's interrogation cells right now," he says.

"They're stupid. Stupid and impulsive," the woman says.

"It's going to be OK. The girl will save him."

She pushes away from the man, shaking her hands out as she walks backs to me, then kneels next to the boy to lift the bandana from his face. As she changes position, the cloth shifts and a fragment of his face is revealed. Five o'clock shadow. A defined jawline. She sees me looking and adjusts the fabric so that it blocks him from view again.

It's difficult to concentrate. The huge man who carried me most of the way here is pacing in the shadows like a death sentence.

I take the suture bot from my bag. Until I press go, it's just a simple plastic frame about the size of my hand. I line it up over the wound, getting the hole as close to the center as possible to give the needles a chance to do their best work. It beeps when I place my finger over the print reader, and the red light flares. From the inside edges of the frame, two lines of articulated needles stretch like the legs of a spider being roused. The needles grip the sides of the wound, pinching the edges closed, pressing tiny dimples into the boy's flesh. The bot begins to sew, passing gossamer-thin suture silk from one leg to another. The stitches are more delicate than anything a human could produce, even a human as good at suturing as me. The wound is an almost imperceptible puckered thread once the bot has done its work.

I need an escape plan. I can literally see the poison spreading through the boy's body; his heart is pumping it through his circulatory system. The clock's ticking for us both. He'll die, if I wait too long.

We're not in the part of the ship I call home. This metallic room isn't on the residential decks; it was never meant for people to live in it. It feels more like a workroom with all the pipes and machinery. And it doesn't feel as if it's part of a small boat, like the ones on the flotilla. There's not enough movement for that. It's not off the service corridor either, with its old music, its cooking smells, its menacing atmosphere.

My dad took us to that slice of chaos once. He'd heard about some black-market pork chops, and he left May and me standing beside a stall selling live hens, while he headed into the throng. I watched him haggle with a woman wearing an ancient orange life jacket over her clothes. May held my hand and glared at anyone that came too close. That was the night Mom and Dad had one of their rare fights—about whether the risk was worth the reward. We all enjoyed the meat though.

I wipe my face again. My stomach twists because I've figured it out. I know where they've brought me. Far below deck, deep in the belly of the ship. I'm in Neath territory. Normal people don't set foot down here, not even for pork chops. I'm so far from home no one will ever find me.

There are stories of below-deck people who never see the sun, their skin like fish scales, their eyes pale. It's enough to terrify any above-deck child.

I need them to take me somewhere else. Above the waterline, out of Neath territory, with enough people around so they won't be able to kill me without attracting attention. I need them to take me to the market.

"Work," the big man growls. Each step he takes, black boots pounding the ground, makes panic tighten my chest.

Step 3: aftercare. Or in the case of me and this boy: mutually assured survival.

"Will he live?" the woman asks.

This is the moment. I have to be like May. I have to muster every ounce of strength and ferocity that I have. I need to make this woman believe that, if she doesn't give in to my demands, I'll let another human being die.

I take a deep breath. "Probably." I shrug. "If you treat the venom in time."

She flinches and lets out a noise so loaded with anguish that I waver. Can I live with myself if I do this? I don't know. But I want to live.

"See the traces of blue under his skin?" I pull back the tattered rags that are the remains of the boy's shirt, still damp with blood.

"The bullet carried a toxin into his system. I've patched him up, but in a few hours it will reach his brain. Once it gets there …"

"You are going to save him," she says.

Her voice is hard, but there are tears pooling in her eyes and soaking the scarf that covers the bottom of her face.

I unwrap the bullet from its gauze and hold it up to the light in a pair of tweezers. I need to lay this on thick.

"See the way the end's split open? That's so the toxin is released on impact. A blast of poison delivered right into your boy's chest. It's government-issue. A very specific neurotoxin. Deadly. Agonizing. A horrible way to go. They're banned in the Federated States, but the Coalies get away with using them on the ships."

Even as I say it, my stomach knots in horror. The Federated States has to take a hard line against its enemies, but I'm not sure anything justifies inflicting this kind of torture on a human being. I drop the bullet back into the gauze and force myself to look at her face.

"Take me to the market. Once we're around people, I'll tell you how to save him."

For a few seconds, I'm not sure what she's going to do. They went to a lot of trouble to save the boy, but maybe this is just one step too far. Maybe my survival isn't something they can risk.

"I won't tell anyone," I say, voice almost a whisper. "If I go to the Coalies, they're just as likely to arrest me as you."

She looks at me now, searching my face. "It's a deal."

Relief, like drinking cold water. I've won, but I'm not home yet.

The big man lunges at me. One massive hand wraps around my neck. My feet lift from the deck. I squirm like a hooked fish, legs thrashing in the air. Pressure builds in my head, every second closer to exploding. My neck muscles strain against his fingers.

His eyes flash with hatred. He wants to watch me die.

Pinprick stars burst into my vision, only to be swamped by a wave of blackness that sweeps in from the edges. My hands drop from his arm.

"There'll be no killing," says the robotic voice of the newcomer.

I crumple to the bare metal floor, coughing while air and blood resume their normal course, making my head swirl. The man's fingerprints burn like a noose mark around my neck. The two men square off. They're a match in height and bulk. The bottom half of their faces are covered, both of them staring and fierce.

"I won't let her live. She'll be blabbing as soon as she sees daylight," says the man who brought me here. His fists clench and unclench, making meaty balls studded with dark hair.

"If we kill her, she can't tell us how to save him." The new man's voice is calm, almost soothing.

"Give me three minutes with her, she'll talk." He looks down at me hungrily.

Terror crawls over my skin. I'd do anything to get away from this man. My rational mind blinks and flashes. Cowering, I inch backwards until my hand touches the boy lying on the floor. Every fraction of an inch I can put between me and those fists is a blessing.

The new man shakes his head. "We can't afford to attract attention, not when things are getting serious. She'll be looked for. Girls like her don't go missing without anyone noticing. Especially not ones being trained by the government. There'll be pictures of her bloated body floating on every digiscreen in the Federated States.

Promising young medic viciously murdered by Neath gangs. They'll say enough's enough and send an army in. Hadley will start with your territory—you can be sure of that."

I shudder at the thought of my ballooned body being pecked at by fish.

"This was a bad job from the start." The big man jabs a sausage finger at the boy. "If he lives, you take him in hand. We're close to the end, and I don't want *this* being linked to my territory. The next time he comes down here, trailing Coalies, he won't get out alive, you hear?"

He pounds to the hatch and spins the handle, then looks back—at me. "No good can come of letting her live."

With the rush of cool air that comes through the door, I let go of the tightness in my chest. I can't believe I pulled it off. I stared a gang of criminals in the face and demanded that they let me live.

The boy's breath rattles in his chest.

"We can't lose his support. We need his firepower. We need access to his territory," the other man says through his mask.

"I'll smooth things over, offer him more incentives," says the woman. She turns her attention to me. "We'll take you to the market, and you'll tell us how to save him."

The boy stirs by my elbow. His eyelids flicker open, and I find myself staring at him. He's trying to speak.

"Esther," he whispers.

The hood is pulled over my face, and I'm dragged away.

CHAPTER 11

ESTHER

My toes clip the floor, and I stumble. The man in the mask steadies me, his hand tightening around my arm so that I don't fall. He's different from the man who wanted me dead. Still urgent, still determined to get his way. But he's not enjoying this.

In his haste he hasn't noticed that my hood is riding up. I can see a slice of floor, our fast-moving feet, the light when we pass bulbs. But I can't pay attention to the route right now.

That boy knows me.

We splash through pools of darkness and over crumpled cardboard and trash. The air is stale and loaded with muffled noises, slamming doors, singing or shouting or screaming nearby.

How could he, a boy with a government-issue bullet in his chest, know my name?

The man drags me up a short stretch of stairs, and we burst

through a door. My fragment of floor floods with early daylight, and I feel a flash of hope.

He pulls the hood from my head, and I'm blinded by the intensity of the morning. A glimpse of the gray shining sea, liquid clouds. I can hear the gulls circling. There's the ship's railing, so close I could touch it. I've been missing for an entire night.

"Keep your eyes forward," he says. "This is almost over, but you have to keep moving."

For the first time since they kidnapped me, I feel a bud of compassion from one of my captors.

He moves so quickly that I'm always a few steps behind. Then my feet tangle and I trip, hang from his hand and slam into the deck. Strips of pain flare on the skin of my hand, and something spikes the inside of my lip. I spit. A chunk of tooth, slimy with saliva and blood, drops on to the deck. The man pulls me up and makes me continue.

Familiar features of the ship swim around me as we near the market, and the distant hum of people grows to a tumult. We slow down and pass beneath the twisting and rusted steel archway that marks the entrance, with its flowing image of a person, midstroke among blue-and-white waves that are far tamer than the sea that surrounds the ship. A sign points left for the men's changing area, right for the women's.

The market was once the ship's swimming pool. Long drained of water, the floor and walls are still lined with tiny tiles in shades of blue. At the deep end, the pool's sheer sides tower above the market stalls. There's a concrete block with old metal fixtures where the diving board used to be, and the remains of a lifeguard station stands proud at the far end.

The place swarms with life. A line of Neaths and ticket holders snakes from the baozi stand, steam gushing skywards in great clouds. There's an oil-slick smell of smoking fish. Spices—cumin and coriander—thicken the air. We earn angry yells as we barge through a huddle of people waiting to buy pickled herring. The only group of passengers you'll never find in the market are the ticket holders from the topmost decks. They'd never rub shoulders with strangers down here. They have people to do their shopping for them.

Gap-toothed Neath kids dodge in and out of people's legs. They gather scraps from the floor and pick pockets given the chance. With the man pulling me on, I almost trip over a scrawny girl carrying a piece of bread as big as her head. She looks up at me with happy eyes and smiles. There's a row of pulpy gums where her teeth should be. Out of habit, I feel for my med bag. You have to watch these kids.

The downward slope of the floor sends me off balance, and threads of dizziness swirl inside my head. Throbbing pain radiates from the front corner of my mouth. I have to grit my teeth to avoid retching.

Keep it together, Esther.

Pages from textbooks flit through my head. I compare the bullet from the boy's chest, and the tangled web and knots of blue under his skin, to things I've seen before. When I find the right memory, I close my eyes and hold it in place until it's set.

The man stops in the center of the market, our feet scuffing the tiny orange and aquamarine tiles of an octopus mosaic. He twists me around so that I'm facing away from him and grips my wrists. His face touches the side of mine, sending shivers of electricity running along my ear. I fight the urge to pull away.

"Tell me how to save him," he says.

It's a shock when I hear myself say, "No."

"No?"

His surprise fires me up. "No," I say more forcefully. "Who was that boy? How did he know my name?"

"You're in dangerous water," he says.

"How do I know you're not just going to grab me the next time one of your criminals takes a bullet?" I strain against his hands, ignoring the pain of his grip on my wrists.

"We know where you live, Esther. Your family. Your boyfriend."

Anger charges down my sternum, searing hot.

"Do not threaten my family," I say through clenched teeth.

"Perhaps I should have let him kill you," he says, but his grip loosens. "It would give me no pleasure to see you harmed. But you shouldn't doubt the ruthlessness of my associates. They *will* kill you if you don't cooperate."

My skin crawls. I need to get away from him. "But why me? There's thirteen trainee medics in my class. You could have taken any of them."

"I can't tell you any more. If you let him die, there will be retribution. It won't be pleasant."

"Esther?"

Alex's voice rises above the din of the market. He's standing a few yards away with his med bag over his shoulder, textbooks tucked under one arm. He takes in the man behind me, still holding my arms. Tension ripples through him. "Get your hands off her."

"Tell me, now!" the man says, pulling my attention away from Alex.

The sight of my best friend brings reality thundering into the nightmare. I shake. I'm exhausted, and I can't figure out what my next move should be. Alex drops his bag on the tiles. The pages of his textbooks flap in the breeze.

"I said, take your hands off her."

The man's grip falters for a split second, just long enough for me to rip my arms free and run to Alex's side. Alex steps into the gap between me and the man, bristling with suppressed rage.

Over Alex's shoulder, the man's eyes stay fixed on mine. The soft leather of his mask moves imperceptibly when he breathes. People flow around us as though nothing's happening. He gives me a final glare and turns toward the chaos of the market.

"Wait!" I shout. "Lactrodectus. You need Lactrodectus antivenom." I push Alex aside so that I can speak to the man.

"Administered into a vein?"

"Yes."

His eyes ping-pong between mine. "What else?"

"Antibiotics to stop infection. Fluids on a drip until he can drink. Morphine."

"Thank you. You did the smart thing. Now go to school and pretend this never happened." He marches away. Within seconds, he's swallowed by the crowd.

My knees buckle. Alex holds me up.

"What the hell was that? Are you OK?" He's watching the place where the man disappeared into the crowd, frowning.

Think fast. A lie or the truth?

"Nothing," I say. "He saw my uniform and wanted to ask a question."

"About antivenom?"

I nod. If I speak again, I won't be able to hold myself together. I can already feel my insides unfurling. The shard of my broken tooth is jagged in my mouth.

Alex gathers his things from the floor and swings his bag on to his shoulder. "Come on. Don't want a late demerit on our records."

"I'm not feeling good—must have eaten something spoiled at the Lookout. I'm going to skip class today."

I scrunch my fingers into a ball and wince at the sting of raw flesh from where I fell. I was kidnapped. They tied me up. They wanted to kill me.

Alex presses the flat of his hand against my forehead. "You're not running a fever," he says. His forehead furrows in concern.

My chin wobbles. *Hold it together.*

He stares at me, assessing my condition. "Come on. I'll fix you some breakfast. You always get shaky when you don't eat enough."

"Thanks," I murmur.

Alex's eyes dart to my mouth, and I realize what he's looking at a second too late. I roll my top lip to hide the fractured tooth.

He presses his thumb against my lip, revealing the broken canine. "Esther, your tooth. How did you manage that?"

Lie, Esther. Lie and figure it out later. "Jogging," I say. "Slipped on a patch of wet deck and cracked my face on the railing."

"Looks nasty. Let me come with you next time, OK? I know you like to go by yourself, but it's not safe. Anything could happen. I'll even run behind you. You won't know I'm there."

I've no energy left to argue with so I nod weakly.

"Come on. You can shower at my place. Eat something, and if you're still not up to class, I'll figure out a way to cover for you."

Alex puts his heavy arm over my shoulder and steers me up the slope and toward the exit. I'm too drained to do anything but let him move me, so I concentrate on putting one leaden foot in front of the other.

"You would tell me if something bad happened? You know we can figure anything out," he says.

I swallow hard, blood running slick down my throat, and try to paint a smile on to my face. "Of course," I manage to say.

CHAPTER 12

HADLEY

The captain of the *Arcadia* is late.

Interesting.

Hadley has a meeting with him every Monday morning at 8 a.m. Like clockwork. This has never happened before.

He takes the opportunity to try out the captain's high-backed chair. The leather squeaks as he leans back to rest his feet on the desk. Comfortable and well-worn.

On the desk, there's a bottle with a miniature ocean liner inside. Solid turquoise waves hold the ship up, its black-and-red chimneys spewing fossil-fuel smog in a cotton-wool line. An analogue clock emits a soothing *tick-tick-tick* from inside its glossy wooden case.

Hadley compares this paneled office complex on the top level of the ship to his own scruffy headquarters hidden on a nondescript middle deck at the stern. Doesn't sit right that the captain, an overblown administrator who hands out rations and organizes the market, gets all of this. What does Hadley get? A cramped bunk. A bullpen shared with the rest of his officers. All close enough to the cells to smell the slop buckets the detainees use.

Your time's up. What the lowlife dealer said has been playing on his mind. It had taken Hadley all of two minutes to reject the idea that the captain might be trying to get rid of him. The captain's little more than a puppet, passing down the commands of the Federated States. Keeping the ship's population in line by making them feel like they're self-governed. Hadley's the one who's really in control here. The captain would never risk upsetting the status quo, but he does have his finger on the pulse of this ship, access to places Hadley can't get near. Increase the pressure by the right amount, and the old man might yield information about the real culprits behind the leaflet drop. Time to see how far the captain of the *Arcadia* can be pushed.

Hadley doesn't budge when the captain strides into the office. The old man stops short, shoulders rising as he struggles to catch his breath. Usually, he has a layer of composure that Hadley finds difficult to penetrate. But today he's tired. Ruffled. His neatly trimmed beard wilder than it should be. And that might mean something's happening, behind the scenes.

"Made myself comfortable," Hadley says. "Don't mind, do you?"

"Not at all."

The captain's dark eyes roam. He's looking for the bot. Hadley's very own surveillance camera is never far behind him. "My apologies for the lateness. I was dealing with some confusion over the distribution of rations. It seems this week's shipment was missing a significant volume of food."

The captain finds the bot hunkering on top of a bookshelf. He watches it for a moment before turning his attention back to Hadley, shifting so that he's facing away from it. "Did Gareth offer you tea?"

"As always," Hadley says. "New regulations are on your digiscreen."

"More restrictions. The longer you're aboard, the more things you find to ban, Commander Hadley."

The captain takes the digiscreen and sits down in the smaller, less comfortable guest chair on the wrong side of the desk. He scrolls through the list of new restrictions.

Hadley puts his hands behind his head and leans back, enjoying the rhythm of the clock and the quiet. No shouting prisoners. No officers with their constant banter. No *clack-clack* from the bot shadowing him. Maybe he'll keep the clock as a memento of his time aboard the *Arcadia*. Once he's dispatched the captain.

"Impossible," the old man says.

Hadley whips out of his daydream. "Which part?"

"I can't reduce the per-head ration by another two hundred calories a day."

"You're resourceful. You'll find a way."

"You want to ban reading in public?"

"A dozen people were caught with propaganda leaflets in the Lookout yesterday. It can be difficult to tell whether someone's reading an illegal document or a legal one. This way my officers can be certain that anyone reading in public is, in fact, a criminal."

"Perhaps if your government allowed some movement of people ashore we would be less inclined to read...propaganda. Fewer than five hundred of us have been allowed to leave. Most of those were prisoners you sentenced to hard labor at the camps." The captain throws the digiscreen on to the desk.

"Quarantine of the *Arcadia* is necessary to protect the Federated States."

"There have been no cases of the Virus here in living memory. And yet you hold us, against our will, based on the overblown fear that we might be carriers."

"It's not a chance we're going to take," Hadley says.

He knows as well as the captain that the threat from the Virus is minimal, but it's a neat way to demonize the ship's inhabitants that Hadley is quite happy to go along with.

The captain eyes Hadley steadily. "If we'd known we would never be granted asylum, we'd have gone elsewhere. You've kept us in a state of hardship and poverty for decades, and now we can do nothing but wait."

"We've made significant improvements to conditions on the quarantined ships. We've trained dozens of your young people and given them the chance of a new life."

"And most of them have met violent deaths patrolling your southern border walls."

Hadley bristles. The old man's starting to irritate. A seed between the teeth.

"I'm old enough to remember what things were like before you and your Coalies came aboard, Commander."

"When the gangs rampaged unchallenged, and your passengers died by the dozens trying to swim to land."

The captain smiles. "Thankfully, those days of disruption are behind us."

"Absolutely. I certainly wouldn't relish a return to lawlessness. Without the rules I implemented, it was just about impossible to decide who was a normal passenger and who was a criminal."

The captain remains silent.

"I recollect that even you had some questionable associations back then."

"I'm old. I've had many acquaintances over the years."

"I don't doubt it. But I'm thinking of a particular case about five years ago. A young couple that you were close to. I remarked at the time what a nice pair they made."

The captain stands. "If that's all, Commander—"

"He was popular in the community. Well loved, you might say."

"I have a lot of work to do."

"Lall. That was their name."

The captain stiffens. His eyes flash to Hadley.

"I remember because they had a little one—a boy. Such a wholesome family. Such a shame one of them was rotten."

The captain's face blanches. He swallows hard, as though his mouth is dry.

"What was he accused of again?" Hadley says.

"My memory fails me."

Liar. The old man's as lucid now as he ever was.

"Planning a mass escape, wasn't it? Maybe not. The father was delirious, barely knew what he was saying after he'd been interrogated. The wife was a pretty thing. It can't have been easy not knowing where her husband was all these years. Maybe I'll pay them a visit. See how that little boy is growing up. He'll be, what, sixteen by now?"

"The boy is under my protection. I vouched for him personally when you took his father. Your superiors agreed that the child should not be punished for the father's activities."

"Things change, captain. People stray."

"We're done for today." The captain stands straighter, making himself look bigger.

Hadley rests his elbows on the desk.

Stop struggling, Captain. You're not going to win.

"Not quite. I want you to find out who did that leaflet drop."

He pauses to gauge the captain's reaction. The older man raises his eyebrows, but keeps his mouth shut. "Some egregious fake news was spread. Call a meeting of the ship's council. Find out who was responsible."

"The news was fake?"

"Of course. Official news comes from me to you. I'll tell you if there's anything you need to be concerned about."

"Are you saying the *Oceania* wasn't destroyed?"

"I'm saying it's none of your business until I say it's your business."

"Very well. I will prepare a report of my findings."

Hadley smiles across at him. He's riled the man. Pushed him to cut their meeting short. Doesn't happen often. He must really be having a bad day to be stung by the mention of an acquaintance who was arrested years ago. Hadley's next move might tip him over. He takes a box from under the desk and tosses it to the captain. "Present for you."

The captain opens the unmarked lid of the box, and Hadley watches for the flash of dread on his face. The bot climbs out, legs first, and crawls over the captain's hand. The old man shudders visibly, shaking his arm until the bot clatters across the desk. In a couple of seconds, it rights itself and twists so that it's watching him.

"It's my job to look after you and the other council members as you carry out your work of keeping the ship functioning. You'll have no objection to a surveillance bot? For your own safety and security, of course. That way, I can send help if you need it."

The captain wipes a hand across his face, trying to compose himself in front of Hadley. "Of course," he says.

"You have a duty to the Federated States, Captain. I want these agitators found and handed over for interrogation. Otherwise, I might have to reconsider your position on the ship."

"You have no power in matters of ship governance. The deck representatives appointed me, and only they can remove me."

Hadley takes the few steps around the desk and leans back on it, folding his arms. "There are unofficial ways to force a change. It would only take one dissatisfied Neath with an oyster shucker, and the deck representatives would have to elect a new captain."

"Get out of my office."

Hadley allows himself a smile. "See you next Monday, Captain."

He claps the old man on the back as he strides out of his office.

Good afternoon. The time is 12:00 hours
on Thursday, October 28, 2094.
This is the captain of the cruise ship Arcadia.
The outlook for the rest of today is unsettled, with
choppy seas and a high of 54ºF expected.
All passengers be advised that the daily food
allowance is now 2,000 calories per adult.
At midnight tonight, a new regulation comes into effect, and
the following activity will now be outlawed: reading in public.
Daily reported Virus cases: zero.
Days at sea: 15,938.

CHAPTER 13

NIK

My head's about to explode. Literally blow to pieces.

"Was she OK? When you let her go? And why her? What were you thinking?" I ask, and I pull myself up, which is a mistake, because it sends pain tunneling into my chest. I flop against my pillow.

"Please calm down, Nikhil. It's not good for your stitches. She was the correct choice. I needed someone with a connection to our organization. I needed to be sure she wouldn't go straight to the Coalies and turn us in. The girl will have forgotten all about you by now."

"I know Silas, Mom. He's a piece of work." I rub my eyes, trying to keep the nausea at bay long enough to have this argument. Don't often win a fight with my mother and this time I'm weakened by the fact I just got shot.

"'Mom', Nikhil? You know I find 'Mom' disrespectful. It makes you sound like a Neath." Her mouth pulls down when she stretches out the *Mom*.

"Dad is a Neath," I say under my breath. She heard, but she's choosing not to react.

"Injury is not an excuse for sloppiness, Nikhil."

"I can't believe you just grabbed her off the deck. She must've been terrified."

"I'll have to live with your disapproval," she says crossly. "I can't believe that you orchestrated such an ill-advised prank when we're so close to achieving our goal. Silas almost pulled his support."

"People need to know what's happening on the other ships," I say.

"No, they don't. People need a way off *this* ship. And that's what we'll give them if we succeed. Our plans will give everyone—Neaths and ticket holders—a brighter future. We'll be free from Hadley."

At the mention of Hadley, my mother's mouth tightens at the corners. I get it. I have the same gut reaction to the monster that rules the *Arcadia*.

Mother sighs. She's folding my T-shirts into crisp rectangles. "Without the support of the major gang leaders, we'll have neither the firepower nor the access to the lower decks that we need to complete our plan. The engine room is in Silas's territory. You come and go only because of his good grace."

"Come off it! The only reason Silas and Enid aren't at each other's throats is the rebellion. There's no way he'd back out and let Enid get all the glory."

Even as I'm saying it, I know she's right. The ship's engine room is buried deep inside Silas's territory. I work there because he lets me. If his support is gone, below deck becomes out of bounds to me.

Mother purses her lips and slaps the folded clothes into a pile just hard enough to let me know how angry she is. The pieces of machinery on top of the chest rattle, and a handful of screws roll and drop to the floorboards. I've been dissecting one of the Coalies' spider-legged bots to see if I can figure out the power source.

Mother's hands fly to her hips as she stares at it with undisguised disapproval. "Rest now. That's an order. We still have a lot of work to do."

"I want to see May."

Mother's nostrils flare. She smooths her already neat black-and-silver hair with her hands. "I would drop Cadet Crossland, if there was time to recruit another candidate."

Unbelievable. After everything May's risked for the rebellion, she's still willing to excommunicate her for dropping a few leaflets. And it's obvious that the clock is ticking. My mother and the other leaders of the rebellion must be expecting the Coalies to act soon, and that means our mission gets more urgent with every day that passes. I'll ask Enid what she knows ASAP.

"So can I see her?" I say, trying not to sound hopeful. You never let my mother know you want something; she'll stop it if she can.

"As her handler, it was your job to supervise Cadet Crossland." *Don't react.*

I twist the blanket in my fists. "And it's a job I take seriously. I know how important she is to the rebellion. That's why I need to see her. To make sure her head's in the right place."

Mother gives me a searching stare. That got her attention. "If you suspect she's having second thoughts, it's your duty to inform me."

"No, *Mom*, that's not what I meant. You know May's as loyal as they come. But she's worried about what happens if she fails her mission. And she's worried about her family. Something that you've probably made a hundred times worse by involving her little sister."

"Every member of our organization understands the risks. Cadet Crossland accepted that when she joined us."

"She didn't sign up for our own side kidnapping her baby sister, and you know it. Dad would never allow it."

"It's been five years since they took him. Your father is dead, Nikhil."

"You can't know that for sure."

"I know the Coalies. I've seen them make people disappear. Then they dangle hope in front of the ones left behind, using it to make us compliant."

"But what if he's—"

"Enough, Nikhil!"

I cut my losses before she gets any angrier. It's not like we haven't argued about this a hundred times before.

Mother picks up an empty glass, straightens the book on my bedside table and runs her eyes over the room. "Now, get this mess tidied up. The last thing we need if we're raided is for the Coalies to find one of their machines in pieces."

"What about seeing May?"

"You'll remain here until I've had chance to consult with the rest of the leadership about your actions. When you do finally see Cadet Crossland, I hope you explain that what has happened to her sister is a direct consequence of your prank. Make sure she understands that her sister's safety, and the safety of everyone in the rebellion, depends on Esther keeping this fiasco a secret. A lot of people have sacrificed everything to liberate this ship. The sooner you stop treating this like a game, the better."

She exits the room and slides the door closed behind her.

I flop down on to my bunk and rest my hands across my chest, careful not to brush the gunshot wound. I haven't seen May since I fell through the elevator shaft. Don't remember getting shot. Just remember her holding me and the smell of her orange soap. Somehow, she got me below deck and into an unused service room. Then my mother and her cronies found a med student to patch me up. Esther. May's kid sister. By my mother's account, it sounds like Esther managed to do some damage to Silas's face in the process.

The tannoy *bing-bongs*. Midday. Time for a captain's announcement. Every room in every cabin has a plate-sized speaker on the wall somewhere. The captain keeps us informed about what's happening on the ship and whatever scraps of news from the outside world the Federated States allows us to hear. My speaker's at the foot of my bunk.

I need to see May. She has to know I had nothing to do with what happened to Esther. And now I'm starting to worry that Silas won't tolerate being shown up by a girl, especially one who works for the Federated States. There's not much the gangs like less than a collaborator.

As gang leader, Silas controls a huge swathe of Neath territory and goes unquestioned most of the time. His word is law down there. But, for all his power, he's bound by a code of honor. If someone crosses him the way Esther did, he has to retaliate. An eye for an eye. I can't lie here any longer, wondering if Silas is going after her.

Usually, I like hearing the captain through the speaker. It's solid and unshakable. Today, his voice feels like a reprimand, and I have zero appetite for listening to anything that's coming from Hadley anyway. Everybody knows the captain isn't allowed to give us any real news. He won't be allowed to tell us the *Oceania* went down. He won't mention the leaflet drop.

Can't turn the speaker off, but I don't have to listen to it. I lean off the bed and grab a T-shirt from the pile my mother just folded. Pain groans in my chest as I reach forward and pry the cover off the speaker with my fingernails. It comes away with cobwebs streaming behind it. I jam the T-shirt inside. The captain's voice is muffled to a deep drone by the cloth. Job done.

I bully myself out of bed, fighting the sicky whirling sensation in my gut again. Acid crawls up the back of my throat as I barefoot it the three steps to the door. Locked. She locked me in! Unbelievable!

"Mom, are you kidding me?" I shout, smacking the door.

My head spins, and acid floods my tongue. It's claustrophobic enough being trapped on the ship, but being locked in my room as well makes me feel like I'm suffocating. I have to get out of here. Breathless, I inch back to my bed and sit down. I ease open the drawer of my bedside table. My multitool is somewhere at the bottom. I pull a handful of socks out and toss them around the room, underwear too, then I kick the blankets into a pile and let them fall off the bed. The mess'll drive her crazy.

It doesn't take much jimmying with the screwdriver tool before the lock gives way. Mother knows it won't hold me; she just wants to make it clear I'm not allowed out.

The captain's voice floods from another speaker as I venture into our front room. Everything's tidy. Stowed away or put on a shelf. Mother's bed folded back into a couch, plain blue cushions arranged perfectly on top. The kitchenette sparkling.

My mother's parents were from a well-to-do Punjabi family. They were ticket holders and landed this sweet cabin on Deck Seven, along with respectable jobs in the administration and organization of the ship's food supplies once the Coalies started sending stuff in. My paternal grandparents ran a restaurant near the Liverpool docks, serving the Punjabi food of their homeland. When the bioweapon attacks started, they made a run for it with my dad and clambered on to the *Arcadia* just as the anchor was being hoisted. They weren't ticket holders. They didn't get a cabin, and they were never assigned jobs, so they got as comfortable as they could in the service corridor and started cooking the recipes they'd brought with them. Even though Dad was a Neath and Mom's from an upper deck, they found each other and fell in love over my grandparents' butter chicken and golgappa.

Our cabin wasn't like this when my dad was around. It wasn't so sterile. His laugh was like thunder—it filled a room with life. And he cooked a huge dinner every Sunday. Even when food was short, he somehow managed to make it feel like a feast. When he disappeared—was taken—my mother put away everything that reminded her of him. Most days I manage to put what happened to him out of my mind. Sometimes it's all I can think about.

There's a box of paper by the front door. I scrawl a note with the stub of a pencil: A. 16.

Arboretum. Four o'clock.

May will get it.

It's too hard to put my boots on without passing out, so I stay barefoot.

I stand on the welcome mat my mother has laid outside the front door, the bristles like pins in the soles of my feet. Sunlight filters through gauzy clouds. It's good to be out on deck after my stifling sickroom. Someone's strung limpet shells up on the railing, long pieces of twine passed through the holes they've painstakingly made in the top of the creamy white cones. The twine's all wet from the spray, and the shells clink in the wind. There must be thirty of them all along the deck, dangling from the top rail to the floor. They're supposed to keep evil away. Don't figure they work.

Holding the collar of my jacket tight around my neck, I start an old man's shuffle along the deck. It should be an easy five-minute walk to the front end, past the line of identical cabin doors and front windows, but today it feels like miles.

A drone buzzes through the air a few yards off the ship, sprinting past on its way to ruin someone's day. I get a rise of paranoia. A few days ago, I took a Coaly bullet. Have they got a photofit of me? Are they watching? What's my escape plan? Can't fight. Can't run. Over the railing then and hope one of Enid's people fish me out before I'm shark bait. Wish I'd brought my zip cord with me.

Footsteps drum behind me. Booted steps. The thought of the coal-black uniform that goes with them breaks me out in a sweat.

The steps move faster. They're coming for me. The world spirals, colors mixing like wet paint. My knees go.

Fingers grasp me above the elbow.

"All right, soldier?" May's voice trickles into my ear. She slides her arm around my waist, and I lean into her. Soft. Orange soap. "Wow. You look like crap."

"Just a scratch."

She smiles and presses a hand against my back to adjust my course, turning me toward home.

"That's what your mother said. You're really milking it."

A bout of wooziness takes hold. May grips my elbows to stop me swaying. "Nauseous?" she asks.

"Yup."

"That'll be the antivenom. Looked it up in one of Esther's textbooks. Side effects include, but are not limited to, muscle aches, vomiting, fever—"

"Check, check, and check."

"—damage to the nervous system, muscles, kidneys."

"Something to look forward to," I say.

She laughs. "Idiot."

"Was leaving you a note. In my pocket."

We stop, and May pulls the slip of paper out, smirking as she reads. "How were you planning on getting all the way up to the arboretum? And that was your code? Honestly don't know how you're still alive." She scrunches the paper into a ball and lets the ash drift off.

"Well, General, for that I have you to thank."

Her smile drops. "That was too close."

"Agreed."

She hugs me. I bury my face in her neck and hold on to the moment.

"I can't lose you," she whispers. "Try not to get shot again, 'kay?"

"Sir, yes, sir."

"We shouldn't be hugging like this. Negates the whole leaving-secret-messages thing."

"Yeah. But my legs have the strength of seaweed. If you let go, I'll hit the deck."

May snorts. Wisps of hair curl out from her ponytail. Sharp as a pin in her cadet's uniform. Green vest, camo-print trousers with a matchbox-sized Federated States flag sewn on, black boots. And something's bothering her.

"Ask the question," I say.

"What makes you think there's a question?"

"I'm your handler, have been for years. So ask me the question that stopped you sleeping last night."

May looks over her shoulder. Red blotches bubble up from her collarbones to her neck. "Are we going to be reprimanded?"

"Yes. My mother already confined me to quarters."

"Dammit," she says, and she stares, unfocused, at the ocean.

"Don't worry about it," I say. "May, look at me. They're not going to do anything."

She's chewing on her lip in a way that looks painful.

"Seriously, what are they going to do? Throw us out of the rebellion? No. Without you, there's no way to get into the base—"

"—which means there's no way to get the codes—"

"—which means there's no way to bring down the Coaly

surveillance system," I say. "And that makes the bigger plan unviable. They've been working on it too long to abandon it over a few leaflets. Think about it. What can they take?"

I'm saying all this to May and trying to reassure myself at the same time.

"Let's get you back to bed," she says.

I haven't convinced her, but it's a relief when she takes my arm. My head feels like a balloon. We reach the front door of the cabin, and I lean against the frame.

"It's not too late to back out. We could run. Start a farm, grow stuff."

"Even if we could get off the ship without getting caught, you have no idea how to plant a seed, do you?" She laughs again. The breeze takes loose strands of her hair and sets the limpet-shell wind chimes ringing.

"We'd have time to learn."

"And where would this farm be?"

"I've heard the outskirts of Amritsar are nice. No Coalies out in Asia either."

"And no Sickness Wars fallout," she says.

"And no cruise ships. It's totally landlocked."

I take her hand. Her glove's all covered in gray powder. I dust it off, then I let my fingers fall between hers. For two heartbeats, we're really looking at each other. She runs her thumb over my knuckles. Then she lets my hand drop. I scratch the back of my neck for something to occupy my buzzing palm.

"I'll check in on you tomorrow," she says, walking backwards down the deck. "And please figure out a better code next time."

"Sir, yes, sir." I salute. It tugs at my stitches, and I flinch, wincing.

May shakes her head. "I can think of one thing they can take from me," she says.

"Yeah? What's that?"

"They could take you." She looks at me, head tilted like she's still figuring out who I am.

Then she's jogging down the deck, the wind playing with her ponytail. I watch until she's an ant-sized dot at the end of the ship.

There's still time before she graduates and leaves for land. But until then the rebellion's most valuable asset is my responsibility. If she dropped out of her government training program and told my mother to forget the undercover mission, I'd be facing more than house arrest for a few days. If the rebellion loses May, we lose this battle.

Still, part of me wishes she'd back out. That she'd stay here, where I have a chance of protecting her. I know—I've always known—that I have to let her go. Just not ready for it yet.

CHAPTER 14

ESTHER

Three bodies, cross-sectioned, stand at the front of the classroom. Holographic flesh tones glisten on the ed-display's life-sized images. The human muscular system. The human skeletal system. The human circulatory system. We've been studying them all morning, and now my neck creaks when I move my head.

Corp's a good couple of inches shorter than the holograms. She stands on tiptoe to swipe her hand through the menu bar above their heads. The first image snaps off, and she moves to the next one. Crisp white bones.

Corp turns to face us. "Next week's test will make up sixty-five percent of your grade for this term, so I shouldn't need to tell you how important it is. Those of you who perform well will be one step closer to achieving the goal of this program: the chance to leave the ship and complete your medical training at our most prestigious university. I urge you to study as though your future life depends on it."

As she turns off the remaining display, my heart flutters against my ribs. Thirteen of us have been offered a chance for *the life*. Land. Freedom. We get to be part of the world instead of spectators watching it from the sea. In exchange, all we have to do is study, follow the rules, and shape ourselves into the best medics the Federated States could want. It strikes me that by helping that boy, instead of reporting the incident, I might already have messed everything up. The memory of my name on his lips chills me once more, but no amount of worrying has brought me any closer to figuring out who he is.

I force my attention back to Corp. Other than her rank—corporal—we know agonizingly little about the woman who has taught us for the past five years. No name. No details of her life. She shares her accent with the Coalies: all soft Ds and rolling Rs. Nothing like the hard-angled accent of the Stranded. She was fresh out of med school when she started her assignment here. That first week of training, I was so distracted by her that I learned nothing. Lesson after lesson, I built an imaginary life for her. She grew up in a house with a flower garden. She had a dog that she walked around the neighborhood. She likes ice cream (does it feel like eating snow?) and movies (do you talk to the other people in the movie theatre?), and that strange pastime that land people enjoy: hiking. I'm certain I'll enjoy hiking when I finally get the chance to do it. Walking with no boundaries.

A thrum runs through my comglove. It's set to silent during class, and this tickle tells me I have a message. From Alex. Who's sitting a few feet away at desk number one. I've got a surprise for you. My stomach does a flip that isn't entirely pleasurable.

I was distracted, and now Corp's standing in the space between our desks. She snatches my hand, turning it palm up to read the message. "Passing notes in class will not be tolerated, Ms. Crossland—one demerit."

I burn with shame. Not only did I betray the Federated States by giving aid to its enemies, but I've let myself be thrown off balance by distractions. It's been four days of looking over my shoulder and feeling a flush of anxiety every time I spot someone who could be a gang member. Four days of wondering how that boy knows me and whether he's still alive.

"Yes, ma'am," I say.

My classmates gape. I feel Kara shift in the next seat. She's a Deck Five girl, sharp, and she'd be happy to slip into my place beside Alex. She won't gloat though, not in front of Corp, so she stares resolutely ahead.

"All rise for the oath," Corp says. She stands at attention in front of us, chin high and proud.

The thirteen of us get to our feet. We speak as one: "I offer myself as a servant of the Federated States and vow to defend it with my breath and with my life."

As soon as the last word fades, we pack away our textbooks and screens.

"Cadet Crossland. Mandatory physical examination," Corp says.

My stomach drops, but it's perfectly routine. Nothing to worry about.

Kara squeezes past me, clutching a book to her chest. "A few more demerits and we'll be switching places, Number Two. I'm hot on your heels." She grins, eyes shining.

Don't snap back, I tell myself. Corp's within earshot. And anyway Kara's right. A couple more demerits, and we'll be tied for second place. A few more and I'll drop to number three.

"Hey, Kara, my girl's going to nail every test they throw at her. So why don't you concentrate on yourself instead of trying to drag everyone else down?"

Kara's face is set, but her eyes betray her. She'd love nothing more than to beat us both to seat one. I get the feeling she'd like to be the one holding Alex's hand too.

Alex kisses me on the forehead. "See you later."

Corp catches my eye as Alex leaves, and the rest of the class streams out. If she has an opinion about us, she's never shown it. Alex and I have been friends since our first awkward day of training. Once we were officially boyfriend and girlfriend, he started calling us a *power couple.* Alex and Esther. Esther and Alex. By a whisker, I scored highest on the entrance exam. That landed me seat one. Alex came in second. Kara got seat three. We've switched around twenty times over the years. It's almost a game.

Corp moves around the training room, rooting through our stash of supplies to find the things she needs. We still use the ship's original infirmary, but it was only ever meant to treat vacationers who'd picked up a stomach bug or overdone it on the sun-deck chairs. Not thousands of refugees and not for decades. It's not even adequate. If we ever had to deal with more than a handful of patients at once, we'd be spilling out into the hallways.

"Dammit, this place is a mess. You all can tidy up in here after class tomorrow. Where's the—? Got it," Corp says.

My eyelid twitches. Mandatory physicals always make me anxious, and on top of that I'm severely sleep deprived. For four nights, I've listened to every creak of the cabin, jolting awake with each gust of wind. Imagining the Neaths coming to finish me off. The gang member ready to cut my throat. I thought about confiding in May, but what would it accomplish? Absolutely nothing. And I can't tell my mom or dad. They'd lose their minds. I'd be under lock and key until the end of time. There's no one I can talk to about this.

"Sit on the desk," Corp says, wheeling over the tall obs machine that will record my details. She sits on a stool and scrolls through my medical records on her digiscreen.

Corp's uniform is a replica of mine: a medical jumpsuit in unflattering green, belt at the waist, thick-soled boots, Federated States flag on the left sleeve. A badge above the breast pocket shows the ancient symbol of medicine: two snakes wrapped around a staff topped with outstretched wings. The caduceus. Her black hair is tightly braided and pinned in a bun at the back of her head.

While Corp unpacks the machine, I smush my tongue into the gap left by my broken tooth. I can feel the clot of blood capping the wound. A jagged point of enamel. It's revolting and impossible to ignore. A constant reminder that the boy knows my name. His friends will come for me if he dies.

"You were fine at your last check. Swab," Corp says, holding a cotton bud out. I take it and run it around the inside of my cheek. It leaves an irritating tickle that I scratch with my tongue. Corp drops the swab into a tube and clicks the lid closed.

Random physical exams make sure we haven't come into contact with the Virus that brought Europe to its knees. The *Arcadia*'s isolation has lasted four decades. Long enough for my grandparents to die and my parents to grow up here. Every generation hoping that the Federated States will finally believe we're not Virus carriers and let us go ashore. But, even after all this time without an outbreak, we can't shake the *infectious* label. Some people in the Federated States still campaign to send us back to the wastelands of Europe, or to some barren, rocky island to be forgotten. If only they could see how hard some of us work, how much we want to be good, productive citizens, maybe they'd let more of us leave.

"Has anyone ever actually tested positive?" I ask.

"Not in my time."

"So it's gone, hasn't it? The Virus?"

"Our scientists think there's a chance it entered dormancy. You learned that the first week of training."

"For two generations?"

"Look, I don't make the hoops, OK? I'm just here to give you the best shot at jumping through them. And, if it helps, I have to inject myself in the thigh every day to make sure I don't get infected."

"Everyone could go ashore if they were given the same injection as you."

"It'd cost millions of dollars, and not even the most pro-ship-rights politicians are willing to pay through the nose to open our country to Neaths. Why the sudden interest?"

I bite my tongue, realizing I've stumbled dangerously close to questioning the wisdom of the Federated States. I shrug.

"A few more weeks, you'll pass your exams, and you'll be on land. Hang in there."

I spark with anticipation at the thought of going. Fear and excitement indistinguishable.

"Temperature," she says.

I open my mouth and let her tuck the end of the thermometer under my tongue; the other end trails a wire into the machine. She Velcros a cuff around my arm for blood pressure, a clip over the end of my finger for my heart rate. This is the only part of being a trainee that I hate. Having this machine literally see inside me. All my bodily functions reported straight to the Federated States.

The cuff around my arm wheezes as it inflates, squeezing until I feel my pulse raging in my fingertips.

Corp's eyes linger on the bruises around my mouth, now ripening to a sickly yellow that was impossible to cover with makeup. She pulls a stool over and sits down, digiscreen on her knee, eyebrows raised while she inspects me. "You've been off your game the last couple of days. Part of my job is pastoral care. Is there anything you want to talk about?"

I shake my head mutely.

The thermometer beeps. She takes it from my mouth and stows it on the side of the machine. "Fine. Don't talk. But you should know that I'm obligated to report anything unusual regarding my students."

"Unusual how?"

"Anything that could indicate they're no longer an ideal candidate. Unexplained bruising. Broken teeth. A sudden drop in ranking."

My chest constricts. "Have I dropped?"

She lowers her voice, leans in. "Not yet. But if I know something's going on with a student, I might be able to help. Has something happened that I should be aware of?"

My heart races. On the monitor, the line that records my heart rate dances with extra peaks.

Corp glances at the green line and then back at me. "Well, that was damning," she says. "Look, I can't force you to confide in me. Just know that you can come to me."

"And you'll report me?" I say. I know the answer because I should have reported all of this myself.

"That's at my discretion," Corp says, pulling the Velcro cuff apart. It gives me a dash of hope. Maybe Corp wouldn't be so quick to sell me out after all.

I fidget, hands in lap. "Something did happen. The other day, I—"

There's a knock at the door. Through the square pane of glass at the top, I catch a glimpse of a black helmet, visor flipped open.

Corp tuts. "What do they want?" she murmurs as she walks over and opens the door wide enough for the Coaly to look in. He takes in my face, the wires leading to the obs machine.

"What do you need?" Corp says. She's brusque with him, but is that because they're both military efficient or because she dislikes the Coalies just as much as the rest of us?

"There's a transport scheduled for you. Tomorrow, fifteen hundred hours."

"A transport? For what?"

"No idea. All program leaders to report to the helipad before 3 p.m."

"OK. Thanks."

The Coaly looks at me again. Corp pulls the door so that it's almost closed, blocking his view of me. "If there's nothing else, I'm in the middle of this month's mandatory physical."

She slams the door and takes her seat on the stool again, looking me straight in the eye. "All I'm interested in is training good doctors and helping your cohort exceed expectations. Tell me what got your heart rate going."

I want so much for Corp to be on my side that my heart aches. She's the one I've tried to emulate for five years. My role model and measure of success. If I can trust her, then I won't be alone anymore. Maybe we can go to the Coalies together and explain what happened—that they threatened me into helping them—and everything will be OK again. They'll see that I'm loyal. They'll see it was all beyond my control.

Still, something makes me hesitate. Corp builds us up and makes us work, and she's our only chance of a life in the Federated States. But she seems fiercely loyal to her homeland.

I can't tell her yet. I need to work around the edges of the truth until I can figure out whether she'll keep me safe. I press my hands together. Take a breath.

"Is it true? Is the *Oceania* gone?"

"You know I can't discuss outside news with you."

We stare at each other, Corp looking to see whether I understand. Me trying to find some clue as to where her heart lies. With her students or the Federated States. She can't always be loyal to both. If she finds out what I did, I don't know which she'd choose to protect. And it's an uncomfortable realization that I'm in the same position, torn between my dedication to the Federated States and the fact that I gave aid to their enemies.

I find myself staring at the obs machine, listening to my heart rate transformed into a series of blips.

"Things are about to change for you, Esther. Don't rock the boat now."

CHAPTER 15

NIK

The pliers slip off the rusted bolt, and I catch my thumb on the metal. "Dammit!" I shove it in my mouth. Does nothing for the pain. So sick of this. Sick of hiding from the Coalies. Sick of living my life under the shadow of this engine. Sick of being ordered around by my mother.

What May said about our higher-ups taking us away from each other has been eating away at me. My mother's given me the silent treatment for twenty-four hours. Don't get me wrong: I can live without having to talk to her most of the time, but, when I'm waiting to hear what punishment the crime of insubordination will carry, I wish she'd be chattier.

Frustration boiling over, I grab the pliers off the floor and throw them, hard as I can. They ricochet off the wall by the door—narrowly missing someone's head.

A few inches more and I'd have taken out the captain of the *Arcadia*. He's standing in the doorway to the engine room.

I shoot upright and straighten my back, clasping my hands behind me and trying not to let the pain show on my face. "Sorry, sir," I say, frustration melting to embarrassment.

"That wasn't the welcome I was expecting. And you should be taking it easy. The suture bot did an excellent job of repairing the damage, but that was not a minor injury." He steps through the door and swings it shut behind him. He hands me the pliers.

"Bolt's rusted on. Need to get in there to check the fuel lines," I say.

He throws something down on the long table I've been using as a workbench. A bot, long legs bent the wrong way, the lens smashed from its crushed body. "A consequence of your misadventure the other day. Commander Hadley is having me followed."

I rub the back of my neck, too late to realize I've spread grease all over myself. "Sir, I'm sorry. We didn't mean for that to happen."

It's a weak response, and the captain knows it. I want to fall through a hole in the deck.

"I appreciate that."

I swallow the lump in my throat. "Won't you get in trouble for smashing it?"

"Hadley will send another one, no doubt. But he won't risk arresting me yet. It would destabilize the ship, and he wants to keep everything in order until he gets the go-ahead to clear us. It could embarrass him, if it looks like he's not in control."

The captain looks around the engine room. It really is a beast. Has to be to move something like the *Arcadia*: 300,000 tons of floating city. Seven thousand passengers were supposed to be on board when it set sail, but the number was much higher than that in the end.

The engine's taller than either of us, a mass of tubes and dials and wires. It was stainless steel and gleaming once, but I've added so many new and scavenged parts that it looks like Frankenstein's monster. All mismatched and stapled together. By the time I started working on it, a lot of the engine had already been rebuilt, and it was my task to continue the job. I've spent five years getting it back in fighting shape. It's almost ready.

"You've done good work here," the captain says.

"Just doing my job."

I pick a rag up from the floor and wipe the grease off my hands, for something to do. I know I'm about to get chewed out, and the wait is killing me.

"Your loyalty has never been in question. Your patience, by all accounts, needs work."

He turns his steady eyes on me. This is it. The reprimand I've been dreading. From my dad's best friend. My godfather. The captain of the *Arcadia* and the leader of the rebellion. I want to crawl into the engine chamber so he can't look at me anymore.

The captain scans the surface of the *Arcadia*'s engine. Runs his fingers along a patch of metal, then sits down on the folding chair I take my breaks in. "You know how I met your father?"

Every strand of muscle in me tenses. "No."

"Seventeen years ago, I saw him standing on a wooden box in the market, shouting about freedom. Bold as brass. You weren't even born yet. He'd just married your mother. The day before, it had been announced that the government was sending a task force to clean up the ships."

"Hadley?"

"That's right. Ostensibly, Hadley and his Coalies were coming to protect us. After years in quarantine, the *Arcadia* was in danger of sliding into anarchy. People were giving up hope of ever being allowed to leave, and the ship's engine was dead from neglect and scavenging, so we could no longer move on even if we'd wanted to. Silas was rising to power. He had taken control of the starboard gangs in a bloody fight of succession, but he was still a ways from realizing his ambition of controlling all the below-deck territory. Enid, of course, had not yet inherited power from her father. And the gangs were lawless. A mosaic of violence and illegality. Above-deck people were swelling the gang's ranks too."

"Things were becoming more desperate by the day. There had been several delays in food shipments, and everyone on board was hungry. Some tried their luck at swimming ashore, only to be shot in the water. Your father saw that the Coalies coming aboard marked the start of martial law. So he took a box, stood on it and tried to persuade everyone else that we needed to fight against government control."

The captain taps a dial and watches the pointer flicker. "The first drones were being launched, and I knew that if your father was spotted, the Coalies would go after him. Hadley, the new Coaly commander in charge of the *Arcadia*, wasn't really interested in Silas and the other gang leaders as long as they didn't cause him too much trouble. He had a sadistic streak and a pathological hatred of ship folk, and he was interested in people who talked about hope and freedom. The ones who wanted to escape."

Trying to stop myself from panting. Trying not to look at

him. Don't want anything to break the spell of what he's saying. My mother won't tell me about my dad, and I've given up asking. His disappearance broke her, and it's too painful to go over again. That's why she removed every trace of him from our lives.

"Then what happened?" My voice scratches.

"I dragged him off the box and told him that he was about to get himself arrested."

"You're saying I'm just like my father?"

"No. No. You are nothing like your father."

That feels worse than a punch in the gut. Worse than getting shot.

"Your father knew when to shout and when to shut his mouth. After that one lapse in judgment, he kept his head down. We knew—him, your mother, and me—that someone had to take charge of the future. And that meant planning and organizing. It also meant waiting for the right moment to act."

Tears prick my eyes, and the shame burns so fierce I want to smash my fist into the wall. He's right. So's my mother. I get caught up when I'm with May. I don't think things through. And it makes me stupid.

"You and Cadet Crossland risked the plan that your father started and your mother continued and that you have been working on since you were a child. Your father would never have been so reckless."

I turn away from the captain and wipe my nose on the back of my hand. Trying to control the storm of emotions I'm feeling. Guilt that I could have messed everything up. Fear of losing May and of the rebellion failing. And beneath it all is the smoldering hatred. An ember that's been burning since my dad was taken and that can only be extinguished by destroying Hadley and everything he's built on this ship.

"None of us saw his arrest coming. And it was our lack of foresight that meant you, an eleven-year-old child, were the person with the most knowledge of the engine your father had been working on. You have done an admirable job, but, in hindsight, your father should have been teaching as many of us as possible how to work on it."

He spins me around, so that I have to look at him. Right now, part of me wishes I was still unconscious.

"Hadley took your father and your childhood, and that isn't fair. Don't hand him your future too. I have a feeling that you and Cadet Crossland feed off each other's enthusiasm. Don't be knocked off course. Keep your father at the front of your mind. Think of everything he gave up for this ship. Everything he gave up for you."

Feels like something is broken in my chest. One part's May; the other's my dad and the rebellion.

I have to finish what he started.

"From now on, I must avoid visiting the engine room. Hadley has asked me to find the ones responsible for the leaflet drop."

I feel the blood wash from my face as the reality of what we've done hits me.

"Don't be concerned. I can put on a show that will throw him off the scent without implicating you or Cadet Crossland. What should concern you more is that shortly after the council meeting tomorrow night there will be a second secret congregation. You will both stand trial in front of the rebellion leadership. You will be asked to explain your actions. Silas and Enid won't be pleased about being called—Silas is close to withdrawing his support. Do not expect them to be lenient."

My stomach bubbles with acid. This is exactly what May was worried about.

The captain takes a socket wrench from my toolbox and pushes the head over the bolt I've been trying to remove.

"Tried that already," I say.

He gives me a smile and slides a piece of waste pipe over the wrench handle, doubling the length. He pushes down. The bolt grates. Flakes of rust shower out. The captain turns the bolt.

"Cadet Crossland is the right tool for the job. Just like you are the right person to rebuild the *Arcadia*'s engine. It isn't fair. But it is necessary. You need to find a way to be content with your roles." He drops the bolt into the palm of my hand. "Don't stand in her way."

CHAPTER 16

ESTHER

Alex is leaning on the railing when I get home. "Time for your surprise," he says, grabbing my hand. He's excited. I can feel the faint buzz in him.

"Great," I say, trying to sound enthusiastic. All I really want is my bed and my blanket and a giant mug of tea.

Ten minutes later, we're on the opposite side of the ship, hopping up a staircase to Residential Deck Ten. An angry wind tugs at my hair, thick with the smell of the ocean. Alex has the collar of his uniform turned up to shield his neck. The weather is coming from the open water and surging around the decks like they're wind tunnels. Whistles and bangs and creaks.

Halfway along the deck, there's an old, orange-hulled lifeboat raised on a stand. A relic of the time when all the passengers were supposed to make it off the ship. Most of the ship's lifeboats were stolen decades ago, and either reused or broken down for scrap. You can still see some of the lurid orange roofs nestled in the flotilla.

Alex jumps up on the railing and checks for airborne drones.

"You're making me nervous," I say.

"Everything's fine," he says.

Alex punches a code into a number panel attached to the side of the lifeboat's hull. The door swings upward, and he climbs in. Keeping my feet firmly on the deck, I poke my head in after him, blinking while my eyes adjust to the gloom.

Cardboard boxes are piled in columns, floor to ceiling. Every space rammed so that there's barely room for passengers. On the side of each, the words Humanitarian Daily Ration are stamped alongside the Stars and Stripes. Inside the nearest box, I find meals vacuum-packed in silver foil. The first one I pick up is labeled red beans and rice.

"Think of it like an emergency survival kit." Alex takes the ration pack from me and closes the box lid. "And it's all organized, so don't mess with it."

"This isn't a survival kit. This…this…" I scan the piles of boxes. "It's enough to feed someone for months."

He pauses and turns so that we're face to face. "It's enough to feed two people actually."

My face flushes.

"Or more. It's to keep us going if there's a food shortage. Lots of people have them."

"Lots of people have an extra bag of pasta. This—where did it all come from?"

He's moving boxes around. "Been saving for years. Every time someone paid me for tutoring, I bought food and stashed it here."

"Is that legal?"

He hesitates. "It's not exactly illegal."

"But the Coalies wouldn't like it."

"Probably not, but it's worth the risk."

I'm so distracted by the towers of food, I don't realize Alex is pulling my comglove off until it's gone.

"Hey!"

Cold air plays over the skin of my hand. I flex my fingers and compare my hands. The skin on my comglove hand is sickly pale.

My skin puckers in the cold. Without that glove, I'm vulnerable. No money. No way to communicate. And no ID. If I get stopped by the Coalies, I won't be able to prove that I'm me. Or that I'm not a criminal.

"I need that!" I say.

"This way no one will know who we are. You'll be OK without it for an hour," Alex says, taking his comglove off too, and stowing both of them behind a box. And then, as though he's done it a thousand times before, he produces another comglove and puts it on.

"If you get caught pretending to be someone else, they'll throw away the key," I say.

"It's just a fake ID. And I don't plan on getting caught." He gives me a straight-toothed grin. "Your mouth's open."

I snap my teeth together. "We'll be thrown out the program if Corp finds out."

"Can't make an omelet without cracking a few eggs," he says, sitting down with his back to me, so I can't see what he's doing. This does not feel right. It feels dangerous.

"If we run into trouble on the way, let me do the talking," he says over his shoulder.

The *Arcadia* can be a risky place to live, and it feels even riskier since I found out a boy with criminal connections knows me well enough to call me by my name. I can count the number of people I trust on one hand. May. My parents. Corp is borderline. Alex? I trust him.

"All right," I say.

"That's my girl." He finishes whatever he was doing and jumps out onto the deck. "It'll be fine," he says. I step out of the way as he closes the door and punches in the code to lock the lifeboat.

Alex bounces excitedly ahead as we take the stairs down, passing each numbered door until I feel panic in the pit of my stomach. "We're getting awfully low. Want to tell me where we're heading?"

"We're here," Alex says. I stop dead in my tracks halfway down a set of stairs, and stare at the door on the next landing down: Service Corridor. This isn't turning into a good kind of surprise.

"Are you serious?"

"Always." He reaches out to open the door, but before his fingers touch the steel handle it swings open. And in the space of a second we're face to face with ourselves—reflected in the cold visors of a Coaly patrol. Terror lurches in my stomach. It grips my throat. The thing I was most afraid of is here and real and far, far, worse than my nightmares.

I clench my naked, comgloveless hand and shove it behind my back.

Alex snaps to attention. He stares ahead.

Don't scan us. Please don't scan us.

"Officers," Alex says. He gives them a wholesome smile, and his cheeks are ruddy like everyone else's, and somehow it makes him look healthy instead of wind-battered.

There are two of them. I stare at myself in one of the visors. Wind-ruffled hair. Reddened cheeks.

The Coaly's visor creeps from my face to my boots and back. It lets go of its weapon, a black rifle slung from a strap, and reaches a black-gloved hand toward me. I close my eyes and try not to faint. *Trust Alex. He told you to trust him, now trust him.*

The Coaly moves the front of my jacket aside to look at my uniform underneath. It taps the double snakes of the caduceus badge.

"State your business, medic." Coalies only have one voice. Deep and desolate. Not quite human.

"There may be a measles outbreak on this deck. We're here to determine whether to quarantine," Alex says. Smooth and convincing and like he owns the place. But Corp didn't give us this assignment, and there's been no report from this deck. He's lying.

I focus on the epaulette on the Coaly's shoulder. Seconds stretch out painfully.

After what seems like hours, the Coalies step around us and continue on their way.

Alex grabs my hand and holds me in place. "Wait," he whispers. Their footsteps fade away. The door separating the staircase from one of the decks slams above us.

"Jerks," Alex mutters. "Come on."

"If they'd scanned us, we'd be on our way to the cells right now."

"I know, and I'm sorry. That shouldn't have happened. But everything's fine now."

"Can we please just go back and get my glove?"

He hesitates, turning to face me. "We're almost there. If we go back, we might run into them again."

I look up at him, weighing Alex's steady reassurance against the nakedness of my hand. "OK," I say.

He grins. As he leads me through the door, I nurse a nasty hollow feeling. My instinct's telling me something is very wrong. I've only been in the service corridor once before, and it's as crowded and smelly and unpleasant as I remember. It's so busy, so full of shuffling people and scared animals. Worst of all, it's almost impossible not to touch strangers. The mixed odors of food and unwashed humans are so unpleasant I clap my hand over my face. If there was ever an outbreak of the Virus down here, it would be impossible to slow the spread.

Alex pauses outside an unused elevator. The steel shell of it is stopped permanently on this floor, and just visible inside is an old woman. The walls are wrapped in plastic sheeting. The woman spots us. "You're late," she says.

Alex pushes me forward. Inside, the light is dingy, and something rancid is half masked by the smell of disinfectant. There's an examination bed in the center of the elevator identical to the ones we use in the infirmary. It's bathed in yellowish light from a lamp that's suspended from a hook in the ceiling. The woman sits on a stool, gloved hands held up in front of her. The plastic sheet on the floor crackles beneath the stool's wheels.

"Jump up, darlin'. Let's have a look at you."

She pats the bed. She grins at me. Her teeth are unblemished white and look like they belong to someone else. Her eyes flick to the caduceus badge on my uniform. "Not often I meet a fellow medical professional."

It clicks. She thinks she's a dentist.

Too late, I step back toward the corridor, but Alex stops me from running.

"Give it a chance," he whispers, taking me by the arm and steering me back into the elevator.

"It'll cost a fortune," I say.

"Don't worry. I've got some credits saved up."

"I'll never be able to pay you back."

He stops and looks me in the eye, surprise raising his eyebrows. "You don't have to pay me back. It's ours. We're in this together."

There's a lump in my throat and pressure building behind my eyes, so I bite my lip until I don't feel like crying any more.

The pillow is covered with splashes of yellow and brown. A hundred heads must have rested there before mine. I imagine lice burrowing into my hair.

Alex shrugs off his coat and spreads it over the pillow. Outside the elevator, a crowd of Neath kids has gathered to watch me climb onto the bed.

"Open wide," the woman says. She holds a magnifying glass over my face in one hand, a thin flashlight in the other. "Been a lot of you down here recently," she says to Alex.

"Medics?"

"Coalies. More bots too, truth be told."

"We're not Coalies."

"As good as. There any truth to these rumors the *Oceania*'s been sunk?"

"How would we know?" Alex says.

"No need to get snippy. Just thought your friends might keep you in the loop."

"We aren't friends with Coalies. We're being trained by the Federated States."

"In my day, we called it collaboration." The old woman sniffs, still looking into my mouth. She wheels backwards. "How'd this happen?"

"I fell. Cracked my face on the railing."

Alex shifts somewhere near my head. He's accepted the story that I slipped on a patch of wet deck and smacked my face as I went down. It's believable. But I catch him watching me sometimes, like he's trying to figure me out.

"Yep, that'd do it. Not enough left to save the tooth. But I can yank it out from the root and give you another one."

Yank it. A tremor runs through me.

"From where?" Alex says.

The woman glances past him at the kids jostling to see. They whisper and giggle. "Depends on your resources. Extraction for half a day's rations. A pre-loved organic canine will set you back a full day."

"She's not having a second-hand tooth."

Second-hand tooth. I grip the sides of the bed.

"My transplants are all good quality. Freshly erupted, checked for caries and cleaned of plaque. I'll send out for a donor if you want one."

I never understood the gappy smiles of the Neath kids. So many of them have missing teeth, I assumed it was due to poor nutrition. The truth is so much worse.

"No way," I say with a sob, pushing myself up. "I won't take a kid's tooth. People live with worse than this." I shake my head and try not to break down.

"Give us a minute?" Alex says to the woman. She purses her lips and wheels herself away on the stool.

Alex leans over me. In the murky light, I can see the stubble on his chin. "Think about it. Would Corp be without a tooth? Would anyone from land? They're going to assess everything about you. Grades. Late marks. Demerits. We can't give them any reason to reject us. And May's graduation ceremony is coming up. Anyway, you shouldn't have to live with it." He takes my hand, running his thumb over mine. "You deserve better."

My heart skips. He seems so determined to look after me. I trace the spike of tooth with my tongue, and I wish he was wrong. Maybe no one will care that I have a broken tooth. Or maybe they'll put a big red rejection stamp on my application form.

I can do this. For med school. For my future.

"Sorry to interrupt your *tête-à-tête*, but I've got other patients to see," the dentist says.

"OK," I murmur.

Alex grins at me. "Give her a synthetic implant."

"Three days' rations."

The woman holds her hand out to Alex. There's a ping as the funds are transferred between their comgloves. The kids gasp at the cost of it. All I can feel is relief that I won't be getting a secondhand canine.

The woman lifts up a syringe, squirting a drop of liquid. Alex grabs her hand. "That black-market crap causes nerve damage."

She sneers, tosses the syringe on to a tray and picks up a pair of pliers. "This is going to hurt."

Fear, primal and creeping, claws at my chest.

CHAPTER 17

NIK

May passes me a sheet of brown paper cradling three steaming bao. I wrap my fingers around the buns and lean back, one foot against the wall. May stands next to me, looking past so that she can see the service hatch without having to crane her neck. It's a huge rectangular metal door with a circular handle in the center, and it takes two people to swing it open.

"What's the time?" She blows steam between her lips as she eats and talks.

"Fifteen fifty-five."

"It'll be docking now."

On the other side of that service hatch is the main gangplank. A long, sloping runway that goes down to the ocean. Once a day, dead on at 4 p.m., the supply barge comes up close to the *Arcadia*, attaches itself to the end of the gangplank and unloads enough food to feed the ship. Well, they pretend it's enough food. Really, there's plenty of people on the *Arcadia* that go to sleep hungry. The shipments bring other stuff too. Crappy secondhand clothes. Electronics that were state of the art ten years ago.

I look down the corridor. The air's hazy with the smog of old cooking oil from the fish and chip stand, and the busker that wanders the length of the corridor is somewhere close by with his out-of-tune fiddle. Disused elevators line both sides of the corridor like the spines of vertebrae. A little over a week ago, I got shot and plummeted down one of those shafts. Nerves tighten in my neck. Don't remember the slam of the bullet. Don't remember the fall.

Usual policy is to stay a long way away from any Coaly patrol. Today, that's exactly who we're waiting for. May takes another bite of dumpling, showering dough on to her scarf, and watches the hatch.

"By the way, all that stuff you asked for is ready. It'll be at the safe house. Don't think you'll need it though," I say.

"Fail to plan, and plan to fail," she says without taking her eyes off the hatch.

Her training kicks in whenever we're on one of these missions. It's like she has an instinct for it. She can watch without it looking like she's watching. And you should see her with a rifle. She'll hit an empty bean can from 200 yards.

"You sound like my mother," I say.

"It's a contingency plan."

"You need to believe you can pull this off."

"I do."

She flicks a glance at me, and—for the briefest second—I see through the swagger: she's seventeen and scared and about to go on the adventure of her life.

What I won't tell her is that my mother hasn't got another way of completing May's mission. If May fails to bring back what we need, the next part of our plan is going to be 100 percent more dangerous.

So fast I don't even see it happening, May twists around and grabs a pickpocket by the wrist.

"Don't mess with cadets, kid," she says quietly, hard as steel.

The girl looks terrified. She's about eight with blonde hair matted into a single braid.

"Next time, just ask." May folds the paper over what's left of her buns and presses it into the girl's hand.

The kid stares for a second, then sprints off, gathering other hungry kids as she runs. Just before she disappears, I see her cramming the food into her mouth.

We've been staking out this supply delivery for the last three weeks because May needs to feel like she's taking action. For her, it's not enough to have a mission to complete at some point in the future. She needs to stick it to the Federated States now, even if it's just going over the mission plans like we're doing at this moment. That's what started the leaflet drop. She came up with the idea, and I went along for the ride. In hindsight, the whole thing's caused way more trouble than it's worth. But at the time I wanted to make her happy. And I guess I was pleased to be actually doing something for the cause instead of hiding away in the engine room, tinkering with the machines and plotting Hadley's downfall.

"Where do your parents think you are this afternoon?" I ask.

"At war-games training."

"Didn't Hadley cancel that class months ago? Something about not wanting guns to fall into the wrong hands?"

"Yeah, well, I didn't bother to enlighten my parents." She scans the width of the corridor. "Look for bots, will you?"

I turn to face her so that I can look over her shoulder and try not to get distracted by how close together we are. I check the corners of the mold-blotched ceiling as far as I can see, looking for the spidery legs of mobile surveillance bots, then switch to scanning the ground. Nothing but a scraggly ship's cat going after a mouse.

"You need to tell your sister about the mission now," I say.

I've been feeling more than a little guilty that Esther got a bomb detonated under her life, and she doesn't even know why. Maybe, if she knows about the rebellion and how we're going to make things right for everyone, she might feel better that her world's imploding.

"Tell her what? That I'm part of an illegal rebellion? That I'm a traitor to her beloved Federated States? That I'm not the good collaborator I'm supposed to be?"

She's checking out the ground behind me, the elevator across from us where a Neath fries dumplings on a sheet of hot metal. There's nothing.

"I prefer the term *freedom fighter* to *traitor*," I say. "Can't you find a way to soften the blow? Explain to her. Show her that not all of us live in a Federated States bubble."

"Introduce her to the sights and sounds of the ship? Make her realize how wholesome and down to earth life can be if she just embraces the world of the ship?"

Now May stops searching for surveillance bots, and I find myself leaning on the wall, face to face with her. Looking into her eyes. She has freckles over the bridge of the nose. A cupid's-bow mouth. She's laughing at me. "I could bring her down here and feed her baklava made by Neaths, and she'll realize there's more to life than going to med school."

"All right, all right, I get it," I say.

"Can you imagine her down here? Can you imagine the look on her face? No. It's going to crush her when she finds out our plan and realizes she's never going to med school, and nothing will soften the blow. Switch."

We nonchalantly swap places so that we can cast fresh eyes over the corridor. May leans on the wall again. I wish she'd look at me a second time.

"It'll be easier on her if she knows. Especially after what happened the other night," I say.

"What happened the other night?"

"I got shot for one thing."

"Sure, but what's that got to do with Esther?"

I open my mouth and snap it shut again. And I know it's too late. *Damn your big mouth, Nikhil Lall.*

"What's that got to do with—? Wait—which medic worked on you?" Her cheeks flush pink.

"How would I know? I was unconscious." I look away. Look at the sawdust-coated floor. Look anywhere but at her.

"Nik," she says. She rests her hand on my arm, and it's like she found the chink in my armor.

"Nothing. Forget about it. That's an order."

"Nik. Tell me."

I stare at what's left of the bun in my hand. "After you left, I was in a bad way—"

"I know. One of Silas's people fetched your mother. She threw me out as soon as she got there."

"Well, she needed to get someone to look at me."

"So she went and got Corp, because Corp's our very own highly qualified medic with access to the best medical equipment on the ship."

"No. We can only use Corp if it's an emergency—-"

"This was an emergency!"

"She's too valuable where she is. My mother wasn't willing to risk blowing her cover." My mouth's like dry crackers. "My mother sent Silas to look for Esther. Grabbed her off the deck."

May's face is frozen in an expression of cold rage while she processes what I've told her.

"I'm going to kill her," she grunts through clenched teeth.

"You're going to kill your sister?"

"I'm going to kill your mother. And then I'm going to kill my sister for not telling me what happened. How could she keep that secret?"

She paces across the corridor until she almost hits the elevator, then paces back again. Her face flashes with rage, and her fists are clenched rigid at her sides. "All the medics in that class, and she chose my sister?"

"It was a time-sensitive situation." I decide not to tell her that my mother targeted Esther because she thought May would keep her quiet.

"Don't you dare defend her. We had an agreement, Nik. You came to me, and you asked me to stake everything—my life, my future, *everything*—on this rebellion. Your mother literally asked me to give my life for the cause. And what did I say?"

"You said it would be your honor to serve."

"I said I'd lay down my life, as long as my family was protected."

She's getting too loud. People are staring. Even without surveillance bots, we don't want to draw attention to ourselves.

"May, cool down."

"I'll cool down when your mother fixes this."

"She can't fix it. It's done. And, much as I'd like to see you take my mother down a notch, you've really got to quiet down. They're here."

Down the corridor, marching in unison, a unit of Coalies appears. People shy away from them, pressing themselves against the walls. The kids don't ask Coalies for food. Don't try to pick their pockets. That would be a one-way ticket to the prison camps.

"If that creep Silas touched her, I'm going to kill him too."

"He didn't hurt her. The captain was there. He made sure," I say.

The Coalies are getting closer. I check the time: 16:00 hours exactly.

May's agitated, so I herd her back to our spot by the wall. I hold my breath until the unit passes us, and try not to attract their attention, dropping my chin into my scarf in the hope that they won't recognize me. When they reach the big service hatch, the soldiers take up position, staring out into the corridor. A kind of hush descends. People stand still and watch. A Coaly hammers on the metal door, three ringing bangs. It squeals open, and waiting outside is a container packed with cardboard crates marked with the Federated States flag. A guy pushes the container into the ship. Next come a line of people—ten, maybe fifteen of them—each carrying a box.

"Sixteen oh four," May says. "Like clockwork."

The Coalies and the guy pushing the container check the boxes, and for a few tight seconds no one's paying attention to anything but the food. "That's it. That's the moment. You need to hang outside until everything's onboard. Once they start moving, you can slip through and go the opposite way. We've already transferred a bribe to the captain of the supply barge."

Someone slams the hatch shut, the light from outside blinking off.

"It's going to be tricky," May says. "Those Coalies can't turn around for anything."

"I'll be here. If it looks like you're going to get caught, I'll cause a distraction."

"Fine. See you later." She walks off, hands in her pockets.

"Come on, May. Don't be pissed at me. Where are you going?"

"I'm going to check on my family," she says.

CHAPTER 18

HADLEY

Hadley swallows a handful of painkillers. It's getting dark early, rain beating against the ship so hard it makes his head ring. He leans over the sink in his cabin and stares into his own bloodshot eyes. Maybe it was interrogating that girl who acted so much like Celeste. Or maybe he's just tired from watching the captain's surveillance feed. But Celeste got into his head last night, so when the sun broke over the horizon, he knocked back one of his precious few memory suppressants and climbed into his bunk. Now it feels like the inside of his skull is on fire. He burns with hard-edged memories of her. This is what happens if you run out of pills and don't have enough to keep your dosage up. The memories snake their way out of your subconscious.

Celeste in their apartment.

Celeste buying groceries.

Celeste in the interrogation room.

The memory of her confession rushes to the fore. Crystal tears in blue eyes. Blood billowing from white skin. Couldn't bring himself to touch her during the interview. He watched while the others interrogated her, and when they dragged her off to the gallows, he covered his ears, so he couldn't hear her shouting for him.

He presses his scorched forehead against the cold of the mirror.

"They're ready to start, sir." The deputy's voice comes through the crack in his cabin door.

"Just a minute."

Hadley splashes his face with water, then forces himself to walk along the narrow corridor to the bullpen.

Lieutenant Grimson assesses his condition as he comes in. She knows what drugs he uses to get through the bad nights. She knows he'll be groggy and plagued by phantom memories and disembodied voices. She knows that he'll snap into memories so vivid, he won't be able to tell they're not real. And she forgives him and picks up the slack.

Still, he shies away from her judgment. Pretends to focus on the wall panel showing the captain's surveillance feed.

There's another flash of their last day together. Celeste was stirring a pot on the stove, the air a fog of steam and garlic and herbs.

He presses his fingers into his eyeballs until the nauseating food smells clear.

There's a crackle from the digiscreen in front of him, the ghosts of lowered voices. Figures appear wearing scarves and heavy winter coats. Rainwater is shaken off. Hijabs are rearranged. Gloves are removed. They take their seats in front of the captain. The ship fled from Liverpool forty years ago, and the council reflects that city's multicultural heritage. The descendants of every continent are here tonight, but to Hadley they're all as bad as each other. They all came from the same place. Europe.

The old man has called the meeting in the grandest restaurant, ceiling arched and painted as though it's the Sistine Chapel. The chairs have been arranged on the stage in a horseshoe shape with the captain standing in the middle like the conductor of an orchestra. On either side, the stage curtains sag from their rail, red velvet edged with gold tassels.

"Thank you for coming to this council meeting," the captain says from the front of the stage.

Hadley sways on the spot. His eyes are fixed on the feed from the captain's surveillance bot, but his mind hears Celeste whispering, *I was born on the* Arcadia.

It didn't matter. He loved her. Still loves her.

The room spins. Hadley's empty stomach writhes with acid.

On the digiscreen, the captain looks directly at the surveillance bot. Straight at Hadley. The conniving old fox has destroyed three bots in as many days. The snippets of footage Hadley has seen have been a waste of time. Full of the captain doing paperwork. But he's got precious little else to go on. Every attempt to find the source of the antivenom has been a dead end. He's no closer to catching the culprits, and he's got precious few clues about who's working against him.

"Who've we got?" Hadley slurs. Sweat is beading on his face.

Grimson's dark hair is coiled tightly at the back of her head. "No surprises, sir. Representatives from the residential decks."

She pushes a glass of water into his hand.

He chugs it down and wipes the drips from his chin. "The Neath representatives? Silas Cuinn? Enid Hader?"

"No, sir."

Hadley watches the meeting. There are fourteen upper-deck representatives, one from each of the residential decks. Elected by the passengers, the representatives in turn appointed the captain. Funny thing is most people on the *Arcadia* despise the captain for being a collaborator, while Hadley hates him because he represents the ship.

The captain calls them to order. "Commander Hadley asked me to gather information about an alleged leaflet drop carried out a little over a week ago. I will yield the floor to each representative. Please provide any information you have on this matter."

First is the representative of Deck Four. A slender woman with brown skin folded around her eyes. "I know nothing about this matter." She retakes her seat.

That's how this will go. No comment from any of them. No clues as to who was involved. Ship's councils are mandatory; there's one on each of the vessels anchored along the coast. They do all the organizational work necessary to keep the *Arcadia* from imploding. Carry out the census. Deal with petty crime. Organize maintenance. It's supposed to make Hadley's life easier. But what if they're working against him? Uprisings have happened before. Soon after he got here, he was forced to execute a gang leader who thought he could raise a militia and force his way off the ship.

The pressure gains traction in his head, anger mixing with the aftereffects of the memory suppressants in a blinding swirl. This is for his benefit. Planned and rehearsed, to show that they're going through the motions. They have no intention of giving him anything.

After all his years in exile aboard the *Arcadia*, he knows the one thing all ship scum have in common: you can't trust them. Deception is hard-wired into them.

He snaps into a memory. He's bounding up the stairs to his apartment, a bunch of fresh train tickets in hand. Their bags are packed and ready. They're going to run, he and Celeste. Straight to the Maine border and out of the Federated States. Over and free. But then the memory fractures.

Celeste left him for dead.

He's falling.

Grimson's ready with a chair.

He opens his eyes, and he's in the bullpen, Grimson by his side, the deputy studiously avoiding eye contact. On the digiscreen, another representative stands up.

"This is pointless. Turn it off," Hadley says. "Do a roundup. Get together a list of people who have been informed on in the last week."

"Yes, sir. Which crimes?"

"Doesn't matter. Just make a list. I want twenty arrests. Make sure we hit every deck. Each person on this ship needs to know someone that gets picked up. Let's tighten the grip."

Hadley rolls things around in his mind. He's got no new intel. But this was a planned obstruction. They're united in their determination to keep him in the dark, and someone told them how tonight was going to play out. Someone orchestrated the whole thing, and he has the sneaking suspicion that this is about more than a few leaflets. It's becoming clear that the captain of the *Arcadia* is working against him.

CHAPTER 19

ESTHER

revel in the sensation of the comb pulling across my scalp, and I've managed to convince myself that any lice that crawled on to my head don't stand a chance. I can scrape away the memory of the stained pillow.

Scrape.

The old woman's weight as she pulled my tooth.

Scrape.

After the dentist, Alex brought me home and ordered me to take a nap. I've been sitting here, combing my hair, since he left, the daylight turning oily with the sunset.

The towel is free of bugs when I swipe the nit comb across it. No lice. No eggs. Still, my head crawls. And the new tooth feels smooth and wrong in my mouth. Until a few days ago, the route from here to med school was a straight line. Good grades and a clean record would get me there. Now it feels like any moment could knock me off course. Need to keep my eyes on the prize. Head down. Power through. Tonight, I'll make sure I have no lice. Then I'll pass the test. Everything will go back to normal.

May's home. She slams the front door behind her and drops her bag in the middle of the floor. Her face glows with sweat. Saturday is war-games training day for the cadets, and she'll have spent this afternoon in a simulated shoot-out with her classmates. Preparation for when she joins the army and goes to defend bleak border walls that were erected when the Federated States seceded from the United States in an argument over immigration. The Federated States was so concerned that immigrants from the south might carry disease that it fractured the union. Since then, it has done its best to keep outsiders out, including us.

May's face is striped with shadows, as she stands next to me in the half-light, glaring.

"What?" I say.

"Got something to tell me?"

Before I can answer, the cabin door opens again, and this time it's Mom, trailing the smell of rain. Droplets flick against the window like gravel. It's going to be a hard storm.

"You're both home. Good," she says with a tired smile.

May and I have Mom's eyes, minus the crow's feet. And her hair, minus the gray. Her rounded shoulders are different; the slight hunch caused by years of physical work. Circles of mud stain her knees from crouching in the dirt around the vegetable beds she tends. I stretch my neck from side to side in the hope of avoiding the same posture.

"May, do you have to leave your stuff in the middle of the floor?"

Mom tuts and throws May's bag into the space by the sofa, then hooks her coat on the back of the front door. She takes a jam jar of yellowish liquid out of the top cupboard. "Put this on while you're combing—it'll kill any eggs."

The unfinished conversation fizzes around us.

"Give me the comb," May says.

She arranges herself behind me on the sofa and spreads the towel on her knee. Getting rid of lice takes diligence. Front to back. Roots to ends. Swipe the comb on the towel at the bottom of each strand. May rubs the oil through my hair. It's cold and tingly on my scalp, the smell deliciously sweet.

I close my eyes against the clutter and mess of four overlapping lives and listen to the rain while May works out my tangles. She yanks through a knot. "Take it easy," I grumble.

By *Arcadia* standards, we're privileged. Except for the grand cabins on the topmost decks, ours is one of the biggest homes on the entire ship. Square feet bigger than those on the lower decks, and a world away from the squalor of the Neath territories. But some days, when we argue, the cabin's a war zone. According to the ship's brochure, a dog-eared heirloom that Dad keeps in a drawer, our suite *brings land's greatest luxuries out to sea*. Maybe once, but now our front cabin is a cluttered mess, the kitchenette and the living room and my parents' fold-up bed all vying for supremacy. The walls are lined with junk, our two pans, jars of food, books. We have a two-seat sofa, four fold-up chairs and no privacy.

"I need to talk to you about the other night," May whispers in my ear. Some of her anger seems to have dissipated, and now all I can sense is anxiety. "I'm super pissed that you didn't come to me, but I'll explain everything."

My mind reels with confusion. What can she know? *How* could she know? "What is there to explain?"

"We can't talk about it now. I'm going to fix it, OK? I'm going to make sure that's the end of it. I didn't want you involved—"

"Hold on, involved in what?"

"You two look like the ship's been sunk tonight," Mom says, interrupting us. She'd been folding a pile of laundry while the water steams on the stove, but now she's watching us.

"Just tired," May says.

Satisfied, Mom looks at the front door. She's waiting for Dad, and she won't relax until everybody's home. "Sounds like it'll be a bad storm tonight," she murmurs.

Rain-soaked wind blasts through the door. Dad slams it behind him. His fingers rattle the chain as he pulls it across to lock us inside. He dashes over to the front window, takes a fistful of curtain and looks out. Rainwater beads on his thin hair, turning it black and sticking it to his neck. He's still wearing the long, thick leather welding apron that protects him at work, singed in patches from flying sparks. Something's wrong.

I'm on my feet. May's next to me. And I get that nasty swooping feeling that something bad is about to happen.

"George?" Mom's wringing a tea towel between her thin hands.

Dad's shoulders heave. He drops the curtain and turns to face us. Shadows fill the hollows of his cheeks. "Girls, have you done anything? Anything that might get us searched?"

Anxiety makes my head spin. Where would I start?

The leaflet drop?

The kidnapping?

The new tooth?

So much has gone wrong so quickly.

Dad has that wide-eyed look, clear and glassy. Like the girl in the Lookout. Like our abducted neighbor. And I can't confess. I can't look at his unfiltered terror and tell him that everything they've sacrificed for me, everything we've worked for, might be for nothing. I can't tell him that his nightmares are coming true.

"What's this about?" Mom says.

"One of the guys on my work team…Coalies came at quitting time…His wife had been keeping tabs on him…He tried to run…Blood everywhere."

"His own wife?" Mom says. Her face matches Dad's.

May doesn't miss a beat. "Could they think you were friends?" She's tracking the connections, trying to find any link between that man and our family.

"No. Don't know. Maybe." Dad chews his bottom lip. The permanent lines on his forehead are deepened by the dim light. He looks old.

"What did he do?" I ask.

May glares at me. "He didn't have to *do* anything!" she blurts, losing her cool. Splashes of furious red bloom on her neck.

"Don't start, May. Not tonight. Not when we've got such a short time left together," says Dad.

A surge of pain rises through my fear. It hurts to hear someone say it out loud. In a few days, this life we've shared for sixteen years will be over. May will graduate from her training program and leave the *Arcadia*. The truth that none of us want to face, the truth that feels like it might rip my heart right out of my chest, is that we might never see her again. The graduation ceremony could be the last time we're together in the flesh.

Dad scans the corners of the cabin. My hackles rise. I know exactly what he's thinking. What if their bots are already inside?

"Coalies are putting the screws on. Making arrests. Heard a rumor that the *Oceania* was cleared. They're saying it's gone," he says.

My mind flashes to the leaflet with the black lettering, the tilting ship spewing smoke. I see it disappear from the edges of the paper and turn to dust on my hands.

"We've proved we can be trusted. Two hard-working girls. Clean antibody checks. Clean records," Mom says. "We have nothing to worry about."

May catches my eye.

"You're right. You're right." Dad clasps Mom's hand. "Let's do a sweep for cameras anyway. Esther, check the bathroom. May, you do your bedroom. Your mother and I will start in here."

This is a ritual we've practiced for years, ever since our neighbor was arrested. We've done it dozens of times, scouring the cabin for signs that we might have been infiltrated. Every time trouble comes so close that it might have tarred us by association. We've never found anything, and it brings peace of mind, even if it's just for an evening.

Dad moves to start the search, but Mom holds him back. "What if we find a camera, George? What would we do?"

"Get rid of it. What else?"

"And what would that achieve?"

My dad's face twitches in confusion.

"Are you suggesting we don't check for cameras?" May says. Her eyebrows are pulled up together in an expression of incredulity that would be funny if this whole thing wasn't terrifying.

"Let them watch if they want to. We've got nothing to hide," Mom says.

I've got something to hide. I aided a criminal. Then I kept it a secret. That's treason.

"That's the most ridiculous thing I've ever heard. We've always checked before. Why stop now?" May says.

"Because something's changed. They're upping surveillance."

May folds her arms. "Dad agrees with me. Don't you?"

Dad presses his lips together, his face pinched with stress as he thinks. "No. Your mother's right."

"Are you serious? We *let* them watch us?" May says.

"Think about it. Even if we find something, there's nothing we can do. We can't get rid of a surveillance bot; they'll know. The other option is we continue. We keep acting exactly the same," Dad says.

"That way, all they see is a loyal family," Mom adds.

"And in the meantime we live under their eye?" May says.

"We always live like that."

"Esther, back me up." When I don't say anything, she turns to stare at me. "Seriously?"

"I don't know," I say. "Maybe it makes the most sense."

Much as I hate to admit it, when Mom wants us to bow to every new restriction, every indignity and rule, all she's thinking about is us. We're being good citizens, and May and I will be rewarded with new lives. But something else brings a bitter taste to my mouth.

The word the dentist used this afternoon set me on edge and it's been growing with every passing minute: *collaboration.*

"It's decided. If they're watching, all they'll see is four people following the rules. Now set the table, please, girls."

May makes a sound like anger grating across her vocal cords. She grabs her bag off the floor and pulls the chain back from the front door.

"Where are you going?" Dad asks.

"For a run."

She swings the door open, letting in a fresh tumult of rain, and slams it behind her.

"She's too headstrong. Not careful enough," Mom says.

"She'll be safer once she graduates." Dad rubs his stubbly jaw, cheeks drawn with stress.

May said she needed to talk to me. She said she knew about what happened the other night.

Looks like I'm not the only one with something to hide.

CHAPTER 20

NIK

May and I are on trial. Literally. Everyone in the rebellion knows it was us that did the leaflet drop. It's not like it's the first time we've acted out.

We're in the hallway outside what was once the most high-end restaurant on the ship. Carefully scanned and cleared of the surveillance bots Hadley has been using to keep his beady eye on the captain. Two double doors you could drive a forklift through—smooth and made of oak or mahogany or something—separate us from the upper crust of the rebellion. Inside, the captain, as well as my mother and the representatives of each different part of the ship, are talking about our stunt and what should be done about it.

May stands against the wall, kicking one boot heel against a patch so soggy it dents with each blow. A rainstorm's been hammering the *Arcadia* all day, and water drips from her hair.

"They're going to slap our wrists, and that'll be the end of it," I say.

The rebellion can't do without May any more than it can do without me. It's a finely honed plan, the confluence of years and missions stretching back to before the Coalies took my dad.

"You know what pisses me off about all this?" she asks.

"Got a feeling you're going to tell me."

"It's that we're the ones actually *doing* something, while the representatives sit and wait. And now they're going to judge us."

Not much I can say to that. In the rebellion's view, we were reckless. We could have sunk the whole mission. And I have to agree with them. It was a stupid risk that I took because I wanted to make May happy. Now I can feel the ripples of it spreading through the rebellion, and it's not giving me a good feeling.

There's a sound down the corridor, and I look up to see a group of Neaths jogging toward us.

"Almost time," I say to May.

She nods, setting her face in a flat expression that only I can recognize; she's trying to control her feelings.

The Neaths come face to face with us and, before I know what's happening, they pin me and May against the wall.

"Get off!" May snarls.

"It'll only take a minute," the one holding me says. One of the others passes a scanner over May's livid face, hovering around her pockets and her boots until he's satisfied she doesn't have any surveillance equipment on her.

Another group appears at the end of the corridor. The entourage surrounds a tall, straight-backed thirty-something with long black hair that falls in thin braids and thick waves down her back. With her pale skin and wild hair, she always looks like she's just come in from a storm. Enid.

The minions in front wield disc-shaped scanners on long poles, attached by wires to headphones. This whole place will have been swept and searched by fingertip before she arrived, every fraction of an inch checked to make sure Hadley isn't watching. He gets to see exactly as much as the captain wants him to. Obviously wasn't good enough for Enid, so she's brought her own little mobile search team with her.

She stops in front of me, staring forward at the door, surrounded by her muscle. One of them hammers on the door.

I hold my breath. Enid's a friend. Some days. Other days, she's the leader of a highly trained, ever-loyal criminal militia.

"You've been playing the fool, Nik my boy," she says without looking at me. At the outer edge of her eyes, black makeup sits in the creases of her skin. "Don't appreciate being called up here to vote on whether you're thrown off the team."

Enid doesn't raise her voice. Ever. She doesn't need to.

"Enid, I—"

"Shut up," one of her bodyguards says. She swings the bot detector around, skimming my face until I bat it away.

The doors open from the inside. Enid turns to May. "When his mother starts flapping her mouth, stand your ground."

She continues on into the dining room, and I let out a breath as the doors slam shut behind her.

We wait. May kicks the wall.

The door opens. "You can come in now," says Gareth, the

captain's right-hand man. He's got the stooped shoulders of someone who's taller than everyone else and doesn't like the fact.

May goes ahead of me, striding through the dining hall.

I trot after her. The broken-down grandeur of this place always makes the hair on the back of my neck stand on end. Red carpets covered in circles of water damage. A constant drip of water from the ceiling. Half a crystal chandelier, the lower parts plucked bare of crystals, the upper parts dangling with ropes from where people have tried to nab the rest. All the tables are piled in one corner, snapped legs and cracked tops. They're covered in sooty patches that look like someone's tried setting fire to them. The whole thing's dominated by a semicircular stage, gold-trimmed red velvet curtains still dangling at the sides.

The captain uses this place to hold meetings because none of the leaders have a territorial claim to it. Means there's less chance of things descending into a fist fight if the gang leaders start arguing.

May bounds up on to the stage like she's about to perform. By the time I follow her up, she's already standing at attention in front of the leaders of the rebellion. They sit in a horseshoe shape, all stony faces and crossed arms. Somehow, the original ornate chairs survived the pillage of the dining room, and that's what they're sitting on. The fabric's covered in a layer of greenish mold, and the whole place has an oniony aroma.

Silas Cuinn's already installed on one of the dining chairs, a gang of scruffy-looking Neaths lounging nearby. Enid's sitting now too, but her followers are doing another sweep of the place with their devices, obviously not yet satisfied that all of Hadley's surveillance equipment was picked clean after the meeting of the ship's council. The two groups from rival gangs stay warily away from one another. The rest are the deck leaders. All of them have been persuaded to act against the Coalies.

My mother gives me a single ice-cold glance and returns to looking at the sheet of paper in her hand. I've been trying to keep calm for May's sake, but now my mouth goes dry. I feel like I'm shrinking.

"Nikhil Lall, Cadet Crossland," the captain says. There's a crushed bot at his feet. "You understand what you've been accused of?"

"Yes, sir," I say. "Cadet Crossland and I made leaflets announcing the destruction of the *Oceania*. We distributed them in the Lookout."

A murmur goes around the horseshoe. Someone tuts.

My mother's unmoved, her back poker-straight. "As you know, our organization is close to realizing its goals. As such, we issued a blanket ban on any activity not directly related to our overarching mission in the hope that we would avoid the attention of Commander Hadley," she says.

"Hearing news from the other ships is important for the survival of the people of the *Arcadia*, ma'am," May says.

My mother lifts her eyes to May, and it's at that moment I realize tonight will not end well. May and my mother are coming face to face for the first time since Esther was kidnapped.

"I think I speak for everybody here when I say that you do not have permission to speak freely. We are not interested in your opinions. We do not wish to hear your philosophizing. Whose idea was the leaflet drop?"

"Mine," May and I say simultaneously. I hide a smile, despite my nerves.

"Your actions have had repercussions. Commander Hadley has placed the captain under surveillance, making our operations infinitely more difficult. In addition, he has further tightened his restrictions—"

"That wasn't because of us," I say.

"–has further tightened his restrictions on the ship," my mother continues, quiet and all the more sinister for it. "Nikhil, as Cadet Crossland's commanding officer, you sanctioned this action. Correct?"

"I take full responsibility," I say.

"Garbage," May says, looking at her feet, shaking her head.

"Don't," I murmur.

"I won't stand here while she blames us for Hadley tightening control. He's added new restrictions every week for five years. Does anyone really think a few leaflets made things worse? More likely he's getting ready for the clearance. And that's exactly what people aboard the *Arcadia* should be doing too."

"Cool down," I urge.

My mother stands up. "You have reinforced the idea that there is an organized rebellion. For years, we worked hard to keep our activities secret from Commander Hadley, and we had hoped to remain hidden for weeks to come. Instead, you revealed to Hadley that we receive radio communications from outside the ship, and that we have the resources to produce leaflets in high volume. Most people onboard don't have access to recycling paper. What's more, he knows Nikhil was shot with a toxic bullet, and that he would need antivenom to survive. If he investigates where antivenom might be sourced, he could be led straight to one of our major assets. Finally, you exposed yourselves to arrest and interrogation. If either of you falls into the hands of the Coalies, Landfall *will* fail."

May's fingers bunch up at her sides. "Get on with it," she says.

"Excuse me?"

"Give us our punishment. You're dying to."

"I think what Cadet Crossland means is we acknowledge the unintended consequences of our actions. We apologize unreservedly for our unsanctioned mission," I say.

My mother breathes out through her nose. "You are forbidden from speaking to one another."

"What? We've got a mission to complete. I'm the one meeting her when she comes back onboard!"

"Not anymore. Someone else will take your place. From now on, you will not see each other. You will not speak to each other or otherwise attempt to communicate."

Feels like the ground's opening under me. "This is bull," I say. Another murmur from the leaders. I catch the captain's eye and find sympathy, but no help.

"What an eloquent counterargument. From now until further notice, I will act as Cadet Crossland's handler."

"She's graduating in four days," I say, trying, and failing, to keep my cool. "We've got work to do. We're supposed to be getting ready for her mission." *And it's our last few days together*, is the thing I stop myself saying.

"A consideration that should have been at the forefront of your mind before you carried out such a blatant act of provocation. That will be all, thank you," my mother says.

May's face hardens at the dismissal. Her fingers flex at her side. Here it comes.

"You had my sister taken," she says.

Mother looks at the ceiling. "This is neither the time nor the place."

"I told you when this all started that I'd take on whatever mission you assigned to me. But I wouldn't risk my family. I wouldn't let you recruit my sister. That was our agreement."

"Your behavior threatened the mission. Perhaps with your sister now part of the rebellion, your dedication will be renewed."

"My dedication? I've given my life for this. I've proved my loyalty over and over."

"That was low, even for you, Mother," I say. "You traumatized a sixteen-year-old girl."

My mother looks at me for a split second, and it's obvious she feels absolutely no remorse. "I made the difficult decision to use Esther because I believed Cadet Crossland would stop her reporting the incident to the Coalies. Involving Corporal Weston in your care entailed too much risk of her being exposed. It remains to be seen whether the antivenom she stole—the antivenom that saved your life—will result in her cover being destroyed."

"I'll kill you!" May screams.

She lurches toward my mother. I leap after her, grabbing her around the waist to hold her back. She strains against me. I feel her lungs pressing out with each breath.

"May, stop!" I say.

"Does she know anything she shouldn't?" Mother's voice is like silk, but there's danger in it. The hint of a threat.

From his place at the side of the stage, Silas stares at May like he's growling silently. Waiting to hear whether Esther is a problem he has to deal with.

I step in front of May and pull her into me, half holding on to her and half stopping her from getting at my mother. I can hear her raspy breaths, feel the heat of her anger. I put my cheek against hers. "She's relying on you keeping Esther quiet. It's messed up, and it's wrong, but you have to make them believe you'll be able to do it," I say into her ear, so quiet only we can hear it.

She's breathing hard, shaking with rage, but she raises her chin as I take my place at her side again. "No, she only knows what happened to her. I haven't given her any details about our organization," she says. She glares at my mother without flinching.

"And has she been talking to anyone about her experience? Her boyfriend perhaps?"

"She hasn't spoken a word. And she won't."

"Keep it that way. Get her out of here." My mother gives a signal, and a couple of men emerge from the shadows.

"They can't do this. They can't keep us apart. Nik, do something," May says. The men usher her down the steps. "Wait! Let me just say something to him. Please, I'm leaving. Please let me just say one thing."

There's no sign of emotion from my mother, not a scrap of sympathy for either me or May.

Halfway across the room, May tries to get back to me. All I

can do is stand and watch as the men grab one arm each and pull her backwards. The doors are opened. She shouts something I don't catch.

In fifteen seconds, our last days together have been torn away.

I'll never forgive my mother for this.

Good morning. It is 06:00 hours on Monday, November 1, 2094.

This is the captain of the cruise ship Arcadia.

It has come to my attention that a quantity of illicit material was distributed in the Lookout café a week ago. I will provide all possible assistance to Commander Hadley of the Arcadia *Special Task Force as he works to apprehend the culprits.*

I urge all passengers to remain vigilant at this time.

Daily reported Virus cases: zero.

Days at sea: 15,942.

CHAPTER 21

HADLEY

Hadley crouches in the shadow at the end of the corridor. The floor is layered with sheets of cardboard. A useless attempt to soak up wetness. Anticipation makes him light as air, even though he's weighed down by his extra layer of body armor.

In front of him, Grimson uses a mirror to peer around the corner, checking the corridor for Neaths. This is an internal deck, no windows, no sea view. Shoebox cabins open straight onto communal corridors with their peeling paint and dim light. Would've been the cheapest fare you could buy when the ship was used for vacation cruises.

Grimson signals for the team to advance, two fingers flicking toward the door. *Go! Go! Go!*

They move. Long strides. Weapons pointing. Reaching the cabin in seconds, Grimson steps to the other side of the door, her hand clutching a cylindrical flashbang. Other officers take up position, covering them from every angle.

Hadley kicks the door as hard as he can. It splinters around the flimsy lock, ancient wood giving barely any resistance. It slams back against the inside wall. Grimson throws the flashbang inside.

Hadley waits for the explosion, so loud it rattles his eardrums even through his helmet. The flash like a solar flare. Then smoke blooming from the doorway.

His officers flood inside. The screaming starts.

There are ways to get things onto the ship. Throw the crew of a sewage tanker a bribe, and they'll turn a blind eye to a couple of boxes changing hands. Extra food gets slipped into the official rations. Every now and then, someone tries sending things in on a small motorboat or even a rowboat. Once it's on the *Arcadia*, stuff follows the smuggling routes that grow through Neath territory like weeds. They reach the market and the residential decks. There's not a person on the ship that's innocent. They've all tasted a fresh apple or bought a couple of pills to treat a toothache.

Hadley pretends not to see most of it. He doesn't care about a few extra calories, or a bottle of antibiotics, or even the steady trickle of unauthorized screens and comgloves. He watches the connections until he needs his meds or some piece of intel about what's going on in the underworld. Like now. He wants to know who's been trying to get hold of antivenom. Smugglers will give him the answers.

After a few seconds, he walks into the cabin, keeping his visor down over his face to shield himself from the stench of piss.

Officers drag two Neaths out from a back room and throw them, quivering and sniffling, onto the floor in front of Hadley. An old couple. Coughing on the smoke. Their eyes stream. The woman's long gray braid snakes between her bony shoulder blades.

Hadley watches the deputy flip up his visor, the skin of the younger man's face pale with sweat and guilt. The kid's not getting into the swing of these raids. He's still oozing compassion. The old Neath couple watch Hadley from the floor. He feels his mouth curl in disgust. Filthy smugglers. Filthy Neaths.

Grimson's smashing cups exuberantly in the kitchenette. That's how you're supposed to conduct this kind of raid.

"Search the whole place. Throw whatever we don't need over the railing. Make a show of it," Hadley says into his visor. "And take the deputy with you."

Grimson pauses as the order is relayed into her helmet. She picks up a pile of clothes and tramps to the door, trailing stuff behind her. Hadley catches a glimpse of the deputy's tear-filled eyes before the kid closes his visor and follows Grimson's lead. *Pathetic.*

"Jared Alba," Hadley says. The old man looks up at him, white beard against wrinkled skin. "I'm looking for something specific, Mr. Alba. And I've heard you're involved in the unlawful movement of medicines."

"Not me, not me." The old man wobbles his head and keeps his eyes pinned to the ground near Hadley's feet.

"We've got meds, sir. All kinds," Grimson says. She throws him a pointed glance as she drops a box onto the ground in front of the blubbering Neaths before marching off.

Hadley stoops, snatching up a bottle with a label he'd recognize anywhere. He holds it up to the light, the tiny blue pills inside glistening as he turns the bottle.

"I need to know about antivenom," he says, turning his back on the Neaths momentarily, so that he can slip the bottle into his pocket. That stroke of luck will keep him going a little bit longer.

"No. I wouldn't smuggle anything like antivenom. Only criminals would need antivenom. I only do medicine. Only the things people really need, Commander Hadley, sir," Alba says.

Hadley opens his visor. The smell of the cabin floods in. Wet cardboard and urine. He grabs a few of the meds and reads the labels on the vials, throwing them down one after the other. Tranquillizers, painkillers, anti-inflammatories. No antivenom.

Another dead end. If the shooting was fatal, his officers would have found a body when they went down that elevator shaft the next day. There'd have been a funeral. Or at least whispers about someone dying violently. Ship people aren't good at keeping their mouths shut. No, his gut tells him that whoever it was crawled off to lick their wounds—they had help, and they got the antivenom they needed. So why can't he find any trace of it?

"The respectable face of drug smuggling. You just want to help people, don't you, Mr. Alba? Maybe your boss will know more."

"No." The old man's face jerks to Hadley's. He's trapped. There's Hadley and there's his boss. Rock. Hard place.

"I've heard you work for Silas Cuinn. I could let him know you sent me over to see him."

"No, please. We don't know anything about antivenom. I pick up the medicines from the captain of the sewage tanker. I take them to the service corridor and sell them. I leave the money at a drop point. I never see Cuinn. I don't go down there."

The old man's telling the truth, and it's nothing Hadley couldn't have figured out himself. He's a two-bit drug dealer with no access to the real power. And there's no whiff of antivenom in this cabin or anywhere else.

"Aw, Jared. You've spilled your guts, and I didn't even get chance to chat with the lovely Mrs. Alba."

The woman's eyes widen. He drinks in her fear.

"Are you aware, Mr. Alba, that the Federated States has supported the ship with food and resources?"

"Yes, sir."

"And we've educated your children? And repaired damage to your hull, and given you materials to improve the places that you live in?"

"Yes, sir."

"It would be an ungrateful person who took all that was offered, consumed resources that could be used by the Federated States' own citizens, and then ignored the very reasonable requests of their generous host country."

The old man's mouth works silently. Hadley waits.

"Yes, sir."

The woman throws herself at Hadley's leg, smearing dirty tears on his uniform. Hadley kicks her off. Her sobs irritate. They're too needy. He likes defiance. He likes the pain of someone trying not to break. "Grimson, make her shut up."

Grimson grabs the old woman by the hair and drags her out into the corridor between the rows of cabins. Her cries become quieter as she gets further away.

Everyone on the ship will share the same fate soon enough. Hadley despises the Neaths, but he doesn't discriminate. He hates the rich upper-deck passengers who pretend to be Federated States citizens as much as the have-nots who live on the lower decks. The ones at the top are deluded enough to think their status means something. That somehow they're better than the others, and that it will save them. In the end, they're all the same, whatever deck they come from. Scrounging Europeans.

They've all been sucking life from the mainland ever since they dropped anchor. Taking without giving anything back. The ships caused a rift that almost tore the Federated States apart. Half the citizens wanted to let the refugees in. The other half wanted nothing to do with them. While the arguments raged, the ship's food ran out. And what were supposed to be rations to stop the ships starving on their doorstep turned into daily transports of food the Federated States could barely afford.

It has its own problems. Its own battles. The southern border wall needs protecting. The farmlands produce only just enough food. It has plenty of poor and old and sick to take care of. Even if it didn't, why should his people look after the feral displaced population of some far-off continent? It wasn't their war. They didn't bomb the hell out of each other. They didn't reduce a whole continent to wasteland.

Every few years, there's a new campaign, a new petition, a new debate in Conclave. A group of citizens opening their arms in welcome. Another faction insistent that the refugees will be used to score points against the Federated States, if they fall into enemy hands. There's even some that argue for the ships to be returned to Europe, but that's never happened, unfortunately. He's watched it seesaw twenty times, all from within the ship. And, while they argue, the ships stagnate.

Alba whimpers. "Please, we've done nothing. Silas ordered us to keep our heads down, and we've done nothing—"

Hadley freezes at the door of the cabin. He turns back to look at the old man. "Silas Cuinn ordered you to keep your head down?"

Alba looks up at Hadley, his eyes dancing with hope. "Yes, sir. Yes."

"Just you?"

"No, sir. Everyone. He's ordered everyone that works for him to lie low."

"Why?"

"Don't know. Please, I don't know. My wife knows nothing. Please."

Hadley inches closer, leaning in so that the man's personal space is eroded. "What exactly are your orders, Alba?"

"He's ordered everyone to keep quiet. We do a few deals. Nothing big. Just enough to make it look ..." He trails off.

"Talk, Alba."

"Make it look like business as usual." The old man shakes and collapses on the ground, sobbing violently.

Hadley steps out into the corridor. Faces pop out of doorways to see what's happening and vanish as fast as they appear. One of his officers is attaching a board to the wall next to the cabin door. It will list all of Mr. and Mrs. Alba's crimes. The smuggling and the drugs. And, once Hadley has sentenced them, the punishment. Death or deportation for hard labor at one of the prison camps.

Hadley stands with his hands on his hips. An unpleasant suspicion settles on him that what started out as a few leaflets dropped in a public café is actually something much more disturbing. Silas

Cuinn has ordered all his people, the vast network of criminals and smugglers under him, to *make it look like everything is normal*. They're setting something up. Hadley's starting to see the shape of it, but he can't figure out the punchline yet.

He needs the clearance order, and he needs it soon, otherwise his plan to get off the ship will go down the drain. Whatever they've got in the pipeline will be ruined as soon as he gets the go-ahead to clear the ship. The first thing he'll do is put a bullet in the captain and the rest of the council members. That will end this rebellion.

Further down the corridor, Grimson has the old woman kneeling on the ground with her hands cuffed behind her back. She strides back to Hadley, pulling off her helmet as she walks, so that she's no longer connected through the audio system. "There were memory suppressants in that box. They should probably be confiscated," she says.

"I saw them. Thank you, Grimson," he says. He checks for the bottle of pills stashed in his pocket. "Do the neighbors too. Let all the scumbags know what happens to those who don't show proper respect for the Federated States."

CHAPTER 22

ESTHER

Alex's eyes pin me as soon as I walk into class. I know what's happened before I look at the class ranking. My grades have slipped. Above Corp's desk, flickering in the autumn light from the open window, are the holographic representations of me and my classmates beside our names. A reminder of our success. Or, in this case, my failure.

1. Alex
2. Kara
3. Esther

I've dropped to number three. Kara has taken my place. My hologram smiles out from her new position, cadaver-blue and unaware that she's plummeting.

Raw shame burns through me as I drop into seat three, the

empty place between me and Alex now reserved for Kara. I hide my humiliation by rifling in my med bag for my digiscreen and find it too quickly. The embarrassment overwhelms me, and I grind my hands into my temples, wishing the imprint of the miniature blue Esther would disappear.

At least she's blue. Blue is good. Blue means pass. Blue means safe. If she turns red, I'm really in trouble. Red would mean I dropped off the threshold for a visa, and nothing short of perfect would let me claw my way up to a passing grade. I try to focus on the cooling breeze, let it chase the panic away.

Behind me, Seth, the pale red-haired kid from Deck Fourteen, is talking in hushed tones. I hear *Oceania*, and *clearance* and *dawn raids*.

Another voice, this time belonging to Anna, rises indignantly. "I just don't believe it," she says. "There'd have been an announcement if a ship was destroyed. Anyway, where would all the people go?"

"I heard they've got specially built quarantine camps. Basically, prisons, and if you're sent there, you have to work for the rest of your life," Seth replies.

"Come on," Anna says. "That's a conspiracy theory. It's as stupid as people saying the drones can shoot you."

Alex is watching me—I can feel it—like he's analyzing me. He suspects I'm not being honest about the events of the past week.

He gives me an *it's OK* half-smile. "Ready for the test?" he says.

Oh no.

Dread lurches in my stomach. I swallow hard.

I forgot about the test. It got pushed out of my mind by the thought that the Coalies might be watching us. I'm unprepared. Didn't even open my textbook. If I fail, I won't be scrabbling for the number-two spot any more. I'll be lucky to stay above tenth place.

Alex's face flickers, and I see he already expected this. The weight of shame pushes me lower into my chair.

He leans over the chair between us so that our heads are almost touching. Everyone else is caught up in their own conversations about ships and drones, disinterested in what Alex and I are saying to one another. "Don't worry, I've got your back," he whispers.

He slides his hand onto my thigh, the gesture blocked from everyone else's view by the back of the empty chair. When he leans away again, there's a small metal box balancing on my leg. I open it and, inside, a delicate glass dome rests on a foam pad. Its surface swims with oily color.

"I'm not a cheat," I say. Anger jostles against humiliation. How can Alex think I'd use that?

"I know you're not," he whispers, taking a look over his shoulder to make sure no one's listening. "You'd ace this test if you'd studied. But you've got a lot going on. I can tell you've been distracted because May's leaving. Can't be easy for any of you thinking you might never see her again after graduation."

"It doesn't matter. I'm not using it," I say. "Take it back."

I try to push the box back into Alex's hand, but he keeps his arms firmly crossed, his face determined. As the room fills up with our classmates, I start to panic. One by one, they see the projection. One by one, they check my face for signs of anguish before they take their seats.

"It's barely even cheating, more maintaining your well-earned position," Alex whispers when he gets the chance. He glances at the class ranking. The Kara hologram smirks at me. "We only get one crack at these tests. One opportunity to go ashore, and you're choosing to fail."

"I can't fail," I say, and my words end in a tiny involuntary whimper.

"Class has begun."

Corp's clear, ringing voice shuts down any further discussion as she strides across the front of the room and slams the window. The strip blind jangles in protest.

I can't catch my breath. There can be no getting out of it now, no begging to take the test another day. I slide the box between my leg and the chair, trying not to crush it with my weight. It sits there, like a trapped moth. At least it's hidden.

Kara arrives late. She murmurs a hurried *sorry* to Corp and scooches into the chair next to me. *My* chair until a couple of minutes ago. I stare at my hands so that I don't have to see her victorious glow. I can feel it though, when she flashes Alex a breathless smile.

Alex returns Kara's smile and adds a nod of congratulations. I'd like to throw a bucket of oyster slops over her.

The thought makes me ashamed all over again.

Corp taps on her digiscreen while the class waits in silence. I watch her face, willing her to cancel the test.

Cancel the test, Corp. Cancel the test because I won't cheat. I can't cheat.

For the first time in five years, Corp's mask slips. For a horrible second, I'm convinced she knows about the little cheating device hidden under my leg. I check the corners of the room for cameras. Corp rests on the edge of her desk and looks at the ceiling, clutching the digiscreen to her chest. She sighs, presses something on her digiscreen, and the class ranking blinks off.

It takes me a second to figure out what's changed when the faces reappear. All of them, except for Alex and Kara, have turned red.

I'm red. My face is red.

The classroom falls away, and I'm watching myself from outside. Dizzy. My nails dig into the flesh on my thigh.

There's the echoing scrape of a chair. "What's this?" Alex yells.

"Sit down, Mr. Hudson."

Corp's tone leaves no room for argument. Alex brings his indignation under control and thumps down on to his chair.

"This training program has been canceled."

It's like we take a breath. All of us. And then the whole class erupts in a torrent of protests. Anguished and bawling.

"No new ship students will be accepted for training. Please—" Corp raises both hands, palms out, to quiet the class.

I stay in my seat, trying to ground myself. Trying not to think about my hologram shining with blood-red light. Next to me Kara doesn't move. She's watching Corp, stilled by the news that has the rest of the class climbing the walls.

"I managed to persuade my superiors that it would be a waste of resources to cancel your education at this point. Therefore, you will all be able to finish the term, and in their *benevolence*"—Corp forces the word out—"they've agreed that the two most promising students will be offered study visas."

Only two places at med school. Only two chances. Eleven of us are out of luck. The little metal box pushes back against the weight of my thigh.

Kara fidgets and side-eyes me. I know what she's thinking, because I'm thinking the same. It's her against me. Alex is safe. The others could catch us, but it's unlikely. Only I can knock Kara from her place.

"They can't do that!" Alex's voice rises over the din.

"Eyes forward!" Corp barks, slamming her hand down on her desk.

Silence stretches the air. We've overstepped and now, as one, we drop back into line. Except for Alex. He's out of his chair and standing in the aisle.

Corp stares him down. "I know you're upset. But every one of you has a chance to—"

"A two-in-thirteen chance?" Alex says. The skin on his hands is taut around his knuckles.

"Do not test me, Mr. Hudson. I will report any insubordination."

Nausea hits me in waves. Just like that, Corp wheels out the threat of being reported. She's a Federated States officer first, our teacher second.

Alex snorts and drops back into his seat, catching my eye.

Corp doesn't miss a beat. "Let's move on. This test will be sixty-five percent of your grade for this class. It will mean the success—or failure—of your Federated States career."

My fear grows. As I watch my own flickering red-lit face, and weigh my chances, I realize I'm shaking. Two visas. I need one of them. Can I really bring myself to cheat? What if I get caught? Will Corp report me? Will she have me arrested?

Corp roams around the room, tapping each person's digiscreen with her own to pass along the test sheet. Before she can reach me, I shuffle the box out of its hiding place under my leg and raise my hand.

"Yes, Ms. Crossland?"

"Sorry, bathroom break," I say.

"Set timer, three minutes," she says to her comglove.

Scanning the cobwebbed corners for roving cameras, I rush across the corridor. The air in the bathroom is frigid, and I can see hot breath in my reflection. Two chances. One of them has to be mine. I wash my hands in water so cold it stings.

The contact lens stares at me through oily swirls of color. I stare back at it. What would Mom tell me to do? *Keep your integrity?* Or *do whatever it takes to succeed?* What if I can only become part of the Federated States by doing something I know they would consider illegal? The only thing I'm sure of right now is that Mom never expected me to be in this situation.

I need to buy myself some time. I need to tread water until I can get back on track. This is a one-time thing, and if I get through today I'll make sure it never has to happen again.

I lift the contact lens on the tip of my finger. Trying not to shake, I hold my eyelid back and press the glass dome into place over my cornea. It feels like a layer of frost. The glass flexes and pushes against the softness of my eye. It starts fingering its way around my eyeball, under the skin at the edges. The sensation makes me gag. I grasp the sink and pant through the pain.

"I've been top of the class for a year," I whisper to myself, but my voice is as weak as the excuses I'm using to justify all of this. I am pathetic. I'm snatching the chance to escape the ship away from one of my classmates. But I can be pathetic at med school or pathetic here, on the water, for the rest of my life.

My three minutes must be up, and I need to get back to class. The lens is almost invisible. The only way I know it's there is an irritating scratch when I blink. Corp won't notice unless she's looking for it. I splash water on my face and run my hands over my ponytail to tame it.

When I'm as neat as I can be, I return to class. Face down. One foot in front of the other. Don't attract attention. Corp taps her digiscreen to mine. The test sheet appears, sliced in half by the crack to my damaged digiscreen. The contact lens flares to life when I look at the on-screen text, taking less than a heartbeat to find the answers and display them on my vision. Answer after answer. Everything I need to get a winning grade.

Everything I need to beat Kara.

CHAPTER 23

HADLEY

Hadley wakes to a camera in his face.

He rubs grit from his eyes and stares. It's on the ceiling of his bunk, right above his pillow. Watching him sleep off a migraine. Maybe someone's at the other end of the feed observing Hadley's whole existence. Maybe no one is. He's given up wondering. His superiors have a penchant for punishments that mess with people's heads. Especially when the punishment is for a crime like his, where your thoughts were the source of the transgression. He dreamed of freedom with Celeste. His superiors made sure his punishment was the opposite.

He scratches his scar. It's cold in the cabin. The blanket too thin and damp, the mattress too hard and uneven. He puts his thumb over the camera's eye. It sidesteps, trying to get away from whatever's blocking its view. Eventually, it stops and crouches on the ceiling, emitting a series of annoyed chirps. He could kill it. He could crush it or drop it over the railing.

The thing beeps urgently. He keeps his thumb in place. This time he'll do it. Forget his life. Forget his apartment. His career. He'll start over, still in exile, but at least he'd be away from this stinking pile and these stinking refugees.

The camera extends an arm, sharp as a needle. It jabs Hadley in the thumb. He snatches his hand away and sits up in his bunk, swinging his legs over the side. Bare feet on the wooden floor. He sucks the bead of blood from his thumb.

There's a soft knock on the door. "Commander Hadley, sir." The deputy's voice barely carries through the wood.

"What?"

"There's a message from the admirals. You have to call them."

Hadley swears under his breath. Another headache for his pounding brain. "All right, Deputy."

It's coincidence. They wouldn't call because he shoved his thumb over the camera. He's done it a hundred times before, and they either didn't notice or didn't care.

The camera watches him put his dress uniform on. There's no such thing as privacy if you've been sentenced to a surveillance order. Still buttoning his jacket, he slides the door of his cabin open and staggers down the corridor to the bullpen. He stands in front of the wall, hands behind his back.

"OK, Deputy, open a line."

The deputy starts the transmission, and a bank of screens is projected on to the wall in front of Hadley. Six panels today. All the admirals will be joining the call.

This is it. He's going to get *the* news. At last, the order to clear the *Arcadia*.

Six screens blink on. All but one shows a person in uniform sitting behind a desk. High, stiff collars. Gold epaulets. Large Federated States flags hang on poles behind them.

The digiscreen in front of Hadley is empty, but he can hear a voice. "I've got to speak to that damned Hadley. Yes, now. And bring me some coffee."

"Admiral Santos, we can all hear you, sir," says Admiral Janek. She's straight-backed behind her desk. Hadley can see pine trees out of the window behind her.

Hadley's hatred for Janek is as bitter as nettles. She was at his court-martial hearing. Concrete-hard and mean too, with her tiny hooked nose and beady seagull eyes.

She was a new admiral then, and she wanted to strengthen her authority, so she lobbied for his sentence to be bumped from five years onboard the *Arcadia* to indefinite. As long as this ship exists, Hadley will be on it. At the start of his exile, in those never-ending nights before he discovered memory suppressants, he imagined all the ways he could destroy Janek. If he ever gets the opportunity, he'll bring Janek's life crashing down around her. And he'll make sure it's public. And he'll make sure it's humiliating.

Admiral Santos comes into view on the central digiscreen. He dodders around, rearranging paperwork, bald head shining through strands of hair. "Ah yes. Hadley. You've done well, Commander. From what I've seen, you haven't been tempted to leniency during your exile."

"No, sir. Thank you, sir."

"It's the opinion of this panel that there are no longer any concerns about your service to the Federated States."

Hadley's chest swells. "That's good to hear, sir."

It's happening. It's over. They're going to tell him the *Arcadia's* to be cleared, the passengers sent to work camps, the ship broken and sanitized and made to disappear. He's going home. Dry land. Life. He can clear the ship in a week. Maybe even a couple of days once he gets the order.

Hadley checks Janek's face, and her unruffled expression puts a dent in his excitement.

The admirals are busy people. They're all distracted by their work. Most of them are still having conversations with their staff off-screen, only half-focused on the call with Hadley. Six careers. Six sets of ambition. Six endgames. Only Janek is watching him. It's like she doesn't want to miss something. Hadley has the horrible feeling he's walking into a trap.

"Now, as you know the *Arcadia* was next in line for clearance. However, we've decided that we're going to skip the *Arcadia*—"

And the trap is sprung.

Hadley loses focus, the heat of devastation making it impossible to think. The voice of Admiral Santos shrinks to a hum. Janek watches him with her mean-gull face. She's smirking. She wants to see him broken.

"It was my turn." Hadley interrupts Admiral Santos.

"Pardon me?"

"How long until you order the clearance of this ship? How long am I going to be trapped out here?"

"Well, that depends on the other ships. You seem to have the *Arcadia* in hand, and the *Jørgenson* has recently seen a growth in unpleasant unrest."

"Due respect, Admiral, the *Arcadia* has its share of problems too," Hadley says.

The admiral raises his eyebrows. "True."

Janek leans forward in her seat. "This is a balancing act, Commander Hadley. Our citizens will tolerate the presence of the ships," she says. "We will provide a level of support in the form of food and sanitation and technology, and the ships will be safe from exploitation by our enemies."

She spreads her hands, palms toward Hadley. "However, we cannot tolerate criminals coming ashore and putting the lives of our people in danger. Right now, the *Arcadia* is under control, except for this minor business of the leaflets. Other ships are more challenging. The Federated States government must act on the most urgent threats to its security first."

A smile flits over Janek's face. "We don't expect this delay to last more than two years," she says.

Hadley can't breathe. His collar's tightening around his neck.

"That's all, Hadley. Keep us informed of the situation on the *Arcadia*," Santos says.

Five screens go blank. Hadley tries to stay calm, tries to hold his position so that Janek can't see the tide of panic that's seconds away from engulfing him.

She watches him for five long seconds before she hangs up.

He drops into a chair, grabbing at the buttons at his throat, trying to loosen his uniform. Two more years. The roving camera twitches on the wall by his head. He's worked hard. He's done well. And they repay him by passing him over. He won't do it. He can't.

He'll burn the ship down himself if he has to.

CHAPTER 24

ESTHER

'm sitting at my desk, trying to force medical details into my brain, when the power goes off. Darkness so complete that shapes of inky black dance in my vision. "May," I say urgently. "May, wake up."

"What?"

"The power's out."

"It's the middle of the night. Go to sleep."

"I need to study."

There's been a kind of strained peace at home in the days since my dad's work unit was raided and his colleague was dragged off. We skirt around anything important because we don't know whether they're listening.

Sometimes, in the suffocating quiet, I waste hours thinking about Kara and whether I've cheated her out of her place at med school. My answer is always *yes*. And that girl from the Lookout keeps getting into my head, and I keep wondering where she is. Whether they hurt her. The only way I've found to drown out the guilt is to study.

I slap the textbook closed and stand up, feeling around the room until I find the door handle.

May's fast asleep again. For all her strength and training, she's the one coping the worst with our new living conditions. For the better part of a week, she's been almost mute. She sits in her bunk with her back turned, and there's nothing I can do to coax her out. I tried to get her to take a walk with me, hoping that she'd open up. She refused to get out of bed. We were best friends once, but recently it's like she has a whole other life she won't let me be part of. It's as if she left the ship months ago.

The front room is just as dark. I can hear my parents breathing in their bed as I tiptoe past. Somehow, I manage to open the front door and find a night of moving clouds lit by the thinnest sliver of moon.

The circuit box for our cabin is shared with our upstairs neighbors, so it's attached to the overhanging ceiling close to the railing. Losing power is a common occurrence, so we keep a communal ladder on the deck for this purpose. Tonight, the ladder's nowhere to be seen.

"Brilliant," I whisper. I could go in search of it, but the thought that this might be a trap forces its way to the front of my mind. What if someone tripped the circuit deliberately so that we'd come out on deck? What if they're coming for me?

I hurry across the frigid deck and climb up onto the second bar of the railing, sitting so that my back's to the sea. My skin aches in the cold.

Wish I'd put my coat on. Working blind, I manage to find the shoebox-sized plastic circuit box, flip open the lid and run my fingers over the row of little levers until I find the one that's pointing the wrong way.

"Gotcha."

Closing my eyes, I reach higher, willing myself to balance. The lever flips down without resistance, and I hear the hum of electricity running back into our cabin. In a split second, my balance is gone. But instead of falling backwards off the ship, and down to certain death, something tugs me back by my T-shirt, and I tumble on to the deck.

"What the hell are you doing?" May says. She looks wild, hair loose and whipping around in the wind.

"You scared me!" I say, making a show of straightening my pajamas.

"Get inside. Now."

"The hell I will. You've ignored me for a week, and now you're suddenly giving orders?"

"You could have been killed. Don't you know how dangerous that was?"

"The ladder's gone. I need to be able to see to study. I tried to wake you, and you basically told me to get lost."

May's face is a storm of anger and concern. "You shouldn't even be out here, Esther. What were you thinking?"

I huff and cross my arms. Now she cares, after a week of giving me the silent treatment. "Don't act like you're concerned."

"Of course I'm concerned. You could have been killed climbing up there. Or, worse, someone could have taken you. It's not safe for you to be out here now."

I feel myself blinking. "What did I do to you? What did I do to make you stop talking to me?"

"Not everything is about you."

"Then tell me what it is about. We used to be best friends; now you can't stand to be in the same room as me."

"You're not the center of the universe," she says, her voice rising, frustrated.

"No. Don't try to gaslight me, May. Something's changed," I say. "You wanted to talk to me about it the other night. Then something happened. And now you're closed up tighter than a clam."

"Stop it. Just stop it." She's pointing at me as she talks. "Nothing's changed. I have nothing to talk to you about. Lock the door behind you." She stomps back into the cabin.

I follow, stopping to close the front door and pull the security chain into place. By the time I find my way back to our room, she's already kicking her blanket over her feet.

"Tell me what's going on," I say.

"Can you keep your voice down? You'll wake Mom and Dad. I just want you to be more careful. There are dangerous people on this ship, and after graduation tomorrow I'm not going to be here to protect you."

"Believe me, I know. I'm not as helpless as you think."

"Funny, because you act pretty naive most of the time."

That hit a nerve. "I am not naive!" I shout, not caring whether my parents can hear us arguing in the next room. "And I'll be glad when you're gone. At least then I won't have someone ignoring my existence."

I regret it as soon as it's out of my mouth. She pulls the blanket up to her neck and turns her back on me.

"May—"

"Turn the light out," she says quietly.

I manage to stop the tears rolling until I'm curled up in my bunk.

Good afternoon. It is 15:00 hours on Friday, November 5, 2094.

This is the captain of the cruise ship Arcadia.

A bittersweet day aboard the Arcadia *as we bid fare-*
well to some of our best and brightest young people.

Congratulations to all those military cadets cel-
ebrating their graduation today.

May your future endeavors bear fruit.

Daily reported Virus cases: zero.

Days at sea: 15,946.

CHAPTER 25

ESTHER

I want to die of shame.

"Just saying we like Alex. He's been good to you," my dad chips in. He's holding his hat in his fist, leaning back on the stove. "You could do worse than that boy."

Mom pulls my hair backwards and pushes a bobby pin into it, scraping my scalp. She's already dressed in her one good outfit: a dress that's twenty years old and hangs from her shoulders. She's lost weight. Her eyes are puffy red.

My bare legs stick to the chair, despite the fact that I'm covered in goosebumps. I'm not used to getting dressed up, but today is a special occasion. We're saying goodbye to May.

I don't want to think about where she might be stationed. Cadets go to defend the southern borders of the Federated States, and the benefits to ship kids willing to fight are enormous. A new life on land. All the food you can eat. And travel to the kind of places most ship people can't even dream of. And, when she's served her time, a house and a job and the chance to build a life in freedom. But there's no escaping the fact that the border walls are perilous. It's where the Federated States and what's left of the United States take potshots at each other.

I lift the hand mirror to see what Mom's doing and catch a glimpse of the tear stains on her cheeks. The taste of our celebration dinner is still oily on my tongue.

Mom starts up again. "It would be a weight off our minds—for me and your father—to know you had someone looking after you when you go to medical school."

She puts her hands on my shoulders and gives them a squeeze. Her face looks old suddenly, the crow's feet permanent now.

"If he wants you to make things official, your father and I would have no objection."

"Stop, just stop." My face burns.

Worse than Alex's mom asking me to get married is my parents talking about it. I try to sink into my chair.

"People like us don't always have the luxury of choice," she says. "Just look at me and your father. You think I would have married him, if I'd had another option?"

"Oi. Heard that," Dad says, and then he twirls her around in our tiny living room, and she laughs. "I'll have you know I fought off a number of suitors to win your mother. She chose me for my good looks."

They smile at one another, my dad's arm wrapped around Mom's waist.

"We did it, George. We got one of them out."

I swallow the lump in my throat and try to smile. I haven't told them about my plummet from top of the class, the awful splash of red on my holographic face...that I might lose my chance to go ashore.

May comes in, wearing her dress uniform. She throws her peaked cap down on the kitchen counter. "Ew, do you two mind?" she says.

"We're just very happy for you," Mom says, releasing Dad and transferring her hug to May. "You made it."

Her voice breaks, and I can tell she's trying not to sob. May's success means she loses her daughter.

May seems to glow with pride. I wish I could feel the happy-sad mix that my parents do. All I can feel is sad-sad. Like my heart is being ripped from my body. May doesn't know how close I am to never seeing land. And the only thing I seem capable of feeling these days is anxious.

Our comgloves let out a screech that shreds my nerves. We look at our hands. **Mandatory Public Announcement.**

Four sets of held breath. Four racing hearts.

"We have to go outside," Mom says. She hands us our coats and unchains the front door.

Outside, it's already starting to get dark. All along the deck, our neighbors leave their cabins and take up position at the railing. A wretched, helpless line.

Public announcements come straight from the Federated States government. They never bring good news. Martial law. Executions. Banned newspapers. Banned communication with the world outside the ship. All of them preceded by the order to come out and listen. *Come out. Hear your punishment.*

A squall of drones hovers around the ship, and I steady myself. Concentrate on the icy rain that's already soaking through to my skin, ruining the hair my mother just finished styling. Eke out the seconds before the announcement begins.

Light washes over us. The line of drones is just beyond the limits of the flotilla. A beam stretches from the bottom of each drone, glancing off the surface of the waves. The rays spread out until they merge into a wall of light.

The Federated States anthem plays, thudding through my gut. I love it. And now I find I hate it too. It brings everything that's happened over the past few days thundering to the front of my mind. I've seen firsthand how brutal and unforgiving the Federated States can be. Tears well up in my eyes. I grasp the railing with both hands and force myself to look at the broadcast.

The man who appears on the projection is recognizable to everyone on the ship. A mythic figure pasted straight onto the sky. A jagged scar slices his top lip, and his mouth is permanently curved in a sneer. It's a face I've never seen in the flesh. And yet it's engraved on my consciousness. He has an air of savagery. I think he enjoys delivering painful news.

"Patriots," he says. His voice is thick and confident. "I am Commander Hadley, head of the *Arcadia* Special Task Force."

The image flickers and flashes in the dark rain. "You may be aware that a quantity of unpatriotic and damaging material was disseminated on the ship recently. Despite the hard work of my officers, the perpetrators of this crime are still at large and living among you. For your protection, I am implementing a series of new laws."

May's fingers curl more tightly around the railing, her knuckles whitening. She's not looking at Hadley; she's twisting her neck to scan the deck. I follow her gaze, but all I can see is the long line of our neighbors.

"Every law-abiding patriot among you will understand and accept that these dangerous times require personal sacrifices. This is a temporary measure—"

"Temporary." Dad snorts. "Like the drones were temporary."

"Please don't," Mom whispers.

"From sunset to sunrise, no person shall be permitted to be outside their cabin. It will be assumed that anyone away from their home during these hours is engaged in criminal activity. They will be arrested or terminated on sight."

Terminated. Blood seeps into my mouth where my new tooth has sunk into my cheek. Just being outside at the wrong time can get us killed.

May pushes back from the railing. She stares down the deck, preoccupied by whatever she's looking for. My nerves crackle.

Or *whoever* she's looking for.

"Unfortunately, due to the ongoing situation, I have taken the decision to cancel this evening's graduation ceremony. All cadets must now make their way to the front of the ship for departure. From the end of this transmission, the rest of you will have thirty minutes to return to your cabins. Thank you for your attention. Good people of the *Arcadia*, together we will eradicate the plague of violence and criminality onboard your ship."

He smiles, and his scar stretches. The anthem plays again. The wall of light shrinks to individual beams that are sucked back into the drones.

May walks away.

"May!" Mom shouts.

"I have to—I need to say goodbye," she says.

"To who?" I call after her.

I feel the lump in my throat grow. The moment I thought wouldn't come for hours is here. And she's walking away without a backward glance.

On my comglove, a countdown timer blinks: 29m55s.

Once May steps off the ship, she can't come back. My only chance of seeing her again is if I get accepted into med school, and then visits will be short and rare. But, in my heart, I know the likelihood of even those short encounters is slipping away. If I don't get a study visa, this will be the last glimpse I ever get of my big sister.

She stops and turns, then she's running back along the deck toward us. We crash together, encircling her with our arms, Mom and Dad crying into her hair. Her cap gets knocked to the ground.

"I'll see you again, I promise," she says.

She presses her cheek against my face, and I feel her push something cold and hard into my hand.

"In case you ever need me," she whispers. She kisses me, scoops her cap back on to her head and marches away.

I watch her go through a haze of loss, straining to keep her in view until the very last second. Eventually, she's indistinguishable from the others on deck.

The tears I've been holding back burst over my cheeks.

I look at the thin brass ring in my hand.

In case you ever need me.

CHAPTER 26

NIK

Helicopters. Six of them. Like beetles with their skittering wings and long bodies. I dip my head as they pass over, hoping that the night hides me from their lights. Feels like they're looking for me, but they're here for May.

Hadley's face is burned onto my eyelids when I close them. The guy who took my father. The guy who drives my mother to do what she does. Without him, maybe she'd have given up on the rebellion years ago. Maybe she'd have been less commanding officer and more mom. Maybe she wouldn't pull all the awful crap she pulls in the name of the rebellion.

Now Hadley's taken May too. My hatred of him is like an ember, always burning hot, ready to ignite into flame as soon as oxygen breathes life into it.

I'm huddled at the front of the ship on an upper deck overlooking the helipad. On my comglove, the countdown reads

2m22s. My thigh muscles ache from crouching, and my knees creak.

I didn't realize until I was watching Hadley's announcement that I couldn't let May go without saying goodbye. It goes against my mother's direct orders, but I've got nothing left to lose. It's time to give May up for the rebellion, but I have to see her one last time.

"Hello, stranger. You shouldn't be out here." May is standing a few yards away, as sharp as a new pin in her dress uniform. Blue with gold on the shoulders, her hair hidden under the peaked cap. She drops her duffel bag from her shoulder, takes her cap off.

I push myself away from the wall, lurch forward and hug her tighter than I've ever hugged anyone in my life.

"I have to go," she says.

But she doesn't let go and neither do I. In this moment, right here, I don't care who sees us or what comes next.

"Didn't think we'd be able to say goodbye," I say. "Needed to watch you leave."

She laughs into my hair. "Well, you weren't going to say goodbye from up here, were you? Lucky for you, I managed to sneak away from my unit."

She lets go, but stays really close. So close I can see the freckles on her nose. We both know we're out of time. As handler and handlee. As Nik and May. Nothing can be the same after this.

"Is it me or does everything feel so much more dangerous now?"

I breathe in, trying to fix the memory of her in my brain. She looks down at the helicopters. One starts to land, touching down gently.

"It's not just you," I say.

"And I was watching Hadley and thinking about how he's looking for you. How at any second you might get arrested. How I might not—"

"Don't," I say.

"But I might not come ba–"

"Don't say it. You're coming back. You have to."

She drops her head. "Because if I don't, the ship's screwed?"

"Did you talk to your sister?" I say, stalling for time.

Didn't sleep last night. Too wired thinking about May leaving. Deciding whether I should tell her how I feel. But what if she doesn't feel the same? What if it throws her off her game? She's got a mission to concentrate on. The most dangerous mission of her life. Straight into the viper's den.

"Couldn't risk it. Your mother's made it quite clear that Esther's safety depends on me keeping my mouth shut."

Another chopper hovers low over the front of the ship, waiting for space on the helipad. Everything's lit up like it's Christmas. Helicopter floodlights twinkle through spinning blades.

"Got her a combat ring though," May says.

"Sweet. Toxic or charge?"

"Charge."

"Will she figure out how to use it?"

"As long as she puts up a fight, it should activate. Hoping she won't need it. Thought we'd have more time, you know?"

She watches me. Her hands are on my back, just under my shoulder blades. I can feel her breathing.

My heart thunders. We're down to seconds. Almost out of grains of sand. *Tell her. Now.*

"May, I…"

"Yeah?"

I swallow, and there's a scratch of cotton wool in my throat.

"See you in two days, General," I say. As soon as it's out of my mouth, I hate myself. I'm a coward.

Her smile falters for a second, then strengthens. She pulls her comglove off and holds out her hand for me to shake.

I hold it. No shaking.

I pull her closer. I run my fingers through her hair, and we're face to face, her breath blowing onto my lips.

"Why didn't you tell me when we still had time?" she says. Her voice is barely a whisper.

"Been trying not to feel it. I was scared you wouldn't feel the same."

"Of course I feel the same. I always have."

She looks down, and I can see each eyelash. Then the countdown timer on my comglove bleats again.

"That's my cue," she says. She twists away from me and grabs her bag from the floor.

"I'm ordering you not to go." I blurt it out, not even sure whether it's a joke. Don't know what I'd do if she said OK. How can I be a hundred percent certain that she has to go, and a hundred percent certain that she has to stay? Only one of those things can be true, and they're fighting it out inside me.

She turns to look at me and smiles. "See you next time, Lall." And then she's gone.

PART TWO

LANDFALL

Good afternoon. It is 15:00 hours on Saturday, November 6, 2094.
This is the captain of the cruise ship Arcadia.
We are enjoying calm waters at present. However, the coast
guard forecasts strong westerly winds by this evening.
Daily reported Virus cases: zero.
Days at sea: 15,947.

CHAPTER 27

NIK

Thanks for seeing me. I owe you one."

"You owe me hundreds, Nik, my boy. Anyone else would be feeding the fishes by now," Enid says, but her black-lined eyes crinkle at the corners so I know she's kidding. Hope she's kidding. Enid's a friend, but she's also the gang leader in charge of the flotilla. You don't get there without breaking bones.

She pours something brownish from a teapot with a mismatched lid. I take the cup, trying not to look around the barge. It's like someone closed the door and let off a color bomb. Flower-covered blankets. Brass ornaments nailed to the door frames for luck. Time-thinned rugs. I don't look closely at any of it. Doesn't pay to be nosy with Enid.

She sips her tea and watches me over the rim of her cup. The barge creaks in time with the swell. Never can get used to the movement down here on the flotilla.

"Your mother know you're here?"

"You think I have a death wish?"

"I'll take that as a no," Enid says. Steam swirls around her face. "I'm assuming your interest in Silas has something to do with your girls?" She munches on a biscuit, coating her lips in crumbs.

"They're not mine. But yeah," I say.

"And specifically Crossland Girl Number Two, I'm guessing, since Crossland Girl Number One is on her way to a Federated States military base. While we're on the subject, it was a rookie move, getting shot. You'd do well to run faster next time."

"Thanks for the advice."

"Welcome. Still not clear on why you want to know about Silas." She dunks the biscuit in her tea.

"Silas grabbed Esther, and in the scuffle Esther kicked him. Square in the nose."

Enid's hand hovers halfway to her mouth. The soggy end of the biscuit plops into her cup.

"Let me get this straight," she says. "You got shot."

"Yes."

"Your mother needed someone to dig the bullet out. And on a ship full of backstreet sawbones, not to mention a half-dozen other kids who are also training to be government medical robots, your mother picks the one that shares DNA with May."

"That's it."

"And then Crossland Girl Number Two turns around and breaks a gang leader's nose with her boot?"

"That's it."

She throws her head back and laughs, so that I glimpse the

fleshy redness at the top of her throat. "I'd pay money to see that," she says, wiping the corner of her eye. Her eyeliner leaves a smudge where she touches it.

This is good. Get Enid on our side. Get her rooting for Esther.

"Mother said she split his nose right across. Pouring blood, she said."

"I have to meet this girl. So that's why his nose is all bandaged up?"

"Yep."

"He'll be spitting bullets, that's for sure."

"That's why I'm here," I say.

"You want to know if Silas is mad enough to bump her off?"

"Yep."

"Oh, I'd say definitely. Yep. For sure. Crossland Girl Number Two's got a big old target on her back, especially now her big sister's not here to defend her. He's got to do something about her, otherwise every wannabe leader in his territory will be trying for a coup d'état. They're all about their code of honor in Silas's world—you know that. Making him seem small is almost worse than attacking him outright. And I wouldn't recommend you go up against Silas either. It'll only cause trouble."

Enid looks into her teacup, tilting it to watch the leaves move in the dregs. "But—and tell me if I'm barking up the wrong tree here—you'll have some noble yet ridiculous notion that you owe her something, won't you?"

"She saved my life."

"Plus, she's May's sister, and you're holding a candle for your little soldier girl."

"It's not like that," I lie.

"Maybe not for May," Enid says. She smiles when she sees the blood rush to my face.

"So can you help me out?"

"I can watch her to make sure they don't snatch her. And I'm willing to let my people do some light scuffling. But I won't go to war with Silas over it, Nik. I'm not raising the militia to go and defend one girl. I've got bigger things to think about."

"Thanks. I won't forget this. Neither will May."

"Certainly you won't."

Enid lowers her eyes so that they're almost closed, stirring her tea slowly so that the spoon chinks in the quiet. I see the moment she makes a decision. Her eyes dart back to my face, crackling with energy. "The girl's a medic?"

Here it comes. How much will Esther's life cost me?

"There's a family lives on the edge of my territory, poor as barnacle scrapers. The youngest kid's sick."

"Enid—" I shake my head.

She's calm on the surface, but the current's stirring underneath. She grins like a shark. I'm in dangerous waters. She leans back in her chair and pushes open the nearest shoebox-sized window with a squeak. "John, can you come in here a sec?" She pulls it closed. She sips her tea.

John climbs down into the barge, bending his skinny frame to get through the door. Salt spray sticks his straggly mullet permanently to his forehead. His mouth is wet and gappy. He sweats the sea.

"Tea, John?"

"Thanks," he says. Most of his teeth are gone, and the ones left are on their way out too.

"Let's do the daily report," Enid says.

Her voice has a mocking undertone that makes me feel like I've walked into a trap. She knew what I wanted before I even set foot on the flotilla. I could kick myself. Of course she knew. She's Enid.

"Coalies been keeping up their normal patrols," John says.

"*Umm-hummm*," Enid mumbles through her teacup.

"Some trouble in the market with one of ours tryin' his hand at stealing fish from Nan Smokey, but I sorted that out, so nothing to concern you. And there's a rumor going around that the Coalies have found a way to mount guns on drones."

"Well, that's a nasty piece of news, isn't it? And do we have anything about Silas this evening, John?"

"Oh yeah." John smiles widely. "Apparently, he's put a price on some fancy upper-deck girl's head. Got everyone in his territory out looking for her. A month's wages to whoever drops her over the railing. Two months if they deliver her alive."

I spring out of the chair, and the partly healed bullet hole in my chest pulls. The china teacup smashes to the floor. I try to dodge past John, but he steps in front of the barge door.

"Let me go," I say with a growl. He shows his gums and takes a noisy swig of tea.

"Sit down," Enid says.

She's so calm. So smug. She's leaning back in her chair, and I could just kick it over. One hard shove and she'd go flying.

"I've got sick people down here. People who might not be able to see a doc. Kids too."

"She's sixteen, Enid," I say.

"We're all just trying to stay afloat. Which is what your girl's going to be trying to do if Silas gets hold of her."

Behind me, John chuckles.

"She's not going to hand over drugs."

"You're a resourceful boy—you'll think of something. Let's start small. A couple of doses of antibiotics."

My eyes skitter around the barge, resting on the teapot, the chintz curtains, the crappy brass ornaments. There must be something else I can barter, something that Enid wants.

"How high was the reward again, John?" Enid says, still leaning back in her chair. Just one kick.

"Two months' wages."

Enid whistles.

Nothing I can do. No other way to get Enid's help. Worry about the medicine later. Right now, I need to get to Esther.

Enid watches me and breaks into a genuine smile. She knows she's won. Getting to her feet, she holds out her hand. I shake it. Tied in.

"John, leapfrog a message up to our people. Get some eyes on the girl, but make sure no one gets involved with Silas's guys unless they're about to clobber her. I don't want to start the next ship war over some girl Nik's crushing on." She jerks her head at the door. "They'll watch her until you get her somewhere safe. Here, take some more biscuits—you're looking bony."

I shove past John and through the tiny door of the barge, breaking into a run as soon as my feet touch the floating walkway. I've got no idea where Esther will be, but Enid's people will only do so much to help her. If Silas gets to her first, she's dead. And it'll be my fault.

CHAPTER 28

HADLEY

Hadley's checking the route from HQ to Neath territory on a drone feed. He needs to see his dealer. The withdrawal's getting too much.

Grimson enters and heads for the coffee jug. She sees what he's doing, knows he's using drones for unscheduled reconnaissance, and chooses to ignore it. She pours two cups of coffee and hands him one.

"Two more years is a long time, sir."

"Tell me something I don't know."

"Permission to speak freely, sir?"

"If you must, Grimson."

"I have a colleague on the *Jørgenson*. It's a small cruise ship made for exploring fjords and fishing villages that's anchored about ten klicks south of here."

"I know what the *Jørgenson* is," he says.

The *Jørgenson* is the ship that took the *Arcadia*'s spot in the cascade of clearances. The one that apparently warrants his superiors' attention.

"There'd better be a point to this lesson in ship demographics, Lieutenant." He looks up at her and sips the coffee. She seems unfazed by the reprimand.

"Yes, sir. My colleague tells me that his ship was scheduled for priority clearance six months ago, but then the commander cracked down on an uprising, executed a few troublemaking drug dealers, and the place entered an uneasy kind of peace. And because the trouble was gone, and there wasn't any smuggling of note on the ship anymore, the admirals decided the *Jørgenson* could stay where it was."

"And why are you telling me?"

"The *Jørgenson*'s review came around a few days ago. My colleague told me that two weeks before review a bunch of Coalies were given two weeks' shore leave. And he says when they came back, every prisoner in the brig had been pardoned and cut loose. Apparently, the commander did exactly nothing for two weeks. Removed all types of surveillance and patrols. Just let the place go to seed."

Hadley sits up, his interest piqued. "Then what?"

"Then, the day before the review, he writes a report detailing a two-week explosion of crime aboard his ship. Smuggling, theft, violence, you name it. And, when they read it, the admirals shifted the ship back up the priority list. Their clearance date was set within twenty-four hours."

"And that's when we got bumped."

"Yes, sir."

Could it be possible that Hadley had taken the wrong tack with the admirals all along? He'd been trying to impress them with how well behaved his ship was when what he should have been doing was letting it run amok.

"Well, it got me thinking, sir. And I thought you'd like to know too."

"Yes, very interesting, Grimson. Dismissed."

She salutes neatly and picks up her coffee cup.

"Grimson."

"Yes, sir?"

"Nice work."

She keeps her expression flat, but Hadley can see the traces of a smile around her mouth. She heads for the cells.

Perhaps there's potential to speed up his departure from the *Arcadia* and make the possibility of a rebellion moot. If there's no ship, there's no rebellion. It'll have to be big. The *Arcadia*'s far bigger than the *Jørgenson*. With far more investment of resources and effort needed on the admirals' part to clear it. It'll take more than a spike in Neath fights or problems with smuggling for them to take action. What he needs is a grand gesture, blamed on the ship malcontents, of course. He needs something that will reverberate on land.

And, if he times it right, maybe he won't need to visit his Neath supplier again after all.

CHAPTER 29

ESTHER

This is where we come to forget we live on the ship. To find a moment of quiet in the chaos of being trapped with thousands of other people in a floating metal box.

Above us, the girders of the derelict glass roof stretch across the sky like the ribs of a long-dead leviathan. There are scrubby, windswept trees and vegetable beds that are empty now that it's winter. Cold earth pushes against my back. The ring May gave me weighs down my hand. I feel fleshless without her. The grief strips me down to a skeleton, and I imagine myself melting into the ground. Freeing myself to the blankness.

Alex's hand finds mine. It's warm.

"You'll see her again," he says.

"I know." I brush away a tear and sniff. "But what if I fail?"

"I'm not going to let that happen."

I sigh heavily and watch the clouds skip across the cold sky.

The arboretum is the closest thing we have to a park. The way the ship's designed means this small fragment of upper deck isn't over-shadowed by anything else, and the noises of ship life don't seem to reach this high. Sky stretches out above us. It has its own gated staircases, and sometimes, in that transitional moment between the end of the workday and the start of the evening, we get the whole place to ourselves.

Wind whistles through the trees and up through the broken roof. I'd have liked to see it when it was still a pleasure garden for the ship's passengers, but that's long gone. Now it grows stunted vegetables and tiny sour fruits that most people will never get to taste. The arboretum is my fallback. My mom will get me a job here, if I don't get into med school.

I concentrate on the chill of the ground until the churning guilt in my stomach lessens. I can't tell which scenario makes me feel worse. Cheating to beat Kara or not beating her at all. If I lose, my hopes of a different life are over. If I win, it's her dreams that are in ruins.

The grass has stained my one good dress with marks that won't come off even if I scratch them with my nail. Tonight, I'm having dinner with Alex and his parents so that we can all discuss *our future*. No real marriage proposal. No awkward, wonderful evening of being asked. No spreading of the happy news. No chance to say no.

Alex rolls over on to his side. He picks a blade of grass and shreds it with his nails. "We haven't talked about it," he says as if he knew what I was thinking.

I stare at the sky. "About what?"

"Getting married."

"I don't want to." I blurt it out before I can stop myself.

"You don't want to talk about it or you don't want to get married?"

"Both. Either."

"Ah." He stares into the distance. That hurt him more than I meant it to. "Is it me or ..." He trails off.

I shoot upward so that we're facing each other and take both his hands. "No, no, Alex, it's not you. It's because we're sixteen. And I'm not saying never. I'm just saying not now."

He smiles half-heartedly, but I can still see disappointment underneath it. "It doesn't have to be a real marriage," he says.

"Are you asking me to be your pretend wife?"

"Guess so. We could continue like nothing's changed. We could still be Alex and Esther, but with a piece of paper that means we get to stay together."

I look down at our hands. His are the strong and dexterous hands of someone who's destined to become a surgeon.

"And there's always divorce," he says when I don't answer.

"You're already thinking about divorcing me?"

"Only if someone better comes along," he says. His face cracks into a grin.

"You rat!" I say, pushing him off balance. He rolls on to his back, and I lie down too, resting my head in the crook of his arm.

"I wouldn't expect anything. I just want us to stay together," he says.

He presses his lips onto the top of my head, and I feel my cheeks redden. Everything's changing so quickly. It feels like we're being sucked along by the current. I close my eyes, trying to hold on to right now.

"Why can't things just stay like this?" I whisper.

I run my fingers over the buttons on the front of his uniform. His comglove bleats, and he brings his hand up to read the message. "My mom wants me to pick some stuff up from the market before dinner."

"I'll stay here a little longer."

"Don't be late."

He leans over and drops a kiss on my forehead, then picks up his stuff, and I listen to his footsteps thudding off toward the nearest exit. A gate slams.

I wonder what May's doing right now. She's been onshore almost a day. Maybe she's unpacking the few things she was allowed to take with her. Maybe she's digging into her first dinner as an inhabitant of dry land.

Even though I know it won't get through, I type a message: Hey, how's life as a landlubber? And press send. Message undeliverable appears in half a second. The distance between us is a few miles, but she might as well be on the other side of the planet.

The inevitable has been delayed long enough. I should go. Grabbing my bag and swinging it over my shoulder, I head for one of the exits on the portside of the ship. There's a thin metal gate at the top of a staircase. This one will bring me out close to Alex's cabin, unless some freak occurrence saves me from the impending dinner with its awkward topic of conversation.

Fear trickles between my shoulder blades at the sight of a figure propped up against the railing at the other end of the arboretum. Someone's been watching me this whole time, while I've been lying in the grass and looking at the clouds. In the half-light, I can't make out any details, just the creepy shape of a thin man in a long coat.

It's nothing, I tell myself. *Just someone enjoying the evening.* My chest thumps like it doesn't believe me, and I find myself running my thumb over the ring May gave me.

At a run, I figure I can make it to the portside staircase in ten seconds. Going through the middle of that radish bed will shave another second off. Slamming the gate behind me will buy me a couple more. Escape plan formulated.

But in those seconds of scanning the area, I took my attention off the figure, and now he's disappeared. He could be anywhere. He could be coming up behind me. The hairs on my neck prickle, and I twist, trying to find him again.

Breathe to loosen your muscles. Walk to the exit. You're being paranoid.

I'm almost at the gate, and there's no sign of the skinny figure.

Ahead of me, two men emerge from the staircase. Recognition crosses their faces even through the bars of the gate, and I know: they're here for me.

The gate's hinges squeak.

I run, aiming straight across the arboretum for the exit on the opposite side. My dress whips around my knees. Feet pound behind me, dull thuds against the earth-topped deck.

I'm ten strides from the other gate. Seven. Six. The promise of safety. But then a woman emerges, separating me from the exit. She grins horribly, long locks swaying.

My feet skid on the earthy ground. Air screams through my throat. "What do you want?"

The woman shows the inside of her rotting mouth. Her cheekbones press against her skin; there's not enough flesh over them. "I want you," she says.

I sense the two men stopping somewhere behind me. At the sight of them, the woman's grin drops.

"I found her first," she spits, flecks of saliva spraying the air in front of her.

"Don't mean you'll be the one to deliver her," one of the men says.

They split up and start moving around me like sharks. Circling closer.

The woman's face folds into a grimace. She gobs phlegm on to the ground. "Compromise. Three-way split on the reward."

Reward?

"Why should we split it with you?" says the jowled man.

"Cos otherwise I'll help missy here slip away, and you'll get nothin.'"

"Let's take her to Silas then. The reward's two months if we deliver her alive."

"Don't say his name out loud, you imbecile!" the woman says.

Who the hell is Silas? And why would he want me alive? Why does he want me at all?

"I'm not going anywhere with you," I say.

"You're as good as dead already, so shut up," the woman snarls. "Too much trouble getting her all the way below deck. Coalies could stop us; drone might see. Let's just drop her over the side."

"What's he paying you? I'll pay more, or, or" I scramble for a lifeline—"or get you medical supplies!"

All three of them stop pacing and snap their attention to me, hungry eyes darting.

"What kind of medical supplies?" the woman asks.

"Anything. Vaccines, bandages—"

"Drugs?"

"Anything."

Her eel's tongue moves in and out of a gap between her teeth. Seconds pass. "Nah, not worth pissing him off. Let's throw her over now and be done with it. Fifty-fifty split?" She extends a hand to one of the men. He steps over to her and shakes it.

The arboretum turns around me. I can't feel the ground under my feet. I won't let them take me. Not again. An electrical hum shudders through my hand and into my arm. I look down at my fist in confusion. The ring May gave me is buzzing with life. The bands of metal move smoothly over one another to reveal a line of hair-thin needles. They stick out of the smooth surface like thorns. I hear May's words: *In case you ever need me.*

"Got to take something off her, to prove we did her in." The man's voice drags me back to the present.

"Hair?" says the woman.

"That'd be least messy."

I stare at her. My mouth opens and closes stupidly.

They pounce. Their hands are on me, pulling me down, down, until my knees buckle, and I thud to the ground.

In case you ever need me.

I twist my arm free, pain ripping through the muscle, and slam my fist as hard as I can into the nearest man. It's a pathetic blow that's like punching clay, but he screams as the needles pierce his skin. Without me doing anything else, the ring releases a charge that makes him jerk and twists his face in agony. He falls to the ground.

I struggle to pull myself up. The woman grabs me by the hair and pushes me so that my cheek squashes into the dirt. Her weight presses down on me, knees on my arms so that I can't move. The other man forces the ring from my hand, scouring skin from my finger. I won't get the chance to use it again.

I taste soil: musky and lifeless.

The woman tugs at my hair, gathering it above my head with one hand.

Huffing, I try to topple her, but she's so heavy she hardly moves, and now the man is pinning me too.

"Hold her," the woman says with a grunt. She reaches inside her coat and brings out something that makes me scream inside. A small brown handle. She holds it in front of my face, presses a button and the blade flicks out.

CHAPTER 30

NIK

I t's creepy, all those rusting girders penning you in. Everything streaked with seagull crap. Seriously questioning why Esther would hang out up here, but I've checked everywhere else.

My chest's a pit of burning pain by the time I slam through one of the gates into the arboretum. Good thing Esther used a suture bot to close that gunshot wound. If she'd sewed it by hand, I'd have been stuck in bed for months instead of running around the ship, trying to save her life.

I scan the place. *Dammit. Too late.*

Two heavies are pinning Esther to the ground; another one lies on the floor, twitching like he's been zapped. She figured out May's ring. *Good girl.* The woman sitting on Esther's back is struggling to hold her down. The woman's fist punches the air, and my blood runs cold; they've cut off a handful of Esther's hair. As proof that they've killed her, it could have been so much worse.

One of Enid's guy's leans on the railing, wearing a long coat and chewing a piece of grass. They call him Scratch or Sniffer or something.

"Why the hell aren't you helping?" I shout.

"My orders were not to engage."

"Engage now, or Enid'll hear about it."

Sniffer pushes himself up and spits out the grass.

I charge at the woman. We plow into the ground, air whooshing from her chest as we land in a heap. Esther's hair showers to the ground. The woman rakes at my face with her nails, screaming. I yank her arms down behind her back and use my knees to hold them while I unwrap the scarf she's wearing. I snake it around her wrists. The few teeth she's got gnash and snap.

Sniffer lands a good punch on the other man's cheek, and he drops to the ground. But Sniffer doesn't stop, and now he's standing over the man, pummeling his bloodied face. He's lost in bloodlust. The woman must have dropped her knife when I hit her, because now I see Sniffer raise it over the man's chest, crazed eyes staring out from blood-splattered skin.

"No!" I shout.

I let go of the woman and kick Sniffer in the chest hard enough to send him off balance. He gives me a disgusted glance before wiping his face and turning his back. The man lies still, face red and shining with blood, but not dead. Silas doesn't take kindly to people murdering his employees, and after the thing with Esther kicking him, it'd be like spraying gasoline on a fire. It would be all-out war. No one would be able to help Esther then.

"Get out of here!" I scream to Esther. She's already gone. Her chopped hair disappears down the nearest staircase.

The woman's already getting up, the scarf dangling loose from one hand, and she's looking like she's going to follow Esther. I shoulder-barge her and then manage to get hold of the scarf, pulling it as tight as I can into a knot around her wrists. It won't hold her for more than a few seconds, but it'll be long enough for us to get away. I follow Esther, leaving the woman to curse herself hoarse.

Hardly touch the ground on the way down the stairs, and at the bottom I realize she's not heading for home. Maybe she's aiming for the market. Or the Lookout. Public places. Smart but wrong. Everywhere will be crawling with Silas's people.

She needs to change direction. And then we need to hole up together, until they give up looking for the day. I figure sunset ought to do it. Most of them won't risk being on an upper deck after curfew. I have to make her go home.

On the bend of a stairwell, I grab her by the jacket and swing her around.

She screeches, and her fists slam into my face.

"Esther, stop!"

She focuses on me, all bleary with tears, and the look on her face knocks me breathless; she's the image of May.

"I'm a friend, OK? I'm trying to help."

"OK," she says, and she stops wriggling so I relax my grip. That's when she brings her knee up between my legs. Exploding pain. I double over. She punches me square in the nose. Star-studded blackness.

Esther leaps down more stairs. If she gets away from me, I won't be able to protect her. I force myself to keep up, running through the pain. We reach our home deck, the stretch of cabins, the rows of boots outside the front doors.

Esther fumbles for her keys, and I'm nearly there. But then she's through. I jam my fingers around the door frame at the last second, and scream through my teeth at the stripe of pain where the door crushes my fingers. I shove it with my shoulder. Esther gets thrown backwards into the cabin. She sprawls on the ground, legs kicking up at me.

I drop on top of her and grab her in a bear hug that clamps her arms down. In my mind, a drone's racing to the deck, alerted by the sound of her screaming or an image of us chasing down the deck. In my mind, there are cameras skittering along the railing. Coalies marching in formation, about to burst through the open door and drag me away.

"Shhhh!" I say. "Keep calm. I'm a friend of May's. People are trying to hurt you, but I'm not one of them."

"What do you want?" She's shaking. Freshly chopped hair falls over her face. Strands stick to the shoulders of her jacket.

"Just want to make sure you're OK." My chest heaves. My fingers are throbbing and fat and seeping, and there's a sick feeling running through my whole body. "I saw them attack you in the arboretum, and figured you might need some help. That's all."

She relaxes. I loosen my grip and kneel up so that I'm not squashing her. She edges backwards, putting space between us. We sit there on the floor, staring at each other, both breathing through the pain and adrenaline.

"Say my name."

"What?" I say.

"Say my name again," she demands.

"Esther."

She grimaces. "It was you," she whispers. "You're the boy. You're with them. The ones that kidnapped me."

I open my mouth and close it again.

She pulls at the bottom of her dress. There's mud smeared on her legs. She stands up and moves crab-like to the kitchenette. The Crosslands' cabin is the same as ours: small front living area with a kitchen on one side and a sofa on the other, single-file corridor through to the bedrooms. It's messier than ours though. Lived in.

"Why did you say you're May's friend? You don't know her."

"We work together."

"You're not a cadet."

"No."

Esther rests her muddy fingers on the counter. Her med bag hangs across her shoulder, covered in dirt from the scuffle. If I can distract her, I might be able to get those meds for Enid after all. I swallow hard. The door's wide open behind me, and I imagine devices peering through. Drones or those creepy spider-bot things.

"I'm gonna shut the door, OK?" I say.

She stays silent.

No sign of Silas's goons when I check up and down the deck. No drones. Nothing scuttling. Once the door's closed, I let myself breathe.

Jeez, everything hurts. Chest. Gut. Fingers. Ego.

I cradle my mangled hand against my throbbing gunshot wound. Wonder if my fingers are broken.

220

When I turn back to Esther, I'm staring at a knife. It's blunt but evil-looking. I hold my uninjured hand up in surrender.

"Come on, doc. You won't stab me—you only just fixed me."

"Want to find out?"

"Think I'll pass."

Esther raises the knife. "Start talking."

CHAPTER 31

ESTHER

The knife hovers in the air between us. My arm's shaking from holding it, and my hand is slick around the handle. I recognize that voice, even without the sickbed rattle. It's been on repeat in my head since I heard him say my name the night I was kidnapped.

What now? Now I get answers. Hoping that trouble will disappear if I ignore it long enough hasn't worked. I have to take action, even if it means doing things I never thought I was capable of.

Like holding someone at knifepoint.

"Start talking," I say, trying to sound like someone who will use a knife if she needs to. It weighs a ton, and I already wish I'd picked the vegetable peeler, but I need shock and awe if I'm going to get info out of him. I raise it so that the point is level with the boy's chest.

He scratches his head, ruffling scruffy black hair that looks like he cut it himself, and puffs his cheeks in exasperation. I realize

I know him. He lives down the deck. We've passed each other a thousand times without ever speaking. His dad was taken by the Coalies a few months before May and I started our training. We watched them throwing the family's possessions down into the sea until Mom shooed us inside.

"What do you want to know?" he says, shrugging.

He's wearing a hoodie underneath a waterproof jacket that's been patched more than once, and the smell of woodsmoke and paraffin lingers on him.

"Let's start with your name, then move on to how you know my sister."

"I'm Nikhil Lall. Nice to officially meet you. And I told you. We work together."

His eyes flick around the cabin. He picks up our tea container from its place on the worktop and sniffs the leaves inside. He wrinkles his nose.

I snatch the tin and snap it closed. "Why was I kidnapped? Why not someone else?"

"How would I know? I was busy being half dead, remember?"

He wanders to the shelf by the front door and pulls a book out by its spine, leafing through the pages before dropping it and picking another one.

"Where does May keep her stuff?" Nik says.

Emotion catches in my throat, raw and hot, but I refuse to let him see me cry. "I'm asking the questions," I say. I jab the knife in the air.

"All right, doc, keep your hair on." He smirks.

My free hand goes to the choppy ends of my hair, and I want to cry all over again. If I had any strength left, I'd punch that stupid grin off his face.

"Who's Silas? Why does he want me dead?"

He scans a book's cover, then drops it on the growing pile by his feet. "That's what happens when you give a gang leader a bloody nose. They hold grudges."

"What?"

"The other night. You kicked him in the face. Ring a bell?"

"He attacked me! I was defending myself!"

"You're a little girl, and you humiliated him. He needs to reassert his power." Another book thuds to the ground. "May's room through here?" He marches past me, pushing my knife hand out of his way.

"You can't just walk in!" I toss the knife on to the counter and chase after him. This is not how I envisioned things playing out.

He's in the tight space in front of our bunks, and I have to stand way closer to him than is comfortable. Adding a stranger to the tiny space usually reserved for me and my sister makes me twitchy with embarrassment.

He stares at May's bunk, the blanket pulled snug over the mattress, the military textbook left open on top. "Come on, doc, where's her secret stash?"

I press my lips together and fold my arms.

"Not playing, huh?"

He opens the top drawer and starts pulling things out. My frayed underwear. My unpaired socks. The things I don't want anyone to see. Heat floods my cheeks. I reach around him and slam the drawer. It almost catches his fingers, and he responds by pulling the covers from May's bunk. I drop my med bag to take hold of a scrap of blanket, and then we're tussling tug-of-war style.

"Get out!" I say, snatching the blanket back and throwing it onto May's bunk. "I'm not telling you anything. Just get out of my room!"

"You're as stubborn as she is," he says, looking directly at me.

He holds up the jar of pens I keep on the desk and rattles it, dancing eyes locked on mine. He upends the jar, scattering pens across the floor, then lobs it over his shoulder.

My stomach flips. Anger and frustration fight for dominance. "What is wrong with you?" I manage to say.

The fear I felt in the arboretum is long gone, replaced by head-to-toe fury. Two weeks ago, I would have done anything to avoid confrontation. Now my chance of med school hangs by a thread, and my relationship with May lies in tatters. So what does it matter if I stand up for myself?

"Wrong with me? You're the one whose idea of fun seems to be color-coding their notecards," he says, picking up a stack of them from the desk and scanning them one by one.

I tense. Hours of work went into those notes. "Don't you dare."

He breaks into a smile and raises his eyebrows, then flings the pile of cards into the air. They separate and scatter across the floor.

I chase them, restacking each one with trembling fingers, trying not to think about the work I've lost and how long it will take me to fix this. I toss them in the drawer and slam it closed. Next he's rummaging in my med bag. I snatch it and throw it on to my bed.

"Stop! Just stop!" I say, holding my hands up in surrender.

He shoves both hands in his pockets and fixes me with a gleeful stare. "How 'bout this? An answer for an answer."

"Fine. Just stop trashing the place. And I'm first. Why did you help me?"

"I told May I'd look out for you until she gets back. My turn—"

"Wait, *gets back*?"

"Fair's fair, doc. An answer for an answer, remember? So where would May keep something hidden?"

He's standing too close, and I try to breathe quietly, so he can't see how tightly I'm wound. If I want to continue with this stupid game of his, I have to give him what he wants. "Behind the drawers. Third panel up."

He eases the chest of drawers away from the wall and crouches in the space behind it. Dust bunnies as big as my hand litter the newly exposed floor. He runs his fingers around the edge of the third wooden panel up, lifting it away from the wall to reveal a hole. May's hiding place. Cold air, damp and mildewy, floods the room.

As Nik reaches in, I watch the back of his head. Would a good whack from a textbook knock him out long enough for me to get away? Probably. But thinking about knocking someone out and actually doing it are completely different. And then I've got the problem of explaining why there's an unconscious boy in my bedroom.

He brings May's shoebox out. I keep an identical one in its own hiding place, but I have no idea what we'll find inside May's box of secrets and keepsakes. Curiosity tugs at me; I'm more than a little eager to know what May treasures.

Nik opens the lid and rummages through the contents, handing me memories. A crackly autumn leaf, bright orange. A shiny purple wrapper with a faded chocolate smell. A piece of paper with a blurred picture of a cruise ship on it. Words blaring in all caps:

CRUISE SHIP *OCEANIA* CLEARED!
HUNDREDS DEAD!

The paper trembles in my hand. All the anger I've been directing at Nik drains away. Dread grows in its place. Day and night since my ordeal, I've been preoccupied with questions about who kidnapped me. Why they took me. Whether they're coming back. And in among them all a nagging suspicion that things aren't quite right with my sister. Now the questions that I've been focusing on fizzle out. There's just one left, circling around and around: is my sister OK?

Nik finds what he's looking for and stands up, the rest of May's unwanted memories falling to the ground. He's holding a gun. Blue-black with a cruel staring-eye muzzle.

"My turn," I whisper, without moving my eyes from the gun. "How much trouble is my sister in?"

He points the gun at the wall and pulls back the top section to reveal glinting brass bullets. "May can look after herself."

"That's not what I asked."

For a second, the cockiness and bravado fade, and I glimpse something else in his face. Fear.

There's a clang from the front cabin. The front door smashes against the chain. Someone's trying to get in.

"They're here. Stay quiet," Nik says, pushing past me.

I wait. Panic so tight it squeezes my breathing so I'm panting.

I hold on to the chest of drawers so that I don't fall. There's only one way in and out of the cabin, so if they get past Nik I'm trapped.

"Esther, I know you're in there. Open up!" Alex's voice rises from the other side of the door.

"Alex!" His name floods out in a torrent of relief that carries me, running, to the front door. I pull back the chain and fling myself at him.

He pushes me away, strides into the cabin and slams the door. His eyes bore into me, my scuffed knees, my cropped hair. I squirm. I straighten the collar of my jacket and pull at the hem of my dress. Relief turns to shame.

Nik sneaks the gun into the back of his belt.

"You'd better have a watertight explanation," Alex says. His voice is flat. I've never seen him this angry before.

"I—?"

"Can you explain to me why you're here. With some guy. Instead of having dinner with my parents?"

"My fault. I'm Nik, by the way. Live down the deck." He holds out his hand and lets it hang, matching Alex glare for glare before dropping it, unshaken. "My mom's sick. I asked Esther for help."

"Don't recall speaking to you."

"Let me explain—" I say.

"I know my mom's been overbearing about the marriage thing, but she doesn't deserve this. She doesn't deserve to sit waiting for you at an empty dinner table."

He's hurt and angry, and it's my fault. I can feel the rage spitting like oil from a hot pan. I can imagine how it feels to be stood up, and then to find me here, with Nik.

Alex grabs me, wrapping his hands around the top of my arms. He squeezes so hard I let out a whimper.

"Hey, take it easy," Nik says quietly.

Alex lets me go and switches his attention to Nik. "Get back to your mother. Or is she so sick we need to call the Coalies for help?" I reel as if he's slapped me. Nik's face blanches. I'm certain it's an empty threat, but no one should be threatened with the Coalies.

"We won't bother you again," Nik says. He edges out of the front door and closes it behind him, his shadow passing in front of the window as he heads down the deck.

I want to chase after him. I want to ask more questions about May. But I need to smooth this over with Alex. I can't stand the thought of there being a rift between us.

Tears gather behind my eyes, aching to be released. I search for what I should tell him. The truth—the whole truth—will mean an end to the few freedoms I have. I imagine Alex talking to my parents. Imagine him saying he'll chaperone me everywhere. They'll agree, of course. It would be for my own safety. And I can't tell him about May. Tell him what exactly? That she knows someone scary? That she had an anti-government leaflet? That she was hiding a gun? No. I can't tell him until I know myself.

"Well?" Alex says.

"His mother is sick. He came to ask if I'd take a look at her."

Alex wheels away. He marches to the front door and yanks it open. "I won't be made a fool of," he says over his shoulder. He slams the door behind him.

I've never felt so utterly alone.

CHAPTER 32

HADLEY

Hadley's been chasing drug smugglers and illegal antivenom for days. It wasn't until a kid walked into HQ wanting to trade information for perks that he realized he'd overlooked another source of antivenom on the ship: the infirmary. The infirmary staffed and stocked by the Federated States.

Excitement pulses through him. There are threads to follow here. And, if he's successful and manages to unravel any kind of organized resistance on the ship, it'll be easier for him to deal with them once the clearance order comes. Because it will come. And he won't be waiting two years for it.

Rein it in, Hadley. It's not done yet. He can already feel the firmness of dry land pressing into his feet. Taste the mineral weight of city air.

The refugees are all squirming to save themselves, and this kid's no different. He sits by the deputy's desk in the bullpen. He doesn't fidget, not even when the roving camera stares at him. He's wearing the uniform of a trainee medic, but his hair's a mess, and he has dark circles under his eyes.

The medical program's a damn stupid initiative started by some bleeding-heart humanitarian charity. Aims to send the *promising* ones ashore so that their potential isn't wasted on the ship. It's a publicity stunt. *Look how compassionate we are. Look how we embrace the poor ship kids.*

Hadley bites down a surge of anger. He thought Celeste was promising: too clever and too pretty to be wasted onboard a ship. Look where compassion got him. A scar across his face and exile out here.

The deputy loiters next to Hadley.

"Did you bring up his records?" Hadley asks him, taking a swig of coffee and refusing to grimace at the earthy tang.

"His name's Alex Hudson. He's on the medical-track training program. They just announced that the program's being canceled."

"He's come to save himself then." Hadley scrapes a hand over his stubble. *Here they come, wriggling out of the woodwork.*

"One other thing, sir. The medics are due to run a booster drive in the market next week. I was thinking they could use some help."

"Some help, Deputy?"

The deputy picks nervously at a scab on his neck. "Yes, sir. With crowd control."

This could be the perfect opportunity to execute his plan. Everything's falling into place. Hadley searches for the roving camera. It's out of range, watching the kid.

"Good thinking, Deputy. Choose yourself a team and brief them," he says, his voice low so that the camera won't pick it up. "Not Grimson though, all right?" he adds, surprising himself that he's just found the line he won't cross. Not surprising. They've worked together a long time.

"Yes, sir."

The deputy can't hide his pleasure as he heads to his desk.

The zit-faced newbie has been a dud since that business with the girl's fingers. Hadley misjudged things; interrogating her was supposed to steel the deputy; instead, it softened him. He got more compassionate. Hadley can't have that on his team. He needs people who will do what's necessary.

Never mind. If his plan works, Hadley's time here will soon be over.

Hadley walks over to the trainee medic, coffee in hand. He wheels a chair around so that it's facing the kid and slides the digiscreen onto the desk. The boy's trim but not starving. Hair trimmed, clothes well maintained. Hadley needs to figure the kid out, discover what's driving him, before he agrees to anything. Not that he's obliged to keep any promises. A long stint in a work camp is how this usually ends. That or the firing squad.

"My deputy tells me you have information that will protect the Federated States."

"Yes, sir."

"Let's hear it then."

The boy hesitates. "I need some assurances."

Hadley raises an eyebrow. "What kind of assurances?"

The kid licks his lips. "A full pardon first. And a place at med school."

"A pardon? For what?"

"For everything. Everything I've done, anything I'll do before I get out of here. And not just for me. For my girlfriend too."

"Let's see what you've got for me. Then we can talk about a deal."

The boy pulls a digiscreen from his medical bag and types on the glass, then holds it out to Hadley. Hadley glances at the girl on the screen. He reads the bio info. Esther Crossland. She's a straight-A medical student. Mother works in the arboretum, father on a maintenance crew. Sister's a cadet, just graduated and gone to the training base outside the city. Interesting. Not the kind of family you'd expect to rock the boat. They're trusted.

"I don't know how, but she's gotten herself into trouble. Twice I've caught her talking to someone suspicious. And I think they're involved in something bigger. Something illegal. I could watch her," he says.

"Or I could arrest you both now, and that would give me two fewer refugees to worry about."

"I could find out who she's seeing and lead you to them."

Hadley considers. If this kid's gut is right and the Crossland girl is involved in something, it might be useful to have someone on the inside.

The kid leans forward, dripping confidence. "Worst case, I find nothing. Best case, I find something really useful."

"Can't argue with an offer like that, can I? Next time you see her, find a way to get a tracker into her comglove."

He leans over to his desk drawer and takes out a box, flipping it open to reveal the lens. Wires trailing. It's a high-tech piece of equipment integrated with a camera. A tracking system. They're made for long-term use on undercover missions, and installing a piece of equipment like this is usually accompanied by a local anesthetic.

"Here's what's going to happen."

He grabs a handful of the boy's hair and yanks backwards, only reining himself in when he feels the kid's neck reach its limit. No need to damage him before he can be useful. There'll be others to have fun with before the end.

He gasps, but doesn't cry out. His fingers clutch the edge of the desk as his chair balances on two legs, his body held up by Hadley's fist on the back of his head.

"First, I need an insurance policy. This lens means that wherever you go, whatever you do, I'll be able to track you. It means you won't be running off and reneging on our deal. And it means that, if you fail, I'll be able to find you. Wouldn't try to remove it if you want to keep that eye. And, just so we're clear, I'll be coming for your family too."

He forces the kid's eye open and presses the lens against it, then holds the boy's face still, drinking in his unfiltered terror. The wires rear and start to burrow into the skin at each corner of the kid's eye.

Hadley lets go. The chair slides from under the kid, dropping him sprawling and panting to the ground. He clutches his eye. Bloody tears drip down his face.

Hadley turns away, enjoying the dense feeling of satisfaction.

He grabs a tea towel they use to wipe up spills from the coffee machine and rubs his fingers clean.

"This is what you're going to do in exchange for the lives of your loved ones."

Good afternoon. It is 16:00 hours on Wednesday, November 10, 2094.

This is the captain of the cruise ship Arcadia.

A reminder that booster vaccines will be avail-
able in the market this evening.

Together we can prevent the scourge of the Virus.

Daily reported Virus cases: zero.

Days at sea: 15,951.

CHAPTER 33

ESTHER

The market crowd presses in on me. A churning sea of strangers. The air's thick and unbreathable, despite the cold wind and clouds in the dusky sky. This is how I imagine drowning would feel. The rising panic. The struggle for air.

Behind me, just inside the arched gunmetal entrance to the market, we've set up a temporary clinic. A three-sided tent of thick green canvas with the Federated States flag stamped on the side. It gives us an air of being official. From inside, we can see our queue of patients as they wait to claim their free medical care.

Alex unfolds a table and clicks the legs into place. Kara sets out line after line of plastic-covered syringes. I push my way into the crowd and open a sandwich-board digiscreen, the gleaming flat display inviting people to come into the tent. Half the ship's population can't even read it. Reading, swimming, first aid: all skills that the Coalies consider dangerous in the hands of ship folk.

The fight with Alex still hangs between us, fresh-edged and raw as a wound. I want to talk to him so much. He keeps looking like he wants to say something too, but neither of us has worked up the courage yet. I can count on one hand the number of arguments we've had, and they're never about anything serious. It shakes me that we can't find a way to talk to each other now. It feels like I'm missing my anchor.

When everything's ready, we hover by the tables, Kara tapping her fingernails in a manic rhythm, Alex staring at the melee of the market so that we don't catch each other's eye.

"It's good that Corp's put me in charge today," I say when I can't stand the tension anymore. "She must still think I'm near the top of the class."

"Yep," Alex says.

He's standing an inch out of reach, arms folded. Kara's noticed something's up. She keeps giving me the side-eye, snatching her gaze away when I make eye contact.

"Is that it then? One argument and we're done?" I say out of the side of my mouth. My stomach's a pit of acid.

"Of course not."

Alex's voice is so level, I can't tell whether he's enraged or trying not to cry. His ability to pretend nothing's happened infuriates me. Guess it's how some of us cope with existing here. "But what were you doing with him?"

"It was nothing," I say. "A misunderstanding."

"It's the second time I've caught you with someone suspicious, and you've brushed me off."

"Caught me with someone? I wasn't doing anything wrong.

And since when do you not trust me?" The heat of anger sparks in my chest.

Alex scratches his head. "No, I didn't mean that. Let's talk later. When we don't have an audience," he says. He takes my hand, but I want to cry.

"Here's Corp," Kara says.

"First up, test results," Corp says when she reaches us.

We gather around, comgloved hands poised. This test result could propel me toward my dream. Or seal my fate.

Kara's right next to me. "Good luck," she whispers. I nod in acknowledgment.

Corp moves along the line, holding out her comglove just long enough for it to bleep before moving on to the next person. Alex gets his result first, sighs, then turns his smile on me. He did well, an almost perfect score. Kara's next, a smile of victory playing around her eyes when she realizes she's stayed near the top of the class.

Then it's my turn. Corp watches my face while we wait for the beep. I open my hand to find the word PASS glowing on my palm. I'm still in the game.

"Excellent work, medic. Your test was flawless," Corp says. Her stare is almost too hard. *Flawless.*

How could I have been so stupid? No one ever gets a perfect score. Why didn't I think to throw in some wrong answers instead of blindly following the lens? Does Corp suspect I cheated?

"All of you are first for boosters," she says, handing me a digiscreen.

I scroll through the details of today's program, barely registering them. Booster vaccinations for the Virus that hasn't been seen on the ship in decades. Pointless, but it's a regulation demanded by the Federated States, and so we'll participate.

It's going to be a long day, made longer because half the class decided there's no point continuing on if they can't go to med school. We're down to seven medics. Can't say I blame the rest for bailing. They've all had their dreams crushed by some lawmaker in the Federated States who has probably never even met someone from a ship.

I roll up my sleeve while Alex bites the lid off a syringe. Green-blue fingerprints mottle the top of my arm, the single physical remnant of our argument. Corp glances at the bruises. Alex pinches the top of my arm. Scratch and pop as the needle breaks the skin. A scarlet bead grows in the hole left by the point.

"A little pain now for security later," he says.

I pull my sleeve back down without waiting for a cotton swab.

"Break it up, lovebirds—you've got work to do," Corp says. She steps between us and starts organizing the crowd into a disorderly queue.

One good thing about today is that I might finally be able to see Nik Lall. This booster is free to everyone onboard, so if he comes to the drive I can talk to him in plain sight. Alex will be busy working on his own patients, and it's a public place, so he'll be able to see there's nothing going on. I need to know what he meant when he said that May was coming back. How is that even possible? More importantly, why does she need to?

Everything's ready. I take a seat, and I'm about to call for the first patient to sit across from me when I see something that makes my heart beat in panic. Three Coalies duck under the awning, but before they can reach me, they're intercepted by Corp. The one in the lead flips his visor open to reveal a young pale face, pockmarked with acne scars. So much for encouraging people to get vaccinated. Most of our patients would rather take their chances with the Virus than a Coaly.

Corp talks to them as if they're normal people. Her hands rest on her hips. She twists and looks at me, and I feel a terrible surge of certainty. I'm the one they're here for. Sweat breaks out under my uniform. She's given me up.

But instead of throwing me to the ground and slapping handcuffs on my wrists, the Coalies take up position at the head of the queue. The effect is immediate. Half the patients break off and melt into the market. And I'm guessing Nik Lall won't risk coming to see me either.

"What do they want?" My voice squeaks through dry lips. "They're scaring our patients away."

"Concentrate on your work," Corp says.

"With them standing so close?" I grumble.

"Don't stare."

As we work, injecting patient after patient, dropping the empty syringes into the waste bucket, my fingers stiffen with cold. It gets harder to push the plunger with each new patient. My movements are tense and exhausting. I can't relax, not even for a second. Not with them standing so close by.

On the next chair along, Alex rolls his neck and shakes out his hands, stretching cramped fingers. My next patient drops into the chair opposite me. I grab a syringe, douse a cotton swab with rubbing alcohol, and look up. Into May's face.

The syringe drops from my hand, clattering on to the floor with a sound as nerve-jangling as a chainsaw. The Coalies spin to look at me.

"What's the problem?" one of them calls.

Speak. You have to speak.

"Nothing. Dropped a syringe," I say, head reeling, threatening to black out.

"Be cool," May says. There's a wildness in her eyes, a flush on her cheeks.

I fumble to pick up a replacement syringe and slide myself back into the chair, my eyes fixed firmly on the Coalies.

"Are they looking?" May asks.

I shake my head. She's wearing a faded gray hoodie and a long, shape-concealing coat. Camouflaged for the dull shades of the ship. The rings under her eyes are so purple they look like bruises.

She should be gone.

"What are you doing here?" I say.

"No time." She's unbundling herself, removing her jacket, pulling up her sleeve so that her arm's exposed. There's a bandage wrapped tourniquet-tight around her forearm. She pushes her hood back, revealing a stubbly buzz cut.

"Did the military give you home leave?" I say, clutching at straws.

I know they didn't. Joining the Federated States army is a lifetime contract. But, if I don't think the word, it might not be true. AWOL. Absent Without Leave. It means a court martial if they catch her. Life in a labor camp if she's lucky. The firing squad if she's not.

"Don't be naive. You're supposed to be vaccinating me," she says.

"What?"

"I'm here for a vaccination."

Forcing myself to move slowly, I make a show of opening the plastic covering on the syringe. Swipe a cotton ball over May's upper arm in long strokes.

"You remember Nik Lall? The boy from down the deck whose dad was arrested years ago?" she says.

May doesn't know what happened in the arboretum, or how Nik trashed our cabin. She's been busy doing other things, and it leaves a tang of bitterness in my mouth. "I remember."

"I need to get something to him."

"And I need an explanation. Tell me you haven't absconded."

"There's no time—they're following me—I'll explain everything when it's safe. But now I need you to trust me. I need you to help me."

The sound of a drone passes close above the roof of the tent. May tenses. I see fear in her eyes. Real fear.

"What's the bandage for?" I say.

"I needed to trap it."

"What?"

She turns the soft underside of her arm up. The bandage is wound so that a tiny patch of skin bulges out, and as I watch I see the ripple of something moving beneath the surface. I clap my hand over my mouth so that I don't gasp out loud.

Before I can stop her, she's slicing into the flesh, the skin opening, blood rising in a thick streak. Corp comes to the table closest to me, counting the vaccinations we still have to administer under her breath. I hide the wound on May's arm with my hand.

May keeps her head down, her face flat and unreadable. As Corp turns to speak to me, she catches sight of May. I watch her eyes creep down to the slick of bright red that's already running under my fingers. We've been caught.

I wait for her to raise the alarm. Wait for the shout that will bring the Coalies to us and send both me and May to a prison cell.

Instead, she locks eyes with me. And then she walks away without saying a word.

What just happened?

May wastes no time. She pushes my hand out of the way and feels inside the open wound with her finger. The only indication that she might be in pain is an almost imperceptible quickening of her breath. When she lifts her fingers out of her skin, she brings up a two-inch-long metal worm that dangles, tail flicking. She takes hold of my wrist and turns it so that the delicate flesh is exposed, shielding the action from the Coalies with her body. Her fingers are all nails.

"Don't cry out," she says.

The worm traces a line along my forearm and, when it rears and presses its pointed front end into my skin, I try to get my fingers around its tail, but May takes hold of my hand and stops me. "If you yell, we're dead," she says.

It breaks a hole in my skin. The pain is unbearable. I clench my teeth and, as quickly as it started, it's over. I look at my arm. The only sign of the worm is a small scar.

"Don't trust anyone but Nik."

"Why does it have to be me? Why can't you do it?"

"I absconded from a military training facility. Every Coaly on the ship will have seen my picture by now. If they recognize me, they'll arrest me. And, if they arrest me, they'll find this. Right now, you can still get around the ship without too much trouble. Find Nik."

"Where will you go?"

"The flotilla, if I can. Tell Nik I'll meet him at Enid's. And tell Mom and Dad I'm sorry. I just wanted to make things better."

Then suddenly she's gone, out of the tent, past the Coalies and into the crowd, her chair empty across from me.

And, like a lightning strike, my world is on fire.

CHAPTER 34

NIK

Where are you, Nikhil?" my mother says through my comglove.

I spin around, looking for the plaque that shows the deck number. "Back end of Deck Eleven," I say.

"And what are you doing?"

"Nothing."

"Do not lie to me. Are you trying to make contact with my agent?"

"She didn't make her rendezvous."

"I'm well aware. I'm also aware that, according to our protocols, in case of trouble, you're supposed to make your way to the engine room."

"May won't be in the engine room."

"Leave this to Enid and Silas. They have teams out looking for May. There's nothing you can do to help the situation."

"Due respect, Mom, I left this to you, and it hasn't gone well, has it?"

Silence.

Everywhere feels weird. Can't tell if it's because May's missing, or if there's something really bad going on. People scurry about. Heads down, shoulders up. Drones worry around the ship like insects.

"Get to the engine room, Nikhil. That's an order."

I jog toward the back of the ship. "Sorry, Mom, didn't catch that. Coalies must be jamming the signal again," I say, and before my mother can screech any more orders, I jab the End Call button on my palm.

Sure, we have a protocol. And, sure, everyone's now supposed to position themselves in the best place for helping the mission. But this time I don't want to follow protocol. I want to find May. She's carrying our only way to bring down the Coaly surveillance system. A set of codes that can be used to ground every single drone in Hadley's arsenal. Without those codes, every action we take, every force we muster, will have to be right under Hadley's beady eye. And, if the rumors are right, and Hadley has deployed military-grade weaponized drones on the ship, we'll be like fish in a very small, very hard-to-escape barrel.

And truth is, right at this moment, I don't care as much as I should about the mission. I care about May. Watching her leave— waiting for her to come back—made me realize that May trumps the rebellion. If it comes down to a choice between her and obeying orders, I choose her. One hundred percent.

Won't let myself think about what happens if the Coalies get to her.

A drone screams over the water. I duck into a doorway, pressing my back against it, and bury my face in my scarf.

Think—where will she go? If she got a hint of trouble, she'd keep away from anyone she might burn. That means me, and my mother, and the captain. No contact. She'll lose herself in the crowd. Keep moving until she's lost the tail. And where's the busiest place aboard the *Arcadia*?

In a flash, I know where she'll be: the market. Busy. Noisy. Big enough to get lost in.

I leave the shelter of the doorway and slink along the wall. It's open deck from here to the staircase, so I start jogging. Fear makes running easy, and when I reach the top deck and see the entrance to the market ahead of me, I've hardly felt my feet hitting the ground.

My gut-crunching fear isn't that May will be killed. The thing that breaks me out in a cold sweat is the thought of her getting arrested. Hadley will try to wring info from her, and he's not known for his gentle interrogation techniques. If things get bad, she'll take her memory scrubber. But the thought of May disappearing like my dad—

No. Don't think about it. Find her.

Gulls circle above as if nothing's wrong; clouds are soft and white in the sky. This part of the top deck is a mishmash of original buildings, all squat and utilitarian, and makeshift shelters thrown up sometime after we dropped anchor. The place is arranged in narrow streets, flimsy huts facing each other. Cooking fires and camping stoves in the doorways. Between the hovels, I get a glimpse right across the width of the ship. And that's when I spot them. Right on the other side of the *Arcadia*, moving parallel to the railing. A unit of Coalies, taking a slow march toward the back of the ship.

What are they doing? It's been my business to know the comings and goings of Hadley's forces, and this isn't on any regular patrol route. It's not every day you see a whole unit deployed unless there's serious trouble onboard. I run to the next avenue and look across the ship again. They're still there. Seems like they're heading the same way as me.

I pick up the pace. Don't want to meet them right outside the market if I can help it. When I get to the back of the ship and turn the corner to the market entrance, they're already coming around on the opposite side of the deck.

There are people here, a lot of them, coming in and out of the steel arch, milling around inside. *Dammit, the Coalies beat me.* They stop outside the arch. They stand at attention.

But here's the weird thing: they aren't interfering.

They're not stopping people going in or out. Not chasing anyone. This is new.

Don't know what they're waiting for, but I do know it doesn't feel right. I need to get in, find May, and get the hell away from whatever it is these Coalies are here for.

But that means taking a slow walk right under the visors of a whole unit. It's enough to make my hair stand on end.

You've got this. You can do it for the rebellion. You can do it for May.

My gut tells me to hunker down and hide my face, but this time I need them to see me. Not suspicious. Not trying to hide. I take a second to control my breathing. Pull my hood down and rearrange my scarf so that my whole face is visible. Holding on to the straps of my backpack so I've got something to do with my hands.

I need to find May, and I'll scour the ship from end to end if I have to. I walk toward the Coalies.

CHAPTER 35

ESTHER

I need a break," I say, my voice ending in a faint quiver that matches the feeling I have inside. I don't wait for anyone to respond before plunging out of the tent and into the crowd. I'm submerged in the noise and smells of the market: scorched meat and body odor; the high-pitched calls of hawkers. I follow what I think is the back of May's head as it bobs away.

I hear Alex calling after me, telling me to stop.

Halfway across the market and I've lost her. I spin around and around, looking for something familiar, waiting for something to catch my eye. The world sways, and the feeling of dread makes me want to curl into a ball. What happens if I don't give this to Nik? What if I cut it out of my body and throw it in the sea? Would that be the end of it all?

No. Nothing can go back to what it was.

What I want doesn't matter.

My loyalty doesn't matter.

I'm a traitor.

Out here, the sky is still angry and gray. The market still vibrates with the sounds of ship life. The world continues as if I haven't got a message for an illegal anti-Coaly organization burrowed into my flesh. Except for May, there's only one other person who can tell me everything: Nik Lall.

My arm's heavy, and I find myself clutching it to my chest like a broken wing.

Someone grabs my hand. I turn and find Alex.

"Wherever you need to go, I'm coming with you. Just tell me what's going on." His eyes plead with me.

I can't tell him yet. What would I say? That his dreams have been dashed on the rocks along with mine? That he might be arrested any minute just for associating with me? That my sister and I have destroyed everything he's worked his whole life to achieve?

"Nothing's going on," I say, and it comes out as a whisper.

I look up at him and see in an instant the heartbreak. The certainty that I'm lying to him. Again.

Corp's followed us from the clinic tent. She's standing just yards away, looking at me like she finds me totally disappointing. Behind her, all three Coalies have turned to face us, waiting to see what happens next. Poised to act.

An unpleasant tingle runs the length of my spine. The clarity hits me so hard I almost gasp. Corp isn't my friend. She isn't even my ally. She's a loyal subject of the Federated States. She knows I cheated, and I'd be willing to bet money that she recognized May a few seconds ago in the tent. She knows everything. It's not about if

I'm going to be arrested, it's when. Any second now, she'll give the nod to her Coaly friends.

Everything stops. Alex, Corp, the Coalies, all frozen in place. A flash lights them from behind. In the same moment, the tent seems to bulge outwards, the poles snapping like twigs, the canvas shredding into the air. A violent ball of flame and smoke spreading to engulf the world. Alex wreathed in black. Then he's gone.

CHAPTER 36

NIK

Walking in front of those Coalies broke me out in a cold sweat of dread. These are Hadley's people. I try to mingle with the crowd flowing under the arch, try to act normal. The sun's going down. I'm in danger of losing the light, and that will make it ten times harder to find May. Once I'm at the other side of the entrance, I dodge left, behind some sort of big green tent with the Federated States logo painted on its side, and run around the edge of the market. Want to be out of here as fast as possible, and it's a better vantage point from the deep end.

There's the lifeguard's chair. A tall metal frame with the jagged fragments of a seat at the top, red plastic bleached to pink from decades in the sun. When I get there, I set my foot on the lowest rung, reach up, and grab the top one, holding myself steady so I have a good view. Don't like how exposed I am up here, so I scan fast. Esther's running out of that big tent by the entrance, followed swiftly by the boyfriend. Something's got them all agitated, and I'd bet money on that something being May.

I drop down and have a scout around for drones and Coalies to make sure I haven't been spotted. When I climb back up, I trace the crowd again, knowing that I'm running out of chances.

Come on. Where are you?

I know her the second I see her. The way she moves. The shape of her. My heart beats a thousand times faster. She's alive.

She's in danger.

Esther's racing after her. That girl sure can attract attention. It's the kind of thing that will get you noticed by the Coalies. May is carrying her coat rolled up in a ball, even though it's freezing. My guess is she's taken the worm out of her arm.

The boyfriend's yelling. Telling Esther to stop, I'm betting. He grabs her hand, and that's when the Coalies join the action. They follow Esther and her boyfriend, presumably to see what all the fuss is about. If Esther wanted to keep a low profile, she's failed.

There's a blast of pure white, an incandescent cloud that swells outwards at a terrifying speed. It's so loud, it feels like it's inside my head. Too late, I shield my eyes and try to grab hold of the metal frame. Then the shock wave hits. It rips me off the ladder, slams me into the ground. My head cracks against the deck. Can't breathe. No air left in my lungs.

It's started.

We're under attack.

Weeks early. No warning. Our network of friends on land should have sent us a message. Someone must have known the clearance was coming today. Unless everyone's been rounded up already. My gut twists. I see them in my head: Rebels handcuffed and kneeling. Rebels under interrogation.

I pull myself up and plant my feet on the deck. My head's whirling like you wouldn't believe. Twenty seconds ago, this was the market, now there's nothing but rubble and fire. My lungs fill with ash. I stagger down toward the place I saw Esther a few seconds ago, smoke thickening as I get closer to ground zero. Everything's in motion. Flames. Air. People trying to right themselves. Those that can are already getting out of here, a torrent of walking wounded. They clutch devastated faces. Blood and ash.

Centered above the market is a drone, recording everything that's happening. I'm guessing I've got seconds until that whole unit of Coalies is in here with me. No time to be stealthy. I look around for anything, anyone, recognizable in the mess. I spot Enid's right-hand man, John, by the entrance, pulling himself along, one leg dragging behind. Getting to him means stepping over debris and ignoring the groans of the injured. Patches of blood slicken the blue-tiled floor. Never did spend too much time thinking about the clearance. Almost persuaded myself that we'd get out of here in one piece.

John looks away when he sees me. "Not here," he says, and he nods toward the drone.

Not much will shake John, but there's an unnerving edge of desperation to his voice. Up close, his leg looks terrible. Ribbons of bloody skin underneath shredded trousers. I clench my teeth.

"Jeez, John. That's nasty," I say. I crouch next to him, trying not to look at the damage to his body.

"I'm not dead," he says, and he collapses back against the railing, heaving on his trousers to bring his injured leg closer.

I hold my fist over my mouth. He's not far from dead. Pale and glassy-eyed.

"May didn't make her meeting," I say.

"She came aboard this mornin', but she had a tail so she's been movin' around."

"Where is she now?"

John lets his head rock backwards, his eyes rolling with the pain. He claws at the top of his thigh. "Lost her just before this happened. Think she was talking to her sister."

I stand and sway against the railing, pulling at the neck of my hoodie to get more air. "Is it happening? The clearance?"

"No. Saw Coalies over there. Dead. They wouldn't attack their own."

"Then was it us?"

"Don't think so. Your mother's got everyone under her thumb. Enid and Silas both know to keep their heads down, if they want their piece of the pie when we're free. Must have been someone else."

"Who?"

"Your guess is as good as mine."

A kid with blood pouring from a finger-sized hole in his cheek walks by, and I grab his coat. He tries to shake me off.

"This is Enid Hader's right-hand man," I tell the boy. "You know who Enid is?"

The boy's eyes are wide with fear. "Yep," he says. There's blood seeping from the corner of his mouth, ash caking the cracks in his lips.

"You take him down to her. You save this guy's life, Enid Hader's going to be grateful to you. She's going to owe you one. Got it?"

The kid nods. Together we pull John up, and the boy slides himself under John's arm. They shuffle toward the exit, John grunting with each step.

A way off, about where Esther was standing when that bomb went off, there are two figures lying on the ground. Esther and her boyfriend. I'm guessing, May's already passed the drone codes along to her sister. So, if the worst's happened and Esther's dead, the codes are lying there in her body. Unprotected. This might be my only chance to get them back.

What I want to do is find May. I want to go after her and make sure she gets through every Coaly checkpoint without a problem. I need to know that she's alive and safe. But I also have to make sure we have the best chance of defeating the Coalies, otherwise this explosion is only the start of the suffering for the people onboard this ship. I have to follow the codes.

CHAPTER 37

ESTHER

Looking up. Strange sounds. Everything smeared, out of reach. Fractured tiles scratch at my fingertips. Chest aches from holding my breath. How long have I been lying here?

Time to get up, Esther.

Warm stickiness in my eyes. Skin tight with pain.

Smoke masquerades as clouds, but darker, angrier. Pushed away by the wind. A drone watches me from above, a dark blurry shape. Something balled me up. Need to unbend all my creases. Flatten out the folds.

You have to get up now.

Is that voice inside my head?

I turn my face to the side. Skin crackles. Alex is next to me. An ashy mask. Lips cracked with pink. Red streaking like lava. Oh God, he's dead.

Esther! Move!

Someone kneels next to me, his knuckles pressing into my sternum, trying to wake me. I click back into the world. Clawing at the deck, I pull myself through the whirring in my head. There's fire. Flattened stalls. Broken bodies. Blood.

Nik's face is close to mine, smeared with grime, glistening with sweat and pinpricks of blood.

Alex is moving, the fingers of one hand smearing the blood on his lips. Somehow, I manage to drag myself over to him and shake him by the shoulders. "We have to go," I say, and I can't hear my own voice through the buzzing in my ears. His eyes flicker open and then close again. "Please, Alex!" I sob. "Please, we have to go. Wake up."

He snaps to and lurches up. I grab a handful of uniform and pull at him. Fire's eating up the stall nearest to me. Nik helps Alex to his feet, and together the three of us scramble away from the flames. Away from the twisted remains of our clinic. Fragments of plastic chairs. Bodies in medical uniforms. Kara's clouded eyes. A Coaly's visor cracked open.

"This is bad. This is really bad," Nik says. He bends to rest his hands on his knees.

"You OK?" Alex says. He's holding on to me, pushing the hair out of my eyes. "You got burned."

He gets a dressing from the pocket of his trousers and unpeels the wrapper, letting it fly away in the wind. He presses it on to my face, and I gasp at the sting before the cool anesthetic kicks in.

Through the wreckage and smoke, I see the figure of Corp. Her hair's come out of her braid, and she limps as she moves from body to body, stooping over each one to check for a pulse. When she gets to one in a Coaly uniform, she grimaces, clamping her teeth together like she's biting back tears.

How could I have been so stupid? Corp's never been anything but a loyal servant of the Federated States. Why did I ever think she might be on my side? Everything she did for me was part of her job description.

"We need to move," Nik says.

There are Coalies flooding through the entrance to the market. The clomping of their boots makes the deck rattle. Each one clutches a rifle to their chest.

"That's the only exit," Alex says.

"Anywhere's better than here," Nik replies.

We pick ourselves up. Nik runs ahead, leading us away from the worst of the destruction, until we reach a stall that's still standing. He pulls us behind a towering pile of shipping pallets.

That blaze will spread. The leather and canvas and wood of the stalls is like tinder. Once fire takes hold onboard a ship like the *Arcadia*, there's nowhere to run.

Alex coughs into his sleeve. There's a cut on his temple, but other than that, he's pretty unscathed.

Through the pallets, I get a good view of where we've come from. The sight of the clinic chills me. Nobody could have survived that. It's obliterated.

"Did you see anyone else?" I say to Alex. I can taste blood and ash thick in my throat.

"I saw Kofi and Anna leave."

"That's it? Just two?" My throat thickens. I have to hold back a sob.

"Can't be sure. There were too many people running. Where did you go?" he asks.

"What?"

"You went off. I came after you. Then this."

"I—"

I can't think of anything but the truth. The truth is that my sister is AWOL, and I'm a traitor against my will. Something destroyed the market. And suddenly I have to decide who I can or can't trust.

Nik drops to his knees behind the shipping pallets, peering through the slats to get a better view of the Coalies. "Why were they here?" he mutters like he's talking to himself.

"They're responding to an emergency. It's their job," Alex snaps back.

"No, they were here before the explosion. They were ready."

"We should go back. Try to help," Alex says.

"Wouldn't advise it until we know what's going on with them. Doesn't look like they're here to provide first aid. We stay hidden until they leave."

As I look through the narrow gap between two planks, I realize Nik's right. The Coalies aren't helping. They're just looking around. One of them relays instructions to the others. I can hear the faint echo of their voices bouncing from helmet to helmet. In among them is Corp. She talks to the Coalies, waving her arms, resting her hands on her hips. Obviously explaining what happened. She helps someone to their feet, a green medical uniform darkened with soot and blood. I try to figure out who it is, but there's ash everywhere and my vision's blurred.

I run my hand over the part of my arm that holds the worm.

"May gave you something," Nik says. He grabs both my hands and tries to turn them so that he can see the underside of my arm. I slap him away.

"How did you get my sister into this mess?" I say.

"We can deal with that later, once we're safe and away from those Coalies," he says.

He grabs my hand again and starts feeling along the fleshy part of my arm. When he finds it—the worm bulging under the skin—he presses it with his thumb. A sharp thrill of pain travels up my arm and I feel the thing wiggling away.

"Esther, who the hell is this guy—wait, what is that?" Alex says. He frowns down at my scar.

"Nothing you need to know about," Nik says.

"It's in my girlfriend's arm. I want to know what that thing is, and I want to know now."

"Or what?"

"Or I'll march over to those Coalies and point them in your direction."

Nik laughs. "Good luck with that. What makes you think they won't arrest us both?"

"This uniform for a start."

They glare at each other, both puffed up and bristling. Alex shoves Nik by the shoulders, and then they're locked in a weird back-and-forth pushing thing.

"Keep your voices down," I hiss. I'm trying to maintain control, to keep my voice calm and professional, but that drone is still circling above the market. "Nik, get this thing out. Now," I say.

He straightens his clothes, still glaring at Alex. "Can't. You need to deliver it."

"May said I needed to get it to you. That's all I have to do."

"Well, May wasn't being entirely accurate. Truth is, it has to be cut out. It's programmed to be removed with a specific hook, the one the contact's got. A scalpel would work, or I can cut it out with a knife, but the thing will move around inside, and I'd probably have to slice up your arm chasing it."

"How did May get it out without the right hook?" Alex says.

"She had it trapped with a tourniquet and made the cut with a knife."

"We could do it in the infirmary," Alex says.

"And how are you going to get over there? It might only be two decks down, but the place is already swarming with Coalies and drones."

Alex rubs his forehead. "I want to know what we're dealing with before she goes anywhere with you."

I look at Nik. He shakes his head, warning me to keep my mouth shut.

"OK," I say, taking a shuddering breath. "May's involved in something. Something big."

Alex raises his eyebrows.

"Esther," Nik says.

"It's OK. I trust him."

Nik throws his hands in the air and paces around, shaking his head.

"What are we talking here? Is it smuggling?" Alex says.

"I'm not a smuggler!" Nik says.

"Maybe not. But you are trouble. So I'd rather hear this from Esther, if it's all the same."

"Stop bickering!" I say. "I don't know exactly what she's involved in. All I do know is she doesn't want the Coalies to catch her. She went ashore, and she came back with something hidden under her skin. And now it's hidden under mine."

Alex turns to Nik.

"My lips are sealed," Nik says.

"Is May a traitor? Because you know they execute traitors in the Federated States."

Hearing Alex say that makes everything painfully real. "I don't know," I say.

"I've got a scalpel. This could be over in a few minutes. You call it."

I hesitate, shocked that Alex would risk cutting my arm open. I can't face the thought of someone chasing that thing around my body with a scalpel, a trail of bloody slices following it.

"Let's deliver it to May's contact," I say. "And then I want to see my sister."

"Now we're talking. But only you, doc. Not him," Nik says.

"We're a package deal. If she goes, I go," Alex says.

"Stop arguing and look," I say.

They turn to where I'm pointing, and we watch the Coalies march out of the market, carrying three bodies in Coaly uniforms between them. The dead and dying are left on the ground. There are no stretchers and no med kits. Even Corp's gone. The gate clangs. There's the jangle of a heavy chain being pulled around the steel bars.

"Why are they leaving?" I say.

Nik steps around the shipping pallets. Out into the open. "No," he says. "No. No. No."

Then he's off, running through the market, dodging burning debris. He slams into the gate, setting it rattling against the thick chain that holds it shut. He shakes the bars. Alex joins him, both of them straining to pull the chain apart.

"Here," I say, grabbing a charred wooden pole, the remains of a stall.

They stand back, and I slide the pole through the chain. Alex takes hold with me. We pull downwards. The wood strains under my hands, the chain creaks, each link stretching under the pressure. Then the pole splinters, and we stagger back.

"Get something stronger. Help us, Nik," Alex says.

But Nik's not listening. He's focused on the sky behind us. And I hear it. The high-pitched whine of a drone. No, not one. *Drones* plural. They stir the air. Chase away the smoke that's still bleeding into the sky.

A terrible swarm.

CHAPTER 38

NIK

The sun's going down, but the sky's alive. Crawling with drones. The wind from their propellers is blowing my hair around. Smoke from the burning stalls brings an eerie kind of twilight. The drones rise and circle.

"We're trapped," Esther says. She's panting, cheeks flushed. A white dressing covers one side of her face.

"I can get us out of here," I say. "Just need to buy a minute."

I take her hand, the one with the drone codes, and we run away from the gate. I want to put some space between us and those drones. When I find a patch of railing that doesn't seem too damaged, I lean over to get a look at what's down there. Seaward side, back of the ship. Even in the failing light, I can see there are no hazards between us and a section of the flotilla below. It's nothing more than a floating platform cobbled together from doors and shipping pallets.

Good. Good. This should work.

The drones congregate over the center of the market, turning their bright floodlights on the worst parts of the blast damage. I swing my bag off my back and undo the zip.

"You hear that?" Alex says.

I hear it all right. An electronic voice, far away, but loud enough to be clear. It's coming from one of the drones, bleating out into the dusky air.

"You are guilty of terrorist activity."

"Who's it talking to?" Esther says.

"Let's not find out," says Alex.

"Gotta agree with Dimples," I say.

"Dimples? What the—"

"That's why we're going over the side," I say, cutting Alex off before he can get into being offended by his new nickname.

Esther climbs on to the railing, pausing at the top and closing her eyes like she's getting ready to jump.

"Whoa. Hold your horses," I say.

Alex looks over the side. "It'll be like hitting concrete," he says.

They're both calm. Must be their medical training. When something happens, they switch to work mode.

"I have a way to get us down without breaking any bones."

I find what I'm rummaging for in my bag and pull out the two long black belts. They're all wound up together. *Dammit.* May was always telling me to keep them flat so they wouldn't get tangled.

"To the flotilla? That's Neath territory," Esther says.

"Yep. We'll deal with that problem when we get to it. Right now, I want to get away from those drones."

Under the drone that played the voice recording, I see someone move. A hand raised to block out the beam of light. A figure trying to get up. I fiddle with the belts. Esther jumps down from the railing and snatches them out of my hands, her fingers working fast and calmly to untangle them.

The drone drops lower. The bottom opens.

"Come on, Esther," Alex says.

"Quick as I can," she replies.

Screams. My chest squeezes. A sound like a drumroll ricochets around the market, so loud I can feel it in my stomach. We all duck instinctively and glance at each other, too terrified to look for the source of the screaming.

The rumors were true: the drones are packing weapons.

"Faster," I say. Esther nods.

Injured people in the market find a last surge of energy and move. Some crawl; others manage to get on their feet and hobble. All making for the gate I already know is chained shut.

"Come on," I say. Esther's still fiddling with the belts.

"Almost there, give me a second."

"We might not have that long," Alex says.

The drones move around, find new targets. Another announcement. Another round of firing. I watch a guy climb up on the railing. There's a drone flying lazily behind him. He throws himself over before the drone can finish him off. He falls silently. That's one hell of a drop.

Esther has unraveled the belts and tosses them back to me. Question is: let Alex fend for himself or take him down to Enid's territory? If she's suspicious, she'll kill him on the spot. But if I leave him up here, he's dead meat. And I can't just let the guy die, no matter how annoying I find his face. Damn stupid conscience.

"One for Dimples," I say.

I tighten the black strap around my middle, the shiny steel disc at the small of my back. The flotilla's down there, so far away it's a smudge of brown and black peppered with lights. It's too dark to see the waves. That's good. More chance we'll stay hidden. And with any luck the drones will be too distracted up here to notice us. We'll take a swim if I misjudge, but it's better than taking bullets.

Alex fumbles to copy me. *Not so calm now, is he?*

I'm fifty percent sure there's a platform below us. Forty-five percent sure.

I pull the metal disc, letting out a length of cable, and press the disc onto the top of the railing. It holds fast. Dimples follows suit, attaching his zip cord to the railing a yard or so away.

"There's only two," Esther says.

"For emergencies. Usually, it's just me and May. Dimples, make sure you press the release button before you get to the water or you'll be dangling like a fish on a line."

"Thanks for the tip," Alex says.

We climb up on the railing.

Esther's holding on to Alex on one side. I take her other hand and uncurl it from the railing. She gasps.

"I won't let you fall," I say.

We all stare downwards. Esther's hand twists into the shoulder of my jacket. She smells like May; there's a sweet orange tang to her hair.

"You've done this before?" she whispers.

"Of course," I say, and it's not a lie. I have done it before. Only not so high. And not so fast. And not with a weaponized drone chasing me. And not in the dark.

"Just hold on really tight," I tell her.

Then I feel the push of wind behind us, and I know it's a drone, and I know it's spotted us, and I know if I turn around I'm going to see its gun pointing straight at me. I hook my arm around her waist and pull her toward me. Her expression switches to shock. She grabs hold of me out of pure instinct.

"Ready?" I say, and without waiting for her answer, I jump. Then we're flying.

CHAPTER 39

ESTHER

Air rushes over me. We're dropping through the darkness, the ripcord barely slowing us down. The fall sets me alight with exhilaration. I squeeze Nik around the neck. Reassuringly warm. Reassuringly alive. Grabbing me like that was a dirty trick, and I should be angry. I'm not.

The side of the ship is a cliff. Waves rush closer, frothy and colorless in the dusk.

Above us, Alex whirs down his own line, facing straight down toward the ocean.

I spot a rough platform of shipping pallets beneath us. Water sloshes between the slats. Nik leans back, and the motion slows our descent so that my toes skim the platform before touchdown. We stand together, breathing synchronized and cheeks glowing. Nik laughs, and I laugh too. For a nanosecond, I forget that my life has imploded. He releases me, and the moment of peace is gone. I can feel the weight of my body, the danger we're in, the absence of May.

Nik presses a button on the zip cord, and the mechanism winds it in. Excitement makes my cheeks feel like they're scorched, so I turn to watch Alex descending his line. I don't want Nik to see.

Alex is like a spider on gossamer. He's still several yards short of the water when he reaches around and presses the zip cord release button. He shrieks, plummeting down the side of the ship and splashing into open water.

Nik snickers.

"Alex!" I yell, running to the edge of the platform. "You did that on purpose!" I spit at Nik. He raises his hands in mock submission.

Above the washing of the sea comes the exaggerated splashing of a nonswimmer. Alex dog-paddles to the edge of the platform. The thin layer of trash that coats the water around the flotilla parts in front of him. When he starts to haul himself out on to the platform, the stuff sticks to him.

"It's OK, I can manage," he says under his breath when I lean down to help him. His skin's mottled red, and his hair hangs limply over his face.

Nik doesn't even try to hide his glee.

Alex is fit to explode. He seizes Nik by the collar, pulling him close with gritted teeth. This has been coming since the moment they met in my cabin. They were always going to end up fighting.

Nik shoves back. They start another ridiculous scrambling-pushing-grunting battle.

Idiots.

"As much fun as it is watching you boys fight," says a voice, "think we'd better get somewhere a little bit safer, don't you?"

A lantern flashes on in the dark, illuminating a group of people standing on the next platform. A few feet of water separates us.

Nik and Alex give each other a final bulging-eye glare and push apart. Nik rakes his fingers through his hair. Alex rubs water off his face.

The new people are positioned in a defensive horseshoe around a woman wearing a dark hood, her eyes circled with kohl. In the lantern light, her pale skin seems to glow like bone.

"Enid?" Nik says, squinting into the darkness. "How did you know we were coming down?"

"I have spies everywhere, Nik my boy."

"Someone else jumped when they started shooting," Nik says.

"I know. Already sent someone to fish him out." The woman cocks her head at me and lifts the lantern she's holding, so that she can inspect my face. "This the girl that bloodied Silas's nose?"

"The one and only. Esther, this is Enid Hader."

Am I supposed to know her? My confusion must show on my face because Nik clears his throat anxiously and whispers, "You know, leader of the portside gangs."

"It's all right, Nik. Can't expect my notoriety to extend as far as the upper decks, can I? Girls up there have better things to think about than the woman in charge of the ship's only outboard territory."

I'm not sure what to do, so I take a step forward and hold my hand out over the gap between the platforms. Enid shakes it, hard, raising her black eyebrows with a faint smirk. She yanks on my hand, pulling me off balance, so I'm forced to jump the gap. When I'm standing right in front of her, she holds my hand in a vice-like grip and peers intently at my face.

"Nice to hear someone drew blood from that old turd."

I can't think of anything to say, so I mutter a lame, "Thank you." It brings another grin to Enid's face.

"Well, you're welcome," she says, dipping her head.

God, she's intimidating. She'd be intimidating even if she wasn't the leader of a criminal militia.

"Who's the swimmer?" she says to Nik.

"That's Dimples," Nik says. He steps across the gap and stands shoulder to shoulder with Enid. "Esther's boyfriend," he says. There's more than a hint of contempt in his voice.

"It's Alex. Pleased to meet you."

Alex holds out a soggy hand. He watches Enid intently for a few seconds, then blinks before dropping his eyes. Enid eyes him like he's a mosquito. Eventually, he steps across the gap and stands next to me.

"I want to see my sister," I say.

"Figured."

I wait for her to continue. "I saw her in the market. She said she was coming down here, then there was an explosion. Did she make it?" My voice trembles. I can't control it.

The corner of Enid's mouth curls upward. She gazes at me, weighing my value. "Your girl's still breathing," she says finally.

Relief. Strong as a storm surge. Nik lets out a breath. Alex squeezes my hand. His fingers are like ice. I need to get him warm. Hypothermia is a real threat out here.

"Do you know where she is?" I say.

"I do."

The silence stretches on and on, and I have the strong urge to fill it. Enid watches me with her gentle smirk. I don't know whether I'm supposed to speak. This doesn't feel like a conversation.

"What's happening right now?" Alex says.

Nik sighs. "She wants something."

"I don't have any money," I say.

"You get nothing for nothing down here, darlin', friend or not. Nik still owes me for the last favor I did him. And you're racking up quite a bill too."

I'm racking up a bill? I didn't even know I'd opened a tab.

"Me?"

"Yep. You didn't think Silas had suddenly given up on the idea of bumping you off, did you?"

Nik takes something out of his pocket and holds it up for Enid to see. I know what it is without reading the label: antibiotics. *My antibiotics.* He tosses them to Enid. She inspects the vial in the light of her lantern before pocketing it.

"You stole from me?" I say, and I'm so angry that my voice shudders. "That's why you trashed our cabin? You were distracting me, so you could go through my med bag?"

Nik doesn't even glance my way. And now I know how Alex feels. I could punch Nik in his stupid double-crossing, thieving—

"One course?" Enid says. "Just about covers what you owe. And I'll need the same again for this little escapade."

"Wasn't easy getting that, and now you've let my only source know I helped myself," says Nik.

277

Enid considers. "Ah, you're right. Can't expect you to get more now I've let the cat out of the bag. I'll take your zip belts instead." She holds out her hand.

"You know how hard these are to get?" Nik says with a furrowed brow. He's clearly pissed off.

"I'm aware of their value."

"This is way out of order, Enid. This is BS," Nik says, unbuckling his belt. He throws it to her. She waits while Alex does the same.

"You let him get hold of meds, and you didn't report it?" Alex says.

"He stole them. I didn't know until a second ago," I snap back. But he's right. It's pharmaceutical security 101: no one gets access to medical bags. If you suspect someone might have, you take an inventory and report any losses immediately. I screwed up. I know now that I saw Nik do it, but I was so distracted it didn't even register.

Alex huddles into himself. His lips are tinged blue, and he's shuddering. He glares at Enid and her people from beneath his dripping hair.

"Take us to May," I say, through gritted teeth. I square up to Enid. Too exhausted and too scared to care about who she is. "Or get out of the way so we can find our own way back onboard."

Enid laughs. "Your girl's got some nerve, Nik."

"She's not my girl," he mutters.

A drone passes over far above, skimming us with weak light.

"Whatever. Seems to me you've got a job to finish before I extend my hospitality," she says.

CHAPTER 40

HADLEY

The air in the infirmary is bitter with disinfectant.

Hadley feels taller. He can stand up straight for the first time in years. Two officers flank him, amped up and angry after moving the bodies of their fallen colleagues to the morgue. His young, wet-behind-the-ears deputy is dead. As are two other low-ranking officers that Hadley sacrificed in the market attack. Worth it to get his life back.

There's screaming and crying. Harsh lights and splashes of color. The surviving medics flit from stretcher to stretcher. The ship's infirmary was only supposed to deal with half a dozen patients at a time. Now it's groaning with people from the market blast. They sit on the floor, share blood-stained cots in the narrow corridors. There must be a shortage of drip stands too, because more than one patient has been left to hold their own IV bag in the air.

There's something going on with these trainees; Hadley's

encounter with the disloyal medic told him that much. He just hasn't figured it out yet. He cursed himself when he realized he'd overlooked the medics in his search for an antivenom supplier. Maybe one of them has turned traitor. Maybe it's the whole class. First order is to figure out whether their leader's in on it. Then he'll take a look at this Crossland girl.

He takes hold of one of the trainees as she passes, scrunching the girl's uniform in his fist. She won't look at him. She closes her eyes so that he can see the blue veins on her eyelids. "Where's your corporal?"

"In—in there," she stammers, motioning to a set of double doors with cracked off-white paint and chipboard where the windows should be.

He lets the girl go and strides through the doors with his two officers.

Weston stands next to a bed with a charred figure lying on it. On a stand next to her is a model of a heart rendered in deep pink for muscle, red arteries, blue veins. She squeezes it rhythmically with one hand, the signal carried down a set of wires into the man's chest. Weston's eyes flick from the heart to the man to the display above the bed.

"Weston," Hadley says.

"What?"

She concentrates on her patient, cheeks shining, lips parted with exertion. Sweat stains the armpits of her uniform, and there's blood almost up to her elbows. She didn't stop to put on gloves. A blue line on the display above the bed blips each time she squeezes the replica heart.

Hadley has arrived at the perfect moment. It might have been hard to rattle Weston, an experienced medic, used to working under pressure. She can manage distractions. Noise. Blood. Machines. But what about having her hands tied? It's almost too easy.

He yanks her away from the patient and swings her against the wall on the opposite side of the room.

"Get your hands off me!" she screams, forcing herself against his shoulders.

The medical display beeps in protest at the sudden absence of input from the heart.

"Hold her," he says quietly, scratching at a stain on the front of his uniform with his fingernail.

The officers take one arm each and hold on to Weston as she struggles. "He's dying," she says.

"Yes." Hadley looks the man over. He's probably young under all that burnt flesh. Dark hair singed to stubble on one side.

Hadley brings a chair to the side of the bed and sits, resting his feet on the edge. He did a walkthrough of the market after the drones had finished clearing up, and now his boots are smeared with dirt. He takes a large cotton swab from the tray by the bed and starts wiping gunk from the leather.

Weston is young, pretty, and brilliant according to her official record. Crappy childhood spent studying and scraping around for food. Entered medical school top of her class with a clean record. A perfect example of the rags-to-riches story that Federated States citizens lap up.

Weston stares at him. Her face as fractured and broken as her patient. "I'm a Federated States officer. The regulations say you need a warrant signed by the Admirals in order to take any action against me."

Hadley lets out a snorting laugh, a genuine smile on his face. "The faith you people have in the system. My superiors don't care what happens here, as long as it doesn't make them look bad. It'd be helpful if a few more of you were wiped out before we clear this stinking hole. Less mouths to feed in the prison camps."

Weston heaves against the officers holding her. Fiery. So like Celeste. For a moment, the feeling of betrayal swamps Hadley, even now, years later. "I looked you up, Corporal Harriet Weston."

She stills. Her fluttering breath betrays a deep anxiety.

"And I know where you came from."

"My records are in order. I've committed no crime." She snaps the words out, clipped and rehearsed. She has prepared for this moment.

Hadley gets up and steps so close, he can feel her breath on his face. Close up, her dark skin is dappled with freckles.

"Couldn't care less about your record. Your papers. Your visa. Your exam results. Doesn't matter how integrated you pretend to be. Doesn't matter how good your fake accent is. You are and always will be"—he pinches Weston's face between his thumb and fingers, and blood floods the corners of her mouth—"a vile little ship kid."

Hadley shoves her face away. Straightens his collar. Clears his throat to swallow the feeling of vindication. It's taken less than three minutes to convince him his hunch about her was right. She's a traitor.

"Tell me, if I inventory your infirmary, will I find a single dose of antivenom missing? One that can be used to treat a government-issue toxic round, for instance."

She twitches with understanding, but he can't arrest her without evidence. Can't just kill her, even if she is working for them. On paper, she's an officer of the Federated States government, just like him.

He backs away, slowly, until he's level with the patient on the bed. The man's brain activity plods along. Hadley runs a finger down the side of the heart replica that's still attached to the man's real organic heart.

Interesting piece of technology. Maybe he could use it for interrogations. The med display sets up an urgent beeping that grates on Hadley's nerves.

"Was it you, or was it one of your kids?"

For a moment, it looks like she's about to confess. Then she clears her throat and composes herself. "Most of my students were killed today. I refuse to believe any of them were involved in illicit activity."

"An oversight on my part. Should have found out which one of you did the deed before I set off a bomb next to you."

"You were responsible? Why? What did you get out of it?"

Hadley pinches one of the red arteries between his thumb and forefinger.

Despair washes over Weston's face. "Don't," she whispers. "Stop! Please! You're killing him!" Then she screams, pulling against the officers, teeth bared.

"Hold her here for half an hour. Long enough to make sure she can't bring this one back."

Tears stream down Weston's face. "You're a monster!"

The med-display levels settle to thin blue lines, and the machine emits an incessant monotone.

Hadley wipes his hand on the sheet covering the bed, then pushes open the double doors.

"Yes. I am."

CHAPTER 41

ESTHER

Enid steps, sure-footed, through the tangle of boats and walkways. She's elegant and long-limbed, and the light from her
lantern sways hypnotically.

Like a dark cliff face, the ship brings a creeping, uncanny sensation. We move fast through the streets of the flotilla. It's the first
time I've seen them close up, and every step makes me nervous.
They are, literally, flotsam. Old doors, pallets, unidentifiable pieces
of driftwood all lashed together to form something that can be
walked on. Small boats and barges are roped together like lines of
houses on either side.

The ocean is a forbidding mass beneath us and so unpleasantly
close. Enid's entourage scans the sky and the sea constantly for
signs of movement. I plant every step firmly, not wanting to take
a tumble on the slick wood. I don't want to humiliate myself in
front of Enid.

We take a broad circle and end up near the prow of the *Arcadia*. The sides of the ship are breathtaking. Its skin is made of great metal plates, pinned together with rivets as big as my fist. Streaks of rust look like blood in the darkness. It's dotted with live barnacles and slimed black with kelp, and there's no relief from the pungent smell of rotting vegetation. I'm struck by the fear that I'm lost out here. That I might never find my way home.

"Where is she taking us?" I ask Nik.

"Don't ask questions. Not down here. Not with Enid."

"We have a right to—"

"You don't have a right to anything. You're not on the *Arcadia* anymore. This is Enid's territory, and if you and Dimples aren't careful, you won't see morning. So I suggest you stop talking, do what Enid tells you, and then we can all go and see your sister."

I snap my mouth closed.

Do one thing at a time. Each step takes me closer to May.

We reach a platform that butts up against the hull of the main ship. It's just old pallets roped together and so low that water splashes through the slats. Enid places her storm lantern on the floor, so she can whistle with her fingers. She turns her face up, waiting. After a couple of seconds, a light appears above us.

"Heads!" A voice shouts out of the darkness, and a knotted rope slaps against the side of the ship.

"Here's the deal. Nik brought Alex down without vetting him," Enid says to me as she crouches and pulls a small leather pouch out of her coat pocket. She piles dried leaves onto a rectangle of paper. In the lantern light, I realize she's not wearing a comglove.

"They were shooting people! What should I have done?" Nik says.

"Left him. I don't care. Your choice."

She straightens and sticks the end of the paper roll in her mouth. "What I need to know, Esther, is can he be trusted? And I want you to be sure before you answer."

"Of course," I say without hesitation.

"No nagging concerns? No unexplained activities? Because this is going to be on your head, and on Nik's too. There's a process, you know? We check on people before they're let into headquarters. We follow them for a while, to make sure they're not colluding with the Coalies. You, you're all right. You're May's sister, and I'd trust May to the edge of the world. I know who you are. But him, not so much."

"No concerns," I say. I ignore the lens Alex gave me to help me cheat, the huge stash of food, the backstreet dentist. Tamp the thoughts right down.

"Wow. You must be the first teenage couple in history to be so lacking in drama." Enid rolls her thumb over a plastic lighter and lights the end of the paper. Sweet-smelling smoke fills the air.

We're close together, balancing on the swaying pallets. Enid's smoke crackles in my lungs. She turns her eyes on me, black hollows in the dark. I'm cornered. There's nowhere to escape to. The burning paper glows red in the dark. A smell of aniseed permeates the air.

"He'd never do anything to hurt me," I say.

Nik laughs and shakes his head.

Enid takes a step closer. "Not you I'm worried about, girl," she says. "It's the rest of the people around here that are my concern."

She circles the burning paper roll in the air like she's drawing a protective ring around the flotilla. Shadows dance on her face. In a split second, she seems to have flipped from sarcastic to unstable.

"Tell her, Nik. Tell her Alex wouldn't go to the Coalies," I say.

Nik shrugs. "I don't like the guy," he says, "but I don't think he'd inform on us. It's dangerous for him and Esther too."

"All right. Here's what we're gonna do." Enid pokes a finger into Nik's shoulder, showering ash. "You, Nik, will be in charge of Alex while he's down here. He pees, you go with him. He sleeps, you're lying down next to him."

"Enid!" Nik groans.

"Don't *Enid* me. You brought him here," she says. There's fire and danger in her words. "Watch the kid, or I'll have him over the side."

I feel sick. The platform's swaying horribly. I grab Nik's hand to steady myself. "Please, Nik. Please don't let them hurt him," I say.

"Fine," Nik says. "But you tell him, Esther. I'm out, if he gets too annoying. Don't care if he's thrown in the sea."

"I'm right here," Alex says stonily.

"Talking about you. Not to you," Nik says.

Alex sees my hand on Nik's, and the look he gives me makes my stomach flip. I try to inch away from Nik, cursing myself for giving Alex another reason to be angry.

"Alex—"

"Fine. Whatever," he says, interrupting me. "You won't get any trouble from me."

"Good. Now," Enid says, turning to me, "you're going to get that information where it needs to go. Call it a test of loyalty. Prove you're not about to scamper off to the Coalies first chance you get. Go in, meet May's contact, then you get to see your sister."

She picks up the lantern and steps off the raft.

"Could do with some backup," Nik says.

Enid snorts. The cigarette dangles between her lips. "That's Silas's territory. I'm not going in there. Especially not with two unvetted kids on an unscheduled visit."

"And if we run into trouble? If Silas's people decide we shouldn't be there?"

"Ah, you'll be OK. He won't try anything while she's delivering that thing. And if he does you can call your mommy and hope she gets there while these two still have a pulse," she says.

"I won't call my mother for anything," Nik says. He sounds unexpectedly bitter.

"Still salty about her taking your girlfriend away from you, I see. Well, I stopped caring about this conversation a good few minutes ago. I'll see you later, or I won't."

Nik is May's boyfriend. She has a life in the rebellion and a secret boyfriend. I wonder what else I'm going to find out about my big sister tonight.

Enid takes off into the dark, the lantern dimming to a smudge before it disappears completely.

We all look up. A few yards above us, the rope disappears into a hole cut in the side of the hull, just big enough for a person to climb through, and glowing with weak light from inside.

"You go first. Get yourself warmed up," Nik says to Alex.

Alex takes the rope above the first knot and hoists himself up.

I flip my collar to keep out the cold air. Alex dressed the

burn on my face, but the anesthetic is wearing off, and the skin beneath it throbs.

"What do you see in that guy?" Nik whispers to me as we wait for Alex to reach the top.

"Except for the fact that he's good-looking and reliable, and he's never stolen meds from me?" I say. "It was a stupid thing to do, telling him to press the release on his cord. And you could've sent him down onto a platform too."

"Whatever you say, doc."

What does May see in Nik? He's irritating. And from the short time I've spent with him, he seems relentlessly childish. And cocky. After tonight, if I never see him again, it'll be too soon.

Nik watches Alex disappear into the hull. His smile broadens into a grin. "Funny though, the way he screamed."

"You're an idiot," I say.

"And you're up." He steadies the rope, so I can climb.

With the knots, it's not too difficult. The rope bites into my skin, and by the time I pull myself over the top, I'm out of breath and sweating.

Nik climbs up after me.

We're inside the ship, standing in some sort of unlit corridor. And we're not alone. A group of Neaths stare at us impassively, a collection of motley weapons in their hands. There's a constant *plink-plink* of water from the ceiling. The light from the Neaths' lanterns fizzles out after a couple of yards.

Piles of damp cardboard, trash and mounds of rags dot the ground, cringing against the walls. Some of them move sleepily. Poverty comes as standard in this neighborhood. Faces with sunken eyes peer out of doorways. The hairs on my neck prickle with the horror of being seen.

"Nice neighborhood," Alex whispers. I squeeze his hand, the unmistakable sign for *this will be fine*. He's always been there for me. I should never have shut him out.

"Hands where I can see them, please and thank you," one of the Neaths says.

I put my hands up. Alex and I are in this together now, and I'm going to keep him close. The realization that I should have trusted him from the start makes my stomach churn like the wake of a boat. Facing this together is infinitely better than facing it alone. It's not just friendship. Not just love. It's solidarity too. It's having someone there when things get scary.

One of the men is chewing something brown that coats the corners of his mouth in sludge.

"What now?" I say to Nik.

He clears his throat. "We're here to deliver a package."

"Arrangement was for one visitor, and this wasn't the route that was agreed on."

"The plan changed. Our original agent had a tail. We had to switch her out."

"Fine. Just her then."

Somewhere out of sight, a door creaks on its hinges and bangs. Anxiety ripples through me. "I'm not going with them," I whisper. "Not alone."

"Haven't got all day," one of the men says.

Nik turns his back and lowers his voice so that Silas's men can't hear. "You'll be fine. Keep your head down. Don't talk if you can help it. It's a five-minute job, and then you'll be done."

"Why's it so important?" Alex asks.

Nik looks at Alex like he'd happily shove him from the top deck. "Wasn't about to let Enid kill you, but that doesn't mean I trust you with all my secrets."

"I don't think I can do this." My gut is shuddering in that horrible pre-stomach-flu way. I bend and rest my hands on my knees.

"May has faith that you can get that thing where it needs to go. She wouldn't have given the device to you if she didn't. In and out, OK?" he whispers.

May thinks I can do it.

I can do it.

I pull my hood up and arrange my scarf so that it covers everything except my eyes.

"I'm going with her," Alex announces.

"Nope," one of the Neaths says.

"It's OK," I say to Alex, and it's a hundred percent wishful thinking.

What if they're taking me to Silas? What if they cut out the worm and kill me?

As I follow Silas's henchman, the others take up position behind me. We climb through a warren of narrow corridors and tiny gaps until we reach a door. The chewing man pushes it open, then steps aside to let me through.

"Alone?" I say.

"Evidently," he replies.

I take a full breath of stagnant air and go in. Looks like this used to be a kitchen. There's something clinical about it, even though it's obviously been unused for years. Flat white-tiled walls. Stainless-steel cabinets. Hooks in rows where the utensils once hung. There are strip lights, and it's harsh and too bright after the grimy light outside. They flicker and ping.

At the far end of the long room is a tall figure. Broad, with stooped shoulders. I walk between the steel cabinets. As I get closer, the man turns to look at me, searching my face. Scoops of loose skin under his eyes. And then he marches straight past me and heads for the door. He's leaving. And so is my chance of getting this thing out of my arm.

"Wait!" I shout.

"I was expecting May," he calls over his shoulder.

"The worm's still in my arm. Get it out!"

He ignores me. Before I know it, he's stepping through the open door.

"Get it out!" I scream. I chase after him. I clamp a hand on to his arm. "Get it out!"

He turns on me, a cloud of hostility radiating from him.

"Get it out, or I'll scream blue murder! I'll bring every Coaly on this side of the ship down here. And don't think I won't tell them everything. Starting with a description of you."

"Stop it! Shut your face!" he says with a growl.

He has hold of me, and he mashes his hand over my mouth to stop me shouting while shoving me away. I spin back to face him, and the turmoil that has been growing inside me, the loss of hope, the anger, the fear of losing everything I love, threatens to roar out. I don't feel like myself anymore. I feel fierce.

He grasps my elbow, digging his fingers in so cruelly I think my arm might snap. With his free hand, he presses—hard—round the scar, feeling for where the worm lies. It happens so fast. The hook gleams, a slice of pain—I don't cry out, I refuse to—a twist, and he eases the worm out of my flesh. He produces a glass vial from an inside pocket and drops the device in, screwing the lid on.

The hole in my arm oozes blood. There's no wiping it away, no sutures, no dressing.

"Tell them we'll be ready," he says.

And then I'm standing in the flickering light, bleeding, and trying not to cry.

CHAPTER 42

NIK

Your girl's still breathing.

Never felt relief like it. Now she's lying on a cot across from me with her arm wrapped around her sister and her eyes wide open, staring at me.

Beside me, Alex lets out a ripping snore, like a drone with a bad engine. I give his shin a kick and twist the blanket over me so that he's uncovered. Enid wasn't kidding when she said me and Alex had to sleep together, and she didn't mask her glee when she showed us the cot and handed us a single blanket. The mattress dips in the center, and I've spent the past three hours trying not to spoon with him.

I haven't slept. Couldn't face closing my eyes. I'm never leaving her again.

She climbs out of bed, putting a finger to her lips so I don't speak and rearranging the blanket over Esther. She grabs my hand and leads me away.

We're in a huge open-plan barge that Enid uses as an HQ, a meeting place, whatever else she needs. But every inch of the floor has someone sleeping on it—balled-up clothes for pillows—so there's nowhere to hide. No privacy. We stand against the nearest wall, staying as quiet as we can, so we don't wake people. All I want is to talk to her without a hundred-person audience.

May smiles. She's still holding my hand. "Hello, stranger," she whispers. And she lifts my hand and kisses my knuckles, and I wonder if it's possible for someone to die from their heart beating too fast.

I run my fingertips over her stubbly head. Knew they'd shave it when she got to the military base. Didn't know if I'd mind. I don't. As soon as I touch her head, she blushes and drops her eyes.

"Not looking my best," she says. We're standing so close I can feel the heat of her skin.

"Not gonna lie, it's a ballsy look."

"Shut up," she says, smiling.

She hits me and pushes me away, and then we're standing eye to eye again. Somehow, my hand's holding her cheek. She turns toward it.

"You should have told me how you felt sooner," she whispers. Her breath's hot on the palm of my hand.

"Yeah. Hindsight."

"One of these days, you're going to have to kiss me, Nikhil Lall."

At the front end of the barge, a door opens and closes. We both turn to look. There's a flicker of light as someone starts a fire under a massive pot in the open galley. Oily paraffin taints the air. The barge rocks on the waves.

The spell's broken. The moment's gone. We're back in the real world of danger and Coalies and a barge full of people. I clear my throat.

"So, what happened out there?" I say.

May looks around, then leans in again to whisper, resting her forehead on mine. "Everything went fine to begin with. My class was assigned bunks at the base as planned. Soon as I could, I got into the data archive and retrieved the drone codes. Trouble started when I came back onboard. Hadley's tightened security. It was like he knew something was going down. Patrols everywhere. Think they spotted me as soon as I got on the ship. Your mother sent someone to distract the Coalies, and I managed to get away, but my gut told me I was being followed. Is it possible they know what we're planning?"

I shake my head. "Don't think so. It all feels too general. He's messing with everyone onboard. Nothing points directly to us."

May's thinking. I can see her following strand after strand. Trying to figure out if Hadley knows anything concrete about us and our plans.

"How well do you know this guy?" I say, tilting my head at Alex, still dead to the world.

"I know he'd do anything for Esther."

"That's what I'm worried about. What will he burn to get what he wants?" I say.

She lets out a long breath while she thinks about it. "He's Alex. He's the kid that brings her apples and falls asleep studying on our sofa."

"Listen, we need to make sure he doesn't give Enid anything to worry about. She's already itching to kill him, and I don't want to be responsible for him going for a long swim."

"Didn't realize you cared," says May.

Esther rolls over and rubs her nose with the blanket.

"We'll figure the rest out later," May says under her breath. That's my cue to keep quiet in front of her kid sister.

"What happened?" Esther says groggily.

"What happened is you fell asleep as soon as you sat down," May says, smiling over at her.

Esther sits bolt upright. "Oh no. Mom and Dad are going to hit the roof."

"Don't worry. Enid had one of her people take your comglove aboard to send them a message from it. They think you were at the infirmary all night, caring for the people hurt in the market blast."

Esther stares at her naked hand, then touches the big white dressing on the side of her face. She looks like she might vomit.

"Does it hurt?" May asks.

"Not anymore. The dressing has anesthetic in it. It should be almost healed by now."

"Let me see." May peels the dressing off Esther's face. The skin underneath is baby-pink against the warm tan of her face. Completely undamaged.

"Is there a scar?" Esther asks May, turning her head left and right.

"No. You're good."

"We've got more pressing things to worry about than whether the doc here still looks pretty," Enid says, picking her way over sleeping bodies toward us.

She's carrying a jug and a handful of mugs. Coffee. Smells

so good. She plonks the stuff down on the floor between the cots and flings Esther's comglove at her. "Just had a word with her above."

My heart sinks. My mother. I grab a mug and fill it with coffee. Whatever my mother has to say will be easier to bear with some caffeine in my system.

"Who's *her above*?" Esther asks, still drowsy.

Enid ignores the question. Apparently, kicking Silas in the face is only going to get Esther so friendly with Enid. She tosses May an earpiece.

May looks at it for a second before pushing it into place.

Esther sips coffee.

"You OK?" I say.

"Why is everyone down here?" she asks Enid, ignoring me without a glance. She can't still be pissed about me letting Alex drop into the sea.

"Your girl asks a lot of questions," Enid says to me.

Your girl. Wish she'd stop with the not-so-subtle hints that I like Esther. Esther is May's sister. That's the only reason I'm bothered about what happens to her.

"I just mean, after what happened in the market, it's a lot of people to have in one place."

Enid watches Esther, the corners of her mouth twitching. "Because the second we stop living and start cowering, they've beaten us. I figure people needed to cut loose yesterday."

Apparently, last night they wanted a party. I get it. If you don't blow off steam, sometimes you explode.

Enid gathers her people in the barge whenever there's trouble brewing. And now there is. Never seen anything like it: the bombing; the massacre. Knew the Coalies were brutal, but they usually try to hide it better. And Coalies died too. It's like we're already at war. The *Arcadia*'s days are numbered, that's for sure. Question is: will the story end the way we want it to?

When she pulls the earpiece from her ear, May's face is blank and ashen. I know that look. Half apprehension, half determination. Nobody but me would be able to decode it. She notices me watching and pulls a faux smile on to her face.

"What is it?" Esther says.

That sparks a twinge of jealousy. Obviously, Esther can read her too. They're sisters. But I never really thought about them being close until now. Don't really like someone else having a claim on May. And that's an ugly green monster I didn't know was in me.

"I've got a new mission," May says.

CHAPTER 43

ESTHER

We sit down at a long table, each nursing a bowl of something Enid calls *scran* that seems to be some kind of spiced porridge. It tastes good, but it sits in my gut like concrete. I'm waiting for May to tell me the whole truth and exactly how much danger she's in.

Alex takes a seat next to me. He looks different out of his uniform. Good different. More relaxed. Hair unkempt, his replacement clothes too big, one fingerless glove wrapped around a mug.

I rest my head on his shoulder.

"How'd you sleep?" he asks.

"Not well. You?"

"Nik snores like a train," he says.

"Heard that," Nik says. "And you're not exactly Sleeping Beauty."

He and May are on the opposite side of the table, and I'm pretty sure they're holding hands out of sight. Between us are the remains of breakfast. Piles of toast on brightly patterned mismatched plates. A ceramic coffee pot painted with bright orange flowers.

Alex has dark circles under his eyes, and it's no wonder. Feels like we haven't paused for breath in twenty-four hours. He rubs his eye and takes a spoonful of porridge.

Last night, we slept in this wide barge. The ceiling hangs so low I can skim it with my fingers, and Alex has to duck where it curves lower at the edges. It's all wooden panels—floor, walls, ceiling. The table we're sitting at is attached to the floor. There are windows down both sides with net curtains that filter the sunlight. And it's warm. Not just because there are fires crackling in the pot-bellied stoves, but because it's stacked to the rafters with people. I don't want to be rude, but the odor of hundreds of people sleeping in a warm barge is pungent.

"I want to know everything," I say to May. "Let's start with how long you've been doing this."

She takes a breath. "About three years."

I let my spoon clink into the bowl of porridge. "You've been keeping this from me for three years?"

She has the decency to look shame-faced, a blush of color rising along her cheekbones.

"Who's the rebellion? What do they want?" I say.

"It started as a group of people trying to get more food. They put pressure on the Federated States to let more of us leave. But then the clearances started."

"What clearances?" Alex says.

"All of the ships north of here are gone," May replies.

"Ridiculous. We'd have heard. We'd have been told," Alex says. "There'd have been an announcement. What happened to the passengers?"

"Most of them are being used as free labor in prison camps," Nik says. "But they've started deporting people too."

"Deporting them where?"

"Europe."

Alex snorts. "There's nothing in Europe. It never recovered from the Sickness Wars."

"Don't think they really care about that," Nik says. He holds Alex's gaze. "As for what we want, that's easy. We want freedom. For everybody. We want an end to quarantine. And we're going to start with the *Arcadia*."

Alex pushes his bowl away. "Admirable as that may be, where do you come into this?" he asks May.

"My mission was to retrieve information from inside a Federated States military installation."

"A mission that you had Esther complete for you?"

"If there had been any other way—"

"There was another way," I say. "You could have come to me at the start and told me they were trying to recruit you. You've had years to talk, to be honest. Instead, you lied."

May looks away, biting her lip while tears gather in her eyes.

"Esther, I don't think it's helpful to point fingers." Alex says. "Let's be thankful for the fact that we all survived the past twenty-four hours and figure out where we go from here."

May gives Alex a smile of gratitude. Even Nik seems to ratchet down his dislike of him.

"Did he force you to join?" I say. "I know you've always felt uneasy about us being in government training programs, but—"

"No, he didn't force me," May says. "I chose this. I volunteered."

"Can you unvolunteer?" The need to cry is building behind my eyes again.

May fidgets with the handle of her mug. "Even if I could," she whispers, "I would never give up on the rebellion. It's too important."

"I thought I was important too. You should have told me, May. You should have trusted me enough."

We're all silent. The others seem to edge away from us. Nik looks resolutely into his cup.

"I wish I had. You should have told me about Silas."

I nod. "I was angry at you for pushing me away. Still am."

"Yeah. I'm angry at you too." She takes my hand across the table. "But I'm so proud of the things you've done. Always knew you were fierce deep down." She laughs.

"Don't know about fierce. Thought I was going to pass out when you put that thing in my arm."

May smiles and rubs my forearm where just a few hours ago a metal worm carrying a secret was buried.

"What happens now?" I say.

She takes a deep breath. "I have another mission. The guy that was supposed to be bringing the—" She stops, struggling to find a word that won't give away her meaning to anyone who doesn't already understand.

"Pastrami?" Nik says.

May laughs. "Yeah, the guy that was willing to fetch us the

pastrami has lost his nerve." She raises her eyebrows to make sure I'm following her. "Says it's too dangerous to bring it in on the sewage tanker, since the Coalies have started checking every shipment."

On board the *Arcadia*, you flush the toilet, but there's nowhere for all the human waste to go. So, once a month, the sewage tanker pumps out the waste of the thousands of people that live here. The ferry comes in empty, leaves full.

"And you've been sent out to get it?" I say. "You barely got back safely yesterday."

"Yesterday was bad luck. Felt like the Coalies spotted me when I came through the service hatch. I couldn't risk the information I was carrying, so I had to run—"

"And you passed it to Esther," Alex says. "What information can be so important you're willing to risk your sister's life for it?"

May opens her mouth to answer, then thinks better of it.

"That's need-to-know," Nik says. "And you don't need to."

"Are they looking for you here? Do they know you're on board?"

"No. My comglove's on a truck heading for the border wall. It'll take them a while to find it."

Nik stands up. He scratches his head with both hands, then paces away from the table and back. "I don't like it," he says. "If nothing can come in or out on the ferries anymore, you'll have to use a motorboat. That means sneaking past the drones as well as anyone who happens to be looking out at the sea. It's too risky."

"What's the alternative?" Alex asks.

"May can tell my mother to shove her mission."

"What's his mother's part in all of this?" I ask.

"She's my handler," May says with resentment. "She gives the orders."

Nik scratches the back of his neck. "There's no other way."

That makes my decision for me. "I'm going with you," I say.

I don't even need to think about it anymore. Two days ago, I would have run a mile from this whole situation, but now there's no doubt in my mind: I'm not letting her go alone. Even the seasoned rebels seem to think it's too risky. They all turn to look at me in surprise.

"It's too dangerous," May says, shaking her head. Her eyebrows are wrinkles with worry.

"Well, that makes three," Nik says.

"You're not coming," May tells him. "Neither of you are coming. We won't all fit on a motorboat anyway."

"We'll just have to get friendly then. Anyway, I know the coastline better than you. I know where it's best to get through the net. I know where the safe houses are," Nik says.

May scoffs. "Not going to need a safe house," she says.

"You don't know that. Honestly, this cockiness is going to land you in trouble."

"My cockiness? That's rich coming from you, Nik Lall. I can't be watching out for you two all the time."

"What if something goes wrong? Do you even know how to transport that stuff? Do you know how to deal with it if the casing gets broken? Will you know whether it's even the right pastrami?"

May's silent. Her face is all scrunched up, and I can tell she's starting to lose it.

"What time are we leaving?" I say.

"*I'm* going tomorrow, before it gets light."

"A medic might come in handy. Anyway, unless you're willing to tie me up, there's no way in hell you're leaving the ship again without me."

"Two medics," Alex says.

Now it's my turn to look shocked.

"Two medics. If Esther's going, I am too."

"It's dangerous," Nik says. "And there'll be no returning to your training program afterwards. All your Federated States bridges will be burned."

"Never liked the uniform anyway," Alex replies.

"All right, we're a team of four," Nik says, and he looks like he might actually be glad Alex has volunteered.

May opens and closes her mouth, trying to come up with the angle that will stop us from joining her on the mission. She finds nothing and snaps her mouth shut, folding her arms in resignation.

"Alex, you don't have to do this. Not for me," I say.

He shrugs. "The only thing that feels right is us being together. We're more important than anything else. So that's what we'll do."

I feel like my heart's ready to explode. I throw my arms around his neck and squeeze until he laughs and unpeels my grip.

"All right, take it easy. I was blown up yesterday, remember?"

But he scoops me onto his knee and then reaches around to grab his coffee. I smile so hard my cheeks ache.

"Ugh. And that's my cue to go and get things ready," Nik says.

"I'll come with." May stands up from the table. "You sure about this? There'll be no turning back. If you take on a mission, you're part of the rebellion. An enemy of the Federated States."

"I've seen what the Federated States do to innocent people. I'll never stand with them again."

May raps her knuckles on the table. "Get some rest. It's going to be a long night." She jogs off after Nik.

I take a piece of toast and nibble the corner. Alex roots in his pocket and comes out with a flat, circular piece of fabric. He slides it under the cuff of my comglove. It's so smooth I can barely tell it's there.

"What's that?"

"It's a tracker," he says easily, like it's the most mundane thing in the world.

"A tracker for ...?"

"So that I always know where you are. So I can come and find you if you need me. OK?"

"OK." I take another bite of toast. "By the way, I should check your eyes. Since the explosion, you've been taking an extra second or two to focus on things. Might be a damaged retina."

"I'm fine," he says, and he rubs his eye with one finger. As he does, he dislodges two tiny scabs from the corners. Blood oozes from them.

"It won't take a second," I say.

"I'm OK. Really."

"You're really not. I want to check your eyes, and we'll do a full concussion check at the same time. I'll get my bag."

"Fine. You're the boss," he says. But as I go to stand up he grabs me around the waist, pulling me back down. He grins.

Smiling, I give in. I let my arms rest on his shoulders. Let my fingers play with the short hair on the back of his head.

I forget about getting my med bag. I forget about Coalies and clearances. I forget about the danger that's coming.

I let him kiss me.

CHAPTER 44

ESTHER

I wake to Nik's frowning face. The barge is still and quiet, dim light coming from a lantern by the entrance. He shakes me by the shoulders.

"Where is he?" he says. His face is intense in the darkness.

May sits up next to me, already alert. We fell asleep on our single cot, sharing a thick woolen blanket. Unwilling to be too far apart.

"What's wrong?" May says.

"Your boy, Alex," Nik says, glaring into my eyes, pulling me toward him by the shoulders, so that all I can think about is putting distance between us.

"Did something happen? Did Enid hurt him?" I say. My insides crumple with dread, my mind racing. He's gone. Dead. I've lost him.

"One of Enid's guys saw him slip back onto the ship. We've been searching for hours. He's on the run. We have to leave. Right now."

CHAPTER 45

NIK

We march down the walkway that juts out into the ocean. Saltwater on both sides. The horizon's lost in the fog, and I can only just make out the dark shape of the *Arcadia* looming behind us. Esther's face is washed out. Grayish, like the mist.

"Why do we have to go now?" she asks for like the fiftieth time since I woke her and May up. Her green medical uniform has been replaced by land clothes: jeans, T-shirt, sneakers, jacket.

"Hadley's drones switch every three hours. The ones that have been out are recalled and new ones are deployed. It's not much, but it means there's a window of fifteen or so minutes where they're more interested in their logistics than watching us," I say.

"But what's changed since this morning?"

May can take this one. She stops on the walkway and faces Esther. "If Alex has gone over to them, we can't risk waiting. If we get arrested before the rebellion's ready, or they start the clearance early, the whole plan will go out the window."

"Gone over to them? He hasn't gone over to them. Can't I just send him a com message? Can't I just—"

"No. There's no comglove signal down here anyway. And if he is working with them, he might tip them off." May's tone is harsh. I see Esther's face drop.

"You can't be serious. It's Alex we're talking about. Alex, who I've known since I was twelve. Yesterday, he offered to go with you—"

"Then we've got nothing to worry about. We'll go ashore. You can see him as soon as we get back," May says.

"We've only been down here a day. What could he possibly tell Hadley?"

Don't have time for this. Enid's super pissed off that I lost track of Alex. If he's told the Coalies we're leaving, they could be on their way. Right now. Panic runs over me like something with long legs. I want to get out of here. Fast.

"One, he knows our plan—he could tell them we're leaving. Two, he's seen me and May and Enid and any number of other people. Hell, he could have spent the night making a nice neat rebel shopping list for Hadley. He could turn every one of us in. It's exactly why Enid told me to watch him."

Our feet sound hollow on the wet wood. We're at the straggling end of the flotilla, miles from the main ship and the jungle of boats and barges that make up Enid's territory. A long way from any decent hiding place. This fog's a stroke of luck when it comes to staying hidden from drones—the mist seems to mess with them—but it's doing nothing to keep me calm. Spooked is an understatement.

May spots the boat we're supposed to use hidden under a tarp. She jogs down to it and hauls off the faded green canvas. It'll be a squeeze: the boat's tiny, only just big enough for the three of us to stand up in. The cabin's basically a cupboard with a control panel and a steering wheel. I note the pair of oars stowed along the side, just in case, and I can tell from the coat of fresh white paint that it's a recent addition to the flotilla. It was stolen by one of our contacts and stashed here ready for the mission. Probably belonged to some rich land family who won't notice it's gone until their next trip to the beach.

The top's covered with thin reflective sheeting—another tweak for our mission. It'll mask our body heat and hide us from the drones—we'll look as cold as the air around us, pretty much invisible. Just the way I like it.

Esther's still looking back at the ship. This must be killing her. I get it. Don't know what I'd do if I thought May was an informant. But May wouldn't. Not ever.

My fingers fumble with the mooring rope. We're so exposed it makes my palms clammy, and my skin itches where the rope snags me. Wouldn't see someone coming down that walkway until they were close. Too close to escape. We'll hear them before we see them though.

May steps aboard, and the boat rocks. She glows the way she always does when we're about to start a mission. Her cropped head's hidden under a brand-new beanie, and the dark hoodie she's wearing makes her eyes pop. She looks good in land clothes. Comfortable.

I squeeze past her and go inside the cabin to start prepping the engine. The door clicks closed behind me, and the girls' voices are muffled through the window. Esther's still hesitating. *Come on, doc. We've gotta go.*

"All right?" I ask when May comes inside.

"She'll be OK."

"We need to leave."

"Give her a second. She's never been off the ship before, remember?"

"I know. I remember what it's like the first time. The anxiety. It's just …"

"You're nervous."

"I've got a bad feeling. I bet Dimples is talking to the Coalies right now. Can't think of any other reason he'd do a vanishing act."

"Could be a thousand reasons," May says.

"Could be cause he couldn't get a comglove signal on the flotilla, and he needed to get some info to Hadley fast."

May rubs the patch of skin between her eyebrows. "I know."

"Should never have brought him down to Enid's."

"You didn't have a choice."

"Could've left him."

"You wouldn't have though." She inches closer and takes my hand. For the first time ever, she kisses me. "It's part of the reason I like you."

I breathe out, trying to think straight. "It's nearly six. Go and get your sister," I say croakily.

The boat bobs again as May climbs back out.

It's 17:55. No drone sounds. No footfall in the fog. I start the engine. The low-pitched growl drowns out the girls' voices from the walkway.

From here, I've got a view of their feet. Two pairs of sneakers like the land people wear; not boots, they'd be too conspicuous. The feet face each other. Esther's take a few steps away from the boat, back toward the ship. They stop, turn back. As if she and May are talking. Then they start running away from the boat.

You've got to be kidding me! We don't have time for this!

I poke my head out of the doorway in time to see Esther dashing back toward the *Arcadia*, May on her heels. I push open the door of the cabin, use the rope to haul myself up. We were almost away. So close.

"What's happening?" I call to May. Don't need an answer because down the walkway, fog pooling around his ankles, is Alex. Dread grips me like an icy hand. We've been betrayed. By the guy I brought down here. The guy I almost trusted.

Esther reaches him. She tries to put her arms around his neck, but he grabs her by the shoulders. Looks painful, and I swear I hear her yelp. May steps forward.

I don't want to be right. I don't want Dimples to be an informant, but I know right now, for sure and a hundred percent, that he's sold us out. What he's getting in exchange, I don't know. Doesn't matter. We've got to get out of here, or we'll spend the rest of what will be our short and miserable lives under arrest.

"Let's go!" I yell.

"Not without my sister! Esther, come back!" May shouts.

Her voice is high-pitched and strained with desperation. She can feel, just like me, that this thing is done. The threads of our plan are unraveling faster by the second. Alex is the bad guy.

Come on, doc. Let's go.

The boat's engine is still running at a gentle purr over the whoosh of the sea. It was half untied, ready to go, so the back end starts to drift out. I kneel to haul it back in, and the sound I've been dreading comes through the fog. Heard it a thousand times in real life, and a thousand more in my nightmares. A drone.

"Esther, there's no time!" May calls again.

There's a drone somewhere in the fog. May hears it too, and her eyes roll upward, scanning the blank gray. If we can't see it, it can't see us. But it's coming.

"Esther!" she calls. Esther runs, shouting, but her words are lost in the darkness. Now, Alex has hold of her. She's trying to get away, but he's dragging her back toward the ship.

The hum of the drone gets louder. Any second now, it'll break through the mist. It'll see us. It'll kill us. There'll be no hiding this time. No zip-cording to safety. We could swim, but where to?

And now it's joined by the rhythmic stomp of boots and a faint vibration underfoot. Coalies materialize out of the fog. Black-uniformed. Visors dull and unreflective in the grayness.

We're out of time.

CHAPTER 46

ESTHER

Alex stands at the far end of the walkway. I'm torn between them: May and Alex. The thought of leaving him is unbearable. I can't just walk away.

May calls from behind as I start down the walkway, "Esther, there's no time!"

"I need to speak to him before we go," I say, half turning in my weird rubber-soled sneakers. "Wait for me. I'll be back."

"Dammit, Esther, get in the boat!" May shouts.

All I want is a second, to feel the familiarity of him, to tell him we'll be back. That everything will be OK. I know he has an explanation for where he's been.

When I get close, he grabs me by the shoulders. I reel from the force of his grip. He holds me at arm's length. Before I have chance to speak, he whispers, "Come with me—*now*."

"We have to go. We only have a few min—"

"You're not going anywhere. It's over. I've fixed it."

The sound of a drone engine and then footsteps. The hair on the back of my neck prickles. Alex stares at me, jaw clenched, eyebrows furrowed. Years of friendship and familiarity are built into his face. But there's something I don't recognize. A slick of color that dances on the surface of his eye. A hairline crack that flashes over the center of his pupil.

Everything stops.

"Your eye. Are you wearing a lens?"

He waves a hand over his face, then returns it to my shoulder. "It got cracked in the market. The explosion." Matter-of-fact. Like he dropped a cup or chipped his digiscreen.

My insides scrunch as realization creeps over me. "I have to go," I say, drawing away. I feel like spiders are crawling all over me.

"I made a deal to save us." His voice is stern, and as he pulls me closer he wraps one arm around my waist and twists my hand behind my back.

My confusion is so intense that I let him do it, and we take a few indecisive steps toward the ship. I can't make a sound. My mouth moves wordlessly.

From the corner of my eye, I see May further down the walkway. She seems so small, so exposed. Halfway between me and the safety of the getaway boat. "Esther!" she shouts.

"I did it for us," Alex whispers. "I couldn't watch you throw everything away."

"What have you done?"

"We'll be safe."

"And May? Will she be safe too?"

He grinds his teeth. "I couldn't ask for the world."

"What will they do to her?"

"I'm sorry," he says. "We have to get back on the ship."

His lips brush my hair. The smell of him, once so comforting, sparks a wave of revulsion. I don't need to see the Coalies to know they're coming. I don't need the details of what he promised them.

"You betrayed us," I whisper.

"Not you. Never you," he says, his voice drenched with pain.

"Come with us," I say breathlessly.

He stops, still holding me too tight, too rough. I can see the fight raging inside him, desperation tearing him apart.

"We can go together. We can escape together." I shake his grip off and take both his hands in mine. I still want him to run with me. We can still fix this; it's not too late.

His eyes bore into me. He shakes his head. "We wouldn't stand a chance with the Coalies after us. This way, they'll leave us alone. We can be free."

"She's my sister," I say. Tears run down my face. "Don't make me choose between you."

"I'd never make you choose. That's why I had to make the decision for you. Please. They're coming. We can survive this, but you've got to do what I tell you."

The humming grows louder; there's more than one drone up there. Alex's grip on me tightens.

"May!" I shout. I kick Alex in the shin and pull myself free.

May's face is a mask, her mouth opens in a horrible black circle. "Down!" she screams.

I plunge to the ground, flattening myself, as bullets scream over my head. I press my hands to my ears. Eyes on May.

Red mist swirls around her head. Her body jerks, folding forward like a piece of card. She collapses on the walkway, one hand reaching for me.

There's a terrible noise. A howl of pain. It came from Nik.

I scramble toward May, ignoring the bullets that fly around me. A thick red pool spreads beneath her, dripping between the planks. The beanie she's wearing has a dark, frayed hole in it. Her eyes stare. For a second, the thought hovers that she's lying down to shield herself from the gunfire. With all that training, she knows what to do under attack.

Nik's at my side. He pulls May up by the collar, burying his face in her neck. More bullets fly. Neither of us try to take cover. All I can think of is May.

Nik lays her on the ground. A red streak cuts across his cheek. Tears smudge it, trailing blood down his face. Then his hands are pulling me away from May.

I move, but my feet don't make contact with the walkway.

I don't feel the sway of the boat as we fall aboard.

I don't feel the pain as he pushes me to the floor, my hands and knees crunching into broken glass from shot-out windows.

I don't feel anything.

CHAPTER 47

ESTHER

Nik's face is crooked with anguish as he maneuvers the boat, pushing the engine to a scream.

"Turn us back," I croak.

We bounce so quickly that the *Arcadia* and the flotilla disappear behind us within minutes. The drones must have a range limit that keeps them tethered to the ship because they stop racing after us and turn back.

We travel northwards, keeping the land on our left. Gradually, Nik brings us closer and closer to shore, staying in the rolling waves behind the surf break. We're so close to land it feels like I could almost wade ashore. We slow. I look through the fog to where I imagine the *Arcadia* must be.

"We have to go back," I say.

"What for?" His face is like stone. Dark hair falling over his eyes. Neither anger nor pain breaking through.

"For her." My voice is a whisper.

"She's dead," he says. His voice is flat, the words meaningless.

"But May—"

"We complete the mission."

A high net rises out of the water, its crisscrossed wires slicing through the ocean. Another barrier around the ship that I didn't even know existed. Another way to keep us in. Beyond it, still agonizingly out of reach, is the land.

Nik aims us at the net. He cuts the engine and lets us drift until we bump against it. Unzipping the holdall, he produces a bot with spindly legs that end in nasty-looking metal clips.

Nik climbs out on to the tiny deck. The net is several yards high, and from what I can see it continues on down into the water. He holds the bot above his head, letting its legs touch the strands of wire. It attaches itself. There's a click as the first wire snaps, then the bot feels for the next strand down. Twenty empty seconds and the bot has worked its way down and disappeared into the water, leaving behind a gap big enough for us to steer the boat through.

Nik points us toward the hole in the net. As we bob through the escape route, there's a distant sound, an engine running underwater, getting louder. Nik's face snaps to mine in open-mouthed surprise. He leaves the steering wheel and leans over the edge of the boat, scanning the surface of the ocean.

The noise soars.

A sickening hump of water rises, spreading, moving faster through the fog. A flash of metal.

Nik wraps his body around mine. "Jump!" he shouts.

We leap. No target. Nothing to land on. Just away from the boat.
There's a muffled thud. Flying wood and the smell of oil.
I hit water as hard as bedrock.

CHAPTER 48

NIK

slam into the water. *Don't let it fill your lungs. Don't let it pull you down.* My vision darkens. Roiling sea thunders in my ears, blocking out the world.

She's dead. My May.

I'll stay where it's too dark to see, and too loud to hear, and so cold it stabs like needles, and where I don't even have to breathe. Until I can't feel anything.

My eyes drift open, the lids burning with salt.

It took seconds for the world to be snuffed out. She was there. She was gone.

I want to end. I'll stay here until I'm done. Because I can't exist if she doesn't.

They say it doesn't take long once you stop fighting.

I push the air from my chest to make it happen faster. Bubbles escape me and stream over my face.

May's in the water with me. Her eyes glow through the gloom; her hair swells around her head. And when she holds out her hand to me, I take it.

She pulls me along.

CHAPTER 49

ESTHER

Water presses in. Breath screams to get out.

Tumbling over and over with the waves that suck the strength from my muscles.

I've got no fight left.

I thump against something in the water. The waves whip it away. As it comes back, I make a grab for it, wrapping my deadened hands around it. There's fabric, a sleeve, then fingers. Nik. I hold tight, not knowing whether it's to help him or myself. All I know is that he feels solid, and I don't want to let go.

My foot glances against something firmer than water. A lightning flare of hope. Just in time, I realize my head is in the air, and I manage to gulp down a breath before the water drags me back again.

I lose the surface. I lose solid ground. I keep hold of the hand.

The water is rhythmic. It sucks, lifts, falls. With the next drop,

I touch the seabed again. We must be close to the shore or at least something that's not bottomless water.

Almost out of energy. Almost out of air. My head fills with specks of light. Every moment stretches to hours. Nothing exists but me and Nik and the never-ending, rolling blackness. I kick, searching for the surface. A final push, holding tight to Nik's hand.

Both feet hit something solid. I let the water carry me forward, and when it starts to pull me back, I force my feet against the ground, grinding in my toes as hard as I can.

The next wave carries us onto the beach. I collapse, feeling the whole weight of my body. One hand scrabbles to hold on to the shifting sand, the other twists around Nik's arm. I swallow massive gulps of air. My chest is a swamp of fire and salt. I vomit seawater on to the sand.

Nik lies on his back, his chest heaving like the waves.

I'm on dry land. A lifetime spent dreaming about this moment. There's solid ground beneath me. Not deck. Not water. Sand and bedrock. I could walk to the city. I could walk out of the Federated States. I could disappear, hold my own life in my hands. I'm finally free.

And my only wish is that the sea had taken me.

CHAPTER 50

HADLEY

He got the order.

Hadley picks up the bottle from its stand on the captain's desk. Inside is the miniature ocean liner. He sits down, inspecting the details of the model ship. The captain is on the other side of the broad wooden desk. There's no trace of anxiety in him. No beads of sweat or shortness of breath, despite being under surveillance for days. Despite the fact that his ship has been attacked.

The room smells the way everything on the *Arcadia* does given enough time: wet wood, wet paper, wet metal.

Hadley's heart purrs.

Thirty minutes ago, the admirals told him that the terrorist attack on the *Arcadia*'s market had pushed things his way. That they'd been persuaded of the urgent need to clear the ship before any political repercussions reached their privileged offices in the capital.

Hadley's chat with a journalist helped. Planted the idea that the violence could spread to the city if not nipped in the bud. The head-lines sang about the danger to citizens. The tabloid regurgitated the story of the fresh young deputy cut down in a cowardly terrorist attack. It was enough for resources to be diverted to the *Arcadia*. Helicopters full of extra officers.

Jackpot.

Janek looked like she was chewing glass through the whole conference call.

It's time to pull the trigger.

When they told him, Hadley held his nerve. If he went in guns blazing, he could mess it up. His appetite wouldn't be satisfied with a handful of criminals. He wants to bring them all to justice. Let the world see what happens to those that rise against the Federated States. The rebellion is a weed that's infiltrated the whole ship, and he wants the entire network. All the way down to the roots. That means biding his time.

He's closer than ever to tracing the tendrils of it. The gangs are involved somehow. The medics. The captain. He'll arrest them all soon enough, but he'd rather leave them in place for as long as possible. That way, it's less likely that any will escape. And it seems more satisfying, somehow, to take them all out in a single catastrophic attack.

The dead girl lying in the mortuary at HQ is young and pretty. Good teeth. But Hadley doesn't know yet how she's involved, and Alex Hudson ran off before they could interrogate him.

"What can I do for you, Commander?" the captain asks. His voice smooth. Authoritative. Showy, Hadley's always thought.

Showy traitor. He'll enjoy finishing him when the time comes. Might even do the deed himself.

"You're aware there was an explosion in the market yesterday?"

"Of course."

"There's evidence that it was part of a feud between the Neath gang leaders," Hadley lies seamlessly.

They stare each other out.

"What do you want, Hadley?" the captain says.

Hadley places the bottle back on the desk. The tiny ship stands on end.

Play this right. Don't alert him.

"Yesterday evening, we intercepted a group of rebels attempting to leave the *Arcadia.*"

"Indeed." The captain raises his eyebrows. "As we both know, from time to time, individual inhabitants of the ship attempt to circumvent the normal rules for entry into the Federated States. If you can provide me with some information about these escapees, I'll ask the council to look into it."

Escapees. Hadley suppresses a snort.

"*Criminals* is the correct term here, Captain. One of them was killed during our attempt to arrest them. At least one other left the *Arcadia* and is being tracked by our teams on land. We'll have them in custody within the hour."

Hadley watches the captain. And there's his reward. A tiny flicker. The draining of humor like a plug has been pulled. He knew they were leaving. He cares that one of them is dead.

Bingo.

He could arrest him now. Set up a kangaroo court. Have the

old man executed. But that would tip off whoever he's working with, and Hadley wants more. Hadley wants to see the whole organization burn. He wants to make sure they can't go through with whatever it is they're planning. He wants to find every last one of the sneaky, disloyal—

"I'm sure your team will have no trouble apprehending a couple of hungry refugees from the lower decks. Now, if that's all, Commander, I have a lot of work to do before this evening's sewage tanker shipment." The captain stands.

Hadley gives the old man one of his warmest smiles and takes the ship-in-a-bottle from the desk. He marches out of the office with it tucked under his arm.

Grimson is waiting for him outside on deck, her rifle resting over her stomach.

"Set up three more surveillance bots. Monitor all his communications. I want to know if he tries to warn anyone," Hadley says. "And keep following that tracking signal. I want to know where they're heading."

"Yes, sir. The kid, Alex Hudson, who told us about the escape? He tried to run, but we picked him up. What do you want me to do with him?"

Hadley looks at the bottle he took from the captain's desk. He tosses it over the railing, the glass glinting as the ship flips toward the sea.

"See what you can get out of him. Find out where they're going. Then he can be the first official execution of the clearance."

CHAPTER 51

NIK

A flash of blood. She crumples on to the walkway. Blood creeping, black and thick as tar, from a hole in her head.

I force my eyes closed and dig my fingers into the sand. The ground sways underneath me. Screams tear at my throat. Does nothing to dull the pain that's pulling me atom from atom.

The tug-push of the surf moves my feet in a sick rhythm. Can't move. If I move, I exist. And she'll be gone.

Beside me, Esther spews a bellyful of saltwater on to the sand. Pitiful sobs.

Something rises amid the agony: *hatred*. She got May killed. Her and her traitor of a boyfriend.

I'll lie here and wait for a government-issue bullet in the head. I'll welcome it. The memory of May holding on to me when I got shot, the way she wrapped her arms around me after I fell, keeps rising to the surface, threatening to bring other memories with it.

I can't lose you. Try not to get shot again, 'kay?

May wanted me to live.

She wanted her sister to live.

The world is gray on gray. Thick fog and churning sea, and I hate it all for existing. I want to pull it down. Smash it to pieces. Set fire to everything and watch until it's a pile of ash.

A snake of pain slithers up my arm. Blood mixed with salt water covers my hand, and a gash runs from the crease of my thumb across the center of my palm, edges ragged like torn paper. It opens wider when I press my fingers into it. The surge of discomfort masks the agony of loss for half a second. Anything is better than thinking about her.

Esther cowers on the beach, snot and tears running into the layer of sand on her face. She's pathetic—a jelly mess wallowing in self-pity. How can she be related to May? I resist the urge to kick her.

Dizziness makes me sway, as I lumber to my feet and blink at my comglove. A bright red arrow hovers in 3D at the center, pointing north. It shifts when I move. I twist around until I'm facing the right direction, two and a half inland. We'll be lucky to stay hidden for a fraction of that distance. It's getting light but the morning's still shrouded in fog. It might be a literal lifesaver though, if the Coalies are looking for us.

"Get up," I say to Esther.

She moans. Her sobbing has faded to a gentle whimper, shoulders quivering like an animal.

"Get up!" I shout, and she flinches.

I don't have time for this. May wanted her sister to live, so Esther's going to survive whether she likes it or not.

I pull her up. She stands slack, wet-nosed and sniffling.

Pathetic.

Pushing Esther in front of me, I start in the direction the arrow is pointing. Our feet leave deep scratches in the wet sand. If the Coalies pick up our trail, it'll be easy to follow us. Nothing I can do about that right now. Don't have time to cover our tracks.

A sand dunes rise above our heads and reaches into the distance without a break. No way to move inland without climbing over it. We scramble up the side, using dark green tufts of grass to pull ourselves up. I reach the top and look down. There's another stretch of undulating dunes and beyond them a ribbon of tarmac.

According to the map on my comglove, there should be a narrow river on the other side of that road, and if we follow it upstream, it'll bring us to the safe house. That's if the Coalies don't find us first.

Esther drops to her knees next to me. "Where are we going?" she asks, panting.

I want to tell her I hate her. Instead, I slide my way down the other side of the dune and start up the next hill of sand. By the time my feet make contact with the tarmac, I'm out of breath, and the chill of the sea has been replaced by cold sweat. Fog closes the road off in both directions, limiting visibility to a couple of hundred yards.

"Come on!" I call back to Esther, and she follows, dragging her feet.

Just like the map says, there's a river moving through the undergrowth beyond the road. Swollen from the rain and with a layer of twigs and leaves and plastic trash swimming along its surface.

Esther joins me on the bank and looks down at the water.

"It's garbage," she whispers.

"We'll walk along the road. It'll be easier than trying to get through the—" My heart skips a beat as the low growl of an engine vibrates in the distance. How did they find us already? And how did that thing, that torpedo, find us out in the water?

"It's them," Esther mutters, her breath puffing in gray clouds between blue-edged lips.

"No kidding. Get back into the dunes," I say. My eyes dart around, looking for a better hiding place. There's nothing.

"How did they find us so quickly?"

"You'd have to ask them. And you'll have the chance to if you don't move."

Esther's glued to the spot, staring down at her comglove. "If someone put a trace on a comglove, would it work all the way out here?" she says.

"What?"

"He knew we were leaving the ship, but no one told him where we'd be going from. There must be fifty places we could have launched that boat."

"So how did he pinpoint us?" I say.

She stares down at her comglove.

Tingling horror. I understand. The reason they managed to torpedo us out of the water. The reason they've found us now. Esther's got a tracker. I grab her by the wrist and yank the comglove from her hand.

"I'm sorry," she says. "I didn't think—"

"He's been tracking you the whole time."

"I'm so sorry—"

"Don't say sorry to me. May's the one you got killed by trusting him."

The engine sounds get louder. I skid down the riverbank and splash waist-deep into the stream. Can't tell how far away they are. Need to buy time.

I grab a plastic gallon bottle with a red lid and a picture of a cow on the label. The swamp of trash and vegetation flows past me, and the water's fast. Strong enough to push me off balance. It threatens to take me along with it. I wrap Esther's comglove around the bottle's handle and knot it, then I lob it as far downstream as I can. It makes a faint splash before being carried away by the flow of the water.

My sneakers slip against the muddy riverbank, as I try to haul myself up. Esther disappears over the top of the sand dune on the opposite side of the road, leaving a trail of deep impressions. Unmistakably the marks of someone climbing up. I'm about to make a run for it when the sound of engines breaks through the fog to the north. They're too close. I throw myself back down the bank and lie flat against the side, fingers digging into the mud to stop me from sliding.

The engines stop. I peek through a gap in the ivy, trying not to ruffle the leaves with my breathing.

Four, five, six Coalies on motorbikes. Two of them get off their bikes and flip their visors up. The others rest in their saddles, feet skimming the ground, hands revving the engines.

I hold my breath. They've stopped right where Esther climbed the dune. None of them have noticed the pockmarked path that would lead them straight to her.

The two Coalies talk to each other in a low murmur, their voices drowned out by the rushing water behind me and the bike engines. They're looking at their comgloves. One of them points downstream to where by now Esther's glove is rushing along and doing a good impersonation of someone running away.

My muscles ache from pressing myself up against the bank of the river. My saltwater-bruised throat burns from holding my breath. It feels like forever until the motorbike engines roar off, following the signal of Esther's tracker.

Opposite me, Esther's face pops up over the top of the dune. I haul myself up the riverbank, and we meet in the middle of the road, her showering sand, me dripping mud.

"Let's keep moving," I say.

"What's the point?" She shakes her head and flops down at the edge of the road, clasping her hands around her knees. "I've lost everything."

An explosion of anger and hatred. This girl does not get to feel sorry for herself. She doesn't get to wallow.

"*May* lost everything. While you were playing doctor and bowing to the Federated States, she was fighting for everyone on the ship! You used your privilege to make your own life better. She used hers to change other people's lives. Should be you with a bullet in your head!"

Esther's face crumples in pain, and I enjoy it. Let her suffer like I do. Twisting the knife feels good.

"You got her killed. You and your boyfriend. Why didn't you get back in the boat? She was calling you, and you just stood there." Anger flows easily, bubbling like lava.

She doesn't say anything. She sits there, dazed and mute.

"She's dead because of you!" I rail at her. "All May wanted was to keep you safe. She's dead because you were stupid. You told us he could be trusted, every time we asked you. But you never looked any closer, did you? You wanted so much to believe him. Now you're going to get on your feet, and you're going to walk to the safe house, and then we'll figure out where you go from there. May would be ashamed of you."

She winces at the final strike, but I feel no sympathy for her.

I march in the direction of the safe house. Behind me, I hear Esther get up and start following me.

I know what I have to do. Get Esther to the safe house. Get her away from the Coalies. Out of the country.

Esther will live.

Alex will die.

CHAPTER 52

ESTHER

Through the tree trunks and naked winter branches, I glimpse a house. It's surrounded by undergrowth and looks abandoned. No lights in the windows. No smoke from the chimney.

Everything on land is in shades of brown, and splashes of dark green. Some of the trees hang with acrid red berries that scream poison. Before we started walking through the trees, I expected forests to be still. But there's constant motion: birds chatter and swoop, living things rustle among the leaf litter. You can't get away from the sound of water, even here, but the stream's voice is delicate compared to the constant rumble of the waves. The air is saturated with an earthy smell that reminds me of the arboretum, just more. A heady soil and leaves and water concoction, all on the edge of decay.

We've been following the stream for hours, tripping over roots and hugging ourselves to keep warm. My clothes have stiffened as they dried. My toes are so numb I can barely feel the ground. Lines of pain throb wherever the sneakers rub against my flesh.

The Coalies blasted off on their motorcycles, leaving a cloud of gasoline fumes behind, following the tracker in my comglove. Nik yelled at me until his voice was cracked and hoarse, and I wanted to curl into a ball until it was over. Then he fell into the heavy silence that has enveloped us the whole way here.

"Stay there," Nik says without looking at me. His voice is out of place in the forest. Too loud and too human after so long without speaking.

He creaks up the steps to the porch, windswept leaves crunching beneath his feet.

I hunch my shoulders and hug myself, eyeing the thorny vegetation surrounding the house. I'm on edge. The ground feels strange—too solid. Everything is too unbounded. I miss the ship's railing and the security of knowing where the edges are.

Nik opens the screen door then waves his comglove close to the lock under the door handle. A red light flashes, and he disappears. "All clear," he says.

Inside smells of dust and cobwebs. The entrance hall opens on to a room on either side. Straight in front, a set of stairs leads up to another floor, the walls lined with framed photos. On my right, a kitchen with an enormous wooden table. To my left, a living room. A wicker sofa. A stone fireplace. A deer skull on the chimney breast.

Nik closes the door behind me. He taps a code on to a digiscreen set into the wall. It beeps in recognition and flashes to a series of surveillance images: the front door, the back of the house, the top of the driveway. Somewhere behind the house there's a big gray barn with an open front.

"There'll be supplies in the kitchen," Nik says, pushing past me toward the fireplace.

My stomach turns at the thought of food. "Not hungry."

He stops next to me, gritting his teeth and breathing through his nose, an expression of disgust burning on his face. "Keep out of my way."

He hates me. It's nothing more than I deserve.

I drop onto the sofa. Dust puffs into the air. I unlace my sneakers and find the source of the pain; these land shoes have cut deep, bloody grooves into my heels. My socks stick as I peel them away from the damaged flesh.

Nik works methodically, stacking split logs in to the fireplace and packing the gaps with straw. He sets the kindling alight by striking two glassy black stones together. Flames take hold of the dry wood. He feeds it, piling more and more onto the precarious triangle as it's consumed. I wonder if I'd feel my hand burn if I plunged it into the fire.

Nik's favoring his left hand; the right he keeps balled up and pressed against his diaphragm.

"Let me look at your hand," I say. My voice scratches out of my throat.

He's been ignoring the deep gash that still oozes blood and plasma. From the glimpses I've seen, it could use stitches. And I want to feel the monotony of work. I want to go through the motions. Right now, I'm numb. What happens when the feeling returns?

"Don't need anything from you."

An alarm sounds through the house, and my heart hammers so hard it feels like it will never stop.

Nik drops the piece of wood he's holding and rushes to the surveillance digiscreen by the front door. There's a gentle knock from outside, a pause, two more knocks.

He swings the door open. "Mit," he says, hugging the man that steps inside.

With unblemished black skin and a neat salt-and-pepper crew cut, nothing about him screams rebel, except for a long pink scar that runs front to back along his scalp.

They hold on to each other. When they break away, Nik's mouth is a twisted line. He's trying to control himself.

The man looks around then lets his eyes settle on me. "We were expecting May."

I push down a flare of emotion. *Not yet. I'm not ready to face it yet.*

A woman appears in the doorway, and after all the years spent watching her in the classroom, I'd recognize that neat black hair and those delicate freckles anywhere.

"Corp?" I say.

Confusion makes me sway. The things I knew are suddenly smoke. I'm trying to grab on to reality, but every time I think I've got hold of something real it moves and thins and disappears. I can't piece this all together. Is she here for me? Is it some cruel twist that they're sending her to arrest me?

"Esther?" she says. She searches my face. "What happened?"

"Esther's boyfriend ratted us out," Nik says.

Hearing it out loud leaves me breathless. The world flips upside down, and I'm hanging on by my fingernails, pieces of my life falling away. I fold in on myself. Corp grabs me by the elbows, holding me up.

"Alex did this? I can't believe it. He's a good kid. He'd wouldn't turn someone in to the Coalies. He knows how brutal they can be. He couldn't live with himself if someone got hurt because of him." She claps her hand over her mouth, eyes wide.

"I thought it was you," I say to her. "I thought you were the one who'd reported me."

"I wouldn't," Corp says. Her face flickers with pain. "I'd never." She holds on to me, and I feel myself starting to unravel.

"Last we heard, May was coming," Mit says. His voice weakens. I'm traveling away from it.

"Coalies jumped us while we were trying to get away," Nik says.

"Is there any chance this safe house has been compromised?" Corp says.

Nik shakes his head. "No. Alex knew we were leaving. He had no details of the mission."

"Have you had enemy contact since leaving the *Arcadia*?"

"We were hit by a torpedo coming through the net. A patrol almost caught us just after we made it to the beach."

Corp and Mit tense. A look I don't understand passes between them.

"Twice? You're being tracked," Corp says.

"I know. It was in Esther's comglove. I sent it down the river."

"There should be a scanner in the kitchen," Mit says. He leaves, and I hear him opening cupboards in there.

Corp's fingers tighten around the fleshy part of my arm. Her eyes search my face while she talks to Nik. "What happened to Cadet Crossland?"

Nik doesn't speak. From the corner of my eye, I see him sag against the wall. His face has aged by years.

Realization dawns on Corp's face. Her eyes fill with glassy tears, and she shakes her head in disbelief.

"I didn't want to believe he could do it," I whisper.

"Tell me, is there any chance May could give away the location of this safe house?"

"I don't understand," I say.

"She's asking if they could have taken her alive," says Nik.

Grief explodes through me, a searing white-hot core. I return Corp's grip. Remembering the horror of the hole in May's beanie. The blood running from her head.

"There was too much damage to the frontal lobe."

Corp flinches. She takes my face in her hands, wordlessly scanning my pupils for signs of cognitive damage, my head for concussion. She stays there when Mit comes back. "He needs to scan you," she says.

"Keep still," Mit says. He circles me, waving a cylinder, which whirs gently.

"Why are you here, Corp?" Nik asks.

"My cover's blown. We've got to assume that we're all burned. The captain included. For some reason, Hadley didn't arrest me straight away, so I called in a favor. Lucky for me, I'm friends with the guy who takes the bodies from the *Arcadia* for incineration at the central crematorium. He zipped me into a body bag until we got to shore."

Corp takes a breath like she's still trapped inside the bag and seems to wrestle to control herself. "There were a lot of bodies after what they did to us in the market."

"You've been part of the rebellion this whole time?" I ask.

"I had to hide in plain sight for five years."

"Five years of knowing they could find you?"

Corp nods, mouth pressed into a thin line.

"And there are more of you?"

"On every ship. And on land. All over the country."

"How?" I'm coming apart. How much of my life is real?

Corp guides me down on to the sofa so that my head rests on a cushion and pulls a blanket over me. It smells of mildew. She kneels on the floor next to me.

"But you're my teacher. You're an officer. You're one of *them*."

"Until today. But I was born on the *Oceania*. I grew up on the next ship along the coast from you, I followed a training program just like you, and then I went to med school in the Federated States. I was recruited before I left, just like May."

"And the captain? He's part of this?"

"He started it all, this whole rebellion. With Nik's parents. They were in contact with the other ships and with a network of allies on land."

"May should have told me. I might have been able to protect her," I whisper.

I press my face into a cushion and convulse, giving in to loss. Someone presses a pill between my lips, makes me drink water. I feel Corp lie down next to me, her hand slipping into mine. She pulls the blanket over us both. The pain in my chest swells, trying to find release. I'm wracked by sobs so painful it feels like they come from my soul.

My sister is gone.

CHAPTER 53

HADLEY

The kid's head sags, blood dripping from his lips. "Tell us what they were planning," Grimson says.

Hadley leans against the wall. In the moments between blows, the kid, Alex, stares out from under his ruffled hair.

"Is she alive? Is Esther alive?" the kid says, voice rattling through liquid.

Grimson gives him another backhanded slap, knocking his face sideways and almost tipping the chair over. He groans.

Hadley bends so that his face is next to the kid's. "I'll put a bullet in her head as soon as I get hold of her."

The kid blusters; the handcuffs holding him to the chair rattle. "Don't touch her! We had a deal!"

"Our deal was that you'd bring me information about the rebellion's plans. So far, all I've got is half a dozen people I already knew were criminals and a dead girl." Hadley straightens and turns to Grimson. "What's he said?"

"Not much, sir. A list of names—no more details of what they're up to. Seems he's grown a conscience. Just keeps asking if that girl's alive."

"And is she?"

"Last contact with the fugitives was five hours ago, sir."

"Five hours? You lost them."

Grimson's face tightens. She shifts her weight. Hadley enjoys seeing her squirm. "Yes, sir. We found a comglove. Tied to a bottle and floating downriver. I've ordered the team to keep searching."

"They could be miles away by now. Could be across the border even, if they had help. Wrap it up."

"Yes, sir," Grimson says. She hesitates. She looks unflinchingly at the damage she's done to the kid.

"What's your gut saying, Grimson?"

She frowns, gives a tiny shrug of her shoulders. "That it all feels bigger than a few criminals making a run for it, sir."

"Exactly."

Hadley steps in front of the kid. After half a day in custody, he's drenched in the pungent odor of a prisoner: stress-filled sweat, the bite of iron. The loose ends are nagging at Hadley. He can't figure out what the rebels' endgame is. Surely they're not just trying to smuggle people out? All of this—the gangs, the captain, the council, the medics—just to get a few of them off the ship before the clearance? Doesn't make sense.

"What's your girlfriend up to, eh?" Hadley turns back to Grimson. "Let me see that list of names."

Grimson hands him a clipboard. Bloody fingerprints at the corners of the sheet of paper. He scans the list, and when he reaches the middle of the page, a name stops him. He feels rage bubbling in his gut. A rage directed inwards. Lall. Nikhil Lall. That boy that he's known about for years. That boy the captain protected. That boy who Hadley only noticed when he wanted to rile the captain up. He's one of them. He was on the flotilla with Enid Hader's lot. And then he left with Esther Crossland.

Hadley's learned his lesson. He might have overlooked these kids before, but now he's going to bring down his full force on them.

"Do an automatic sweep of the area near where you found the comglove, quadrant by quadrant. And get the description of Nikhil Lall and Esther Crossland over to the border force in case they try to leave the country."

"Yes, sir."

"You're wasting your time," the kid says.

Hadley and Grimson turn to look at him.

"What was that?" Grimson says.

"They're bringing something back."

Now this is interesting. Maybe he has something useful to say after all.

"And what would that be?" Grimson towers over him, casting her shadow over his face.

"Don't know. They wouldn't say in front of me. I can still find out what they're up to. I can still…I can still …" The kid's head sinks to his chest.

Hadley considers him: the crusted blood from some uniden-tified wound under his hair, the shallow breathing, the hand-cuffs. And he sees himself, after Celeste betrayed him. That utter desolation. In those moments after, when she was gone and he was alone, he would have clung to any scrap of hope.

He goes to the intercom by the door and pushes the call button. "Someone bring in some water!" He pauses. "And the prisoners from cell two." He releases the button. "Let's talk, Mr. Hudson. Let's see if we can figure this out together."

A glimmer of hope flickers in the kid's half-closed eyes.

"Don't get excited. This is a temporary reprieve."

An officer enters, carrying a mug of water. He hands it to Hadley, who crouches and lets Alex slurp noisily.

"You're here because you got sucked in by a girl, aren't you? I did too. Her name was Celeste, prettier than the stars, and clever. Too clever, in the end. So I know where you're coming from. You'd do anything just to be with her. You'd fight anyone. Work your butt off. Sell everything you have. And what does she give in return? Nothing. Strikes out on her own."

Hadley's aware of Grimson hovering behind him. She knows all this, of course, but it still feels like he's exposing a part of himself.

"I forgave my Celeste, even when she told me she was a ship escapee. We were planning to run. I was going to give up every-thing—my career, my family—just to be with her. Our bags were packed and waiting by the front door. She sent me out to buy food for the journey, and when I got back there were a bunch of rebels in my house. See, Celeste wasn't happy with us just having a life together. She wanted more. And when I wouldn't betray my country, she let her friend smash a bottle over my head and left me for dead. Turned out we weren't the team I thought we were. Celeste had other plans. Your Esther, she doesn't appreciate the sacrifices you've made. And she's been carrying on behind your back. Betraying you with other people."

At the mention of *other people*, the kid's body jerks. That touched a nerve.

"I sometimes wonder what would have happened if I'd gotten another chance to persuade my Celeste. So I'm feeling generous. I'm rooting for you, kid. What I want to know is, what are you willing to do for her?"

"Anything."

Hadley raises his eyebrows. "I'm going to give you another chance to save yourself and the girl."

The door opens and a line of prisoners are led in. Five Neaths arrested in a random raid. Bruised and bleeding and downcast.

Hadley sees Grimson's mouth twist at the sour piss and vomit stench that fills the room. These are the dregs of society, even on a ship like the *Arcadia*. They don't appear on any lists; there's no census of them or registration. They've not even been counted. If one disappears, it'll be like they never existed in the first place. As insignificant as a raindrop in the ocean.

Hadley uncuffs the kid from the chair, the skin raw and sliced where the metal has bitten into the flesh of his wrists. He pulls him to his feet and pushes him in front of the line of prisoners.

"Choose," Hadley whispers into his ear.

Alex glances at the men lined up in front of him, dragging his eyes from one to the next. "For...what?" he asks.

"One of them's slated for execution. You get to decide."

The prisoners keep their heads bent, none of them willing to make eye contact with Hadley. An old man with a short gray beard mutters what might be a prayer, lips barely letting the sound escape.

"Why me?" Alex says. Hadley can hear the disgust in the kid's voice.

"Call it a show of loyalty."

"No. Can't." Alex shakes his head, eyes closed and face down.

"All right, take Mr. Hudson back to the holding cell. And process the execution order for his girlfriend. Don't worry, they'll make it quick," whispers Hadley in Alex's ear.

The officer manhandles Alex toward the door of the interrogation room.

"No, wait."

Alex raises a shaking finger at the prisoner closest to him, a youngish man with straight black hair falling over his shoulders. The man's face snaps up, eyes wide and lips parted in shock. He makes a grab for Alex's finger, pushing it down and away, a vain attempt to stop himself being chosen.

Hadley tilts his head at the officer. The officer grasps the man by the shoulders and drags him from the lineup, his feet scuffing and squeaking along the floor as he fights to stay. As though somehow getting back into the line of prisoners will change his fate.

"Please!" he yells, but he's cut off as the door slams behind him.

The remaining prisoners stand in silence, shoulders sloping, wretched.

Breathing hard through his mouth, Alex watches the door the man was dragged out of. He's clutching both fists to his gut like he's been winded, his face sickly and pale beneath its mask of bruises.

Hadley turns to Grimson. Giving her a smile, he ignores

the judgmental frown she's fixing him with. He takes the taser that's attached to her belt. Her expression turns to a question. He wouldn't take this attitude from anyone else, but Grimson's been with him a long time. With his back to the kid, he unscrews the battery pack from the taser, gives Grimson a smirk and turns back to the kid.

"You say she's coming back? Go and find her. Bring her to me, and I'll pardon you both," he says. He pushes the taser into the kid's hand. "Bonus points if you can bring her friend Nik Lall along too."

"What's this for?" The kid stares at the taser.

"Give you a sporting chance."

Hadley strides out of the interrogation room, feeling even taller than when he entered. Grimson follows.

"I'm going to destroy them, Grimson. I'm going to crush them, and I'm going to make sure they feel every second of it."

"Yes, sir," she says, and Hadley can sense her ruffled feathers. They've known each other long enough for him to know when she's got a problem.

"Something to say, Lieutenant?"

"Is it wise, sir? Letting the kid go? Why not execute him now, tie this up before we start the clearance? We can pick Lall and Crossland up with the rest of the rebellion. This vendetta you've got, this need to see them suffer—"

Hadley body blocks Grimson in the narrow corridor between the interrogation room and the rest of HQ. "What did you say to me?"

"Nothing, sir." Her cheeks are ruddy, and up close Hadley can see the roughened skin around her lips. She smells of cheap deodorant and a long shift spent sweating inside her uniform.

"That's what I thought," he says.

He continues down the corridor, anger burning his scalp, then hears her take a few steps after him.

"But due respect, sir, it doesn't achieve anything. Does it? All these games. They don't get us anywhere. They're a distraction—"

He turns on her, slamming a fist against the wall so that the bones of his knuckles burst with pain. If anyone else spoke to him like this, anyone else challenged his authority, they'd be court-martialed.

Grimson stands her ground.

Hadley composes himself. He coughs, pulling on the collar of his uniform that's suddenly a size too small.

"He won't get anywhere. Probably won't even find the girl. Best case, he brings them in, and I kill them all. Worst case, he runs around the ship, asking questions, trying to find out where she is. Causing trouble. Giving the rebels a little something extra to worry about. It will increase the psychological pressure. Let them know we're on to them, and they might slip up. That OK with you, Lieutenant?"

"Yes, sir." Grimson licks her lips and fixes her eyes on something over Hadley's shoulder.

A brief challenge, then everyone's back in their rightful place.

"And it's more fun this way," he whispers to her.

CHAPTER 54

NIK

No one's touching May's sister." I grip the hammer and give the machine a whack. Outside, the sun's going down, and the trees surrounding the safe house are eerie columns in the failing light.

"You'll break it," Mit says.

Bugs circle and bump against the light bulb. Cobwebs hang in the high corners of the barn. Straw makes the dirt floor scratchy.

Not fixing it. Destroying it. There's a pile of torn metal and smashed parts next to me. My hands are covered in grime. Even the dressing that Corp stuck over the gash in my hand is filthy. Came outside to clear my head and found this ancient machine, all rusted and choked with weeds. Looks like the blade underneath is supposed to turn. Some sort of cutting tool. Don't know what for.

Corp stands behind Mit, leaning on the edge of a long tool bench, arms crossed. They both ignore the fact I don't want to speak to them. Can't stand the way they look at me. Can't stand the pain reflected back. Want to smash this thing and be left alone.

Mit squares his shoulders. He paces back and forth across the open front of the barn, his boots scuffing a line on the dusty floor. More agitated by the second. He doesn't like people disagreeing with him. "I'm not saying we kill her."

"You're not touching her. End of story," I say.

"I'm not saying we hurt her," Mit says. "But she's brought trouble to our door. She's caused a rift with Silas that might have lost us half our firepower and access to the engine room. She brought a tracker ashore. She got May killed. And you, almost. Dammit, Nik."

I give the machine another whack. The impact vibrates through my arm.

Light shines off the scar on Mit's head. Long. Baby pink. Hairless. Front to back along his scalp. Other people would grow their hair to cover a scar like that. Not Mit. He wears it as a reminder of where he came from: the *Arcadia*. He thinks his battle scars make him special. Plenty of the rebels think it does, too. They listen when he starts spouting off. That means Esther's in danger.

"Scrub her brain. Put her on a train. Get rid of her. She's a loose end, and we can't risk keeping her around. Corp can do it." Mit nods the conversation over to her.

Corp stares out of the barn toward the main house. Deciding. There's a light on in the bedroom where Esther's zonked out on a sedative.

I weigh the hammer in my hand. Sometimes the rebellion wants to remove someone without executing them. There are memory-wiping drugs for that. The higher the dose, the more time you lose. We could scrub hours. Or days. Years, if we need to. Take Esther back to before she was kidnapped. Take her back to when she was a kid. Snip out every trace of the rebellion. Drop her off somewhere safe: some cheap motel or a small town out in the sticks. She'd be confused as hell when she woke up. But she wouldn't be our problem anymore.

We could cut out every trace of May.

"It's too risky," Corp says. "I might scrub too much and cause brain damage. Anyway, I've known Esther a long time. I don't believe she poses a threat."

"That's what Esther said about Alex," I say.

Silence as it sinks in.

Mit perks up. He thinks he's won.

"Don't know whether Esther would betray us. But I do know May wouldn't let you scrub her sister. And I won't either. End of conversation."

Mit shakes his head, looking at the floor. "I'll pull rank to get this done," he says.

I smash a bolt with the hammer. Technically, he outranks me. But I can count on one hand the number of times he's acted superior. We're in this together. At least, we have been up until now.

"There'll be a vote," he says.

Another crash of metal.

"Nik?"

I drown him out with another hard whack at the machine. He glares like he'd happily give me a whack with a hammer right now. Without speaking, he marches over to where I'm sitting with the machine on the floor in front of me, its innards and pieces spread all over the place, and swings a kick at a canister of bolts. It flies like he dropped an air grenade in there.

"You talk to him," he says to Corp, then he strides out of the barn, across the yard, and into the house, letting the screen door slam behind him.

"He could have you up on an insubordination charge," Corp says quietly.

I smash the machine's cover. Over and over. When it's all bent out of shape, I throw the hammer at it and pick up a saw.

Corp watches me. And I know she's thinking about May and what I've lost. And it feels like she's looking right at the pain. As if my grief's exposed for everyone to see.

Do the decent thing and avert your eyes. This is my pain. You've no right to look at it.

"One of these days, you're going to piss someone off, and you'll wish you hadn't," Corp says.

"Doubt it."

Headlights beam into the barn and swing around through the trees. Corp looks toward the drive. "People are arriving," she says.

I stand up and wipe my fingers on a rag. There are things swooping around the house, in and out of the bulb light. Bats, maybe? Don't care.

"Are you going after Alex?"

No comment.

"Take it from someone who's lost people: what you're feeling now, this is it. Forever. They will tell you it gets easier. It doesn't."

"Good talk," I say, shutting her down.

"The pain never goes away. It might change in time. You might get better at living with it. And you think killing Alex will help it heal, that him dying will somehow stop the grief. But the hole that May left will always be there."

Another car arrives, washing light over us. The crunch-slam of car doors bounces through the trees.

"The thirst for revenge does terrible things to people. Makes them hard and twisted inside. It'll turn that May-shaped hole into something awful. And it will sour every moment you had with her. Every memory will be tainted," she says.

There's a lump the size of a fist in my throat. "You won't talk me out of it," I say.

And she won't. Alex is going to pay for betraying us. For killing May.

"Did your mother ever tell you why Hadley hates people from the ship as much as he does?"

"My mother's not big on talking."

Corp nods in agreement. "She's a hard woman, your mother. She loves you though."

"Yep. I'm a solid second place to the rebellion."

"I've only heard about it secondhand. I was still a med student when it all happened, still trying to find a way off the *Oceania*. Celeste was one of us, in the early days of the rebellion. Your father came up with this crazy plan that if the rebellion could somehow recruit Coalies, we'd be able to speed things up. We might get the engine rebuilt years sooner than we'd planned. Security wasn't as tight back then. There were no drones, for one thing. It was easier for people to sneak out."

"Celeste was one of the first rebels to leave the ship. She and

Mit were smuggled off the *Arcadia* on an empty supply ferry back before the Coaly checks were so thorough. Their mission was to befriend an up-and-coming Coaly and persuade him to join us. We weren't asking for anything big to begin with. He'd just let a few things slide in the early days, bend the rules. Let a few extra crates of food in. Allow an extra bottle of pills to come on board without doing the paperwork."

"It wasn't long before Celeste found a good target. A young officer by the name of Hadley. Two months after she made contact with him, she told him she was an escapee from the *Arcadia*. Everything was running smoothly. Hadley loved Celeste enough that he was willing to run away with her. This was back when the borders were still crossable. He was willing to leave the Federated States and start a new life with her."

Corp pauses. "The trouble started when the rebellion tried to recruit him. Celeste was sure that he was a good man just following orders, and that he'd be willing to help when he understood the conditions on board the ships."

"She was wrong," I say.

"It was a disaster. Mit and Celeste told him everything. Hadley went ballistic. In the fight Mit got that scar, but Hadley came off worse—you've seen his face. Mit and Celeste thought Hadley was dead, so they ran for it."

"But why'd they punish him if he refused to join the rebellion?"

"Because in the eyes of the Federated States, Hadley had done the worst thing possible. He'd chosen Celeste over his country and was prepared to run away. His refusal to join the rebellion saved his life. They exiled him to the *Arcadia*."

"They sent him out to sea to think about what he'd done."

"Exactly. And Hadley wanted revenge. He wanted to prove that he wasn't weak. He wanted to hurt Celeste, but he'd missed his chance. So he started torturing the people on the *Arcadia*. And you never saw such a twisted and nasty piece of work as Hadley has become in the years since Celeste tried to turn him."

"I'm not going to end up like Hadley."

"All right. But I wouldn't be a good friend if I didn't try to warn you," she says, resting her hand on my back.

There are voices through the trees, people going from the cars to the safe house.

"If Mit calls a vote tonight at the meeting, scrubbing Esther won't be your choice anymore. It'll be up to everyone else."

"We'll see."

"No, listen. As your superior, I'm telling you: Esther Crossland will be scrubbed if the vote decides it. There'll be nothing I can do to stop it. So if there's something you want to talk to her about, you'd better do it before then. If there's anything you want to ask her... about May, now would be the time to do it."

She gives me a final pat on the shoulder, then she crosses the yard and jumps up the steps to the house.

On the top floor, I see a face looking out, and for a split second it's May, not Esther, staring down at me.

Her face is a skull. Hollow, bruised eye sockets. Sagging cheeks.

I can't forgive Esther for her part in getting May killed. But I have to protect her.

CHAPTER 55

ESTHER

Nik looks up from the yard and catches me watching him. I drop the curtain.

My body feels like an open wound. Everything grates against me. Every creak of the floorboards. Every brush of the blanket. Pain and pain and pain. I can't stand being alive. I tried to be brave. I gambled everything. And I lost it all.

I climb into the bed and pull the blanket up to my ears and try to find some relief in stillness and the absence of thought.

On the small table by the bed there's a bottle of pills, a jug of water and a package. It's addressed to me, my name written in May's handwriting. The package taunts me. It tries to pique my interest, but without May it doesn't matter what's inside. Opening it will only sharpen me. It will bring the grief into focus. And I want to be dull.

If I'd fought harder, would she still be alive? If I hadn't trusted Alex so completely?

It's clear to me now: the life I wanted was never going to happen. Even before Nik got shot, even before I started cheating, and before the market was destroyed, I was never going to make it ashore. It was a delusion. The cogs had already been set to turn, and my chance was gone before I was even aware of it.

It took me so long to realize. Did I suspect what Alex was capable of? Yes. I did. And it sickens me. The evidence was all right there. I knew about the lifeboat. I knew that he would help me cheat. And I knew he'd follow the rules, until it didn't suit him anymore. I let him get away with it because the thing that he wanted was me. He loved me, so I ignored the warning signs. I ate the apples he brought me. I smiled with the new tooth. I beat Kara.

The realization that I'm complicit is a rock in my throat. I chose Alex, and...oh...it was the wrong decision.

A door slams. Footsteps climb the stairs, fast, taken two at a time, and then the door of the bedroom flies open. Nik stands in the doorway.

Fury ripples from him. "Get up! What are you doing?" He grabs the blanket and wrenches it off me. "Get up! Your sister's dead! Your boyfriend betrayed you!"

He's screaming. Spitting through gritted teeth. "Why aren't you angry?" he says. "She'd be raging. She'd be fighting everyone. She'd be back at the ship, baying for blood!"

He slams to his knees next to the bed. "Why don't you want to burn the world?" His voice is coarse, a grating whisper now. His breath is sour.

I reach past him for the bottle of pills and unscrew the cap with trembling hands. Another one will let me slip into a quiet gray unreality. Before I can tip the pills into my mouth, Nik slaps the bottle from my hand. The tablets land on the floorboards like hail.

"No one who looks so much like May should be this feeble," he says. The words rumble in his throat. Gruff with the emotion he's trying to control.

He's angry because May's dead. And he's angry because I'm alive. And I don't know how either of us will survive this.

"What would May say about you treating me like this?"

"Tell me where to find Alex."

"No. How's that for feeble?" I say.

He stands up and paces away, rubbing his face with both hands. And then he's crying. He drops to the floor, head in hands, wracked by sobs.

I get out of bed and sit down too. "Tell me how it started," I say. "I want to know how my family was destroyed."

He scrapes his fingers through his hair. "The captain, my mother, my father. They started it. They needed someone inside the military facility to get the drone codes. The cadets were researched, followed, watched so that they could figure out which one was most likely to help. Not too poor. Not too desperate. Which one—" He stops and looks at me.

"What?"

"Which one had a family they wanted to keep together."

My stomach twists. I remember the endless discussions with May and my parents, all of us trying to figure out whether being together on the ship was better than being apart on land. May never wanted to go alone.

"Go on," I say.

"Then she was recruited."

"By who?"

He's chewing his lip. His fingers scrunch into each other, white knuckles pressing through the skin. "By me."

"Did she know your friendship was a sham?"

"It wasn't a sham."

"You made friends with her because you needed her," I say.

"To start with. But we were friends. I told her what happened to my dad. What the Coalies were planning. It took nothing to persuade her. She believed in the rebellion. She believed we were going to save people."

I push myself up. I can't sit still while I'm listening to this. "How old was she? Fourteen? Just a kid."

"May knew what she was doing. And if you think I could've manipulated her into doing anything she didn't want to, you didn't know her at all."

"Why couldn't you go instead? Why didn't you apply for the training program?"

He throws his hands up and lets out a grunt of exasperation. "Because they wouldn't have accepted me! My dad was a criminal. It was lucky enough that they left me and my mom alone after he was taken—we couldn't draw any more attention to ourselves. If I could've taken her place, I would have done so like a shot."

I bite my teeth together until they creak. "She'd still be alive."

Nik crumples, the pain written across his face like it's fused to him. Impossible to remove.

"At least she wouldn't be ashamed of me," he says, getting to his feet. He strides away and slams the door.

The thought of May being ashamed of me makes me want to fold in on myself.

I grab the package from the bedside table. The thick paper yields under my fingernails. Four passports drop out. I pick them up and open them one by one. Holograms of my parents, of May, then of myself look out from the pages. Names I don't recognize. Unfamiliar addresses. A pile of train tickets slip to the floor. It's an escape plan. The train tickets trace a route north, passing through the border wall of the Federated States and ending up in the safety of neighboring Maine. She planned every detail of our escape. New identities. New lives.

I collapse, clutching the passports and the tickets into my ribcage. Crying and shaking with the pictures of my destroyed family.

Something new surfaces in my mind.

I can't bring her back, but I can take her mission.

I find a nucleus of rage. It swells and intensifies until it fills every empty pocket, every pore and cell. It shines out of me.

Rage because May planned my life.

Rage because she left me.

Rage because they took her.

CHAPTER 56

NIK

L et's start." Mit eases a metal case onto the scratched and ring-marked wood of the kitchen table. Collected in this room are the key players in our organization. If a bomb dropped now, it'd take out half the rebellion. Corp's here in her civvy clothes. She's the link between the rebels on the ship and the rest of the outfit on land, at least she was until yesterday, when her cover was blown. Mit is head of the mission on land, my mother's dry-land counterpart. Most of the rest I know by sight, but not by name. Each one of them works undercover somewhere in the Federated States.

"First of all, I'd like to welcome the contingent from the *Oceania*. We were all saddened to hear that it'd been attacked," Mit says.

One of the group—a middle-aged guy with sallow skin and stubble—nods in acknowledgment. They're rebels. They tried to save their ship. They failed. Numbers are still coming in on how many died when the Coalies attacked, and how many have been locked up. Corp figures it's thousands.

"It's taken hundreds of us to bring this plan to fruition, on ships and on shore, ship folk and allies. We've sacrificed things that can't ever be replaced. And it's with great sadness that I have to tell you that yesterday, we lost one of our most treasured members. May Crossland was murdered on Commander Hadley's orders. She died fighting for our dignity and freedom."

A surge of pain threatens to floor me. I try to block out the gasps and cries of shock.

Mit waits for the hubbub to die down. "In this case is the last part of the puzzle. Nik, if you would do the honors?"

After the Coalies took my dad, my mother devoted her life to organizing the rebellion. May spent years training to infiltrate that military base and take down the drone system. Enid and Silas set up the smuggling routes we needed to get stuff onto the *Arcadia*. All of it led to my job: the engine.

I put my hands on the case. *Breathe. Easy.* A satisfying click, and the catches pop open. Inside, resting on a bed of foam, is a bundle of dull metal rods the length of my arm.

"They're intact," I say.

There's a murmur of relief from the people crowding the table. Fuel. Stolen from a shipyard in Japan and smuggled halfway across the world. It'll bring excruciating death if we handle it wrong. Drop one rod and we're all dead in a pool of tinkling glass and radioactive ooze.

Corp spreads a digiplan out on the tabletop. A map of the coastline floats into view, white land against the background blue. The *Arcadia*'s outline sits inside the curve of a natural harbor.

"Until now, you've been kept in the dark about much of our

plan, for the security of the mission," Corp says. "It's time to put the final part into action. Nik will brief us."

My mouth's suddenly dry. "Codename Landfall. Our aim is to start the *Arcadia*'s engine and take the ship out to sea."

I pause. Murmurs rise and then die down. Someone mutters, "You have got to be kidding ..."

OK. That wasn't exactly the reaction I was hoping for.

"At top speed, we can make it to international waters in an hour."

"And what's to stop the Coalies from coming after you? Or blocking you in?" It's the man from the *Oceania*.

"We'll be out of reach before they have time for any of that. And they won't risk entering enemy waters, so once we're outside Federated States territory, they'll stop chasing."

"What about them attacking from the air?" someone says from the back of the room.

"The *Arcadia*'s gang leaders are with us. They will bring all available firepower to the top decks. It should be enough to keep Hadley's helicopters on their toes. Thanks to May, the drones won't be a problem. We're banking on the fact that the Federated States government won't scramble bomber planes from Andrews Air Force Base until it's too late," Mit says.

"And if they do?"

"If they do, then God help us because there's nothing we can do against a bombing raid."

The room goes silent. I take it as my cue to continue.

"The Maine government controls the closest stretch of non-Federated States coastline. It's agreed that we can make landfall on the coast, here. That's six hundred miles of open sea."

I poke the map just outside Federated States territory. From what I've heard, it's gray and rocky up there. But at least they'll let us get off the ship. If we make it as far as Maine, we'll be free.

Someone laughs, a high, scornful sound. It's Esther. She's standing in the doorway.

"This is the most idiotic—let me get this straight. You think you're going to start a hundred-year-old engine, fight off the Coalies, and navigate open ocean, all the while being chased by everything Hadley can throw at you? And you're going to *hope* that they don't launch an air attack?"

Mit turns back to the map, making it clear he won't be engaging with Esther.

Good. Cut her off. Throw her out. She shouldn't get to speak.

"Maine will let us come ashore, but they won't risk a full-scale battle with the Federated States by actively helping us. If the engine doesn't get us there, we'll be dead in the water," I say.

"Is this what May died for, Nik?"

My mouth's like sand. If I messed up the engine rebuild, or if it doesn't hold out until we're clear of Coaly jurisdiction, I've sentenced everyone on board to a slow death in the middle of the ocean. And May died for a doomed plan.

No pressure.

I try to be the bigger man and control my anger even with Esther's eyes boring into mine.

"I come aboard on the flotilla, timing it so that I arrive between drone patrols. Enid will be waiting in case I need backup, but we're still hoping I'll get back without alerting the Coalies. Once I'm in the engine room, I'll install the fuel rods and start warming her up immediately. The captain won't lift a finger until he gets the signal from us that the mission is going ahead. Once the drones come down, Hadley will know something's wrong. And if the engine won't start, we'll have wasted our one chance. It's going to take an hour or more for it to be ready. Any less and the system could explode. I'll let you imagine what happens to anyone in the engine room if it goes off," I say.

"What if you haven't got an hour?" someone asks. It's one of the new people from the *Oceania*, a middle-aged woman with blonde, matted locks almost down to her knees.

"We're speeding up the timeline: two days from now," Mit says.

The newcomer shakes her head. She runs both hands over her head. "They surprised us on the *Oceania*. And since that bomb went off in the *Arcadia*'s market, there's been rumors that the Coalies will move sooner. Corp's cover is blown. We'd be fools to assume we've got time. So, what if Nik hasn't got an hour?"

"He'll have to make the call," Corp says. "Start the engine or destroy it. That's the reality. I've spent years on the *Arcadia*. So long that it feels like my ship and my people. But we can't risk the government finding out that we've rebuilt the engine. We can't let them know we've stolen the drone codes, or that we've infiltrated one of their bases. If we fail in our mission to start the engine, it's essential that we hide all evidence of our activities. We'll have to sacrifice the *Arcadia*."

You could cut the silence with a spoon. Destroy the engine? An explosion like that would take out three decks and start a fire that will tear through dozens more. Even more terrifying, it could punch a hole straight through the hull. Would I sink the *Arcadia* to protect the rebellion?

"So the people are collateral damage to you," Esther says. "Like my sister."

Pain crosses Corp's face. "That's not fair. We all lost a friend yesterday."

"Our organization *must* remain intact. If we fail on the *Arcadia*, the baton will be passed to the next ship. But if we're discovered, if they destroy the rebellion now, there'll be no one to help the next ship in the cascade. It might mean that this time, this ship, isn't the right one," Mit says.

Esther frowns. "Then do it now before Hadley has a chance to strike first."

"You just said it was idiotic," I say.

"Oh, it is idiotic. And you're all going to die. But if you miss your chance, my sister died for nothing."

All eyes drill into Esther. She's going to get herself scrubbed. No one's going to vote to save her after this display of ridicule.

"No," Mit says. "We're sitting put until we have everything in place. We need the engine fueled. We need the captain poised to bring the drones down. We need our network on land ready to help us once we reach Maine. Enid needs time to evacuate the flotilla."

I need to change the subject before he brings up scrubbing Esther.

"I've got something I need to raise," I say. Everyone looks at me. "That rumor about them weaponizing the drones? It's true. Saw it myself. They took out the whole market in fifty seconds. We only just made it out."

Tension tightens the room.

Mit folds his arms. "Well, that makes things more difficult for us. But if May did her job, it won't matter. The captain will take out every drone along this section of coast. They'll be blind and weaponless. Our bigger problem is what we do with her." He jabs a finger at Esther. "She knows plenty. She's seen all of us. I'm calling a vote. We'll decide whether she needs to be scrubbed."

Corp steps between Esther and Mit. A human shield. Glaringly obvious whose side she's on. Corp's going to protect her student, even if she knows it's pointless.

Esther looks like she could deck someone. "What vote? What do you mean *scrubbed*?" She's getting agitated. Clenching her fists. Looking from me to Corp.

"Mit wants to remove your short-term memory," Corp says.

"And, let me guess, you both agree with him." Esther throws me an acid glare.

"I don't, but it's not up to me. Mit called a vote," I say. "Give everyone an hour to consider."

Mit nods.

One hour. After that, any info about Alex could be gone forever. That means I need to talk to her. But she's storming from the kitchen faster than if the Coalies were chasing her. Chairs creak. Everyone's talking at once.

Esther's in the hall, then she's out the front door without bothering to enter the code. The alarm screams.

I should go after her. If Mit wins the vote and Esther ends up with scrambled eggs for brains, she won't be able to tell me where to find Alex. I need to find her, get the info, then lock her somewhere safe for the night.

I'm about to head after her when Mit grabs my arm and pulls

me to the bottom of the stairs. "You're going to persuade Esther to take the treatment willingly, or she'd better sleep with one eye open from now on," he says. Then his head whips around like he's been punched, as the front door smashes open.

Esther's standing there. "Something's happening."

I run outside. The air swarms with helicopters and drones. A huge black flock with lights as bright as stars.

All heading for the ship.

CHAPTER 57

ESTHER

We stare at the sky. Noise from the helicopters drowns out the world. They swing low over the safe house, brushing the treetops with their lights. A murmuration of black metal.

I stand amid the chaos. People start to jump into the vehicles that brought them here. Car engines rise to match the helicopters' noise.

"Go, get in the truck," Nik says, giving me a shove. He sprints back inside. I follow him.

Corp and Mit dance through the house, following a rhythm that sees them pick the place clean of anything that might be a clue. Paperwork gets piled into the fireplace. Comgloves go the same way. Corp wipes the digimap, and the sharp lines of the *Arcadia* disappear. She folds it roughly and pushes it into the grate.

Nik crouches in front of the fireplace and sets a corner of the blank digimap alight. "Either help cleaning or get out of the way," he says to me.

Smoke curls out. It catches in my throat and drags me back to the market. The burning stalls. The blood.

There's a yell from outside, a voice shot through with fear.

"We're compromised!" someone shouts through the open front door. "We gotta go!"

By the time I run outside, Corp has a pistol in her hand and is firing into the trees. I can't see what she's shooting at. Bullets whizz into the brambles. One hits a tree nearby, and it explodes in a cloud of splinters and the sickly smell of sap.

Now I see the forest on the other side of the river is squirming. Terror glues me to the spot. I don't want to know what's coming. Things that walk up tree trunks. Things that skitter over the ground. Things that are getting closer.

I charge up the porch steps two at a time, shouting, "Nik!"

Mit's clanking around in the kitchen. The rest of the rebels have already piled into trucks and revved off into the night.

May's package of passports and train tickets sits on the coffee table in front of the sofa.

The smell of gasoline, dense and heady, clouds the air. Mit sploshes liquid around, dousing the curtains, the carpet.

"Something's coming," I say.

Short, hard breaths and the smell of the gasoline make me dizzy. So scared I'm shaking.

Keep it together.

"What?" Nik says.

"Bots. A lot of bots. Like spiders."

"Mit! They're doing a sweep!"

"What the hell's a sweep?" I say.

"Something you don't want to get caught up in," Nik says. He grabs the package from the table and holds it out. I've already decided I don't want whatever May arranged for me. I start to turn my back, but he pushes the package into my hands.

Fire stretches its fingers from the grate, sucking on the gasoline-laced walls with a hungry *woof*.

"Move!" Corp shouts from outside.

Nik clasps the metal case that holds the *Arcadia*'s fuel rods to his chest, and we run from the safe house. The alarm still sounds its useless warning. The surveillance panel gives a glimpse of the house surrounded by a heaving forest floor. Corp's on the porch, still shooting. Smoke comes thick and angry out of the windows as the fire rises behind us.

All around the house, the undergrowth scurries with bots. Hundreds. Thousands. Running on insect legs through the leaf litter. They reach the river, horribly close, and the first few splash into the water, climbing up the near side without missing a step. Corp lets off another volley, taking out the nearest bot in a shower of sparks. They keep coming.

Nik doesn't slow when he sees them. He drags me toward the last truck. "Mit, we've got company!" he shouts over his shoulder.

Corp vaults into the driver's seat. I jump on to the flatbed, ignoring the pain when my shins hit the metal. Nik climbs in next to me. By the time Mit emerges from the house, there's a river of bots streaming over the ground between us and him.

"Hold tight!" Corp shouts. She spins the truck, doors swinging wildly. I dig my fingers into the edge of the flatbed to keep from flying off. Bots crunch under the tires.

Mit's cut off. He grits his teeth and sprints, kicking bots before him. He's almost with us.

A bot attaches itself, tightening its legs around his shin, scratching its way upward. Then another and another until he's dragging the leg behind him. When he realizes he won't make the truck, he lets out a horrible shriek. He falls to the ground, swatting at the bots that crawl over his body. Red patches bloom through his clothes. They're stabbing him.

Anger spills from me in a scream that sounds like a war cry. I jump off the truck. The few steps between me and Mit feel like a mile.

Don't think. Move fast.

Mit's trying to throw the bots off, but, each time he gets free from one, another takes hold.

I yank and throw, taking a bot in each hand. When I pull, there's a sickening tug that feels like they're taking flesh with them.

They reattach too fast. One spiders its way over Mit's face. A puncture wound to his jugular vein and it will be game over. I have to get him to the truck. Pulling his arm over my shoulder, I try to stand. He's too heavy. A slicing pain through my calf and I know one of them has got me. They're going to swarm over me—

Nik's here. We pull Mit to his feet. And somehow we're moving. And we're heaving each other on to the flatbed of the truck. And the truck is skidding through the trees, and Nik's shouting, "Go!"

I pluck bots from Mit and throw them onto the road.

Something's climbing up my back, following the trail of my spine. Nik whacks at the bot as it crawls on to my shoulder.

The safe house disappears behind us, its location marked by a plume of smoke that climbs into the sky. The three of us lie panting and bloodied in the dark.

CHAPTER 58

NIK

I sit still in the flatbed. One of them got me in the foot. Pain pulses through my leg, and it's wet and wrong.

Mit groans. His trousers are ribbons streaked with blood. Esther pulls the fabric back: a mess of bloody holes. Have to force my hand over my mouth to keep from hurling.

"Give me your jacket," Esther says. Her face is red and shiny.

I pull it off and pass it over. The axles of the truck rattle, all squeaking steel and rust.

"You got a knife or something I can cut with?" It's like Esther's a different person. Her voice is neat and confident and completely unshaken. "Nik?"

"Um, yeah, hold on," I say. I root in my pocket for my multitool and hand it over, nearly fumbling it in the jumping truck.

Esther cuts a notch in my jacket, then pulls it apart, ripping it into strips. She throws some back to me. I watch her snap the penknife shut and drop it into her pocket.

"Look alive, Nik. Mit's losing blood."

"What?"

"Pick a wound. Tie it around," she says. "And stop staring at me."

"I'm not. Didn't mean to, but—"

"Spit it out or forget it. Whichever you decide, get some pressure on those wounds, if you don't want your friend to bleed to death."

"It's something May would do. Jumping down to help Mit like that. Even though he wants to scrub your memories," I say.

Esther's face tightens. She winds the DIY bandages around Mit's messed-up legs. I do the same, trying not to touch the blood. It's hot and sticky under my fingers. Mit groans when I start to bind a wound on his shin. My hands shake, and every time we go over a bump my insides crunch.

Don't look at the holes. Don't look at the flesh.

"That's the best I can do until we get him somewhere with more medical supplies," Esther says when most of the wounds are covered. Mit looks like a filthy mummy, scraps of fabric hanging, blood-soaked and ragged, from his legs.

"He gonna be OK?" I ask.

"Doesn't look like anything major was hit. We'd have lost him already if they'd nicked an artery."

She takes off her own jacket, rolls it into a ball, and pushes it under Mit's head. His skin takes on a grayish hue, and his chest heaves as he breathes through the pain.

We bump out of the forest and onto the road. Corp switches the headlights on. Low beam. No sign of the rest of the rebels. With any luck, they'll already be holed up in one of our other safe houses. Whatever's happening on the *Arcadia* now, none of them will lift a finger. It's not their fault: it's all part of the plan. If we fail, if the ship falls, there'll be people left behind to keep fighting. The next ship will get its chance.

Before long, I recognize the dunes where we washed up, the rough grass and sliding sand. Can still taste the saltwater and grit. The ache of sea in my chest.

A lone helicopter passes above. Esther makes me lie down and pulls a tarp over our heads, hooking it on to the end of the flatbed. We wait in silence in the shallow tent. I can hear the painful drag of Mit's breath. And Esther's too: quieter, calmer.

Is *her* body still lying out on the walkway? Or did the Coalies clean up?

Don't know which is worse.

The sound of the tires changes from tarmac to dull sand. And there's the sea, soundtrack of my life. The truck stops. Corp throws back the tarp. Rocks rise around us in a jagged cliff face. The truck's headlights shine on the yawning mouth of a cave.

Mit pushes himself upright. "I'll keep watch," he croaks.

Esther and I jump onto the wet sand. Corp looks around the clifftops before disappearing into the cave, sloshing knee-deep in the surf.

I turn to Esther. She's staring at the ocean. The lights of the *Arcadia* twinkle out at sea as though nothing's happening. As though no one on board realizes there's a storm coming. The Coalies will be rendezvousing somewhere along the waterfront, massing their forces for the attack.

"You've got your passport?" I ask Esther.

My voice seems to take her by surprise. "Don't need it," she says.

"You won't get through the border without it."

"I'm not planning on running for the border."

When Corp emerges from the cave mouth, she's hauling a tiny boat through the shallows. Wooden boards, an underpowered outboard engine, barely room for a couple of people. It's all I need to get back on board, and the smaller the better. Less chance I'll be noticed.

"There's no time for sneaking around now," Mit says, like he read my thoughts. "Point her at the ship and go. If they haven't jammed communications yet, I'll get a message to Enid, ask for her help."

His voice creaks with pain, and his skin is ashy gray. That's blood loss for you. Hate seeing him like this, even though two hours ago we were ready to throttle each other.

"The docs will look after you. You'll be OK. This one did an all-right job of fixing me up one time," I say, nodding at Esther.

Esther is beat up and exhausted, but her face is as wild as a storm. Without speaking, she stomps over to the boat, sets her shoulder against it, and starts pushing. It doesn't move. Not even a little. Me and Corp share a look. Mit watches Esther struggling.

"What's she doing?" he says. His face is a deep-lined grimace. "Get back in the truck."

"No," Esther barks back.

"Get in the truck, or I'll make you."

Mit reaches inside his coat and when he raises his hand, he's holding a gun, deep black and brutal.

Esther inches away, holding her hands up half-heartedly, her back against the little boat.

My mouth is dry. "Told you back at the safe house, Mit, no one touches May's sister."

"She knows enough to bring down our whole operation. Not just this ship, all the ships. Thousands of people. Not going to let her sail straight into Coaly hands with the stuff she's carrying around," Mit says.

He brings something rattling out of his pocket and tosses it to Esther.

Esther makes a clean catch. She holds a bottle of pills up, squinting in the half-light.

"Take one. It'll wipe your short-term memory, just the last forty-eight hours. You won't remember the safe house, the plan, anyone you met yesterday."

"Told you no," I say.

This is really starting to piss me off. We don't pull guns on each other. We fight, and we push, and we call each other names. But in the end, we take a vote, and we play nice. Rebels don't pull guns on rebels. The Coalies do enough of that.

"You refused to do what's necessary. Someone had to," Mit says.

There's a sharp whistle from along the beach. "They're coming!" Corp shouts, then she runs and turns off the headlights, plunging us into darkness. My vision takes time to adjust to the weak moonlight. At the top of the cliff, I spot figures, dark silhouettes against midnight navy-blue sky.

"I won't remember how she died if I take it, will I?" Esther says. Her voice is thick in the back of her throat.

We're all silent. The waves tumble. It smells like home. Saltwater and seaweed.

Finally, Corp says, "No, you won't remember."

We're out of time. There are figures crawling down the

cliffside now, following a path that will bring them right down on top of us.

I charge at Mit's gun hand. It's an easy grab given how weak he is. I pull him away from the truck, and we fall to the beach, carving a gash in the smooth sand. I thud his hand into the ground until he drops the gun, then I grab it and move away from him, pushing the gun into the back of my jeans.

"You don't point guns at other rebels, Mit. End of story."

Without warning, Esther swings her arm and lobs the bottle into the sea. It flies over the nearest waves and out of sight. "There. Decision made. Let's go."

"You idiot!" Mit says. His face is covered in a layer of sand.

"Go!" Corp shouts, and she runs to Esther and folds her into a hug.

I dash to the back of the truck and grab the metal case that holds the *Arcadia*'s fuel rods.

By the time I'm back to the boat, Corp has helped Esther move the boat, and Esther's already wading up to her waist. Corp runs back and hugs me tight.

"Switch the truck out, soon as you can," I say.

"I'll be fine, Nik."

"OK, but Hadley will be looking for you at the border, so make sure they can't pick your face up on the surveillance system."

"We'll be fine. The people getting us across the border know what they're doing. Now go. I'll see you in Maine."

She lets go, and I wade out, trying not to let my emotions bubble over. I set the case into the bottom of the boat and hold to the side, helping Esther maneuver it through the freezing waves.

Feels like the sea's trying to hold on to me, as I pull myself into the boat. Hoping all of this hasn't been too rough on the fuel rods, or we'll be going nowhere but down with a bout of radiation sickness. Mit's still glaring at Esther like he could kill her. "She'll give us all up before they kill her!"

I pull on the engine starter cord. It roars, then starts a deep and healthy rumble. Esther climbs into the boat, breathing hard and dripping seawater.

"Nice of you to join me, doc. You sure about this?" I say. "You might die."

"Not sure of anything anymore," she says. "But I'm going to do it anyway."

Completely determined. In this light, with that look on her face, she could be May. And I know, just like I knew with May, that not even the hounds of hell will turn her from this path.

"You're in way over your head!" Mit screams from the sand.

I push the tiller and point us toward the ship. A smudge on the horizon hints at the new day.

The wind pushes Esther's hair back from her face. She doesn't take her eyes off the lights of the *Arcadia*. I realize I want her to live, and not just because I need her help to destroy Alex. I just want her to live.

We plunge through the breakers, flecks of saltwater stinging my face. Won't deny it, there's a thrill in my chest. I'm heading for home. I'm heading for a fight. I'm heading for Alex.

Won't deny this either: I'm glad Esther's with me.

CHAPTER 59

ESTHER

'm all in. Racing toward the ship, uncertainty flies away from me like it's being stripped by the wind. I don't know my path, but I'm done treading water. No more shying away from the inevitable. No more hiding.

The *Arcadia* comes into view like a great rock rising from the ocean, the weeds of the flotilla clinging to its sides. Along the shoreline closest to the *Arcadia*, all along the waterfront that is so familiar, is a black cloud. Boats and black-uniformed figures. Helicopters, lights blinking in the dark. A swarm of drones. And a black boat already steaming toward the flotilla.

"Hurry, Nik!" I shout.

He revs the engine harder, and we fly across the water.

Nik aims at the seaward side of the ship. As we approach, a familiar sound, the buzzing of giant insects, breaks through the engine noise. Drones. They notice us, one by one, and break from their paths to fly in our direction.

"When we get close, jump and run!" Nik shouts.

I grip the side of the boat. Almost there. Almost there. Almost—

A drone zips down, matching our speed to fly along with us. Others join it, and in seconds there are half a dozen metal monsters watching us.

A hatch opens in the bottom of the nearest drone, and a mechanical arm unfolds. It ends in a gun barrel that twists and zooms until it has us locked in its sight.

"Nik!" I grab the only thing on hand and swing, realizing too late that it's the case containing the *Arcadia*'s fuel rods. The case smashes into the drone. It explodes in a spray of blades and glass, its crippled body crashing into the ocean. Water rises in a splash where it hits.

"Maybe avoid smashing stuff with the radioactive fuel rods, doc!" Nik shouts.

I won't have to swing again. The drones have learned already, and they retreat from us, just out of reach. I crouch in the boat, not that it will protect me when those guns open fire. All around us, the drones deploy their weapons.

Nik doesn't slow.

We're fifty feet away.

Still too far.

A drone explodes. Another one spirals out of control and crash-lands in the waves.

Before I can figure out what's happening, the flotilla zooms into view.

"Jump! Now!" Nik shouts.

Still clutching the case, I put one foot on the side of the boat and propel myself toward the walkway.

My head smashes against the wood. My teeth knock together. Nik crashes down on the planks behind me.

"Get up! Run!" he shouts.

Gunfire. That's what took those drones out. I scramble to my feet, catch a glimpse of the ship and force myself toward it.

Figures appear ahead of me.

Keep running.

Enid! Drones swoop in to attack. Enid and her people fire round after round. Most shots sail past without hitting anything, but it's enough to draw the attention of the drones.

We barrel onwards, a gap opens to let us through, and Enid claps me on the back as I pass. I keep running, one of Enid's people leading the way. My breath comes in tight gasps. I can sense Enid on my heels, hear it when she fires into the sky. We jump aboard a barge as a stream of drone bullets bites holes into the walkway behind us.

"Keep going, Nik my boy! They won't lay off for long!" Enid shouts.

We jog through the inside of the barge and out the other end. Across a moving bridge of planks above open water—no time to worry about falling—and in through a hole in the side of the ship. Someone slams a patched metal door closed behind us.

Then there's only the sound of five people breathing heavily in the stillness of the corridor. I collapse on the filthy floor, clutching the fuel-rod case to my chest.

Enid laughs. A loud and joyful sound that makes the corridor we're standing in feel like a living place. Nik laughs too. Then we're all laughing. And Nik and Enid hug, slapping each other on the back.

Enid breathes with her hands on her knees. "You do like cutting it close," she says.

"Thanks for the backup," says Nik, wheezing.

Enid turns and grabs me, pulling me in so that we're face to face, almost touching. She squeezes my shoulders with both hands and looks at me hard, for a moment letting go of all the pretense and machismo. "Your sister. She was one of the good ones. She'd be bursting with pride at you stepping into the thick of things. OK?"

I nod, holding a wave of tears back.

She slaps me hard on the top of my arms. "Better keep moving. They might've seen where we came in, and it wouldn't take much for them to get through. I've already given the evacuation order. The old people and the kids are all off the flotilla and hunkering down in safe cabins on the ship. Coalies will only find fighters when they get here."

Enid leads the way down the corridor, taking us deeper into the ship. The spartan, undecorated walls and floor tell me this was never a public part of it. These are working corridors. The air's dank and moldy.

"Need to signal the captain," Nik says. He opens his hand and taps out a single word. Landfall.

His glove gives a dull beep and flashes red. He tries again. Message not delivered.

"They're blocking comglove signals," Enid says.

"You must've known they'd do that when they attacked," I say.

She stares at me with her black-lined cat's eyes. "Yeah, but we hoped we'd be starting the engine before the attack, didn't we?"

"So what's plan B?"

"Someone's got to go up there and tell the captain we're a go. Even if he realizes the Coalies are attacking, he won't act until he's sure the engine's up and running. He won't risk letting the Coalies know what we're planning."

"I'll go," I say. Nik stares at me in surprise. "It makes the most sense. You need to get to the engine room. Enid's more use down here. And, frankly, she looks like trouble. She'll end up fighting her way through an army of Coalies."

"Not scared of a fight," Enid says.

"I didn't mean that, but there's no point attracting attention. I look...respectable."

"Respectable? You're trying my patience, girl," Enid says with a trace of glee in her voice.

"You know what I mean. No one will notice me."

Nik and Enid consider. A *put-put-put* of gunfire sounds in the distance. This is real. They're really attacking us.

"It's too dangerous," Nik says finally.

"You don't understand. I need to bring Hadley down. I need to stamp out everything he's built."

I'm holding my fists up in front of me, trying hard to stay calm. But the sudden intensity of my hatred for Hadley is dizzying.

"I can't fight, and I can't start the engine. But I can help you beat him. I need to do this. I need it because of what he's taken from me."

"Ah, let the girl go," says Enid. "Do your sister proud."

"I will."

She holds a hand out to John. "Give me a route orb."

John searches in his backpack and plonks something in Enid's palm. An apple-sized metal ball with buttons on the outside. She presses them in sequence, then places the orb gently on the ground in the middle of the corridor. It spins around and around, finds its course, and rolls off, stopping after a few yards.

"It's programmed to take you to the captain's complex. Pick it up once you get above deck, or it'll attract too much attention. And don't lose it—I won't tell you what I traded for it," Enid says.

I walk toward it, and as I get closer, it speeds away, staying a few steps in front of me.

"Esther!" Nik calls.

My heart leaps. I'm heading into danger, and he needs to say something to me before I go. I turn back. He's staring at me like we've got unfinished business.

"Yeah?" I say.

"I need the case."

I jog back, the route orb waiting.

Nik takes the case from me.

"You're on your own, doc. See you after," he says.

CHAPTER 60

NIK

"What is it about that family?" Enid says as we watch Esther run off down the corridor, hot on the route orb's trail.

"What?"

"I have to spell it out? You've been puppy-dog in love with May for years. Now you're standing guard over her sister like she's a priceless relic."

It's a fight to control my anger. Enid really can rub salt in the wound. And it hurts like hell. "We've got work to do," I snap. "Which way's the engine room?"

"Follow me." A smile tugs at her mouth. The sound of gunfire fills the air behind us. I see Enid's face flicker and reset. I know Enid, and I know she'd fight tooth and nail to protect her people. Must be killing her to leave the flotilla behind, knowing that our success means its destruction.

"It'll be OK," I say.

She side-eyes me as we walk. "No. It won't. But thanks for saying it anyway."

Usually, the corridors down here are empty, but now they're alive with people. Everyone in Neath territory understands what's happening. They've had to prepare for it. I almost feel sad for the people who live above. No one's told them what's about to happen. They might have heard some buzz about the *Oceania* going down, but they won't be expecting what's coming their way this morning.

The engine-room door gives nothing away. You'd never know anything important was inside. Smooth metal with a wheel handle in the middle. The metal's bubbled with rust, and I took the Engine Room sign down a couple of years ago. The wheel spins easily. I step through and leave the door open for Enid.

Now we're here, I'm electrified. This is the culmination of my life's work. I look over at the engine. Giant and complicated and the result of years of sweat and blood. A mass of tubes and pipes higher than my head. Restored piece by piece by my own fair hand. Hour upon hour spent studying in secret, or working down here by myself. Or with May. A memory blooms before I can stop it; May sitting on the floor with a textbook on her knee, while I fiddle with the engine.

"Get on with it then," Enid says. She's leaning against the wall, arms crossed.

I lay the metal case on the ground. Time to find out whether Esther's brush with that drone pulverized the fuel rods. The case has a massive dent in the middle and deep scratches where Esther smashed the drone out of the air. A pretty cool move, but has it killed us?

Deep breath.

I thumb open the catches. Inside, there will either be intact fuel rods or seeping radioactive death.

I lift the lid. The rods are pristine, bound together with metal straps, and still cocooned in their protective foam. Not a single one looks damaged. I wipe sweat from my forehead with one sleeve.

Enid cranes forward to get a closer look. "We good?"

"We're good."

I press the release button on one of the metal straps, and the fuel rods separate into twenty-three pieces, each as long as my arm and as thick as a finger.

"What do you do with them?"

"One rod in each of those canisters," I say, nodding at the metal tubes lined up on the wall.

"That's it?" says Enid.

"That's it."

"Seems a little anticlimactic," she mutters.

"Give me a hand, and we'll be done in no time," I say, ignoring Enid's gibe. She's like a sister. An annoying sister who thinks she's cleverer than me and doesn't get tired of showing it.

Enid goes to the first canister and twists the lid, spinning it until it pops off.

I grip the end of a rod and ease it out of the case. My armpits and back sweat as the nerves kick in.

Don't drop it.

I slide it into place. Enid screws on the cap and moves to number two.

"Mit was hurt," I say while I'm sliding out the second rod.

Enid freezes. Her eyes go wide and clear, all the bravado stripped away. In this moment, she's not a gang leader, she's just Enid. "How bad?"

"His legs were pretty messed up. But he'll live."

She presses her lips together. Nods. Moves on.

We continue in silence. Twenty-three rods, twenty-three canisters. We work fast. Enid takes the lid off, and I—carefully, carefully—insert the fuel rod. Enid puts the lid back on.

The whole time, Esther keeps flashing into my head. Wish there was a way I could have kept her here with me. Where I know she's still in one piece.

"We done?" Enid steps back and looks at the bank of canisters. Her forehead glistens. It's hot as hell in here.

"Now we heat the system."

I cross to the control panel, a big metal desk with levers and switches and buttons, and set the target temperature by turning a red wheel valve. Enid and I turn back to look at the canisters, waiting for the moment of truth. If this fuel doesn't work, if I've messed up even a tiny part of the engine build, everything we've done over the past half a decade will come to nothing.

Come on. Come on.

Finally, there's a hiss of steam. The sound of movement inside the pipes that lead from the fuel canisters and up through the engine. The pipes shudder and thunk, but hold. No explosions yet.

"How long will it take?" Enid says.

"An hour, maybe more."

"Too long. The Coalies will overrun the flotilla any minute. It'll take them time to secure the place, but we can't wait an hour." She wrinkles her forehead. "What happens once it's heated?"

"Then I turn this key to access the main control panel."

"Show me."

I hesitate with my hand over the key.

"Ah, come on. We've time to kill. Educate me."

"I turn the key, flip these three switches to on, and set these sliders to control the reactor temperature and system pressure."

Enid looks at the controls like she's running through it all again. "That it?"

"That's it."

"All right, boys," she calls through the open door. "You can take him now."

Two of Enid's guys pile into the engine room. They grab me by the arms.

"Enid! What the hell? Enid!"

CHAPTER 61

HADLEY

Hadley stares at his digiplan of the ship, unfurled like a tabletop sea. Everything's going to plan. Forces deployed. Arrest warrants for the rebels being enforced. The drones surrounding the *Arcadia* appear as darting red crosses, each programmed with precision, letting him see or attack, as needed. He chooses one that doesn't have anything else to do and presses his finger down on it, then slides it over to the seaward side of the ship. The real drone will fly through the air to give backup to his ground forces.

Hadley sings quietly to himself as his hands glide over the digiplan, moving drones around, sending orders for a unit to advance or retreat. It's a good day.

His units move around the ship, red dots on the blue digiplan. He'll concentrate on the arrests first. Then he'll go—step by glorious step—through the ship, sweeping every inhabitant before him.

"Unit two," he says, speaking into the communicator resting on the edge of the map.

"Unit two, responding."

"Once you've completed your arrest list, get some ropes up in the arboretum."

"Ropes, sir?" comes the electronic reply.

"From the trees. No point wasting bullets when ropes will do the job."

A beat of silence. "Yes, sir."

Alex Hudson's testimony added new names to the wanted list, Nikhil Lall among them. The rebels can be dispatched quickly and without fuss. None of the admirals will question the necessity of their executions.

He frowns at the map. The gangs are putting up more resistance than he expected. They mobilized fast, and from the reports he's had so far, they seem to be well organized. Until yesterday, he'd still have believed that the gang leaders were self-serving. Enid Hader would defend her floating hovels. Silas Cuinn would retreat into the dank unknown below deck. Apparently, they've put their differences aside and are mounting a coordinated defense.

Doesn't matter.

There's nowhere for them to go. The gangs can kick and scream as much as they want. Rats in a barrel.

"Sir." Grimson marches up, in full uniform and wearing her gun across her chest. He can tell it's Grimson from her gait. She flips her visor open.

"What have you got for me?"

"The sweep you sent to look for those escapees. It turned

up a burning house. Footage of a meeting breaking up. Lall and Crossland escaped on a truck."

"Dammit, Grimson. What was the gunfire about?"

"Sir?"

"Half an hour ago. There was gunfire off the seaward side of the flotilla."

"Yes, sir. Drones intercepted a small vessel. It had backup from Enid's gang. Should we divert a unit to investigate?"

Hadley stares at the familiar shape of the *Arcadia*. He's planned today so thoroughly. Down to the tiniest detail. He'll be damned if he's going to let some Neaths derail him.

"It was them. Alex Hudson was telling the truth. They've come back aboard. But what are they up to?" he says, half to Grimson, half to himself.

"Not sure, sir," Grimson replies.

"Tell unit four to forget about bringing the captain down here. Give them the kill order. Let's wrap this up. And you get down to the flotilla. Find out where they went and deal with. Got it? Not dead or alive. Just dead."

He'll have to forgo the pleasure of a final meeting with the captain. *Never mind.* A clean clearance is what's important.

Grimson marches off, relaying new orders through her helmet to the rest of the team.

On the digimap, a red dot represents unit four. He watches it moving toward the captain's offices. The knowledge that he's out-maneuvered the old man makes Hadley giddy. In the end, Hadley has won.

There's no time to dwell on the fact now. Hadley needs to end this.

CHAPTER 62

NIK

Enid gives a half-smile and slams the engine-room door shut. The wheel creaks around as she secures it from the inside. Built that locking mechanism onto the inside of the door myself. There's no getting in without a barrel of explosives.

"Enid!" I shout so loud my throat zigzags pain. She's going to get herself killed.

I kick out as the goons she's set on me drag me away. These stupid land sneakers won't grip, and I might as well be trying to run on ice. These guys are enormous. They pull me as far as the end of the corridor, then throw me down in a heap. I jump back at them, trying to push my way through, but it's like fighting a solid wall. She had this planned out. One day, one day, I'm gonna be a step ahead of Enid.

"What the hell is this?" I shout. They barely register my existence, just draw their weapons and stand with their feet too far apart. A barrier between me and the engine room. Between me and Enid.

"Got a message for you from Enid. She says, respectfully, 'Get lost.'"

I spin around to find John leaning against a wall, chewing his finger. His injured leg is still wrapped in bandages from the attack in the market. He spits out a piece of skin and goes back to chewing.

"Need to start the engine." My voice is wheezy, and there's a heavy pounding in my head.

"*You* don't need to start the engine. Doesn't really matter who does the actual starting, does it? Long as the starting gets done at the most efficient moment."

I sway on my feet, ball my fists. "She's going to kill herself."

"Maybe. Maybe not," says John, shaking his head. Like he doesn't care. We both know he does. We both know he'd chew glass if Enid needed him to.

"Let me go back in."

He snorts. "No chance."

"Come on, John. Let me go help her."

"Enid was very clear in her orders. She wants you as far away from this potential explosion as possible. Don't ask me why." His eyes run from my sneakers to my face.

"She'll burn. If she starts the engine before it's ready, it'll go up."

John sniffs. "She made her choice, and I don't make a habit of questioning my boss. We'll hold off the Coalies as long as we can. Then she'll start it up."

"Why? Why did she do this?"

"Who knows. Maybe it's 'cause family does for family."

"We're not family."

"Good as, in her eyes. Though, if it was up to me, I'd have gotten out of this whole rebellion game a long time ago. Anyway, she said you've got things to do. Better scamper off and do them."

A burst of gunfire echoes nearby and sends electricity spiraling down my backbone. The two guys guarding the engine room pan the corridor behind me. Close, but not close enough to worry them. Yet.

"This isn't right. She can't do this. It's not her job," I say. It's my job. It's always been my job.

"Yeah. Well. Ours is not to reason why, lad. She's given her orders. By the way, that guy, Alex? Apparently, he's secured himself one of the old lifeboats on Deck Ten. If you was wanting to know his whereabouts. Apparently, he's been asking after that girl, Esther, too. Trying to find out where she might be."

John flashes his gummy smile at me. He's a stubborn one. Nothing I say will make him go against Enid's orders.

"You gonna stand there, batting your eyelids, or you gonna go do something useful?"

I grind my teeth. No point staying. They're not letting me back in. They're not going to stop Enid from following this crazy course she's plotted. Just hope she has enough time before the Coalies get here. Hope she makes it out in one piece.

I've got Alex to deal with.

I turn my back on the engine room and head for Deck Ten.

CHAPTER 63

ESTHER

I t's nervously quiet on board the ship. Like everyone's holding their breath.

I concentrate on following the route orb. Dark, unfamiliar corridors stretch out in a maze. Every now and then, there's the rattle of gunfire, or shouting, and once something like an explosion in the distance. I taste smoke.

When the orb comes to a ladder, it opens itself up and grabs the edge of the metal with its legs, pulling upward with the whir of some internal mechanism. I climb after it, pushing open a rusty cover that reeks of iron and drops flecks of orange onto my head. I peer through the hole. It opens into fresh air on the top deck, the captain's complex rising like an iceberg in front of me.

The complex is a relic of the cruise-ship days, a rounded brick of offices sitting proud on the uppermost part of the ship. A contradictory place that's essential to the smooth running of ship life, but hidden from its view. You can't see it from the Lookout, or the market at the back of the ship, or the bridge that sits above the prow.

No Coalies stare back at me, so I push the cover past its tipping point, and regret it immediately. It crashes to the deck like a giant cymbal.

Don't panic. You can do this.

I pull my hood up and duck down on the ladder, hiding inside the hole until my nerves stop ringing. Not wanting to piss Enid off, I scoop the route orb into my pocket.

Out here, the air is restless. It smells of storms and thunder. Drones swarm everywhere, more than I've ever seen, blocking out the sky. I wish it was darker, but the drone lights make it bright as midday. I summon my courage and climb onto the open deck. I have to expose myself to them. Faced with walking right under their watching eyes, my thoughts spiral out of control. They're watching me. I can sense them staring, their lenses like the eyeballs of great flying insects.

Walk normally. Don't attract attention.

My fingers reach for the reassurance of a wall, but I force myself to drop them without touching it. Skulking along the wall will only make me look suspicious. My only chance is that they're too busy dealing with everything else to notice an upper-deck girl walking calmly around the ship.

There's the entrance: glass swinging doors with bar handles across the middle. Once-white walls dulled by decades of grime.

One of the doors stands half open, a cobweb of cracks running through the pane of glass. I edge inside and find the air foggy and sweet with burning paper. As I push the door wider, there's a swoosh and a tinkle from the paper and glass piled behind it.

Light streams from a door at the far end of the room. Creeping, I pass a small desk. Filing cabinets pulled open, their contents spewing on to the ground. A swivel chair. And the sense that someone was here until the second before I came in.

Smoke swirls around the door. The air crackles and spits and seems to warn me against going any further. Something's happening here.

My foot hits something. The floor is littered with the remains of surveillance bots. Legs, lenses and bodies smashed and dismembered. There must be dozens of the things.

Shadows move in the next office. Back and forth across the doorway, carrying armfuls of paper to a smoldering wastepaper container in the center of the room. It puffs smoke and ash into the air with each ream dropped on to the fire.

"Hello?" I push the door open wider. It strikes me that this could be dangerous. The captain might already be gone. These figures could be Coalies destroying things they can't use.

Two men freeze. They stare at me. Not Coalies, at least not ones in uniform. With a jolt, I recognize the rounded shoulders of the tall man I delivered May's worm to.

The other man is tall, too, and broad. He moves as though he owns the ship, staring at me like I'm a trespasser in his space.

"Esther, what are you doing here?" he says.

I teeter. This is the captain of the *Arcadia*. This is the man whose voice I've listened to every day of my life.

"There's no time for hesitation," he snaps. "I'm going to ask you to find strength and tell me what you came here for. Do it quickly."

I shake my head to rearrange the thoughts that are disjointed and threadlike. "Nik's going to start the engine. The plan is going ahead. You need to get to the bridge."

He looks at me carefully. "I know nothing about this."

The wind drops from my sails. I scan the room for help. For something that will tell me what to do or what to say.

"Perhaps if we knew the codename?" he says.

"Landfall," I whisper.

A grim smile spreads across the captain's face. "Thank you. Gareth, weigh the anchor and load the new drone codes into the system. Let's even the playing field."

Gareth drops the pile of papers he's holding onto the fire. He opens a filing cabinet and brings out a tiny box, then swings himself into the wheeled chair behind what must be the captain's desk. He busies himself with a digiscreen. I look away when he opens the box to reveal the metal worm. That's a memory I don't want resurfacing.

"You've played your part. Thank you," the captain says.

"What's next?" I ask.

"Next, we attack the very heart of the Coaly surveillance system. Without their drones, they're as blind as we are."

"Then what?"

"Then I will do something I've wanted to do for the past twenty years. I'll set a course out to sea, and I'll steer the *Arcadia* away from this wretched shoreline and out of this purgatory we've been confined to."

There's a lump in my throat. Emotion making me want to cry. "I can help," I say. "Shouldn't you have people with you? Some guards or something?"

He smiles. "You're right, of course. I have Gareth. We'll be joined by more allies as soon as we finish our work here. You've done enough. Go home. Find your parents and stay out of danger. If all goes well, you won't have to wait long."

I can't believe I did it. I can't believe it's over. I'm suddenly aware of the tension in my jaw and in my neck. I can go and find Mom and Dad. I should pack some things for when we leave. I turn to go.

"Esther." The captain's gentle voice comes from behind me. "I'm sorry."

"For what?"

"For putting you through that night. For everything you've suffered. It's a source of regret that you were treated the way you were. That your life has been so upended. That you've lost your sister."

"I . . . I didn't know it was you. That night. I didn't realize until now."

The captain nods, genuine regret evident on his face.

"Can I ask you something?" I say.

"I think you've earned that right."

"You know Hadley, how much he hates us, what he plans to do. How did you work with him all that time? People call you a collaborator."

Even as I'm saying it, I know I'm not just asking about the captain. For five years, I've been called one too. I never really believed it before. This is my demon to battle, too.

"Yes, I'm aware of that. The pretense of collaboration was necessary for the success of the rebellion. My duty is to work for my passengers. It remains my duty whether they love me or not."

The captain turns back to his work, and it's like I never existed.

I retrace my steps through the outer office, past the desk and the disemboweled filing cabinets. I swing through the glass doors without checking for Coalies. Ten feet from the captain's complex, I lean on the railing for support, gulping fresh sea air. The drones suddenly look festive, strung up like fairy lights.

It's over. That was my last act of rebellion.

Footsteps clomp behind me. An army of them. In my relief, I wandered out onto the deck, and I didn't even think to check who was out here.

Stupid. Stupid.

How could I have let my guard down so quickly? I force myself to turn around and find a unit of Coalies coming toward me along the deck. Smooth as water. Their weapons raised.

I'm paralyzed with fear.

"Out of the way!" one screams, slamming me against the railing, and my ribs burst with pain.

This is it. They're going to take me. I'll be one of the disappeared. There'll be no packing of treasured belongings. No comforting my parents. I just won't be around anymore.

But they pass me by, and I watch, dumbstruck, as they pour into the captain's office.

Shouts from inside. The captain's deep voice raised in outrage. A shock wave that rattles the deck and the air and me. Then gunshots.

Run, Esther!

Too late. As fast as they entered, the Coalies reappear. The leader pauses, hand resting on his rifle. "Sir, this is unit four," he says, talking through the microphone in his helmet. "The captain has been terminated."

The visored face shifts until it's looking at me. Sweat pops up on my top lip, and before I can control myself, I throw my head over the railing and vomit.

A hacking noise comes from the Coaly. He's laughing. "All right, let's move," he says.

I stare down at the sea, so many decks beneath me it feels like I'm staring over a cliff edge. All I can do is concentrate on the harsh in and out of my own breathing and wait. Every second is a lifetime until I sense them moving away down the deck. The railing presses into my chest, but I stay there until I'm sure they've gone. Then, sobbing and shaking, I push myself up and go back into the captain's office.

I have to check for signs of life.

First, I smell fire, then I smell blood. Metallic. Red and warm. A pair of boots, worn at the toes, stick out from behind the desk. This is where Gareth fell. Blood pools on the carpet. I know he's dead. The bullet wounds are too numerous, too catastrophic. I check for signs of life anyway. Kneeling beside him, gently and methodically feeling for the place on his neck where the carotid artery passes close to the skin.

I find the captain's body lying next to the fire in his office. He's stretched out on his back, flames already licking at his fingertips. I can't bear the thought of his skin charring and turning black. The smoke's thickening by the second. With one hand, I cover my face; with the other, I grab the captain's arm and pull. He's like a rock, but I manage to drag him just clear of the flames. As his hand hits the floor, he releases a deep moan. He's alive.

The smoke's getting too thick to stay in here. Heat from the inferno licks my face. My skin tightens. I grab his shoulders. Pull with both hands. It's no good. He's too heavy. I make it a little way, just out of reach of the fire. I can't leave him. But if I stay I'll die here too.

"Esther." A noise croaks from his lips. His chest is a lake of blood, the bullet wounds marked by deep red circles.

My eyes stream and prickle with the smoke. I lean closer, taking his hand.

"The screen...Gareth almost did it...Stop the drones...You have to do it ..." Tears stream from the corners of his eyes.

I'm separated from the desk by a bank of fire. I can feel my hair crackling in the heat as the flames grow fierce around me. I have to find the digiscreen that Gareth was using. I leap over a low patch of burning paper, and I'm standing in front of the wide wooden desk. It's piled up with papers and books. Some of them are already smoldering in the heat, ready to burst into flames. No digiscreen. I pull my sleeves down over my hands and use them to push stuff around on the desk.

Come on, come on, where is it?

Papers drop to the floor in a flurry of sparks. The fire's gathering strength. Every breath harder than the last. The fabric of a chair ignites with a hollow *woof*, and a smell of burning leather fills the air.

It's not here. The digiscreen isn't here.

Breathing is like razor blades scraping through my lungs. I trained for this. What did Corp say?

Get low. Get beneath the smoke.

I drop to my knees, trying to find clearer air. And I spot it, a glassy rectangle poking out from beneath the splayed pages of a book. I grab it, the heat from its metal casing puckering the skin of my fingertips, and turn it over. The digiscreen blinks with blue font: Scan retina to execute command.

The ship shudders. A thrumming sensation rises up through my feet. So faint. Almost imperceptible, but it's there, strange but definite. Nik did it. The *Arcadia* has a beating heart.

Somewhere behind me glass shatters. I have to get out of here. I lift the digiscreen to my eye and stare into the tiny camera embedded on its edge. A flash. I look at the digiscreen: Retina not recognized.

Of course it's not recognized. Why would my eye unlock it?

The fire's taken hold with merciless fury. The floor burns. So do the walls. Through the flames and the smoke, I can see the captain's trousers are alight. All hope of pulling him clear is gone. I rake in a burning breath and clutch the digiscreen to my chest, then I hurl myself at the lowest point of the fire. Heat snatches at me. I collapse beside the captain.

"Captain!" I shout, shaking him by the shoulders.

He doesn't respond. He doesn't blink.

My heads spins. The captain's gone. A foundation of my life, an inalienable part of the *Arcadia*, lies dead on the floor. Murdered. His voice, his guidance, as constant as the ship itself. Gone. Torn away.

Sobbing. Eyes and nose streaming. Grief and pain.

His eyes are closed. "I'm sorry," I say as I push his eyelid up and bring the digiscreen to his face, moving it around until I hear the quiet bleep of the camera scanning successfully. I turn it over: Retina recognized. Drone system offline.

I drop the digiscreen and sprint away from the captain and the flames through the door to the outer office. In five strides, I make it to the glass doors, but as I push them open, I hesitate. On the wall, there's a radio. A rectangular black box with a bank of buttons and dials. Above it, a line of clocks shows the time in DC, London, Tokyo, New Delhi. And there's a digiscreen that displays just a number: 15,954. The number of days the *Arcadia* has been at sea. This is where the captain makes his announcements.

I have no idea how to work the thing, but I grab the receiver anyway, bringing it up to my face and pressing a button on the side. It crackles, and I clear my throat.

"Good morning. It is…a little before six a.m. on…Saturday, November 13, 2094. We've been stuck here for 15,954 days." My voice echoes through the speakers.

My hands are trembling. Why the hell did this seem like a good idea?

"There have been no Virus cases, obviously, because saying we carry the Virus is just another lie the Coalies tell to justify keeping us locked up here—"

Behind me, something cracks and falls in the fire. I can feel the heat of it getting closer. I close my eyes, breathe deep to steady myself, try to figure out what I need to say. I press the button again.

"The Coalies are coming for all of us. Run."

I drop the receiver and sprint out into the open. The miracle of clean air pours into my lungs. I collapse in a heap. The doors swing shut behind me. Smoke builds behind the glass like fog. The flames will take the captain and Gareth soon. A funeral pyre. It's more than most will get today.

I run. I know that every step is taking me further from home. Further from my mom and dad. But Nik started the engine.

With the captain gone, someone has to steer the ship.

CHAPTER 64

HADLEY

Hadley's unit at the prow of the ship flashes orange as it moves across the digiplan. They're under attack, gunfire sputtering in bursts. He touches a drone and drags it to the front of the ship.

His coffee cup holds down one curling corner of the digiplan. He glances at the rippling surface before going back to work. There's a hum nagging at him. Barely noticeable, the hint of a rumble that climbs up his legs.

"Sir, we're encountering more resistance than anticipated at the prow of the ship," comes Grimson's voice, crackling through her helmet. "The rebels are defending the bridge."

"Copy that, Grimson. Backup on its way."

He gathers a handful more drones and drags them northwards to join the—

It's gone.

The drone he sent isn't swooping around the front end of the ship.

Must have gotten diverted. They're programmed to prioritize threats, so it might have spotted something more pressing. He scans the digiplan, looking for the stray. But no, it really is gone. He scratches the stubble on his chin.

He looks at the coffee cup again, imagines the surface of the liquid is jumping.

He swats away the uncertainty. A technical glitch won't dampen his spirits today. On the back wall of HQ, the pictures of the ship's most wanted rebels are arranged in neat columns, and two minutes ago he had the pleasure of setting the captain's image to *Terminated*. It was exhilarating.

Realizing that the old man had spent years working against him, siphoning off resources to fund his two-bit rebel organization, had stung. It made him feel naive. Like he still hadn't learned the Celeste lesson. Hadley got a swell of satisfaction from crushing the man like a louse. Would have been more fun to do it himself, but a leader has to delegate.

"Sir, we need those reinforcements!" Grimson's voice clicks, anxiety crackling through it. Gunfire flares in the background.

"I sent th—" Hadley stops. Now the handful of drones he'd ordered to help Grimson is gone. Disappeared into the blue. "What's going on?" he murmurs.

On the digiplan, Hadley watches the red cross of a drone speed alongside the ship. And then, with his eyes firmly on it, it pings out of existence.

Technical glitch. That's all.

He turns the digiplan off. Waits a few seconds. Turns it on again. Drone locations should update on their own. But when the image returns there are even fewer red crosses. They thin out, disappearing one after another.

Gone.

Gone.

Gone.

Panic tightens his throat. His mouth dries out. This isn't right.

He sprints outside. Drones should be hovering around HQ, set in a defensive pattern. Two—four—six. Just a fraction of what there should be.

He puts his hands on top of the railing. He starts at the faint vibration that travels through his skin. A nightmare thought strikes as he stares at his fingers. They couldn't have started it. It would have taken years to rebuild. They'd have needed to smuggle things onto the ship. They'd have needed the gang leaders on their side. They'd have needed the captain. And the council.

Hadley sways. His mouth is acrid with bile. Everything drops into place.

But where would they go? Where could they take a ship like this?

To sea.

They're making a run for it.

In front of him, a drone stops in mid-air, hovers as if it's taking a final breath, then drops from the sky. Another. And another. They plummet, sending great towers of seawater splashing into the air around the ship.

Hadley roars.

CHAPTER 65

ESTHER

Drones drop from the air like rocks, their lights streaking into the dark water. People stare. They pour from the cabins, alerted by the engine, or the drones, or the gunfire, that something big is happening.

But I'm not watching the sky.

I'm watching Alex.

He's standing in the doorway of the lifeboat he's stocked with supplies. He looks poised to lower himself into the water, hands frozen around a rope, hair ruffling in the breeze. Heroic, almost.

I wasn't prepared for this lightning strike of emotions. The way the yearning for him twists through the hatred and the grief. Even after all he's done, he still has power over me. I crave him. I want to feel the safety of him. I want to lie in my bunk with him, eating apples. I want to go back.

He turns. He spots me, and his expression shifts to relief. The change in him makes me ache. We've been apart less than forty-eight hours, yet his face is drawn and bruised, and his eyes bulge from their sockets. There's a gash on his cheek that leaks blood. He jumps down from the lifeboat and takes a few steps in my direction.

"Esther." His voice cracks.

I inch backwards, my body tense with revulsion. Fight or flight kicks in. I'd feel better facing him if I had a weapon, something to keep him at arm's length. Remembering Nik's multitool, I feel in my pocket and find the handle, cold and smooth. It's better than nothing. I pry one of the dull blades open with my fingernails and take a few decisive steps backwards.

"No, wait!" He hesitates, looking around at the people crowding the deck. If he leaves the lifeboat, someone will take it. Getting it back will mean a fight, and he might not win. He runs to me anyway, stopping just out of reach.

His eyes glisten. His mouth's turned down in a grotesque pout. "Thank God, you're OK," he says, and he takes a step closer, opening his arms.

The thought of touching him sends a shudder through me. I remember the crack running down the center of his pupil. I remember the weight of his hands trying to force me back to the *Arcadia*. I feel the betrayal—raw like burnt skin.

He's lost to me. My Alex, the Alex I loved and love still, is gone. He died with May. I lost them both on the flotilla.

Behind him, a man peers into the lifeboat. All of Alex's hoarded supplies there for the taking.

Alex sees me looking, but doesn't turn around.

"Get in the lifeboat. We can go ..." He trails off.

I laugh. The sound's glassy and humorless.

A shadow of confusion passes over his face. "What's funny?"

"I hate you."

It's true. I hate this thing that was once my Alex. I hate him. I hate him.

He looks out at the sea, licks his lips and rests his hand on a long black cylinder that's strapped to his waist. I've seen something like it before. The Coalies used it to shock people in the Lookout the day I didn't stop to help that girl.

"You're not thinking straight," he says. "We can still be together." He flips open the catch that holds the taser in place.

The wildness in him sends a shiver down my spine. He's dangerous.

"None of this is what I wanted," I say.

"You needed a new tooth. I got you a dentist. You needed to pass a test. I helped you cheat. You wanted a way out of the rebellion. I made a deal that would have wiped our records clean." He's in motion. Every cell, every hair, is alive.

"No. I didn't want it, not like this. You never asked me."

"Asked you what?"

"What I was willing to lose," I say.

"It was for *us!*" he screams in frustration and yanks at his hair with his free hand. "I had to do something. You were lying and sneaking around with Nik Lall. Was I supposed to watch you throw everything away? Ignore lie after lie while you shut me out and went off with him? This is your fault. You killed her. Not me!"

He's hopping from foot to foot. More agitated by the second. I'm aware of people staring at us.

"You're coming with me."

He lunges. The taser comes straight at my gut. Too slow, I push his hand away, but the taser presses in by my belly button.

My eyes flick to Alex's. We stare at each other. There's a faint click as he pulls the trigger, and I wait for the agony. But there's no shock.

His eyes widen with the realization that he had planned to hurt me and failed. In one movement, I sink my nails into the flesh of his hand and jerk sideways, feeling the skin tear. The taser clatters on to the deck and slides away.

I push myself back from him, but he swings and lands a blow on my jaw, snapping my head around. A supernova of pain explodes through my face. I crash to the ground and, before the blackness clears from my head, he's on top of me, his arm pressing into my throat. Flashing. Stars.

Go for the eyes, May's voice tells me.

Blindly, I scratch where his face should be. He lets out a grunt of pain. I use the split second of distraction to shove him away and scramble out from under him. On my feet. *Run.*

Alex grabs hold of my hair and yanks me backwards. He covers my mouth with his hand. I bite, flesh yielding under my teeth. He swears and forces me against the wall. Heavy as a boulder. He's got me.

I suck air through my nose. A trickle of blood rattles with each breath.

"You've made a lot of bad decisions. But we're going to have a clean slate. Forgiveness. I forgive you. You forgive me. OK?"

"Never," I say, grunting, and struggle with one hand scrabbling at his face. The other I hold still by my side.

He snorts a crazy laugh and brings his face up to mine, and for a horrible minute, I think he's going to kiss me. His hand tightens around my neck. Impossibly strong.

"I walked through fire for you," he whispers.

He squeezes. I try to say, "*Alex*," but it comes out as a strangled squeak.

"Either you do as you're told or we have a problem."

I try to say, "*You're psychotic*," but all that comes out is a gurgle.

He slams me again. My head rings, but I get my hand in my pocket and find the multitool. Keep hold of it.

"Do you understand?" he says, and he loosens the fingers that are snaked around my neck.

I nod. The smell of him, once so enticing, now makes me recoil.

"I can't hear you," he says.

I lick my lips. There's blood. "I understand. Perfectly," I say through wet teeth.

Then I stab him.

CHAPTER 66

NIK

Enid did it! Twenty minutes after she threw me out of the engine room and slammed the door, a rumble passed through the ship. And I'm guessing, because there was no fireball explosion, that she's still alive.

Great job, Enid.

Deck Ten. Busy as ration day in the market. I've been jogging along, my gun tight in my hand, dodging around people. Half of them wandering, dumbstruck, staring at the places the drones should be. The other half hustle, carrying lanterns and flashlights and whatever belongings they can manage. Just passed a family pulling an old lady and three chickens in a handcart. Where are they going? Anyone's guess.

Gunfire bounces around, and everyone ducks momentarily. Sounded like it came from the next deck up. A scream comes from above, and then a body drops past the other side of the

422

railing. Somebody yelps. There's a pause while everybody on this section of deck processes what just happened, and then the activity starts afresh.

Most of the *Arcadia*'s lifeboats were scavenged as soon as our ancestors got here from Europe. You can find some of them woven into the flotilla or as orange planks propping up shelters on the poorer decks. Most ended up as kindling during that first hellish winter, and I know a couple of them were used in escape attempts. But a handful survived in one piece. And, according to John, Alex has got himself one. He's probably waiting for the right moment to escape.

There's an ear-splitting scream of pain. I know that voice. Alex.

This is it. I'm going to kill him.

People run from the source of the screaming. That's an easy way for me to find who I'm looking for. Through all the faces, I see Esther standing over a figure on the deck. She's glaring down at him, fierce as fire. Alex, clutching his shoulder, rolls around on the deck. Blood funnels between his fingers.

"You stabbed me!" he screams.

Esther takes a final look at him and steps over his legs. She starts jogging. Her face is ruddy and determined. She sees me and skids to a halt.

"You did it," she says, breathless.

"No. Enid did. You stabbed Alex?"

She wipes her nose on the back of her hand, smearing blood across her face. "Didn't kill him though."

She runs at me and throws her arms around my neck. We hold on to each other, staggering. She smells of burnt paper.

"Did you warn the captain?" I say.

She pushes away from me. "Nik, I'm so sorry."

Feel like I've been punched in the gut. I take a few steps back until my back hits the wall. I press my hands into my eyes. He's gone. My dad's best friend. The man I've looked up to for years. The guy who was going to lead us all out of here.

"The Coalies got to him after I left," Esther says.

Grief washes over me like a soaking of rain. I take it, all of it, and squash it into a ball and push it down as far as I can.

"The engine's running, but there's no one steering," I say.

The words taste bitter and dead. All we've done. All the people we've lost. All for nothing.

Esther's fingers find their way into mine. "Come on," she says, cocking her head down the deck.

"Where?"

"The bridge."

She says it like it's obvious. Like I've missed something. She pulls me to my feet and starts toward the nearest staircase.

"We'll never make it," I say. "Too many Coalies."

"What else are we going to do?"

Good question. What am I going to do?

"Wait." I stop. Somewhere behind me, Alex whines on the ground. My hand's all sweaty around the grip of the gun. "Promised myself I'd kill him," I say.

Esther grabs my arm and applies pressure. A squeeze, not enough to hurt. "You're not killing him. I won't let you."

"He helped the Coalies kill May," I say. There's a slick of bile in my throat.

"I hate him, too. But you're a good person. And good people don't commit cold-blooded murder."

Anger narrows my vision. I close my eyes and press my hands into them. Imagining the snap of the shot. The red of the blood. It swamps me. My jaw aches from grinding my teeth.

Alex has pulled himself up, and he's sitting with his back against the railing. I march toward him, finger twitching along the side of my gun. Alex looks up at me when I reach him. His face is pinched with pain and sickly pale. I aim right at the center of his forehead. Right where May was hit.

I'm going to kill him.

"Don't do it." Esther's voice vibrates with tension. She's a few steps behind me. "Please don't do it."

"Go ahead," Alex says, wheezing. "She hates me. I've got nothing left anyway."

I need to kill him.

"It won't bring her back," Esther whispers.

I *want* to kill him.

"May wouldn't want this for you. She wouldn't want you to become this."

It's like Esther's tipped a bucket of ice water over me. Doubt floods in. I hesitate. I see May's face. Alive. Smiling. She wouldn't want me to kill this kid. She wouldn't want me to twist myself into something hate-filled and spiteful like Hadley. And I don't want that either.

Instead, I bring my foot down, square, on the knife wound in Alex's shoulder.

He screams and grabs hold of my ankle. The veins in his neck bulge.

Esther pulls on my arm. I hear her say my name. The world narrows, and it's all a hazy wash of colors and far-off sounds. I let her guide me. Alex's screams follow us, and it's like hearing him through water. When the fog lifts, we're two decks up.

Esther stops and holds on to me, squeezing with each breath. I bury my head in her neck. And I ugly-cry into her hair. Something's broken inside me.

"You did the right thing," Esther says.

"I know."

"Let's finish what she started."

I wipe my face on my sleeve.

***

We fight our way to the front of the ship as dawn is smearing the sky in the east. Some people are just trying to find a safe place to hide. Others have picked up weapons and joined the fight. At one point, I saw a single Coaly separated from his unit. He was stripping off his uniform and disguising himself in the clothes of a dead passenger. My stomach constricts at the thought of what will happen if a gang member gets hold of him. Sure, he's the enemy. Doesn't mean we have to be monsters.

The bridge juts out at the front of the ship. It circles the front of the *Arcadia*. A semicircle of windows at the top of a curved white wall. The windows stare out to sea like eyes. The closer we get, the louder the gunfire is, until we're on top of a shoot-out. No drones though, not even a distant hum. That's something.

Esther and I round the final corner, panting and red-faced from the run. There's a barricade. It's been cobbled together from stuff and junk, planks and doors and furniture. Just over head-height, it cuts across the deck. Six heads poke up above it as we get close, followed by half a dozen gun barrels.

We freeze and raise our hands. Getting shot by my own side wasn't how I expected to go.

"We're not Coalies!" Esther shouts. "Nik, tell them who you are."

"Shh, give them a minute."

"They could shoot us in a minute," she hisses.

Voices behind the barricade, then someone calling, "'S all right. He's one of ours. Let 'em through." It's John, Enid's gap-toothed second in command.

There's movement, the scraping of furniture, and a hole opens up in the barricade. John's face looks out, and he motions with his gun. "She'll be pleased to see you."

We squeeze through the gap into the makeshift fortification. It's narrow and ends a few yards away in another barricade. There, people are taking turns to shoot over or around a stack of metal sheets and wood. Bullets whistle back, striking with a dull thud or a metallic ping.

"Keep your head down," I say to Esther.

Crouching, I inch forward. The barricades won't hold for long. We'll have to retreat before long. Or not. Either way, we can hold this position for minutes, not hours.

I spot Enid and next to her a figure I'd recognize anywhere. I've never been so happy to see my mother.

"You forget to set your alarm?" Enid says, dipping her head as a bullet thumps into the barricade.

"Glad to see you didn't get roasted," I fire back.

My mother acknowledges me with a tight-lipped nod. Nothing new there. "You had no orders to go ashore with Cadet Crossland, Nikhil."

"Nice to see you too, Mom," I say, making no effort to hide the rage that still fills me. It's like I'm torn in two. I'm glad she's alive, but I can't let go of the fact that she took away my last few days with May.

My mother snatches a look at me like she's taking inventory. Checking I'm in one piece. Head. Two arms. Two legs. A moment of satisfaction or relief, then a return to her hard exoskeleton. "Here's the situation …"

I risk a glance over the top of the barricade. The Coalies are lined up, kneeling on the metal deck. Completely exposed. Every time a bullet looks like it's going to hit them, a flash breaks the air. The bullets crumple like they've hit a brick wall and bounce to the ground.

"We were trying to secure the bridge when this unit arrived. The staircase we need to access it is halfway down the deck," my mother says. "They're using some sort of shield to protect themselves. Happily, they don't seem to be able to shoot or advance while the shield is deployed."

I look over the top again in time to see the Coalies drop their protective field and launch a volley of bullets into the barricade, showering splinters of wood. Everyone ducks. When the shooting stops and I look over again, the Coalies have moved another two feet closer to the stairs that cling to the outside wall of the bridge. If they get to that staircase before we do, it's a short climb to the bridge. They'll take control of it, and that'll be the end of the mission.

"We can delay them, but we've had no success in driving them back. And reinforcements will be on the way. As soon as the captain gets here, we need to find a way to get him up there," my mother says.

"He's not coming," says Esther.

My mother looks at her with eyebrows furrowed. "You're sure?"

"I saw him die myself."

"Ah, shit," Enid says, and she fires a string of shots over the barricade, shaking her head when she's finished. Her mouth's fixed in a thin line. She starts firing again.

My mother doesn't miss a beat, but I catch the tightening in her face. The pain. "With the captain dead, I am now head of the rebel army," she announces. "We continue with the plan. Let's get up to that bridge."

The Coalies shower us with bullets and advance toward the staircase.

"We're not going to push them back far enough to take the stairs," Enid says.

I glance around. I look up at the bridge door. A narrow landing runs all the way around the bridge, enclosed by a handrail.

"You still got that zip cord?" I say to Enid.

She unstraps the belt from her waist and tosses it to me. "Pay me for it later."

I fasten it around my middle with the metal disc at my belly. The cord unravels when I pull. I aim at the railing outside the bridge door, spin the disc on the end of the cable and throw. It clangs against the metal, but doesn't hold. Try again. No cigar. My back's sweating. Third time lucky. The disc holds fast, and I give it a hard yank to make sure I'm not going to drop to my death.

"Good thinking, Nikhil. Here." My mother passes me a small

drawstring bag. "You've been trained to use this kind of disabling substance."

I nod and shove the whole thing into my pocket.

"We'll give you as much cover as we can. Hold until I give the order," my mother says.

She takes an egg-shaped grenade from the bag at her hip, activates it by clicking the button, then lobs it toward the Coalies. It lands behind them, releasing a shock wave of electricity that lays out a dozen of them at once.

"Go!" my mother shouts.

Esther grabs on to me. In shock, I pull her close, press the button on the zip cord, and we fly into the air.

CHAPTER 67

ESTHER

We speed through the air toward the bridge. I grab the railing with my free arm as we zip closer, swing myself over, and dart through the door as a volley of Coaly bullets ricochets around me. Nik dives through after me. He bangs the door closed and heaves on the circular handle at its center. It squeaks and stops. Rusted shut.

I look around for something to block the door. The bridge is a semicircle with a long bank of floor-to-ceiling windows. In front of the windows are the control panels that would once have let the *Arcadia* navigate across the Atlantic. It's been unused for so long that one corner has been turned into a storage area, full of boxes and jumbled cleaning supplies.

Fighting rages on the deck below. Enid and the others will hold the Coalies off as long as they can, but they're outgunned. They can't protect us forever.

Nik flops to the ground. A slick of blood runs from his thigh down to his foot. His face is a deathly mask.

Keep your head, Esther.

Step 1: assessment. Nik has a gunshot wound to his leg. He's conscious but weak. Touching the skin of his neck, I can feel his heart pounding. This door might as well be a gaping hole. The Coalies could be here any minute. First, make the situation safe. Secure the door. Slow Nik's bleeding.

Step 2: treatment. Nik tilts his head to a corner of the bridge that's been used to store junk. "Get something to stop the door," he says.

Boxes teeter in a pile. There's a tangle of broom handles.

Nik's pumping out blood at a rate of knots. The urge to treat him is intense, but if I don't secure that door, we'll be surrounded by Coalies any second. I lift his hands and align them over the wound in his thigh. "Press. Hard," I say.

I run to the supply corner and throw boxes aside, spilling bottles and rolls of paper. Searching for something.

Nothing.

Nothing.

A plank? That might work.

I heave the door, jam the plank through the wheel handle and wedge it against the door frame. Splinters pierce my hands. The plank sits tight. Feels like using a Band-Aid to stop a flood, but it's better than nothing.

Now Nik. Blood is soaking through his trousers. I have nothing to treat him with, but I need to slow that bleeding down. He's closing and opening his eyes with a glazed-over expression I don't like one little bit. He's going into shock. That's what happens when you lose a lot of blood all at once. I pull the fabric of his trousers away from his leg, push my fingers through the wet hole and tear downwards, splitting it all the way to the hem. I do the same at the back. He groans as I lift his leg.

"Sorry, sorry," I whisper.

I've got my back to the panel of windows. And there's a sound. A clicking. A tapping on the glass. Panic-sweat pops up under my armpits and down my back.

Push the noise away. Don't think about what it could be. Work on Nik first, then on to the next thing.

I wind the two strips of fabric over and under Nik's leg, pulling as tight as I can to make a tourniquet that will staunch the flow of blood. If I leave it on too long, he'll lose the leg. Without it, he'll bleed out anyway.

At the twist of the fabric, Nik grinds his teeth and rolls his head back. That's good. He's still feeling pain. That means he's not out yet. I push him so that he's lying flat on his back and prop his damaged leg up against the wall to slow the bleeding.

Something slams against the other side of the door. Something heavy and jarring against the metal.

"Gotta take us out to sea. Seal the controls…in here." Nik's voice is raspy. He waves a weak hand over his pocket.

I find the drawstring bag, and inside a ball of doughy rubber attached by trailing wires to a button.

"Spread it over the steering mechanism," Nik says.

Step 3: survival. It's too late for me and Nik. But everyone else has a chance at life.

Another slam at the door.

The clicking sound from the window has turned to hammering.

"Red handle, central control panel, all the way forward."

I get up. I turn. And I let out a strangled, "Oh," as dread swamps me.

Where there should be a view of the ocean through the windows, I find a squirming cloud. Thousands of hand-sized bots, the same as the ones that attacked the safe house, each using a leg to chip at the glass.

"You couldn't have taken the bots out at the same time as the drones?" I say with a strangled laugh. When Nik doesn't reply, I turn to look at him. He murmurs. I'm losing him.

Already, in the seconds I spent barring the door and yanking a tourniquet around Nik's leg, a network of cracks has spread across the windows. Like cobwebs. Deepening with each impact.

And beyond the nasty clicking swarm of bots, on the horizon, I glimpse a black line. Ships on the water. Helicopters in the air. A blockade separating us from the open sea.

We're trapped.

"Nik, they've barricaded the harbor mouth. What do I do?"

No answer.

Panic swirls through me.

Thirty more seconds. Keep your head for another half-minute.

A lightning-bolt crack breaks across one of the glass panes. Another slam at the door splinters the wooden plank I used to hold it shut. The next impact will smash the door open. The bots will be through any second.

I run to the control panel. A dozen neat buttons. A dozen switches to flip. I ignore them and push the red handle forward as far as it will go. Nothing happens. It didn't work. Then movement. Not sure if it's my head spinning or the ship moving.

We're moving!

But where to? We'll be destroyed before we make it out to sea. We can't ram our way through. Even if we made it out, the *Arcadia* is too old and weighed down to win a race to international waters without a head start.

All we need is a chance. An escape route.

There's only one way to go.

In the center of the bridge is a steering wheel. Small, black rubber. Less impressive than I'd imagined. I take hold of it and turn. My muscles scream at its resistance. The *Arcadia*'s gathering speed. I push the doughy ball on to the center of the console, pressing it down with my fingers. I step back to unravel the wires. The trigger feels awkward in my hand. My thumb shakes over the button.

Glass shatters. Deafening and crystalline. Cold air blasts my face. Bots fall among the shards of glass and flood the bridge. Behind me, the plank explodes. Splinters tear through the air.

Through the empty window frames, I get a glimpse of the new day, still pale and silken. And the place we're headed.

Land.

Shouting erupts around me. I turn to face the Coalies. My thumb hovers above the button clenched in my hand. A Coaly raises his weapon.

I press the trigger.

CHAPTER 68

HADLEY

Someone stop this ship!" Hadley screams. He steps onto the bridge of the *Arcadia*. Somewhere below he can hear the uneven *snap-snap* of a firefight between his officers and members of the rebel scum trying to stop the clearance. Wind whips through the broken windows, and the floor is carpeted with deactivated bots. Somehow, somehow, the rebels started this ship's engine and set it on a collision course.

This will be bad for him when his superiors find out. Very, very bad. Janek will smirk through her gullish face as they extend his exile. His heart thumps at the thought of another posting on another ship.

"Sir, they've destroyed the controls. There's no way to stop us from here, no way to slow us."

Hadley grabs the officer by the collar and slams him against the wall. The man's face fills with confusion. "Then get to the engine and blow the damn thing up!" Hadley snarls, ignoring the line of spit that fires from his own mouth.

The controls are covered in a gloopy red substance that hardens with each second. He draws his weapon and fires at close range. Bullets ricochet off and burrow into the walls. His officers duck. Not even a dent in the red stuff.

The girl's lying where she dropped when whatever they used to destroy the controls exploded. She stirs and rolls onto her back. Esther Crossland. The girl he didn't think was a threat. The one he's tried—and failed—to kill is responsible for the most humiliating loss of control by a ship's commander in the history of the Federated States. A humiliation that can only fall on him.

He deactivated the bots before he came up here, and now he kicks through a dead line of them and grabs the girl by her hair. His anger is fizzing hot. He's powerless to stop the ship. Powerless to save himself and his career from disaster. He can at least have the satisfaction of killing this girl. He can look into her eyes when she realizes she's going to die. He can do what he should have done to Celeste.

Hadley pulls her up, and she blinks groggily. He twists his hand into her hair. Strands ping as they're pulled out. She grimaces and whines, and it makes him want to shake her.

This is just the start.

Clamping a hand onto the back of her neck, he pushes her in front of him. Out of the bridge. Out into the fast-moving air. His officers hotfoot it out of the way.

"Get me that zip cord they used," Hadley growls. Outside, he pushes the girl to her knees and stands behind her. She doesn't struggle, more's the pity. Her hair's soft between his fingers, and the speed of the ship, gathering like it's running downhill, sends it rippling in waves. The fighting isn't important now. Clearing the ship doesn't matter. Finally, he's going to do what he should have done before. To Esther Crossland. And to Celeste.

An officer hands him the zip cord. He loops the end. No time for a proper noose, but good and tight so she won't be able to wriggle free.

He's aware of the land, a vague, looming mass. It's over. He's failed. The *Arcadia* slices through the water like she'd never forgotten how to sail. The flotilla drags behind the main ship as it speeds up, walkways and barges and shacks trailing like seaweed.

"Sir!" One of his officers shouts a warning.

"Shut up!"

He slips the circle of cord over the girl's head and attaches the other end to the railing, locking the mechanism so that only a couple of feet of cord will unwind. She lets out a moan that electrifies Hadley. He tightens the cord just enough around her neck; not so tight that she'll pass out too soon.

"Sir, we're about to—"

"You have been found guilty of crimes against the Federated States. I sentence you to death." Hadley runs his hands over her neck, lingering on the vein that throbs against the tightened zip cord. He forces her to her feet.

She turns her head and stares at the land.

He presses her against the railing, enjoying the way he can use his body to force the air from her lungs.

"Brace for impact!" someone shouts behind him.

He only has time to clutch the railing with both hands, pinning the girl in place.

CHAPTER 69

ESTHER

Metal against rock. Shuddering through the body of the ship. Hadley and I are thrown to the deck, his arms wrapped around me. His hands on me.

Get off. Get off. Get off!

We struggle. The zip cord tightens around my throat. One end is still attached to the railing. Desperate, I tear at it, gripping lines in my skin with my fingernails, until I manage to force them underneath the cord. I pull. And—*thank you, thank you*—it slackens. The pressure in my head drops.

Breathe. Breathe.

The *Arcadia* screams like a banshee. Creaking and forcing its way onto solid ground. In the seconds that follow, the world pauses. I breathe through my damaged throat, an aching necklace of swollen skin, looking up at a sky layered in dark clouds.

I'm alive.

Moaning. Shouting. Screaming. The world roars back to life.

Hadley springs to his feet. He stands over me, full of venom and glaring. I'm too slow to react. He drags me up by the front of my clothes and pushes me against the railing again until my feet lift off the deck.

I don't want to die like this.

"Should have finished you off at the start instead of making deals with your boyfriend," he hisses into my face.

Now I cling to him. My nails dig into his skin. He's impossibly strong. The cord is still wrapped around my neck, and in a few seconds he'll tip me over the railing and I'll swing. Tighter and tighter. I whimper.

Hadley jerks. Shots thud into him. One. Two. Three. The noise like a thunderclap.

His body tenses, and he blanches with shock. His grip changes; he's not pushing anymore, he's clinging, pulling me closer. Realization moves over his face; he's dying.

We're too close. I don't want to share this final moment with him. But I can't look away.

He paws at me, trying to hold on to life. His mouth opens too wide, bubbles of saliva crowding the corners of his lips. The urgency seeps from him, and he slides to the ground.

Enid stands at the top of the bridge stairs next to a man built like a bull. Silas—holding a gun that's still pointed at Hadley.

"You could've taken out the girl," Enid chides.

"Would've been a bonus," he says. He strides toward me, shoves Hadley's body away with a boot and slides his fingers under the zip cord to loosen it. "Wasn't about to let someone else enjoy killing you. Doesn't mean we don't still have a problem," he rumbles.

I'm shaking, head to toe, and my hands fumble as I unravel the cord from around my neck and throw it away from me like it's a snake.

"Nik's hurt," I say. It comes out a croak, my voice bruising my throat. I concentrate on not collapsing, using the railing to hold myself up, looking anywhere but at Hadley's body.

Rebels flood up the stairs and through the open door of the bridge. There's shooting inside, then shouting, and through the door I see the remaining Coalies drop their weapons and raise their hands in surrender.

Enid climbs in through the bridge door. Seconds later, Nik emerges carried by two of her people. His skin has a deathly tinge, and there's so much dark blood flowing from his leg that he must be dead.

Please don't be dead.

As they pass in front of me, his eyelids flutter. He's alive.

"Come with me. Now," Enid says.

My feet move beneath me. I leave Hadley's body where he fell on the deck. We hurry toward the back of the ship. It's like I'm floating—this place that has been my home for sixteen years is now thin and unreal. Everything shifts around me. The ground seems to tilt, and my balance is shot. I wouldn't be able to move without Enid's orders.

"Nik's mother's arranged a chopper for us!" she shouts over her shoulder, turning so that I can see the hair flying loose around her face, the splatter of blood on her cheek.

People pour from their cabins. We struggle against a torrent of survivors. Everyone's flooding in the same direction. Toward land.

442

They hum with excitement, carrying whatever precious things they can manage.

I look for my parents. They're nowhere to be seen. Not my mother's dark hair. Not my father's unshaven face. And not May. She won't be among the survivors of the *Arcadia*. I stop in the middle of the deck.

"Enid, I need to find my parents!" I shout.

She stops, comes back for me. "Now listen, you could spend days trying to find them in all this. But they might have left the ship already, and you'd be none the wiser. Come with me now. Get off the ship. We'll find them after. All right? You can't do anything of use from here. But if you come now, you'll have the power and the resources of the rebellion behind you."

Enid continues running toward the back of the ship.

I have to decide. My heart tells me to stay here and find them. My head tells me it will be like looking for a needle in a haystack. I pin my eyes to the back of Enid's jacket and jog to keep up.

Escape routes have been thrown down at intervals from the railing. Ropes and sheets and anything else strong enough to climb down. People climb over and slide toward the sea.

The air sings with screams that are filled with elation and terror. There's fighting. The gentle *phut-phut* of gunfire muffled by the smoky air. The taste of the fire consuming the old wood and metal of the ship.

People slide down the ropes. Below, in the inky mess of the ocean, they try to keep their heads above water. Dying. I'm powerless to help them.

We're almost at the back of the ship. Enid takes a staircase up.

I pull myself after her using the handrail. The men carrying Nik breathe through their mouths and drip sweat. We emerge onto the top deck. Nik's lowered. I check his pulse. Too fast. He's struggling.

"Where is it?" I say.

"Coming," says Enid, panting.

I scan the sky for helicopter lights. I strain to hear chopper blades or the sound of an engine that would tell me help is on the way. Nik's running out of time.

An engine sound pricks my ears. Finally. The sound multiplies until a helicopter springs into view on the seaward side of the ship. Its lights are stars of hope in the night.

"How will everyone else get off?" I ask.

Enid waves both arms to attract the pilot. "Wasn't a plan for this, was there? We were supposed to be heading for safety by now. Your little joyride put a stop to that." She looks me in the eye for an intense second. "You did good, mind."

The wind blasting from the helicopter whips hair around our faces, and I have to force my feet against the deck so that I'm not pushed over. It's small, not one of the big military transports the Coalies use. A single rotor on top, another smaller one on the end of its long tail. In the front, two people are visible, their smooth helmets so like a Coaly uniform it makes my back slick with panic-sweat. The chopper hovers while its landing gear unfolds. Enid's guys pluck Nik from the ground the instant it touches down and lumber toward it, dipping their heads under the blades.

Enid follows. I'm about to jump aboard when Coalies swarm on to the helipad. They move, fluid as water, weapons raised toward us.

"Quick!" Enid shouts. She grabs me and pulls me aboard.

A spray of thuds on the outside of the helicopter tells me the Coalies are shooting at us as we lurch into the air.

Nik is laid out over two seats. His head is propped against an armrest. I drop to my knees next to him as the helicopter wheels around.

Enid throws herself into an empty seat and pulls a seat belt across her chest.

I take Nik's hand. There's nothing I can do for him now. Not without supplies. Drugs. Suture bots. "Hold on," I whisper.

We circle the ship from above. She's monstrous. A beast jutting out from the waterfront. This is the way Hadley has been watching us all these years. A drone's-eye view. We've ended up in the city's industrial harbor. The wharf is edged with enormous rough-hewn blocks of stone. As far away as I can see, there are sturdy, red-brick warehouses. Towers of shipping containers. Cranes. The *Arcadia* has carved a great ravine into the land, slicing through a street and into the building closest to the water. She's cut into great ribbons and bent back like the petals of a flower.

In the gathering light, everything is as raw and sharp as pain. People are in the water. Thrashing. Reaching for air. The sea churns with them. Faces break the surface like the souls of the lost. I train my eyes on them, willing each one to resurface, willing them to survive, but there's too many. They disappear.

"Enid, we have to go down," I say. "We can pick some of them up. We can help some of them." I'm sobbing.

So many. Everywhere I look. A face twisted in agony. A hand reaching into nothing. In among them, I recognize a stubbled, unshaven face. Eyes closed. Floating. The ties of an apron tangled around and around his neck. It's Sim. The owner of the Lookout. Who always wanted to see me escape.

Enid watches, her jaw tightening, her mouth a grim line. "You did this," she says.

"Please, turn us around—we have to help them."

She shakes her head, tears falling down her cheeks. She dashes a hand over her face. "No. There's too many. It's too dangerous."

I hammer on the partition between us and the pilots. "Take us down!" I scream. Desperation closes my throat. "Take us back!"

Enid watches until I collapse on the floor next to Nik. "It's my fault," I say. "It's my fault."

She unbuckles her seat belt and kneels in front of me.

"It is your fault," she says, looking right into my eyes. Staring through an ocean of tears and pain and loss. "You did this. You could've let the Coalies win. And you'd have carried a different kind of guilt. Now you help them—our people. You pick yourself up, and you use that guilt, and you fight for them. You're alive, and there's many that don't have that privilege. There'll be a need for a medic in the next days. There'll be people hurting. You dig deep. Got it?"

The helicopter banks. I watch until the people are confetti on top of gray waves. On the south side of the ship, closest to the city, rebels have taken up position behind broken-down walls and take turns to shoot at the Coalies that are trying to make their way to the ship. Already, rough barricades have been thrown together. The Coalies fire at them uncertainly. They've never seen anything like this.

Nobody has.

The helicopter makes a final sweep. I feel the threads that bind me to the people and to the place. I imagine them as we climb, try to hold them together, so that I'm not torn away. I cry for the people and for everything we've lost. Everything that's been taken.

The *Arcadia* has fallen.

ACKNOWLEDGMENTS

Firstly, thanks so much to my agent Felicity Blunt, who saw something in my manuscript and worked with me through countless redrafts. I'm certain this book would not have reached this point without your insight and patience. I'm also grateful to the others at Curtis Brown, Rosie Pierce, and Roxane Edouard, who read various versions before submission.

Huge thanks to Steve Geck and the team at Sourcebooks for their belief in this book and for their work bringing the inhabitants of the *Arcadia* to a new audience. Thanks also to Tom Rawlinson, whose enthusiasm for *The Stranded* led to so many great new ideas.

I would not have reached publication without the writing community. Extra special thanks go to my writing buddies Carly Reagon, Asha Hick, Emma Clark Lam, Joanne Clague, and Sara Cox. Thank you for being there through all manner of writing emergencies over the past half a decade. Thanks to Sarah

Hindmarsh for welcoming me into your writing group, and for telling me what's what whenever I have a wobble. I promise my pantsing days are behind me. A shout-out too to the WriteMentor community. Thanks to my writing cohort on the CBC novel writing course and our brilliant leader, Suzannah Dunn. Our time together persuaded me that I could finish the book.

Thank you to my former supervisor Umberto Albarella, who unknowingly set me on the path to writing fiction. Many years ago you told me writing science is about finding a good story. It was a snippet amongst a lot of animal bones and archaeology, but it made me think about the craft of storytelling, and I soon found I preferred making stories up to searching for evidence.

Finally, thanks to my family. Nick, who still can't tell me I've written a bad sentence and who has been unrelenting in his support and love. The kids, who have put up with endless hours of me lost aboard a stranded ship. My mum, who has spent forty years telling me I can do whatever I set my mind to. And Sam and Dee for your support in everything, big and small.

ABOUT THE AUTHOR

Sarah Daniels grew up in Derby and has always loved books. After spending many years as an archaeological researcher, she realized making stories up was much more enjoyable than basing them on scientific evidence. Now, she writes books from her home in rural Lincolnshire, UK. *The Stranded* is her first novel.